W9-CFV-229

BRANCH SHIPMENTS

ARC 11/97
B.L.
FER 11/88
FOR
GAR 2/98
HOA
K-T 9/99
McK 2/0
R.D. 11/18
TRN 5/99 3/01
BKM 3/99

EKA

SF
BRADLEY

Bradley, Marion
Zimmer.
Lady of Avalon

29.95 ; 10/97

HUMBOLDT COUNTY LIBRARY

Also by Marion Zimmer Bradley

The Catch Trap
The Mists of Avalon
The Firebrand
The Forest House

Lady
of
Avalon

Marion Zimmer Bradley

Viking

VIKING
Published by the Penguin Group
Penguin Books USA Inc., 375 Hudson Street,
New York, New York 10014, U.S.A.
Penguin Books Ltd, 27 Wrights Lane,
London W8 5TZ, England
Penguin Books Australia Ltd, Ringwood,
Victoria, Australia
Penguin Books Canada Ltd, 10 Alcorn Avenue,
Toronto, Ontario, Canada M4V 3B2
Penguin Books (N.Z.) Ltd, 182–190 Wairau Road,
Auckland 10, New Zealand

Penguin Books Ltd, Registered Offices:
Harmondsworth, Middlesex, England

First published in 1997 by Viking Penguin,
a division of Penguin Books USA Inc.

1   3   5   7   9   10   8   6   4   2

Copyright © Marion Zimmer Bradley, 1997
All rights reserved

Ritual excerpts in Chapters 10 and 23, and the song
in Chapter 19, courtesy of Diana L. Paxson

Library of Congress Cataloging-in-Publication Data
Bradley, Marion Zimmer.
Lady of Avalon / Marion Zimmer Bradley.
p.   cm.
ISBN 0-670-85783-1 (alk. paper)
1. Great Britain—History—Roman period, 55B.C.–449 A.D.—Fiction.
2. Lady of the Lake (Legendary character)—Fiction.
3. Arthurian romances—Adaptations.
I. Title.
PS3552.R228L27   1997
813'.54—dc21   96-51175

This book is printed on acid-free paper.
∞

Printed in the United States of America
Set in Centaur and Colmcille
Designed by Sabrina Bowers
Map by Peter McClure

Without limiting the rights under copyright reserved above, no part of this
publication may be reproduced, stored in or introduced into a retrieval
system, or transmitted, in any form or by any means (electronic,
mechanical, photocopying, recording or otherwise), without
the prior written permission of both the copyright
owner and the above publisher of this book.

To Diana L. Paxson,
without whom this book could not have been written,
and to Darkmoon Circle, the priestesses of Avalon

People in the Story

{Part 1}

Priests and Priestesses of Avalon

Caillean—High Priestess, formerly of the Forest House
(Eilan)—formerly High Priestess of the Forest House, Gawen's mother
Gawen—son of Eilan and Gaius Macellius

Eiluned, Kea, Marged, Riannon—senior priestesses
Beryan, Breaca, Dica, Lunet, Lysanda—junior priestesses and maidens in training
Sianna—daughter of the Faerie Queen

Bendeigid—former Arch-Druid, Gawen's British grandfather
Brannos—an ancient Druid and bard
Cunomaglos—High Priest
Tuarim, Ambios—younger Druids

The Christian monks of Inis Witrin

*Father Joseph of Arimathea—leader of the Christian community
Father Paulus—his successor
Alanus, Bron—monks

---

* = historical figure
( ) = dead before story begins

Romans and others

Arius—Gawen's friend in the Army

Gaius Macellius Severus Senior—Gawen's Roman grandfather

(Gaius Macellius Severus Siluricus)—Gawen's father, who was sacrificed as a British Year-King

Lucius Rufinus—centurion in charge of recruits for the Ninth Legion

Quintus Macrinius Donatus—Commander of the Ninth Legion

Salvius Bufo—commander of the cohort to which Gawen is assigned

Waterwalker—a man of the marsh folk who pole the barge of Avalon

{Part II}

Priests and Priestesses of Avalon

Dierna—High Priestess and Lady of Avalon

(Becca—Dierna's younger sister*)*

Teleri—a princess of the Durotriges

Cigfolla, Crida, Erdufylla, Ildeg—senior priestesses

Adwen, Lina—maidens being trained on Avalon

Ceridachos—Arch-Druid

Conec—a young Druid

Lewal—the Healer

Romans and Britons

Aelius—captain of the *Hercules*

*Allectus—son of the Duovir of Venta, later on Carausius' staff

*Constantius Chlorus—a Roman commander, later Caesar

*Diocletian Augustus—senior Emperor

Eiddin Mynoc—Prince of the Durotriges

Gaius Martinus—an optio from Vindolanda

Gnaeus Claudius Pollio—a magistrate of Durnovaria

Vitruvia—Pollio's wife

*Marcus Aurelius Musaeus Carausius—Admiral of the Britannic fleet, later Emperor of Britannia

*Maximian Augustus—junior Emperor

Menecrates—commander of Carausius' flagship, the *Orion*
Quintus Julius Cerialis—Duovir of Venta Belgarum
Trebellius—a manufacturer of bronze fittings

Barbarians

Aedfrid, Theudibert—warriors in Carausius' Menapian guard
Hlodovic—a Frankish chieftain of the Salian clan
Wulfhere—a chieftain of the Angles
Radbod—a Frisian chieftain

{Part III}

Priests and Priestesses of Avalon

Ana—High Priestess and Lady of Avalon
(Anara and Idris—her second and first daughters)
Viviane—her third daughter
Igraine—her fourth daughter
Morgause—her fifth daughter

Claudia, Elen, Julia—senior priestesses
Aelia, Fianna, Mandua, Nella, Rowan, Silvia—novices in the House of
  Maidens, later priestesses

Taliesin—chief bard
Nectan—Arch-Druid
Talenos—a younger Druid

Britons

*Ambrosius Aurelianus—Emperor of Britain
Bethoc—Viviane's foster-mother
*Categirn—Vortigern's older son
Ennius Claudianus—one of Vortimer's commanders
Fortunatus—a Christian priest and follower of Pelagius
*Bishop Germanus of Auxerre—an enforcer of orthodoxy
Heron—one of the men of the marshes
Neithen—Viviane's foster-father

Uther—one of Ambrosius' warriors
**Vortigern*—High King of Britannia
**Vortimer*—his second son

Saxons

Hengest—leader of the Saxon migration
Horsa—his brother

Figures from Myth and History

(Agricola)—Governor of Britannia A.D. 78–84
Arianrhod—a British goddess associated with the moon and the sea
(Boudicca)—Queen of the Iceni, who led the Great Rebellion in
  A.D. 61
Briga/Brigantia—Goddess of healing, poetry, and smithcraft, Divine
  Midwife, and territorial goddess of Britannia
(Calgacus)—British leader who was defeated by Agricola in A.D. 81
Camulos—a god of warriors
(Caractacus)—first-century leader of the British resistance
Cathubodva—Lady of Ravens, raven goddess, a war goddess, related
  to the Morrigan
Ceridwen—British goddess of the "terrible mother" type, possessor
  of the cauldron of wisdom
The Faerie Queen
The Horned One, Cernunnos—lord of the animals and the dark half of
  the year
Lugos—bright god of all talents
Maponus/Mabon—the young god, Son of the Mother
Minerva—Roman goddess of wisdom and healing, identified with
  Athena, Sulis, and Briga
Modron—Mother goddess
Nehallenia—territorial goddess of the Netherlands
Nemetona—goddess of the grove
Nodens—god of clouds, sovereignty, healing, possibly related to
  Nuada

(Pelagius)—a fourth-century British religious leader
Rigantona—Great Queen, goddess of birds
Rigisamus—lord of the grove
Sulis—goddess of the healing springs
Tanarus—thunder god
Teutates—tribal god

places in the Story

Aquae Sulis—Bath
Armorica—Brittany
Branodunum—Brancaster, Norfolk
Britannia—Great Britain
Caesarodunum—Tours, France
Calleva—Silchester
Cantium—Kent
Clausentum—Bitterne, on the Ictis, near Southampton
Corinium—Cirencester, Gloucester
Corstopitum—Corbridge, Northumbria
Demetia—Dyfed, Wales
Deva—Chester
Dubris—Dover
Durnovaria—Dorchester, Dorset
Durobrivae—Rochester
Durovernum Cantiacorum—Canterbury
Eburacum—York
Gallia—France
Gariannonum—Burgh Castle, Norfolk
Gesoriacum—Boulogne, France

Glevum—Gloucester

Ictis—river that empties into the bay at Portsmouth

Inis Witrin—Glastonbury, Somerset

Lindinis—Ilchester, Somerset

Londinium—London

Luguvalium—Carlisle

Mendip Hills—hills to the north of Glastonbury

Mona—Isle of Anglesey

Mons Graupius—a mountain in Scotland, site of the battle in which
  Agricola destroyed the last British resistance to Rome

Othona—Bradwell, Essex

Portus Adurni—Portchester (Portsmouth)

Portus Lemana—Lymne, Kent

Rutupiae—Richborough, Kent

Sabrina Fluvia—the Severn River and estuary

Siluria—the Silure tribal lands in South Wales

Segedunum—Wallsend, Northumbria

Segontium—Caernarvon, Wales

Sorviodunum—Old Sarum, near Salisbury

Stour River—river that passes through Dorchester and empties at
  Weymouth

Tamesis Fluvius—Thames River

Tanatus Insula—Isle of Thanet, Kent

Vale of Avalon—the Glastonbury levels

Vectis Insula—Isle of Wight

Venta Belgarum—Winchester

Venta Icenorum—Caistor, Norfolk

Venta Silurum—Caerwent, Wales

Vercovicium—Housesteads fort, Northumbria

Vernemeton (most holy grove)—the Forest House

Vindolanda—Chesterholm, near Corbridge

Viroconium—Wroxeter

△ Mons
Graupius

CALEDONIA

BRITANNIA
AD Ist~Vth Centuries

Wall of Antoninus
ALBA
Wall of Hadrian
Vercovicium
Vindolanda   Segedunum
         Corstopitum
Luguvalium

OCEANUS
GERMANICUS

Eburacum   Polaris ☆

OCEANUS
HIBERNICUS

Lindum

Mona   Deva   Branodunum
   Segontium
      ○ Vernemeton   Gariannonum
        (site of)
      Viroconium   Venta
                             Icenorum

DEMETIA
   SILURIA   Glevum
         Venta   Corinium   Othona   Tanatus
         Silurum   Londinium   Insula
              Aquae Sulis   Durobrivae
Sabrina Aest.   Calleva   Durovernum Rutupiae
Inis   Cantiacorum Dubris
Wair   Lindinis   Inis Witrin Venta   Portus
                                 Belgarum   Lemana
        Isca Durnovaria Clausentum
        DUMNONIA Sorviodunum Portus   Gesoriacum
                              Adurni
                     Ictis   Vectis
                     Fluv.   Insula
                OCEANUS
Peter McClure   BRITANNICUS   GALLIA
1997

Sabrina Fluvia

Tamesis Fluv.

Mendip Hills

Sabrina Aest.

Lady
of
Avalon

The Faerie Queen speaks:

In the world of humankind, the tides of power are turning. . . . To me, the seasons of men go by in moments, but from time to time a flicker will attract my attention.

Mortals say that in Faerie nothing ever changes. But it is not so. There are places where the worlds lie close together as folds in a blanket. One such bridge is the place that men call Avalon. When the mothers of humankind first came into this land, my people, who had never had bodies, made forms for ourselves in their likeness. The new folk built their houses on poles at the lake's edge and hunted through the marshes, and we walked and played together, for that was the morning of the world.

Time passed, and masters of an ancient wisdom crossed the sea, fleeing the destruction of Atlantis, their own sacred isle. They moved great stones to mark out the lines of power that laced the land. It was they who secured the sacred spring in stone and carved out the spiral path around the Tor, they who found in the contours of the countryside the emblems of their philosophy.

They were great masters of magic, who chanted spells by which a mortal man might reach other worlds. And yet they were mortal, and in time their race diminished, while we remained.

After them came others, bright-haired, laughing children with burnished swords. But the touch of cold iron we could not abide, and from that time onward Faerie began to separate itself from the human world. But the ancient wizards taught the humans wisdom, and their wise folk, the Druids, were drawn to the power in the holy isle. When the Legions of Rome marched across the land, binding it with stone-paved roads and slaughtering those who resisted, the isle became a refuge for the Druid-kind.

That was but a moment ago, by my reckoning. I welcomed to my bed a golden-haired warrior who had wandered into Faerie. He pined and I sent him back again, but he left me the gift of a child. Our daughter is as fair and golden as he was, and curious about her human heritage.

And now the tides are turning, and in the mortal world a priestess seeks to cross over to the Tor. I sensed the power in her only yesterday, when I met her upon another shore. How is it that she has so suddenly grown old? And this time, she brings with her a boy-child whose spirit I have also known before.

Many streams of destiny now flow to their joining. This woman and my daughter and the boy are linked in an ancient pattern. For good or for ill? I sense a time coming when it will fall to me to bind them, soul and body, to this place they call Avalon.

PART 1

The Wisewoman

A.D. 96–118

Chapter One

It was nearing sunset, and the quiet waters of the Vale of Avalon were overlaid with gold. Here and there tussocks of green and brown raised their heads above the quiet waters, blurred by the glimmering haze which at autumn's end veiled the marshes even when the sky was clear. At the center of the Vale one pointed tor rose above the others, crowned with standing stones.

Caillean gazed across the water, the blue cloak that marked her as a senior priestess hanging in motionless folds around her, and felt the stillness dissolving the fatigue of five days on the road. It seemed longer. Surely, the journey from the ashes of the pyre at Vernemeton to the heart of the Summer Country had taken a lifetime.

My lifetime . . ., thought Caillean. *I shall not leave the House of the Priestesses again.* Six months earlier she had brought her little band of women from the Forest House to found a community of priestesses on this isle. Six weeks ago she had gone back, alone, too late to save the Forest House from destruction. But at least she had saved the boy.

"Is that the Isle of Avalon?"

Gawen's voice brought her back to the present. He blinked, as if dazzled by the light, and she smiled.

"It is," she said, "and in another moment I will call the barge which will take us there."

"Not yet, please—" He turned to her.

The boy had been growing. He was tall for a lad of ten, but he still looked all haphazardly pieced together, as if the rest of his body had not yet caught up with his feet and hands. Sunlight backlit the summer-bleached strands of his brown hair.

"You promised me that before I got to the Tor some of my questions would be answered. What will I say when they ask what I am doing here? I am not even certain of my own name!"

At that moment, his great grey eyes looked so much like his mother's that Caillean's heart turned over. It was true, she thought. She had promised to talk to him, but on the journey she had hardly spoken to anyone, wearied as she was by exertion and sorrow.

"You are Gawen," she said gently. "It was by that name that your mother first knew your father, and so she gave it to you."

"But my father was a Roman!" His voice wavered, as if he did not know whether to be proud or ashamed.

"That is true, and since he had no other son, I suppose as the Romans count such things you would be called Gaius Macellius Severus, like him and his father before him. Among the Romans it is a respected name. Nor did I ever hear anything of your grandsire but that he was a good and honorable man. But your grandmother was a princess of the Silures, and Gawen the name she gave her son, so you need not be ashamed to own it!"

Gawen stared at her. "Very well. But it is not my father whose name they will whisper on this Druid isle. Is it true ..." He swallowed and tried again. "Before I left the Forest House they were saying—it is true that *she*—the Lady of Vernemeton—was my mother?"

Caillean looked at him steadily, remembering with what pain Eilan had kept that secret. "It is true."

He nodded, and some of the tension went out of him on a long sigh. "I wondered. I used to daydream—all the children who were being fostered at Vernemeton would boast how their mothers were queens or their fathers were princes who would one day come to take them away. I told stories too, but the Lady was always kind to me, and when I dreamed at night, the mother who came for me was always *she*. . . ."

"She loved you," said Caillean, more softly still.

"Then why did she never claim me? Why did my father not marry her if he was such a well-known and honorable man?"

Caillean sighed. "He was a Roman, and the priestesses of the Forest House were forbidden to marry or bear children even to men of the tribes. Perhaps we will be able to change that here, but in Vernemeton ... it would have been death for her if your existence had been known."

"It was," he whispered, looking suddenly older than his years. "They found out and they killed her, didn't they? She died because of me!"

"Oh, Gawen"—wrenched by pity, Caillean reached out to him, but he turned away—"there were many reasons. Politics—and other things—you will understand more when you are grown." She bit her lip, afraid to say more, for the revelation of this child's existence had indeed been the spark that lit the flame, and in that sense, what he said was true.

"Eilan loved you, Gawen. After you were born she might well have sent you away for fosterage, but she could not bear to be parted from you. She defied her grandfather the Arch-Druid to keep you with her, and he agreed on condition that it was not known you were her own child."

"That wasn't fair!"

"Fair!" She snapped. "Life is seldom fair! You have been lucky, Gawen. Give thanks to the gods and do not complain."

His face flushed red, and then paled, but he did not answer her. Caillean felt her anger fade as suddenly as it had come.

"It does not matter now, for it is done, and you are here."

"But you do not want me," he whispered. "Nobody does."

For a moment she considered him. "I suppose you should know—Macellius, your Roman grandsire, wished to keep you in Deva and to bring you up as his own."

"Why, then, did you not leave me with him?"

Caillean stared at him without smiling. "Do you want to be a Roman?"

"Of course not! Who would?" he exclaimed, flushing furiously, and Caillean nodded. The Druids who tutored the boys at the Forest House would have taught him to hate Rome. "But you should have told me! You should have let me choose!"

"I did!" she snapped. "You chose to come here!"

The defiance seemed to drain out of him as he turned to gaze out over the water once more.

"That's true. What I don't understand is why you wanted me. . . ."

"Ah, Gawen," she said, her anger suddenly leaving her. "Even a priestess does not always understand what forces move her. Partly it was that you were all that was left to me of Eilan, whom I loved as my own child." Her throat closed with the pain of that. It was a few moments before she could speak calmly again. Then she went on, in a voice as cold as stone: "And partly it was because it seemed to me that your destiny lay among us. . . ."

Gawen's gaze was still on the golden waters. For a few moments the gentle lap of wavelets against the reeds was the only sound. Then he looked up at her.

"Very well." His voice cracked with the effort he was making to maintain control. "Will you be my mother, so that I will have some family of my own?"

Caillean stared at him, for a moment unable to speak. *I should say no, or one day he will break my heart.*

"I am a priestess," she said finally. "Just as your mother was. The vows that we have sworn to the gods bind us, sometimes against our own desires"—*or I would have remained in the Forest House, and been there to protect Eilan,* her thought went on. "Do you understand that, Gawen? Do you understand that even though I love you I may sometimes have to do things that cause you pain?"

He nodded vigorously, and it was her own heart that felt the pang.

"Foster-mother—what will happen to me on the Island of Avalon?"

Caillean thought for a moment. "You are too old to stay with the women. You will lodge among the young apprentice priests and bards.

Your grandsire was a notable singer, and you may have inherited some of his talents. Would it please you to study bard-craft?"

Gawen blinked as if the thought frightened him. "Not yet— please—I don't know ..."

"Never mind, then. In any case the priests must have some time to know you. You are still very young, and your whole future does not have to be decided now—"

And when the time comes, it will not be Cunomaglos and his Druids who decide what he should be, she thought grimly. *I could not save Eilan, but at least I can guard her child until he can choose for himself. . . .*

"So," she said briskly, "I have many duties awaiting me. Let me summon the barge and take you to the island. For tonight there will be nothing before you, I promise you, but supper and bed. Will that content you?"

"It must ..." he whispered, looking as if he doubted both her and himself.

The sun had set. In the west the sky was fading to a luminous rose, but the mists that clung to the waters had cooled to silver. The Tor was almost invisible, as if, she thought suddenly, some magic had divided it from the world. She thought of its other name, Inis Witrin, the Isle of Glass. The fancy was oddly appealing. She would be happy to leave behind the world in which Eilan had burned with her Roman lover on the Druids' pyre. She shook herself a little, and pulled out a bone whistle from the pouch that hung at her side. The sound it produced was thin and shrill. It did not seem loud, but it carried clearly over the waters.

Gawen started, looking around him, and Caillean pointed. The open water was edged by reedbeds and marsh, cut through by a hundred twisting channels. A low, square-prowed craft was emerging from one of them, pushing aside the reeds. Gawen frowned, for the man who poled it was no bigger than he. It was only when the barge drew nearer that he saw the lines in the boatman's weathered face and the sprinkling of silver in his dark hair. When the boatman saw Caillean he saluted, lifting the pole so that the boat's headway could carry it up onto the shore.

"That is Waterwalker," Caillean said softly. "His people were here before the Romans, before even the British came to these shores. None of us have been here long enough to pronounce their language, but he knows ours, and tells me that is the meaning of his name. They make a very poor living from these marshes, and are glad of the extra food we can give them, and our medicines when they are ill."

The boy continued to frown as he took his place in the stern of the boat. He sat, trailing one hand in the water and watching the ripples flow past, as the boatman pushed off once more and began to pole them toward the Tor. Caillean sighed, but did not try to talk him out of his sullens. In the past moon they had both suffered shock and loss, and if Gawen was less aware of the significance of what had happened at the Forest House, he was also less able to deal with it.

Caillean pulled her cloak around her and turned back to face the Tor. *I cannot help him. He will have to endure his sorrow and confusion . . . as will I,* she thought grimly, *as will I. . . .*

Mist swirled around them, then thinned as the Tor loomed up before them. The hollow call of a horn echoed from above. The boatman gave one last heave on his pole, and the keel grated on the shore. He jumped out and pulled it farther, and as it came to rest Caillean climbed out.

Half a dozen priestesses were coming down the path, their hair braided down their backs, gowned in undyed linen girdled in green. They drew up in a line before Caillean.

Marged, the eldest, bent reverently. "Welcome back to us, Lady of Avalon." She stopped, her eyes resting on the lanky form of Gawen. For a moment she was literally speechless. Caillean could almost hear the question on the girl's lips.

"This is Gawen. He is to live here. Will you speak to the Druids and find a place for him for tonight?"

"Gladly, Lady," she said in a whisper, without taking her eyes from Gawen, who was blushing furiously. Caillean sighed; if the very sight of a male child—for even now she simply could not think of Gawen as a young man—had this effect on her younger charges, her attempts to counteract the prejudices they had brought with them from the Forest House had a ways to go. His presence among the girls might be good for them.

Someone else was standing behind the maidens. For a moment she thought one of the older priestesses, perhaps Eiluned or Riannon, had come down to welcome her. But the newcomer was too small. She caught a glimpse of dark hair; then the figure moved past the others into plain view.

Caillean blinked. *A stranger*, she thought, and then blinked again, for the woman seemed suddenly both completely at home and utterly familiar, as if Caillean must have known her from the beginning of the world. But she could not quite call to mind when, if ever, she had set eyes on her before, or who she might be.

The newcomer was not looking at Caillean at all. Her eyes, which were dark and clear, were fastened on Gawen. Caillean wondered suddenly why she had thought the strange woman little, for she herself was a tall woman, and now the other seemed taller still. Her hair, which was dark and long, was fastened in the same way as that of the priestesses, in a single braid at her back, but she was clad in a garment of deerskin, and about her temples a narrow garland of scarlet berries was strung.

She looked at Gawen, and then she bowed down to the ground.

"Son of a Hundred Kings," she said, "be welcome to Avalon...."

Gawen looked at her in astonishment.

Caillean cleared her throat, fighting for words. "Who are you and what do you want from me?" she asked brusquely.

"With you, nothing, now," the woman said, just as shortly, "and you do not need to know my name. My business is with Gawen. But you have long known me, Blackbird, although you do not remember."

Blackbird... "Lon-dubh" in the Hibernian tongue. At the sound of the name which had been hers as a child, about which she had not even thought for almost forty years, Caillean fell abruptly silent.

Once more she could feel the ache of bruises and the pain between her thighs, and worse still the sense of filth, and shame. The man who raped her had threatened to kill her if she told what he had done. It had seemed to her then that only the sea could make her clean once more. She had pushed through the brambles at the cliff edge, heedless of the thorns that tore her skin, intending to throw herself into the waves that frothed around the fanged rocks below.

And suddenly the shadow between the briars had become a woman, no taller than herself but incomparably stronger, who had held her, murmuring, with a tenderness her own mother had never had the energy to show, and called her by her childhood name. She must have fallen asleep at last, still cradled in the Lady's arms. When she awoke, her body had been cleansed, the worst of her hurts become a distant ache, and the memory of terror an evil dream.

"Lady—" she whispered. Years later, her studies with the Druids had enabled her to give the being who had saved her a name. But the fairy woman's attention was fixed on Gawen.

"My Lord, I will guide you to your destiny. Wait for me at the water's edge, and one day soon I will come for you." She bowed again, not quite so deeply this time, and suddenly, as if she had never been there at all, was gone.

Caillean closed her eyes. The instinct which had guided her to bring Gawen to Avalon had been a good one. If the Lady of the Fairy Folk honored him, he must indeed have a purpose here. Eilan had met the Merlin once in vision. What had he promised her? Roman though he was, this boy's father had died as a Year-King, to save the people. What did that mean? For a moment she nearly understood Eilan's sacrifice.

A choked sound from Gawen brought her back to the present. He was white as chalk.

"Who was she? Why did she speak to me?"

Marged looked from Caillean to the boy, brows lifting, and the priestess wondered suddenly if the others had seen anything at all.

Caillean said. "She is the Lady of the Elder Folk—those who are called Faerie. She saved my life once, long ago. In these days the Elder Folk come not often among humankind, and she would not have appeared here without reason. But as for why—I do not know."

"She bowed to me." He swallowed, then asked in a quenched whisper, "Will you permit me to go, foster-mother?"

"Permit you? I would not dare to prevent it. You must be ready when she comes for you."

He looked up at her, a glint in those clear grey eyes that reminded her suddenly of Eilan. "I have no choice, then. But I will not go with her unless she answers me!"

◁ ◁ ◁

"Lady, I would never question your judgment," said Eiluned, "but what possessed you to bring a man-child that age here?"

Caillean took a swallow of water from her hornwood beaker and set it down on the dining table with a sigh. In the six moons since the priestesses had first come to Avalon, it sometimes seemed to her that the younger woman had done nothing but question her decisions. She wondered if Eiluned deceived even herself with her show of humility. She was only thirty, but she seemed older, thin and frowning and always busy about everyone else's affairs. Still, she was conscientious, and had become a useful deputy.

The other women, recognizing the tone, looked away and went back to their meal. The long hall at the foot of the Tor had seemed ample when the Druids built it for them at the beginning of the summer. But once word of the new House of Maidens had spread, more girls had come to them, and Caillean thought they might have to extend the hall before another summer went by.

"The Druids take boys for training at an even younger age," she said evenly. Firelight flickered on the smooth planes of Gawen's face, making him look momentarily older.

"Then let them take him! He does not belong here. . . ." She glared at the boy, who glanced at Caillean for reassurance before taking another spoonful of millet and beans. Dica and Lysanda, the youngest of her maidens, giggled until Gawen grew red and looked away.

"For the present I have arranged with Cunomaglos for him to lodge with old Brannos, the bard. Will that content you?" she asked acidly.

"An excellent idea!" Eiluned nodded. "The old man is dod-dering. I live in fear that one night he will fall into his hearthfire or wander into the lake...."

What the other woman said was true, though it was the old man's kindness, not his weakness, that had led Marged to choose him.

"Who *is* the child?" asked Riannon, on her other side, her red curls bouncing. "Was he not one of the fosterlings at Vernemeton? And what happened when you went back to visit? The most amazing rumors have been flying about the countryside...." She eyed her High Priestess expectantly.

"He is an orphan." Caillean sighed. "I do not know what you may have heard, but it is true that the Lady of Vernemeton is dead. There was a rebellion. The Druid priesthood in the north have scat-tered, and several of the senior priestesses are dead as well. Dieda was one of them. In truth, I do not know if the Forest House will sur-vive, and if it does not, we here will be the only ones left to guard the old wisdom and pass it on." Had Eilan had foreknowledge of her fate, and known that only the new community on Avalon would survive?

The other priestesses sat back, eyes widening. If they assumed it was the Romans who had killed Eilan and the others, so much the better. She had no love for Bendeigid, who was now Arch-Druid, but though he might be mad, he was still one of their own.

"Dieda is dead?" Kea's sweet voice thinned, and she grasped Riannon's arm. "But I was to have gone to her this winter for more training. How will I teach the young ones the sacred songs? This is a heavy loss!" She sat back, tears welling in her grave grey eyes.

A great loss indeed, thought Caillean grimly, not only of Dieda's knowledge and skill, but of the priestess she might have been if she had not chosen hatred over love. That was a lesson to her also, and one she should remember when bitterness threatened to overwhelm her.

"I will train you ..." she said quietly. "I never studied the secrets of the bards of Eriu, but the holy songs and sacred offices of the Druid priestesses came from Vernemeton, and I know all of them well."

"Oh! I did not mean—" Kea broke off, blushing furiously. "I know you sing, and play the harp as well. Play for us now, Caillean, it seems so long since you have made music for us around the fire!"

"It is a *creuth*, not a harp—" Caillean began automatically. Then she sighed. "Not tonight, my child. I am too weary. It is you who should sing for us, and ease our sorrow."

She forced a smile and saw Kea brighten. The younger priestess had not the inspired skill of Dieda, but her voice, though light, was sweet and true, and she loved the old songs.

Riannon patted her friend's shoulder. "Tonight we will all sing for the Goddess, and She will comfort us. At least you have come back to us." She turned to Caillean. "We were afraid you would not return in time for the full moon."

"Surely I have trained you better than that!" exclaimed Caillean. "You do not need me to do the ritual."

"Perhaps not." Riannon grinned. "But without you it would not be the same."

⚭ ⚭ ⚭

When they left the hall it was full dark, and cold, but the wind that had come up with nightfall had swept the mists away. Behind the black bulk of the Tor the night sky blazed with stars. Caillean glanced eastward, and noticed the heavens growing luminous with the rising of the moon, though it was still invisible behind the hill.

"Let us make haste," she told the others, fastening her warm mantle securely. "Already our Lady seeks the skies." She started up the path, and the others fell into place behind her, their breath making little puffs of white in the chill air.

Only when she reached the first turning did she look back. The door to the hall was still open, and she could see Gawen's dark shape against the lamplight. Even in silhouette, there was a wrenching loneliness in the way he stood, watching the women leave him. For a moment Caillean wanted to call out and bid him to join them. But that would have scandalized Eiluned indeed. At least he was here, on the holy isle. Then the door closed and the boy disappeared. Caillean took a deep breath and set herself to climb the rest of the way up the hill.

She had been gone for a moon, and was out of condition for such exertions. When she reached the top she stood panting while the others joined her, resisting the impulse to hold on to one of the standing stones. Gradually her head ceased to spin, and she took her place by the altar stone. One by one priestesses entered the circle, moving sunwise around the altar. The little mirrors of polished silver that hung from their belts glinted as they settled into place. Kea set the silver basin upon the stone, and Beryan, who had just taken her vows at Midsummer, filled it with water from the sacred well.

There was no need here to cast a circle. The place was already sacred, not to be looked upon by uninitiated eyes, but as the circle of women was completed, the air within it seemed to become heavier, and utterly still. Even the wind that had made her shiver was gone.

"We hail the glorious heavens, blazing with light." Caillean lifted her hands and the others followed. "We hail the holy earth from which we were sprung." She bent and touched the frosty grass. "Guardians of the Four Quarters, we salute you." Together, they turned in each direction, gazing until they seemed to see the Powers whose names and forms were hidden in the hearts of the wise ones shimmering before them.

She turned once more to face westward. "We honor our ancestors who have gone before. Watch over our children, holy ones." *Eilan my beloved, watch over me . . . watch over your child.* She closed her eyes, and for a moment it seemed to her that she felt something, like a gentle touch on her hair.

Caillean turned to face the east, where the stars were fading into the glow of the moon. The air around her grew tense with anticipation as the others did the same, waiting for the first bright edge to lift above the hills. There was a flicker; her breath went out of her on a long sigh as the tall pine on the far summit appeared suddenly in stark silhouette. And all at once the moon was there, huge and tinged with gold. With each succeeding moment she rose higher, and as she left earth behind her she grew ever more pale and bright, until she floated free in unsullied purity. As one, the priestesses lifted their hands in adoration.

With an effort Caillean steadied her voice, willing herself to sink into the familiar rhythm of the ritual.

"In the east our Lady Moon is rising," she sang.

"Jewel of guidance, jewel of the night," the others chorused in return.

"Holy be each thing on which Thy light shines...." As Caillean's voice grew stronger, so did the chorus that supported her, her energy amplified by that of the other priestesses, theirs rising as her inspiration grew.

"Jewel of guidance, jewel of the night..."

"Fair be each deed Thy light reveals...." Each line came more easily, power reflecting back from the other women's response to her own. As the energy rose she found herself growing warmer as well.

"Fair be Thy light upon the hilltops...." Now, as Caillean ended a line, she found the strength to hold the note through the answer, and the others, holding their last note, supported hers in sweet harmony.

"Fair be Thy light upon field and forest...." Now the moon was well above the treetops. She saw the Vale of Avalon laid out before her with its seven holy isles, and as she gazed, the vision seemed to expand until it was the entirety of Britannia that she saw.

"Fair be Thy light upon all roads and all wanderers...." Caillean opened her arms in blessing, and heard Kea's clear soprano soar suddenly in descant above the chorus.

"Fair be Thy light on the waves of the sea...." Her sight sped across the waters. She was losing awareness of her body now.

"Fair be Thy light among the stars of heaven." The radiance of the moonlight filled her, the music lifted her. She floated between earth and heaven, seeing everything, soul outpoured in an ecstasy of blessing.

"Mother of Light, fair moon of the seasons..." Caillean felt her perception narrowing until the glowing moon was all she could see.

"Come to us, Lady! Let us be Thy mirror!"

"Jewel of guidance, jewel of the night . . ."

Caillean held her final note through the chorus and after, and the others, sensing the energy building, upheld it with their own harmonies. The great chord pulsed as the singers drew breath, but was sustained.

The priestesses rode the power, sensing without need for signal the moment to bring out their mirrors. Now, still singing, the women moved closer together until they formed a semicircle facing the moon. Caillean, still standing on the eastern side of the altar, turned toward them. The music had become a low hum.

"Lady, come down to us! Lady, be with us! Lady, come to us now!" She brought down her hands.

Thirteen silver mirrors flashed white fire as the priestesses angled them to catch the moonlight. Pale mooncircles danced across the grass as they were turned toward the altar. Light gleamed from the silver surface of the bowl, sending bright flickers across the still forms of the priestesses and the standing stones. Then, as the mirrors were focused, the reflected moonbeams met suddenly on the surface of the water within. Thirteen trembling moonlets ran together like quicksilver and became one.

"Lady, Thou who art nameless yet called by many names," murmured Caillean, "Thou who art without form and yet hath many faces, as the moons reflected in our mirrors become a single image, so may it be with Thy reflection in our hearts. Lady, we call to Thee! Come down to us, be with us here!"

She let out her breath in a long sigh. The humming faded to silence that throbbed with expectation. Vision, attention, all existence were focused on the blaze of light within the bowl. She felt the familiar shift of awareness as her trance deepened, as if her flesh were dissolving away, and no sense but sight remained.

Now even that blurred, obscuring the moon's reflection in the water of the silver bowl. Or perhaps it was not the image but the radiance it reflected that was changing, brightening, until the moon and its image were linked by a shaft of light. Particles of brightness moved in the moonbeam, shaped a figure, softly luminous, that gazed back at her with shining eyes.

"Lady," her heart called, "I have lost my beloved. How shall I survive alone?"

"Hardly alone—you have sisters and daughters," came the reply, tart and a little, perhaps, amused. "You have a son . . . and you have Me. . . ."

Caillean was dimly aware that her legs had given way and that now she was on her knees. It did not matter. Her soul went out to the Goddess who smiled down at her, and in the next moment the love she had offered flowed back in such measure that for a little while she knew nothing more.

The moon was past the midpoint of heaven by the time Caillean came to herself. The Presence that had blessed them was gone, and the air was cold. Around her, the other women were beginning to stir. She forced stiffened muscles to work and got to her feet, shivering. Fragments of vision still flickered in her memory. The Lady had spoken to her, had told her things she needed to know, but with each moment they were fading.

"Lady, as Thou hast blessed us we thank Thee . . ." she murmured. "Let us carry forth that blessing into the world."

Together they murmured their thanks to the Guardians. Kea came forward to take up the silver bowl and poured its water in a bright stream over the stone. Then, going against the way of the sun, they circled the altar and moved toward the path. Only Caillean remained beside the altar stone.

"Caillean, are you coming? It has grown cold here!" Eiluned, at the end of the line, stood waiting.

"Not yet. There are things I must think on. I will stay here for a little while. Do not worry, my mantle will keep me warm," she added, though in truth she was shivering. "You go on."

"Very well." The other woman sounded dubious, but there had been command in Caillean's tone. After a moment she too turned and disappeared over the lip of the hill.

When they had gone, Caillean knelt beside the altar, embracing it as if she could thereby grasp the Goddess who had stood there.

"Lady, speak! Tell me clearly what you want me to do!"

But nothing answered her. There was power in the stone, a subtle tingle that she felt in her bones, but the Lady was gone, and the rock was cold. After a time she sat back with a sigh.

As the moon moved, the circle was barred by the shadows of the standing stones. Caillean, her attention still inward, noticed the stones without really seeing them. It was only when she stood up that she realized her gaze had fixed on one of the larger stones.

The ring atop the Tor was moderate in size, most of the rocks reaching somewhere between Caillean's waist and shoulder. But this one had grown taller by a head. As she noticed that, it moved, and a dark figure seemed to emerge from the stone.

"Who—" the priestess began, but even as she spoke she knew with the same certainty that had come to her that afternoon who it must be. She heard a low ripple of laughter and the fairy woman came fully into the moonlight, dressed, as before, in her deerskin wrap and wreath of berries, seeming not to feel the cold.

"Lady of Faerie, I salute you—" Caillean said softly.

"Greetings, Blackbird," said the fairy woman, laughing once more. "But no, it is a swan you have become, floating on the lake with your cygnets around you."

"What are you doing here?"

"Where else should I be, child? The Otherworld touches yours at many places, though there are not so many now as formerly. The stone circles are gateways, at certain times, as are all earth's edges— mountaintops, caverns, the shore where sea meets land. . . . But there are some spots which exist always in both worlds, and of those, this Tor is one of the most powerful."

"I have felt that," Caillean said softly. "It was like that sometimes at the Hill of the Maidens, near the Forest House, as well."

The fairy woman sighed. "That hill is a holy place, and now even more so, but the blood that was shed there has closed the gateway."

Caillean bit her lip, seeing once more dead ashes beneath a weeping sky. Would her grief for Eilan never end?

"You did well to leave it," the fairy woman went on. "And well to bring the boy."

"What do you want with him?" Fear for Gawen sharpened her tone.

"To prepare him for his destiny ... What do *you* want for him, priestess, can you say?"

Caillean blinked, trying to regain control of the conversation. "What is his destiny? Will he lead us against the Romans and bring back the old ways?"

"That is not the only kind of victory," the Lady answered her. "Why do you think Eilan risked so much to bear the child and keep him in safety?"

"She was his mother—" Caillean began, but her words were lost in the fairy woman's reply.

"She was High Priestess, and a great one. And she was a daughter of that blood that brought the highest human wisdom to these shores. To human eyes, she failed, and her Roman lover died in shame. But you know differently."

Caillean stared at her, scars from taunts she thought she had forgotten awakening to new pain in her memory. "I was not born in this land, nor do I come of noble kin," she said tightly. "Are you telling me I have no right to stand here, or to raise the boy?"

"Blackbird"—the other woman shook her head—"listen to what I say. What was Eilan's by inheritance is yours by training and labor and the gift of the Lady of Life. Eilan herself entrusted you with this task. But Gawen is the last heir to the line of the Wise, and his father was a son of the Dragon on his mother's side, bound by his blood to the land."

"That was what you meant, then, when you called him Son of a Hundred Kings..." breathed Caillean. "But what use is that to us now? The Romans rule."

"I cannot say. It has been given me to know only that he must be prepared. You and the Druid priesthood will show him the highest wisdom of humankind. And I, if you will pay my price, will show him the mysteries of this land you call Britannia."

"Your price," Caillean repeated, swallowing.

"It is a time for building bridges," said the Queen. "I have a daughter, Sianna, begotten by a man of your kind. She is the same age as the boy. I wish you to take her into your House of Maidens as a fosterling. Teach her your ways and your wisdom, Lady of Avalon, and I will teach Gawen mine...."

Chapter Two

"Have you come, then, to join our order?" asked the old man.

Gawen looked at him in surprise. When the priestess Kea had brought him to Brannos the night before, it had seemed to the boy that the ancient bard had outlived his wits as well as his music. His hair was white, his hands so palsied with age he could no longer pluck the harpstrings, and when Gawen was introduced, he had stirred from his own bed only long enough to point to a heap of sheepskins where the boy might lie and then gone back to sleep.

The bard had not seemed very promising as a mentor in this strange place, but the sheepskins were warm and without fleas, and the boy was very tired. Before he had half finished thinking through all the strange things that had happened to him in the past moon, sleep carried him away. But Brannos in the morning was a very different being from the mazed creature of the night before. The rheumy eyes were surprisingly keen, and Gawen felt himself flushing under that grey stare.

"I am not sure," he answered cautiously. "My foster-mother has not told me what I am to do here. She asked if I would like to be a bard, but I have only learned the simplest songs that the children being fostered in the Forest House sang. I like to sing, but surely there is more to being a bard than that...."

That was not quite the truth. Gawen loved to sing, but the Arch-Druid Ardanos, who was the most notable bard among the Druids of his time, had hated the sight of him and never even let him try. Now that he knew Ardanos had been his own great-grandfather, the one who wanted to kill Eilan when he knew she was with child, he understood why, but he was still wary of letting his interest show.

"If I were called to that path," he said carefully, "wouldn't I know it by now?"

The old man coughed and spat into the fire. "What do you like to do?"

"At the Forest House I helped with the goats, and worked sometimes in the garden. When there was time the other children and I played ball."

"You like to be out and about, then, instead of studying?" The keen eyes fixed him once more.

"I like doing things," Gawen said slowly, "but I like learning things too, if they are interesting. I loved the hero-tales that the Druids used to tell." He wondered what kind of stories the Roman children learned, but he knew better than to ask here.

"If you like stories, then we will get on," said Brannos, smiling. "Do you wish to stay?"

Gawen looked away. "I think there were bards among my kin. Perhaps that is why Lady Caillean sent me to you. If I have no talent for music will you still want me?"

"It is your strong arms and legs I need, alas, not music." The old man sighed; then his bushy brows drew down. "You 'think' there were bards in your family? You do not know? Who were your parents?"

The boy eyed him warily. Caillean had not *said* he was to keep his parentage a secret, but the knowledge was so new to him it did not seem real. But perhaps Brannos had lived so long that even this would not seem strange.

"Would you believe that until this moon I did not even know their names? They are dead now, and I suppose it cannot hurt them any more if people know about me. . . ." He heard with surprise the resentment in his own words. "They say my mother was the High Priestess of Vernemeton, the Lady Eilan." He remembered her sweet voice and the fragrance that always clung to her veils and blinked back tears. "But my father was a Roman, so you can see I should probably never have been born."

The ancient Druid could no longer sing, but there was nothing wrong with his ears. He heard the sullen note in the boy's voice and sighed.

"It does not matter in this house who your parents were. Cunomaglos himself, who rules the Druid priesthood here as the Lady Caillean rules the priestesses, came from a family of potters near Londinium. None of us on this earth knows, save by hearsay, who his mother may have been, or his father. Before the gods, nothing matters save what you may create for yourself."

That is not completely true, thought Gawen. *Caillean said she saw me born; so she knows who my mother was. But I suppose that is hearsay, for I have to trust her word that it is true. Can I trust her?* he wondered suddenly. *Or this old man, or anyone here?* Oddly enough, the face that came into his mind at that moment was that of the Queen of Faerie. He trusted her, he thought, and that was strange, for he was not even sure that she was real.

"Among the Druids of our order," said the old man, "birth does not matter. All men come alike into this life with nothing, and whether you are a son of the Arch-Druid or of a homeless wanderer, every man begins as a squalling naked babe—I as much as you, the son of a beggar or a king or of a hundred kings—all men begin so, and all end the same, in a winding sheet."

Gawen stared at him. The Lady of the Fairy Folk had used the same phrase—"Son of a Hundred Kings." It made him feel hot and cold at the same time. She had promised to come for him. Perhaps then she would tell him what that title might mean. He felt his heart pound suddenly and did not know if it were with anticipation or fear.

As the moon which had welcomed her return to Avalon waned, Caillean found herself settling into its routine as if she had never been away. In the mornings, when the Druids climbed the Tor to salute the dawn, the priestesses made their own devotions at the hearthfire. In the evening, when the distant tides of the sea raised the level of the waters in the marshes, they faced west to honor the setting sun. At night, the Tor belonged to the priestesses; new moon and full moon and dark all had their own rituals.

It was amazing, she thought as she followed Eiluned toward the store shed, how quickly traditions could emerge. The community of priestesses on the holy isle had not yet celebrated its first full year, but already Eiluned was treating the ways of doing things that Caillean had suggested as if they had the force of law and a hundred years of tradition.

"You remember that, when Waterwalker came the first time, he brought us a sack of barley. But this time, when he came for his medicine, he brought nothing at all." Eiluned led the way down the path to the storehouse, still talking. "You must see, Lady, that this will never do. We have few enough trained priestesses here to tend those who can give us something in return, and if you insist on taking in every orphan you find, how we will stretch our stores to feed them through the water is more than I can tell!"

For a moment Caillean was struck speechless; then she hurried to catch up.

"He is not just any orphan—he is Eilan's son!"

"Let Bendeigid take him, then! He is her father, after all."

Caillean shook her head, remembering that last conversation. Bendeigid was mad. If she could help it, he would never learn that Gawen still lived.

Eiluned was pulling back the bar that held the door to the storage shed. As the door swung open, something small and grey scurried away into the bushes.

Eiluned gave a little shriek and lurched backward into Caillean's arms. "A curse on the dirty beast! A curse—"

"Be silent!" Caillean snapped, shaking her. "You've no call to curse a creature that has as much right to seek its food as we do. Nor to deny our help to any who come to ask, especially Waterwalker, who ferries us back and forth across the water with no more than a blessing for his pay!"

Eiluned turned, her cheeks purpling ominously. "I am only doing the task you set me!" she exclaimed. "How can you speak to me so?"

Caillean let go of her and sighed. "I did not mean to hurt your feelings, or to imply you have not done well. We are still new here, still learning what we can do and what we need. But I do know that there is no point in our being here if we can only do so by becoming as hard and grasping as the Romans! We are here to serve the Lady. Cannot we trust that She will provide?"

Eiluned shook her head, but her face was returning to its normal hue. "Will it serve the Lady's purposes for us to starve? See here"— she pulled the stone slab from the storage pit and pointed—"the pit is half empty and it will not be midwinter for another moon!"

The pit is half full, Caillean wanted to reply, but it was for just this compulsion to worry about such things that she had appointed Eiluned keeper of the stores.

"There are two more pits, and they are still full," she said calmly, "but you do well to point this out to me."

"There was grain enough for several winters in the storehouses at Vernemeton, and now there are fewer mouths to consume it," Eiluned said then. "Could we send to them for more supplies?"

Caillean closed her eyes, seeing once more the heap of ashes on the Hill of the Maidens. Indeed, Eilan and many of the others would not need to be fed this winter, or ever again. She told herself that it was a practical suggestion, that Eiluned had not meant to cause her pain.

"I will ask." She forced her voice to calm. "But if, as they were saying, the community of women at the Forest House is to be disbanded, we cannot depend on them to support us another year. And it may be best in any case if the folk in Deva forget us. Ardanos mixed in the affairs of the Romans and nearly brought us to disaster. I think we should be less visible, and if so, we will have to find a way to feed ourselves here."

"That is your business, Lady. Dealing out the stores we already have is mine," said Eiluned. She shoved the stone slab back into place again. *No, it is the Lady's business,* thought Caillean as they continued with their count of bags and barrels. *It is because of Her that we are here, and we must not forget it.*

It was true that she and many of the older women had never

known any home but that of the priestesses. But they had skills that would win them a welcome in any British chieftain's hall. It would be hard to leave, but none of them would starve. They had come to serve the Goddess because She called them, and if the Goddess wanted priestesses, Caillean thought with the beginnings of a smile, it was up to Her to find the means to feed them.

"—and I cannot do it all alone," said Eiluned. With a start, Caillean realized that the other woman's comments had become a buzz of background noise. She raised her brows inquiringly.

"You cannot expect me to keep track of every grain of barley and turnip. Make some of those girls earn their keep by helping me!"

Caillean frowned, an idea blossoming suddenly. *A gift from the Lady,* she thought, *my answer.* The girls that studied with them were trained well, and could find a place in any household in the land. Why not take the daughters of ambitious men and teach them for a time before they went out to marry? The Romans did not care what women did—they did not even need to know.

"You shall have your helpers," she told Eiluned. "You shall teach them how to supply a household, and Kea shall teach them music, and I shall teach them the old tales of our people and the Druids' lore. What stories will they tell their children, do you think? And what songs will they sing to the babes they bear?"

"Ours, I suppose, but—"

"Ours," Caillean agreed, "and the Roman fathers who see their children only once a day at dinner will not think to question it. The Romans believe that what a woman says does not matter. But this whole isle can be won away from them by the children of women trained in Avalon!"

Eiluned shrugged and smiled, half understanding. But as Caillean followed her through the rest of the inspection, her own mind was working swiftly. One girl among them already, little Alia, was not meant for the life of a priestess. When she returned to her home she could spread the word among the women, and the Druids could let it be known among the men of the princely houses who still cared about the old ways.

Neither the Romans with their armies nor the Christians with their talk of damnation could prevail against the first words a babe heard in his mother's arms. Rome might rule men's bodies, but it was Avalon, she thought with rising excitement, the holy isle, safe in its marshes, that would shape their souls.

Gawen woke very early and lay awake, his mind too active for sleep again, though the bit of sky he could see through the crack in the daub and wattle of the hut was just beginning to lighten with the onset of day. Brannos was still snoring softly on the other bed, but outside his window, he heard someone cough and the rustle of robes. He peered out. Overhead the sky was still dark, but to the east a paler flush of pink showed where the dawn would break.

In the week since he had come to Avalon he had begun to learn its ways. The men were assembling in front of the Druids' hall, the novices robed in grey and the senior priests in white, preparing for the sunrise services. The procession was wholly silent; Gawen knew they would not speak till the sun's disk showed clear and bright above the hills. It would be a fine day; he had not lived all his life in a Druid temple without knowing that much about the weather.

After sliding out of bed, he got into his clothes without disturbing the elderly priest—at least they had not consigned him to the House of Maidens, where he would be guarded like a young girl—and slipped out of the hut. The predawn light was dim, but the fresh smell of early morning scented the damp air, and he took a deep breath.

As if at some wordless signal, the sunrise procession began to move toward the path. Gawen waited in the deeper gloom beneath the thatched overhang to the hut until the Druids had gone by, then on silent feet went down to the shores of the lake. The fairy woman had told him to wait there. Every day since he had arrived, he had come down to the water's edge. He wondered now if she would ever come for him, but he had begun to love the slow dawning of the day above the marshes for its own sake.

The sky was just beginning to flush over with the first rosy light of dawn. Behind him, the growing light showed him the buildings clustered below the slope of the Tor. There was the long peak of the meeting hall, built in a rectangle in the Roman way. The thatched roofs of the roundhouses behind it glistened faintly, the larger for the priestesses, the smaller for the maidens, and another small building a little apart for the High Priestess. Cooksheds and weaving sheds and a barn for the goats lay beyond them. He could just glimpse the more weathered rooftops of the Druids' halls on the other side of the hill. Farther down the slope, he knew, was the sacred spring, and across the pastures were the beehive huts of the Christians, clustered around the thorn tree that had grown from Father Joseph's staff.

But he had not yet been there. The priestesses, after some debate about what tasks were suitable for a boy-child, had assigned him to help herd the goats that gave them milk. If he had gone to his Roman grandfather, he thought, he would not have had to herd goats. But the goats were not bad company. Eyeing the brightening sky, he realized the priestesses would be stirring soon and expecting him to come to the hall for his morning bread and ale. And then the goats would begin to bleat, anxious to be out on the hillside pastures. The only time he had to himself was now.

Again he could hear in his mind the Lady's words: "Son of a Hundred Kings." What had she meant? Why him? His mind would not let these thoughts alone. Many days had passed since that strange greeting. When would she come for him?

He sat for a long time on the shore, looking out over the grey expanse of the water as it changed to a sheet of silver reflecting the pale autumn sky. The air was crisp, but he was accustomed to cold, and the sheepskin Brannos had given him for a cape kept off the chill. It was quiet, but not quite silent; as he himself grew more still, he found himself listening to the whisper of wind in the trees, the sigh of the wavelets as they kissed the shore.

He closed his eyes, and his breath caught as for a moment all those small sounds that came from the world around him became music. He became aware of a song—he could not tell if it came from outside or if something in his spirit was singing, but ever more sweetly he could hear the melody. Without opening his eyes, he pulled from his pocket the flute of willow that Brannos had given him, and began to play.

The first notes seemed such a squawk that he almost flung the flute into the water; then for a moment the note clarified. Gawen took a deep breath, centered himself, and tried again. Once more he heard that pure thread of sound. Carefully, he changed his fingering and slowly began to coax forth a melody. As he relaxed, his breathing became deep, controlled, and he sank into the emerging song.

Lost in the music, he did not at first realize when the Lady appeared. It was only gradually that the shimmer of light above the lake became edged in shadow, and the shadow became a form, moving as if by magic across the surface until at last it grew close enough for him to see the low prow of the boat on which she stood and the slender shaft of the pole.

The boat was something like the barge in which Waterwalker had brought them to the isle but narrower, and the Lady was poling it with long, efficient strokes. Gawen watched her carefully. He had been too confused to really look at her when they met before. Her slender muscular arms were bare to the shoulder despite the cold; her dark hair was knotted up off her forehead, which was high and unlined, crossed with dark, level brows. Her eyes were dark too, and brilliant. She was accompanied by a young girl, sturdily built, with deep dimples embedded in pink-and-white cheeks as smooth as thick cream and fine hair, burnished copper-gold, the same color as the Lady Eilan's—his mother's—had been. She wore her hair, like the priestesses, in a single long braid. The young girl grinned quickly at him, her pink cheeks crinkling.

"This is my daughter Sianna," the Lady said, fixing him with eyes as bright and sharp as a bird's. "What name did they give you then, my Lord?"

"My mother called me Gawen," he said. "Why did you—"

The Lady's words cut across his question. "Do you know how to pole a punt, Gawen?"

"I do not, Lady. I have never been taught anything about the water. But before we go——"

"Good. You have nothing to unlearn, and this at least I can teach you." Once more her words overrode his. "But for now it will be enough to get into the boat without upsetting it. Step carefully. At this time of year the water is too cold for a bath." She held out her small hand, rock-hard, and steadied him as he stepped into the boat. He sat down, gripping the sides as the punt lurched, but in truth it was his own response to her command rather than the motion that had unsettled him.

Sianna giggled and the Lady fixed her with her dark eyes. "If you had never been taught, you would not know anything either. Is it well done to mock at ignorance?"

What about my *ignorance?* he wondered. But he did not try to repeat his question. Maybe she would listen later, when they had gotten wherever she was taking him.

Sianna murmured, "It was only the picture of an unexpected bath on such a day . . ." She was trying to look sober, but she giggled again and the Lady smiled indulgently, digging in with the pole and sending the punt gliding across the surface of the lake.

Gawen looked back at the girl. He did not know if Sianna had been making fun of him, but he liked the way her eyes slanted when she smiled and decided that he did not mind her teasing him. She was the brightest thing in all that expanse of silver water and pale sky; he could have warmed his hands at her red hair. Tentatively, he smiled. The radiance of the grin that answered him struck through the shell with which he had tried to armor his feelings. Only much later did he realize that in this moment his heart was opened to her forever.

But now he knew only that he felt warmer, and loosened the thong that held his sheepskin closed. The punt moved smoothly over the water as the sun climbed higher. Gawen sat quietly in the boat, watching Sianna from beneath his lashes. The Lady seemed to have no need for speech and the girl followed her example. Gawen dared not break the silence, and presently he found himself listening for the occasional call of a bird and the faint lapping of water.

The water was calm, ruffled only by small ripples as the breeze touched it or the sliding wrinkles that the Lady told him signaled hidden snags or bars. The autumn had been rainy and the water was high; Gawen looked at the waving water grass and imagined sunken meadows. Hills and hummocks poked through the surface, linked in some places by thick reeds. It was past noon when at last the Lady sent the boat sliding up the pebbled shore of one island which—at least to Gawen—seemed no different from any other. Then she stepped out on the dry ground and motioned to the two children to follow her onto the land.

She asked, "Can you build a fire?"

"I am sorry, Lady. I have never been taught that either." He felt himself blushing. "I know how to keep a good blaze going, but the Druids held fire to be sacred. It was only allowed to go out at special times, and then it was the priests who rekindled it."

"It is like men to make a mystery of something that any farmwife can do," said Sianna scornfully. But the Lady shook her head.

"Fire is a mystery. Like any power, it can be a danger, or a servant, or a god. What matters is how it is used."

"And what kind of flame is it that we kindle here?" he asked steadily.

"A wayfarer's fire only, which will serve to cook our day-meal. Sianna, take him with you and show him how to find tinder."

Sianna stretched out her hand to Gawen, closing her small warm fingers over his. "Here, we must find dry grasses and dead leaves; anything which will burn quickly and catch fire easily; little twigs and fallen deadwood—like this." She let go his hand and picked up a handful of twigs. Together they sought out dry stuff and piled leaves and twigs into a little heap in a charred hollow in the damp soil. Larger sticks lay in a heap nearby. This was clearly a place they had used before.

When she judged the pile big enough, the Lady showed him how to strike fire with a flint and steel that she had in a leather bag tied at her side, and it blazed up. It seemed odd to Gawen that she should make him do a servant's work after hailing him as a king. But, looking at the fire, he remembered what she had said about it, and for a moment he understood. Even a cookfire was a sacred thing, and perhaps, in these days when the Romans ruled in the outer world, even a sacred king might have to serve in small and secret ways.

After a few moments a cheerful little fire was sending up narrow tendrils of flame, which the Lady fed with successively larger sticks. When it was burning well, she reached into the punt and pulled from a bag the limp headless carcass of a hare. With a little stone knife she skinned and gutted it, and strung it on green sticks over the fire, which was settling to a steady glow as some of the sticks turned to coals. After a few moments sizzling juices from the hare began to drop into the fire. Gawen's stomach growled in anticipation at the savory smell, and he became acutely aware that he had missed his breakfast.

When the meat was done, the Lady divided it with her knife and gave a portion to each of the children, without, however, taking any herself. Gawen ate eagerly. When they had finished, the Lady showed them where to bury the bones and fur.

"Lady," said Gawen, wiping his hands on his tunic, "thank you for the meal. But I still don't know what you want with me. Now that we have eaten, will you answer me?"

For a long moment she considered him. "You think you know who you are, but you do not know at all. I told you, I am a guide. I will help you find what it is that you are meant to do." She stepped back to the punt, motioning them to get in.

What about the hundred kings? he wanted to ask. But he did not quite dare.

This time the fairy woman drove the punt across open water where the inflowing waters of the river cut a channel through the marsh; she bent deeply to catch the bottom with the pole. The island toward which she was heading was large, separated only by a narrow channel from the higher ground to the west.

"Walk quietly," she said as they eased up onto the shore. She led them among the trees.

Even at the beginning of winter, when leaves were beginning to fall, slipping between the trunks and underneath low branches was no easy task, and the dry leaves crackled beneath any unwary step. For a time Gawen was too caught up in the act of moving to question where they were going. The fairy woman passed without a sound, and Sianna moved almost as quietly. They made him feel like some great lumbering ox.

Her lifted hand brought him to a grateful halt. Slowly she drew aside a branch of hazel. Beyond it lay a small meadow where red deer were cropping the fading grass.

"Study the deer, Gawen, you must learn their ways," she said softly. "In the summer you would not find them here. Then they lie up through the heat of the day and come out only at dusk to feed. But now they know they must eat as much as they can before winter comes. It is one of a hunter's first duties to learn the ways of every animal he follows."

Gawen ventured to ask in an undertone, "Am I, then, to be a hunter, Lady?"

She paused before answering.

"It does not matter what you are to *do*," she said, just as softly. "What you *are* is something different. That is what you have to learn."

Sianna put out her small hand and pulled him down into a little hollow in the grass.

"We will watch the deer from here," she whispered. "Here we can see everything."

Gawen was quiet at her side, and so close to her it suddenly rushed over him intensely that Sianna was a girl, and his own age. He had hardly seen, far less touched, a young girl before this; Eilan, and Caillean, whom he had known all the years of his life, did not seem like women at all to him. Suddenly things he had heard all his life without understanding rushed over him. Almost overwhelmed by this new knowledge, he felt his cheeks flooding scarlet. He was very much aware of this and hid his face in the cool grass. He could smell the damp sweaty fragrance of Sianna's hair, and the strong smell of the crudely tanned hide of her skirt.

After a while Sianna poked him in the side and whispered "Look!"

Stepping high and daintily over the grass came a doe, balanced lightly on hooves which seemed almost too small to bear her weight. A few steps behind her tiptoed a half-grown fawn, its baby spots disappearing into shaggy winter hide. The creature was following in his mother's footsteps, but in comparison with her assured elegance his gait was alternately awkward and all grace. *Like me . . .* , he thought, grinning.

Gawen watched as they slowly moved in tandem, pausing to sniff the wind. Then, perhaps taking fright at some tiny sound Gawen did not hear, the doe flung up her head and bolted away. Left alone in the little clearing, the fawn first froze; it stood for a few seconds motionless, then abruptly bounded after her.

Gawen let his breath go. He did not realize till then that he had been holding it.

Eilan, my mother, he thought, trying over the thought, not for the first time, *was like that doe. She was so busy being High Priestess, she did not even really know I was there, far less who or what I was.*

But by now he was almost accustomed to that pain. More real than the memory was the knowledge of Sianna stretched out at his side. He could still feel the imprint of her small damp fingers clutched in his. He started to stir, but she was pointing to the edge of the forest. He froze, trying not to breathe, and then, at the edge of the clearing, he saw a shadow. He barely heard Sianna's involuntary gasp as, slowly, a magnificent stag, his head broadly crowned with antlers, paraded across the open space. His head was erect; he moved with a great and subtle dignity.

Gawen watched without moving as the stag swung his head, pausing for a moment almost as if he could see Gawen through the leaves.

At his side Gawen heard Sianna whisper half aloud, "The King Stag! He must have come to welcome you! I have sometimes watched the deer for more than a month without seeing him!"

Without having willed it, Gawen stood up. For a long moment

his eyes met those of the stag. Then the beast's ears flicked and he gathered himself to leap away. Gawen bit his lip, sure it was he who had startled the beast, but in the next moment a black feathered arrow arched through the air and buried itself in the earth where the stag had been. Another followed it. But by that time all the deer were in among the trees once more, and there was nothing to be seen but shivering branches.

Gawen stared from the place where the stag had disappeared to the point from which the arrows had come. Two men emerged from the trees, peering under their hands against the afternoon sun.

"Halt!" It was the Lady's lips that moved, but the voice seemed to come from everywhere. The hunters stopped short, staring around them. "This prey is not for you!"

"Who forbids—" began the taller of the two, though his companion was making the sign against evil and whispering to him to be still.

"The forest itself forbids it, and the Goddess who gives life to all. Other deer you may hunt, for this is the season, but not this one. It is the King Stag you have dared to threaten. Go, and seek another trail."

Now both men were trembling. Without daring even to reclaim their arrows, they turned and crashed away into the undergrowth through which they had come.

The Lady stepped out of the shadow of a great oak and signaled to both children to rise.

"We must return," she said. "Most of the day has gone. I am glad we saw the King Stag. That is what I wanted you to see, Gawen—the reason I brought you here."

Gawen started to speak, then thought better of it. But the Queen asked, "What is it? You may always speak your mind to me. I may not always be able to do or tell you everything, but you may always ask, and if it is something I cannot do or allow, I will always explain why."

"You stopped those men from hunting the stag. Why? And why did they obey?"

"They are men of this country, and know better than to disobey me. But as for the stag, no hunter of the elder races would touch him knowingly. The King Stag can only be killed by the King. . . ."

"But we have no king," he whispered, knowing he was getting close to an answer now, and not sure he wanted to know.

"Not now," she agreed. "Come." She started back the way they had come.

Gawen said heavily, "I wish I did not have to go back at all. I am nothing but an unwanted burden to the folk on the Tor."

Rather to Gawen's surprise, the Lady did not at once reassure him about the good intentions of his guardians. He was accustomed to the way in which adults always reinforced what other adults said.

Instead the Lady hesitated. Then she said slowly, "I also wish you did not have to return; I do not want you to be unhappy. But every adult must do, sooner or later in his life, some things for which he has no liking or talent. And though I would consider it a privilege to foster one of your lineage, and I have always wished for a son to bring up with my daughter, it is necessary for you to remain in the temple, as long as is needed for the making of a Druid. This learning is necessary for my daughter as well."

Gawen thought about that for a moment; then he said, "But I do not really wish to become a Druid."

"I did not say that—only that you must receive that training in order to fulfill your destiny."

"What *is* my destiny?" he burst out suddenly.

"I cannot tell you."

"Cannot, or *will* not?" he cried, and saw Sianna go white. He did not want to fight with her mother before her, but he had to know.

For a long moment the fairy woman only looked at him. "When you see the clouds red and angry, you know that the day is likely to be stormy, do you not? But you cannot say just when the rain will come or how much will fall. It is like that with the weather of the inner worlds. I know its tides and cycles. I know its signs and can see its powers. I see power in you, child; the astral tides ripple around you as the water parts above a hidden tree. Although it is no comfort to you now, I know that you are here for some purpose.

"But I do not know what that purpose is, exactly, and if I did, I would not be allowed to speak of it; for it is often in working for or in avoiding a prophecy that people do those very things they should not."

Gawen heard this without much hope, but when she came to the end he asked, "Will I, then, see you again, Lady?"

"To be sure you will. Is not my own daughter to live among the maidens of Avalon? When I come to see her I will visit you too. Will you watch over her among the Druids as she has watched over you in the forest?"

Gawen looked at her in astonishment; Sianna did not at all fit the pattern of Druid priestesses, for whom his model was Eilan, or perhaps Caillean.

So Sianna was also to be one? Did she have a destiny too?

Chapter Three

With the approach of Midwinter, the weather drew in dark and wet and cold. Even the goats lost interest in roaming. More and more often, Gawen found himself close to the beehive huts where the pastureland stretched away from the foot of the Tor. At first, when he heard the sound of chanting coming from the large round structure the Christians called their sanctuary, he stayed in the field, but what he could hear of the music fascinated him. Day by day he came closer.

He told himself that it was only because it was raining, or the wind was cold, and he wanted to watch the goats from shelter. It might have been different if he had had a companion of his own age, but the Faerie Queen had not yet fulfilled her promise to bring Sianna to live at Avalon, and he was lonely. He hid when any of the monks were about, but the long, slow surge of their music stirred him, though in a different way, as much as the music of the Druid bards.

One day a little before the solstice, the shelter of the wall seemed especially attractive, for his sleep had been troubled by nightmares in which his mother, surrounded by flames, was calling to her son to save her. Gawen felt his heart wrenched as he watched, but in his dream he did not know that he was the one she was calling to, and so he did nothing. When he woke, he remembered that he was her son. He wept then, because it was too late to save her, or even to tell her that he would have loved her if he had only been given the chance.

He eased down against the plastered wickerwork of the wall, tucking his sheepskin around him. The music today was particularly beautiful, full of joy, he thought, though he did not understand the words. It dissipated the anguish of the night as the early sunlight was melting the frost. His gaze fixed on the rainbow play of light on ice crystals, and gradually his lids grew heavy, and without warning he slept.

It was not sound, but the lack of it, that brought him to himself again. The singing had stopped and the door was opening. Twelve men came out, old, or at least they seemed so to him, clad in grey robes. Heart pounding, Gawen shrank into his furs, still as a mouse when the owl is flying. At the very end of the line came a little old man, stooped with age, with hair wholly white. He paused, his sharp gaze flickering around him, and far too swiftly fixed on Gawen's trembling form. He took a few steps toward him and nodded.

"I do not know you. Are you, then, a young Druid?"

The last monk before the old man in the line, a tall man with thinning hair and blotchy skin, had turned to watch them, glaring. But the ancient lifted a hand, in reproval or blessing, and the other, still frowning, turned away, like his brothers, to his own little beehive hut.

Gawen got to his feet, reassured by the old man's courtesy. "I am not, sir. I am an orphan, brought here by my foster-mother because I had no other kin. But my mother was one of them, so I suppose that is what I will be too."

The old man surveyed him in mild surprise. "Is it truly so? I had believed the priestesses of the Druids were under a vow of virginity, like our own maidens, and did not marry, neither did they bear children."

"They don't," said Gawen, remembering some remarks Eiluned had made when she thought he did not hear. "There are those who say that I should not have been born at all. Or that my mother and I both should have died."

The old priest surveyed him kindly. "The Master, when He dwelt among us, had compassion even for the woman taken in adultery. And He said of little children that of such was the kingdom of heaven. But I cannot remember that He ever inquired into the birth, lawful or otherwise, of the children."

Gawen frowned. Was even his own soul of value in this old priest's sight? After a moment, hesitantly, he dared to ask.

"All men have souls of equal worth in the sight of the true God, little brother. You as well as any other."

"The true god?" echoed Gawen. "Does your god, whoever he may be, regard my soul as his own, even though I am not one of his worshippers?"

The priest said gently, "The first truth of your faith, as well as of mine, is that the gods, by whatever names they may be called, are but one. There is really only one Source; and He rules alike over Nazarene and Druid."

He smiled, and moved stiffly to a bench that had been set beside the little thorn tree. "We have dealt with immortal souls, and still do not know each other's names! My brothers who lead the singing are Bron, who was married to my sister, and Alanus. Brother Paulus is the lastcomer to our company. I am Joseph, and those of our congregation call me 'Father.' If your earthly father would not object, it would please me if you would call me so."

Gawen stared at him. "I never set eyes on my earthly father, and now he is dead, so there is no knowing what he might say! And as for my mother, I knew her, but not"—he swallowed, remembering his dream—"that she was any relation to me."

For a few moments the old priest watched him. Then he sighed. "You called yourself an orphan, but it is not so. You have a Father and a Mother too—"

"In the Otherworld—" Gawen began, but Father Joseph interrupted him.

"All around you. God is your Father and Mother. But you have a mother in this world also, for are you not the fosterling of the young priestess Caillean?"

"Caillean? Young?" Gawen repressed a snort of laughter.

"To me, who am truly old, Caillean is no more than a child," Father Joseph answered with composure.

The boy asked suspiciously, "Has she, then, spoken about me?" He already knew that Eiluned and the others gossiped about him.

The idea that they might have been talking even to the Christians was infuriating.

But the ancient priest only smiled at him. "Your foster-mother and I talk together from time to time. In the name of the Master who said that all children were alike children of God, I will be a father to you."

Gawen shook his head, remembering the gossip he had heard about the Christians. "You would not want me. I have a second foster-mother, the Lady of the Elder Folk who are called Faerie. Do you know her?"

The old man shook his head. "I am sorry to say I do not have that privilege, but I am sure she is a worthy person."

Gawen breathed more freely, but he was still not ready to trust this man. "I have heard that Christians say that all women are evil—"

"But I do not," said Father Joseph, "for even the Master, when He dwelt among us, had many women friends: Mary of Bethany, who would have been his wife, had he lived long enough; and that other Mary, of the town of Magdala, of whom He said much was forgiven her because she loved much. So of course women are not evil. Your own foster-mother, Caillean, is a worthy woman. I say, not that women are evil, but that they are sometimes mistaken or wrong-headed, just as men are. And if some of them do wrong, that does not mean all women do the same."

"Then the Lady of the Elder Folk is not evil, nor her daughter?" The old man sounded as if he would be no threat, but Gawen had to be sure.

"I do not know the Lady, so I do not know. There are many tales of the Elder Folk. Some say they are lesser angels, who fought neither for God nor for the Evil One when he rebelled, and so were condemned to live eternally here. Others say that Eve, ashamed to have so many children, hid some of them and so they were not blessed by God with souls.

"My masters taught that the folk of Faerie are spirits themselves, who speak for all in nature that has no voice of its own. But surely God created them. And just as men who go to dwell in Faerie never die, those of the Elder kin who cast their lot with men become mortal, and if they live well, the Almighty will grant them a soul. As for her daughter, she is only a child. And if she is partly of mortal race, then surely she has a soul already. Can children be evil? The Master said that of such was the kingdom of heaven."

Father Joseph looked at Gawen and smiled. "You have listened to us singing often, have you not? Would you like to hear us from inside?"

Gawen eyed him suspiciously. His heart drew him to the old man, but he was tired of adults telling him who he was and what he should do.

"You do not have to," Father Joseph added, "but it does sound better that way...." He had spoken gravely, but the boy saw the gleam in his eye and began to laugh. "After the festival of Midwinter, when there will be more leisure, you could even, if you desired it, learn to sing...."

Gawen grew abruptly still. "How did you know? How did you know that I would like that above all other things? But will Caillean give me leave?"

Father Joseph only smiled. "Leave Caillean to me."

⊲ ⊲ ⊲

The big meeting hall was fragrant with the spicy scent of pine boughs. The Druids had gone out to cut them from the trees that grew on the next hill along the ley line that led from Avalon. The line passed through the Tor from the northeast, extending all the way to the farthest point, where Britannia jutted out into the western seas. Other lines of power came through the Tor from the northwest and the north, marked by standing stones or pools or hills, most of them crowned by pine. Caillean had not explored them in the flesh, but she had seen them while traveling in the spirit. It seemed to her that all of them were pulsing with power today.

According to Druid calculations, this night was the time of the year's greatest darkness. Tomorrow the sun would begin its return from southern skies, and though the worst of winter was still before them, one might dare to hope that summer would come again. *What we do here at this node of power*, thought Caillean as she directed Lysanda to fasten the end of a garland to a post, *will send echoes of energy throughout the land.*

And that was true of all their actions, not just tonight's ritual. It was coming to her more and more strongly that this refuge in the marshes was the secret center of Britannia. The Romans might rule its head in Londinium, directing all that happened on the outer plane. But just by being here, the priestesses of Avalon could speak to its soul.

There was a squeal from the other end of the hall, and Dica, red-faced, turned on Gawen and began to swipe at him with a branch of pine. Eiluned, frowning like a thundercloud, bustled toward them, but Caillean was before her.

"I didn't touch you!" exclaimed the boy, dodging behind Caillean. From the corner of her eye the priestess saw Lysanda edging away and grabbed her.

"The first duty of a priestess is to be truthful," said Caillean sternly. "If we tell truth here there will be truth in the land." The girl looked from her to Gawen and blushed.

"She moved . . ." Lysanda muttered. "I meant to poke *him.*"

Caillean knew better than to ask why. At that age, boys and girls were like cats and dogs, two kinds of creature, alternately hostile and fascinated by their differences.

"'You are not here to play, you know," she said mildly. "Did you think we were putting up these branches just for the sweet smell? They are holy, a pledge of continuing life when all other branches are bare."

"Like the holly?" asked Dica, her indignation replaced by curiosity.

"And the mistletoe, born of the lightning, which lives without touching earth at all. Tomorrow the Druids will cut it with golden sickles to use in their magic." Caillean paused, looking around her. "We are almost done here. Go and warm yourselves, for soon it will be sunset, and we will extinguish all the fires."

Dica, who was a skinny little thing and always chilly, darted toward the fire that was burning, Roman-fashion, in a wrought-iron brazier in the center of the room, and Lysanda went after her.

"You must tell me if they tease you too badly," said Caillean to Gawen. "They are young, and you are the only boy their age around. Enjoy their company now, for when they have had their passage into womanhood they will not be able to run about so freely.

"Never mind," she added, seeing his confusion. "Why don't you ask Riannon if any of those sweet cakes she was making for the festival were spoiled in the baking? We who have taken vows must fast, but there is no reason for you young ones to know hunger."

He was still young enough for that to bring a grin to his face, and as he ran off Caillean smiled.

◁ ◁ ◁

Without light, the hall of the priestesses seemed huge, a cavernous expanse of chill darkness in which the humans who had gathered there could be lost. Gawen nestled closer to Caillean, who sat in the midst of them in her great chair. Through her robes he could feel the warmth of her body, and was comforted.

"And so the Giants' Dance was built," said Kea, whose turn to tell a tale it was now, "and not all the powers of evil could prevent it."

Since sundown they had huddled in the hall, and the priestesses had told stories of wind and tree, of earth and sun, of the spirits of the dead and the deeds of the living, and of the strange beings that are neither one nor the other that haunt the waste between the worlds. Kea's story was of the building of the great henge of stones on the windswept central plain. It lay to the east of the Summer Country. Gawen had heard of it but he had never been there. It seemed to him that the world was full of wonders he had not seen, and never would if Caillean kept him here.

But just at this moment he was glad to stay where he was. The sound of the wind in the thatching whispered along with Kea's voice, and at times it seemed to him he discerned a few words. The priestesses said that at this time of darkness powers walked that had no liking for humankind, and, hearing that whispering, he believed them.

"And so the ogres did nothing?" asked Lysanda.

"Not quite nothing," answered Kea, and her voice held laughter. "The greatest of them, whose name on a night like this I will not speak aloud, swore he would bury the ring of stones where we worship the Mother—the one that lies to the northeast of here. One of the lines of power that run through the earth connects us, and this night the folk that live there will be lighting a fire on the central stone."

"But what did the ogre do?" asked Gawen finally.

"Ah—well, I was told that he scooped up a great load of earth and bore it to the circle, but the Lady rose up and stopped him, and so he dropped the dirt in a great pile and fled. And if you do not believe me, you may go and see the hill for yourself. It is just to the west of the ring of stones. We send a priest and priestess there to lead the rites at the equinox of spring."

A stronger gust of wind made the walls tremble. Gawen set his hand to the beaten earth of the floor, for a moment certain that the earth itself was shaking to some ancient, heavy tread. And what of the Fairy Folk, he wondered then. What of Sianna and the Queen? Did they ride the wind, or did they keep the festival in some secret place deep underground? Since that day on the lake he had thought of them often.

"Are we safe here?"

Gawen was glad it was little Dica who had asked.

"The Isle of Avalon is sacred ground," answered Caillean. "While we serve the gods, no evil can enter here." There was a silence, and Gawen listened as the wind whined round the rooftop and faded away.

"How long?" whispered Dica. "How long until the light comes back?"

"As long as it would take you to climb to the top of the Tor and come back down," said Riannon, who, like the other priestesses, had an ability to gauge the passage of time that seemed uncanny.

"Then the Druids who will bring the fire are up there now," said Gawen, remembering what Brannos had said to him.

It was Caillean who answered. "They wait for midnight, braving the cold and the dangers of the darkness. Be still now, my children, and pray to the Lady to kindle a light within your own darkness, for, though you may not think so, your darkness is deeper and more dangerous than this night that wraps the world."

She fell silent. For a long time, it seemed, no one moved. Gawen laid his head against Caillean's knee. No sound was heard but the soft sigh of breathing; even the wind had abated, as if all the world were waiting with the human souls who huddled here. He started as something touched him, then realized it was Caillean's hand, stroking his hair. He stilled in wonder, and something within him that had been as frozen as the winter rime began to ease. As that gentle, regular caress continued, he turned his face against her thigh, glad that it was too dark for anyone to see the tears on his face.

It was not a sound, but some other change, perhaps in the air itself, that brought him to full awareness once more. It was still quite dark, but the shadows that surrounded him seemed to weigh less heavily. Someone stirred; he heard steps as someone went to the door.

"Listen!" The door was pulled open, revealing a rectangle of midnight-blue frosted with stars, and, faint as if the stars themselves were singing, came a breath of song.

> *"From darkness comes the light;*
> *Out of our blindness, sight;*
> *Let shadows now take flight!*
> *Now at the holy hour*
> *the word of power is spoken;*
> *and night is broken. . . ."*

Gawen stiffened, straining to make out the words. Someone gasped and he looked upward. At the top of the Tor a light had blossomed, a tiny, flickering point of flame that in a moment was followed by another, and then a third. The maidens murmured, pointing, but Gawen was waiting for the next verse of the song.

"The year shall cycle round,
The cold earth be unbound,
All that was lost be found!
   Now at the holy hour
   the word of power is spoken;
   the ice is broken. . . ."

The line of light flowed downward, spiraling around the Tor. The voices faded as the light passed around the far side of the hill, and then, returning, grew stronger. As when he had yearned for the music of the Christians, Gawen trembled, hearing these harmonies. But whereas the monks' liturgies were majestic affirmations of order, the melodies of the Druids met and parted, soaring and fading with the simultaneously free and inevitable harmony of birdsong.

"When loss is turned to gain,
By joy transforming pain,
Shall sorrow strive in vain.
   Now at the holy hour
   the word of power is spoken;
   and death is broken. . . ."

They were close enough now so that the torchlight showed him the men who carried them, a line of white-mantled Druids winding down the hill. Gawen swayed where he stood, wanting to be part of that music.

"The blessed tidings bring,
From winter cometh spring,
This is the truth we sing.
   Now at the holy hour
   the word of power is spoken;
   and fear is broken. . . ."

The singers, led by white-bearded Cunomaglos, approached the hall. The women parted to let the men enter. Brannos, his aged features luminous with the ecstasy of the music, met Gawen's ardent gaze and smiled.

I will be a bard, thought the boy. *I will! I will ask Brannos to teach me.*

Pushing back into the hall behind the others, he blinked, confused by the brilliance after so long in the dark. A dozen flaring torches cast their light on smiling faces, but as Gawen's vision sharpened, his gaze fixed on one person. Her fair hair floated in a nimbus around a face as bright as day; her eyes shone. Very slowly a name took shape in his mind—*Sianna*—but this was not the very human girl with whom he had trudged and talked all one autumn day. Tonight she seemed entirely a daughter of Faerie.

Someone handed him a seedcake and he began to eat without taking his eyes from the girl. Gradually, with the nourishment, human senses returned to him. Now he could see the freckles that dusted her cheeks and the smudge on the hem of her gown. But, perhaps because of the hours he had spent in darkness, that first image retained the force of illumination.

Remember! he told himself. *Whatever happens, this is the truth of her! Remember!*

⊲ ⊲ ⊲

Always, thought Caillean, no matter how many Midwinter Nights she waited for the return of the light, there came a moment when she wondered if this time it would not happen, the fire would not kindle, and darkness would overwhelm the world. Tonight, as always, her immediate reaction when the first flicker appeared at the top of the hill had been relief. This year, perhaps, she had more reason to be grateful than most. After so many tragedies, the promise of renewal was especially welcome.

The wood in the brazier in the center of the hall had been lighted; with the heat from the torches, the temperature was rising rapidly. Caillean let her mantle fall open and looked around her. She was surrounded by smiles. Even Eiluned had for once allowed herself to be content.

Father Joseph, his own midnight services completed, had ac-

cepted her invitation with one of his monks, not the sour-faced
Brother Paulus but a younger man, Alanus, beside him.

*In what other bodies, what other lives and lands, have we waited together to greet
the returning of the light?* she wondered. Encountering Father Joseph
often set her thoughts on such paths. There was a curious comfort to
the idea that, despite the confusions and sorrows of their present
lives, something eternal would remain.

She made her way through the crowd to greet him.

"In the name of the Light I return your blessing. Peace be upon
all within these walls," he answered her. "I need to speak with you,
Lady, regarding the training of the lad Gawen."

Caillean turned, looking for him. The boy, his face flushed and
his eyes like stars, was staring across the fire. She felt her heart twist.
Eilan had looked like that after her initiation, when she came up out
of the pool. Then Caillean followed the direction of his gaze and saw
a fair-haired girl, as bright and merry of face as if she had been born
from the flames, and, like a shadow behind her, the Faerie Queen.

Caillean looked from the gawky boy to the luminous girl and *felt*,
in a way given sometimes to those trained as she had been, the com-
pletion of a pattern. After the night on which she had spoken to the
Lady of Faerie, Caillean had thought a great deal about the child she
had promised to take and her possible future here. It was hard enough
to teach girls who had come from the lands of men. How was she to
deal with a child brought up half in Faerie? But Sianna had not come,
and after a time that concern had been overlaid by the demands of
everyday.

"Father—I will speak with you about the boy, but there is
someone I must greet," she said hurriedly. His gaze followed hers,
and his eyes widened.

"Indeed, I understand. The boy spoke of them, but I did not
quite believe. Surely the world is still a place of wonders!" he said.

As Caillean approached, the fairy woman stepped out from
among the shadows to face her. She had that gift of drawing all
attention when she wished, and conversation stilled as those whose
sight had passed over her before suddenly saw her standing there.

"I come, Lady of Avalon, to claim the boon you promised me."
The Lady's low voice carried through the hall. "This is my daughter.
I ask that you take her to train as a priestess here."

"I see and welcome her," answered Caillean, "but, as for training,
that decision must be made by the child herself and no other."

The fairy woman murmured something and Sianna stepped forward to stand before Caillean, head bowed. The firelight glinted on
her fair hair.

"I know that you are here with the consent of your kin. But have
you come among us of your own free will, without threats or coercion of any sort?" asked Caillean.

"I have, Lady," came the answer, spoken in a low voice, but
clearly, though she must know that everyone was staring at her.

"Do you promise that you will live at peace with all the women of
this temple and treat each of them as mother, or sister born of your
own blood?"

For a moment Sianna glanced up. For the most part her looks
were those of her unknown father, but she had her mother's deep
gaze. "The Goddess helping me, I will."

"For the term of their learning the maidens we train here belong
to the Lady, and may not give themselves to any man except as the
Goddess shall require. Will you abide by that rule?"

"I will." Sianna smiled shyly and looked down at the floor.

"Then I welcome you among our maidens. When you are grown,
you may, if the Goddess calls you, take on the obligations of a
priestess among us, but for now these are the only pledges by which
we may bind you." She opened her arms, and gathered the child into
her embrace, dizzied for a moment by the sweet scent of that bright
hair.

Then she stepped away, and one by one the others came up to
welcome their new sister, doubt vanishing and frowns fading, even
Eiluned's, as they touched the maiden. Caillean glanced over at her
mother, and glimpsed a smile lurking in the fairy woman's dark eyes.

She has laid a glamour upon the girl so that we will accept her, thought Caillean. *That will have to end. Sianna must earn her place here or we will be no good to*

her. But there would be problems enough facing the child, who must learn to deal with the temple's discipline as well as the strangeness of the human world. A small spell to get her started off successfully was surely no great wrong.

"This is Dica, and this Lysanda," she introduced the last in line to Sianna. "You three will share the little hut by the cooksheds. Your bed there is waiting, and they will show you where to put your things." She surveyed Sianna's tunic, of natural wool embroidered with a profusion of leaves and flowers, and smiled. "Go now and get something to eat. In the morning we will find you a garment such as the other maidens wear."

She made a little shooing motion, and Lysanda, always the bolder, reached out to take Sianna's hand. The three girls moved off. In a moment Caillean heard the murmur of Dica's voice and a ripple of laughter from Sianna in reply.

"Treat her well, and she will be a blessing to you. You have won my gratitude this day. . . ."

Caillean only realized those words had not been spoken aloud when she turned, and saw that the Faerie Queen was gone. Suddenly the room was full of talk and laughter, as people who had been fasting all day attacked the feast spread out on the boards. To the Romans it would have seemed plain fare, but to the folk of the temple, accustomed to the simplest of boiled grains and greens and cheese, the cakes sweetened with fruit and honey, the stewed hares and roasted venison were almost overwhelming.

"So that is the daughter of the Lady of the Elder Folk, of whom Gawen has told me?" asked Father Joseph, coming to her side.

"It is."

"And you are pleased by her arrival?"

"If I were not, I would never have let her take vows here."

"She is not one of your flock—"

"Nor," Caillean said slowly, "one of yours, Father. Make no mistake about that." She took an apple from the basket and bit into it.

Father Joseph nodded. "That was why I marveled to see her mother here. She is one of the people who were here before the

Britons—some say before humankind. Certainly they were here when the People of Wisdom first came from the Drowned Lands to these shores."

"I do not know for certain who or what the Lady of the Forest Folk may be," Caillean said. "But she helped me once when I was in great need. There is a wisdom in her kind, I think, that ours have lost. I would like to bring the Elder Folk, and their knowledge, among us. And she has promised to teach my adopted son, Gawen."

"It is of Gawen that I wished to speak," Father Joseph said. "He is an orphan, is he not?"

"He is," said Caillean.

"Then, in the name of the Teacher who said, 'Let the little children come unto me,' let your fosterling Gawen be my son as well. He has asked to study our music. If the girl also wishes to learn, she shall be my daughter and Gawen's sister in Christ."

"It does not trouble you that they are sworn to the old gods?" asked Caillean. One of the Druids had brought out his harp and was beginning to play. Gawen stood beside him, watching the flicker of light on the strings.

"I have no objection to the fact that she has taken vows among you," Father Joseph sighed, "though Brother Paulus may not like that. He is newly come among us and feels that even here at the end of the world we should convert everyone we meet."

"I have heard him," said Caillean a little grimly. "Doesn't he believe that if you allow any person in the whole world to remain a pagan, you will fail in your duty? Must I, then, forbid Gawen to have anything to do with any of you? I do not want him to be a Nazarene."

"That is Paulus' belief," said Father Joseph. "I did not say it was mine. A man who forswears his first faith is likely to be apostate also to his second, and I think this is true of women too." He smiled with singular sweetness. "I have great respect for those who profess your faith."

Caillean sighed and relaxed; she knew she could entrust any of her young people to Father Joseph.

"But did I not only now hear you require the maiden to make her own choice? In the end, what faith he follows will be a matter for the boy to decide."

For a moment she stared at him, then shook her head and smiled. "You are right, of course. It is a hard thing to remember that the choosing must go both ways, and that it is not my will only that matters, or even his, but that of the gods...."

She gave the old man her hand. "I must go now and see if Sianna is settling in. Thank you so much for your kindness to Gawen; he is very important to us."

"It is a privilege to be kind to him," Father Joseph assured her. "I must go now as well, for we will rise at dawn to worship our Lord, and then I will have to justify my decision to Brother Paulus, who thinks that I am too tolerant of pagans already. But my Master taught that the Truth of God is more important than the words of men, and in their foundations, all faith are one."

Caillean looked at Joseph, and her vision wavered as if she looked through fire. Then, for a moment, she saw him taller, a man in his prime with a flowing dark beard. He wore a white robe, but the symbol around his neck was not a cross. And she herself was younger, swathed in dark veils.

"'And this is the first of the great truths.'" The words came from the depths of memory. "'That all the gods are One, and there is no religion higher than the Truth....'"

Father Joseph replied simply, "Let the Truth prevail." And the two Initiates of the Mysteries smiled.

Chapter Four

In the winter of Gawen's second year at Avalon, fire raged over the hill. No one knew for certain what had begun it. Eiluned swore that one of the maidens must have been careless when she covered the coals in the hearth of the Great Hall the evening before. But there was to way to be certain. No one slept there, and by the time the light awakened the priestesses, the building was in flames. A brisk wind fanned them, sending flaming brands through the air to set the thatching of the House of Maidens afire.

From there it spread downhill to the huts of the Druids. Gawen was awakened by the sound of old Brannos coughing. At first he thought that the old man was having a worse night than usual, but as he woke, he caught the reek of smoke and began to cough himself. He jumped from his bed and went to the door.

Dark figures scurried frantically against a blaze of light, shouting. A breath of hot air lifted the hair from his brow as the wind shifted. Sparks fell sizzling onto the frosted grass.

"Brannos!" he shouted, turning. "Get up! Fire!"

Gawen owned nothing he would miss but the sheepskin cloak. He pulled it over his head with one hand and hauled the old man upright with the other.

"Come now—get your boots on—" He shoved them onto Brannos' feet and grabbed the sleeping robe to wrap around the thin shoulders. The old bard stood up, swaying, but he resisted Gawen's efforts to pull him toward the door.

"My harp . . ." At last the boy made sense of his muttering.

"You never play it——" Gawen began, then coughed. The fire must have reached their roof, for smoke was beginning to fill the room. "Go," he gasped, pushing the old man toward the doorway. "I'll save it for you!"

A face appeared in the doorway; someone grabbed Brannos and pulled him out, shouting. But Gawen was already turning. A rill of flame appeared suddenly above him, fed by the draft from the door. He started toward the corner where the instrument stood beneath a swathing of hides, recoiled as an explosion of sparks scattered across the floor, then dove forward, swatting the bits of burning thatch away like flies.

The harp was almost as big as he was, and heavy, but in that moment strength came to him and he hauled it back through the blast of heat as flame pulsed downward and hurled himself through the door.

"Stupid boy!" cried Eiluned, her face smudged and her hair wild. "Had you no thought for Caillean's feelings if you had been burned?"

Gawen, his legs chilling from the cold ground even as he perspired from the heat of the fire, gaped up at her, struck dumb by sheer astonishment at her angry words. Then he saw the terror in her eyes and understood that accusing him had been a cover for her own fear. How many of the things people did that annoyed him so, he wondered, were only defenses, as a hedgehog bristles when it is afraid?

I will think of her as a hedgehog, he told himself, *and when she annoys me remember what a timid little beast she really is.*

A few of the Druids were trying to douse the thatching of the buildings that were yet unburned with water from the holy well, but buckets were scarce, and by this time most of the community was standing, watching the fire burn. The long hall stood outlined in fire, and flames shot from the roof of the House of Maidens to lick the sky. The Druids' hall had caught fire as well, as had some of the smaller buildings. The animals had been released from their barns, bleating anxiously, but perhaps those buildings were far enough away to escape the flames.

Women sobbed or sat in stunned silence, watching the flames. "How will we live?" they whispered. "Where will we go?"

Brannos sat weeping, cradling the harp in his gaunt arms.

Why had he risked his life to save it, Gawen wondered, and then, as he considered the size of the instrument, *how* had he done it?

And like an answer, words came to him: *"You will always find the strength for what you have to do. . . ."*

Brannos looked up, his eyes luminous in the flickering light. "Come," he croaked. Ignoring Eiluned, the boy got to his feet and joined him. The old bard reached out and grasped his hand, then set it on the pillar of the harp. "Yours . . . You saved her. She is yours. . . ."

Gawen swallowed. Firelight sparked gold on the wire inlaid into the polished wood and the bronze strings. The voices around him blurred into a soft roaring, like the sound of the fire. Carefully, he reached out and plucked a single sweet note from the glistening strings.

He had not meant to pluck the string loudly, but the note seemed to hang in the air. Those nearest turned, and others, seeing their movement, looked as well. Gawen stared back at them, his gaze going from one to another, seeing them for a little while distracted from their panic or despair by the sweet sound. Among the dark figures he found Caillean, swathed in a shawl. Her face, in the firelight, was furrowed and cragged with anguish. She looked old. She had once told him about the pyre on which his parents had burned. Was she thinking of it now? His eyes prickled with pity for himself, because he had not known what he had lost, and for her, because she had known his mother so well.

And now they were both losing everything a second time.

The harpnote faded. Caillean meet Gawen's stricken gaze. For a moment she frowned, as if wondering how he had gotten there. Then her look changed. Later, in his memory, the only word he could think of to describe what he saw in her eyes was "wonder." As he watched, she straightened, visibly resuming the majesty of the Lady of Avalon once more.

"Lady"—Eiluned spoke for them all—"what will become of us? Will we go back to the Forest House now?"

Caillean stared around her. The Druids were looking to her as well, even Cunomaglos, their leader, who had come to the Tor for a life of peaceful contemplation and had been increasingly unhappy as the community grew.

"You are, as always, free. What do you wish to do?" The voice of the High Priestess was cold.

Eiluned's face crumpled, and for the first time, Gawen found it in his heart to pity her as well. "Tell us!" she sobbed.

"I can only tell you what *I* will do," Caillean said more gently. She looked once again at the flames. "I gave my oath to make a center of the ancient wisdom on this holy hill. Fire can only burn what is visible to the human eye, what is made by human hands. Avalon of the heart remains. . . ." She looked at Gawen once more. "Just as the spirit rises triumphant from the body that burns on the pyre, the true Avalon cannot be contained by the human world." She paused, as if her words had been as much a surprise to herself as to those who listened. "Decide as your hearts counsel. I will stay and serve the Goddess on this holy hill."

Gawen looked from her to the others and saw spines straightening, a new light in people's eyes. Caillean's gaze came back to him and he got to his feet as if she had challenged him.

"I will stay," he said.

"And so will I," came a voice beside him.

Gawen jumped and saw it was Sianna, who had her mother's gift for moving silently. Others were speaking now, promising to rebuild. He reached out and squeezed Sianna's hand.

& & &

Winter was not the easiest season for building. Gawen blew on his stiff fingers to warm them, reached down from the roof of the new House of Maidens for the length of straw rope Sianna was holding out to him, and began to bind the next bunch of straw to the frame. She was shivering, her cheeks, normally so rosy, purpled with cold. In Faerie, she had told him, the weather ranged between the brisk chill of autumn and the sweet warmth of spring. She must be wondering why she had ever agreed to dwell in mortal lands.

But she had not complained, and he would not complain either, even to regret that his lighter weight made him the obvious choice to go up on the roof, exposed to every icy gust of wind. He grinned at her as one of the Druids lifted up another hank of straw. Then he eased sideways, fixed the straw firmly into place, and took another piece of rope from Sianna to tie it down. At least the new building did not have to be as large as the old one. Some of the priestesses were sheltering with Waterwalker and his kin, but others had gone back to their families. The older Druids and the boys were living in Father Joseph's little beehive church. Some of the men had left too. Even Cunomaglos, leader of the Druids, had gone away, seeking a solitary hermitage in the hills. One house for the women and one for the men would shelter them until summer. At least the storage pits and the animals had not been harmed.

He supposed that meant Caillean was in charge. At least nobody had come from Vernemeton to say otherwise. If the High Priestess was disappointed in those who fled, she did not say so. It seemed to Gawen that she looked upon the losses as a necessary winnowing, which would leave them all the stronger. It was the same in the world beyond the Vale of Avalon, he had heard, where Trajan had proved victor in the civil wars and was setting his Empire in order.

The wind was picking up. He shivered violently and crossed his arms, hiding his cold hands between his arms and sides.

"Come down," said Sianna, "and let me do that for a while. I am even lighter than you."

Gawen shook his head. "I'm stronger—" he began. She glared up at him, her color changing as the heat of anger fought the cold.

"Let her do it," said a new voice. Gawen blinked as he realized that Caillean was standing there.

"She can't!" he exclaimed. "It is too cold up here!"

"She has chosen to live among us, and I would fail in my duty if I spared her," said the priestess grimly.

Sianna looked from one to the other, her gaze kindling as if she

could not decide whether to resent Caillean's harsh words or Gawen's
protectiveness more. Then she reached up to grip his ankle and
pulled. Gawen yelped as he began to slide, but in another moment he
was halfway down the part of the roof that was thatched already and
there was nothing he could grab. He landed in a heap at Caillean's
feet.

Sianna leaped back and scrambled, quick as a squirrel, up the
roof. He looked up angrily, but he could not resist her laughter.
Shaking his head, Gawen rose and began to gather the lengths of
rope, and Caillean moved away, still frowning.

That night, as he listened to Brannos and Father Joseph argue
theories of music, it came to him that he had never been so happy.
Warm at last, his belly full of gruel, he huddled into his blankets. He
did not understand all of their discussion, but the alternation of
sonorously chanted phrases and rippling harpsong fed his soul.

The winter passed, and the summer after. The burned buildings
were replaced by others even finer, and the priestesses were beginning
to talk of building in stone. Gawen's first uncertain fumblings on the
harpstrings changed to the beginnings of real skill. He continued, as
well, to sing with Father Joseph and the Christians, his boyish
soprano soaring above their deeper drone.

As the seasons passed, he realized that the uncertainty he had
always felt around Caillean had disappeared. He had stopped
expecting her to be a mother to him, and in truth, as he grew taller,
he no longer desired it. He was not certain what she thought of him,
but as the community of Avalon became more secure, many sought to
join it, and she was far too busy teaching the newcomers to pay him
much attention.

As they grew older, the youths and maidens entrusted to the
Druids of the Tor for training spent their days separately. But for
some things they came together, when there was teaching that both
needed alike, and for the festivals. And so, six years went by.

"I am certain that all of you can name the seven islands of Avalon, but can you say why each is holy ground?"

Alerted by the question in Caillean's voice, Gawen blinked and jerked upright. It was high summer, and the land lay wrapped in a drowsy peace. At this season the folk of Avalon lived mostly outdoors, and the Lady had gathered her students beneath an oak tree near the water's edge. He wondered why. This was lore they had all learned when they were children. Why was the High Priestess returning to it now?

After a moment's surprised silence, Dica raised her hand. From a wiry, sharp-tongued child she had grown into a slender young woman, her foxy face crowned by a cloud of ginger hair. Her tongue could still sting, but she was clearly on her best behavior now.

"The first is Inis Witrin, the Isle of Glass on which is the Holy Tor," she answered demurely.

"And why is it called so?" Caillean responded.

"Because ... they say that when you see it in the Otherworld it shines like light through Roman glass."

Was that true? Gawen's own studies had progressed to include some inner journeying, like a waking dream, but he had not yet been allowed to travel out of his body and look upon the real world with spirit-sight.

"Very good," said Caillean. "And the next?" Her gaze fixed on one of the newer girls, a dark-haired child from Dumnonia called Breaca.

"The second is the isle of Briga, which is great in the spirit though its height is low. Here it is where the Goddess comes to us as Mother, carrying the newborn sun." The girl was blushing, but her answer came clearly.

Gawen cleared his throat. "The third is the isle of the winged god, near the great village of the fen folk. To him the water birds are sacred, and no man may kill them near his shrine. In gratitude, no bird will foul its roof."

He had been there several times with the Lady of the Fairy Folk and seen that it was so. At the thought, he looked back at Sianna, sitting behind the others, as she usually did when the High Priestess taught them. Caillean's gaze had softened as he answered, but when she saw where he was looking, she frowned.

"And the fourth?" she asked sharply.

Tuarim, a stocky, dark-haired boy who had been accepted for training by the Druids the year before and seemed to look on Gawen as his model, spoke up in answer.

"The fourth is the island on the marches which defends the Vale of Avalon from all evil powers."

"The fifth is the isle by the mere, where another village of the fen people is." That was Ambios, seventeen winters old and about to take his initiation among the Druids. Most of the time he held aloof from the younger ones, but he clearly had decided it was time to demonstrate his superiority. He went on, "There is a sacred spring on that isle, growing below a mighty oak tree, and every year we hang offerings in its branches."

Gawen glanced once more at Sianna, wondering why she did not answer, she who had known all this almost from the time she could speak. But perhaps, he thought as he noted her downcast eyes and carefully folded hands, that was why she kept silent. It would not be fair. A light breeze stirred the branches of the oak tree and sunlight flickered through the leaves, kindling in Sianna's bright hair.

I have not seen light glowing through this isle, he thought suddenly, *but I see it shining now in you. . . .* At that moment Sianna's beauty had no implications. Indeed, he hardly connected it with the human girl he had teased and played with in the years before she made her passage into womanhood and was forbidden to be with a male unchaperoned. It was a fact, sufficient to itself, like the grace of a heron rising from the lake at dawn. He scarcely heard Dica answering the next question.

"The sixth isle is the home of the wild god of the hills whom the Romans call Pan. He brings madness or ecstasy, and so does the fruit of the vines planted in this place, which makes a powerful wine."

"The seventh is a high hill"—Ambios spoke up again—"the watchtower and gateway to Avalon. Waterwalker's village is there, and his people have always poled the barges for the priests on the Tor."

"That was well answered," said Caillean. "For you who are about to take vows among them should know that the Druids were not the first priests to seek wisdom on this Tor."

She looked sternly at Ambios and then at Gawen, who returned her gaze limpidly. Two years remained before he would be considered for initiation, and he rather resented the assumption that this was what he would choose. He was making steady progress on the harp, good enough if he wanted to take service with one of the British princely families who gave their allegiance now to Rome but still valued the old ways. Or he could go to his grandfather—the other one—and claim his Roman heritage. He had never even seen a Roman town. They were dirty, noisy places, he had been told. There were rumors that after years of peace the tribes of the north were stirring once more. But on days like this one, when the dreaming peace of Avalon was so intense that it seemed stifling, even the prospect of war attracted him.

"The Isle of Glass, the Isle of Brigantia, the Isle of Wings, the Isle of the Marches, the Isle of the Oak, the Isle of Pan, and the Watch Hill. They have been called by other names by other peoples, but this is their essence, as we were taught by the wise ones who came over the sea from the Drowned Lands. And why is it that these islands and no others are held holy, when, as you can see, they are not all the highest or the most impressive to the eye?"

The young people stared back at her, silent. It had never occurred to them to ask.

Just as Caillean was opening her mouth to speak again, Sianna's voice came from beneath the tree.

"I know—"

Caillean's brows lifted, but Sianna, coming forward to the lake's edge, seemed to have no awareness that she was treading on ancient mysteries. And to her, perhaps, they were not mysteries at all.

"It is easy, really, when you know how to see." She picked up a triangular stone and set it upright in the soft ground. "Here is Inis Witrin, and here"—she took a smaller, rounded stone and set it below the first—"is the Goddess isle. The Isle of Wings and the Isle of the Oak are over here"—she placed a small stone and a larger one a little farther apart from each other to form a slightly skewed rectangle with the first two—"and then we have Pan's Isle and the March Isle"—a tiny stone and a pointed one were placed close together a ways to the left and above the Isle of Wings—"and the Gateway"— yet farther to the left, an even larger stone was set down.

Forgetting Caillean, the youths and maidens gathered round. Gawen agreed that from the air this might well be the appearance of the land, but what did it mean?

"You don't see?" Sianna frowned. "Think of the nights when old Rhys made you look at the stars." Girls on one side of the hill and boys on the other, Gawen remembered, grinning.

"It's the Bear!" exclaimed Dica suddenly. "The hills form the same pattern as the stars in the Great Bear!"

The others nodded as the resemblance became clear to them. And then, finally, they turned back to Caillean.

"But what," asked Ambios, "does it mean?"

"So you want wisdom after all?" asked the High Priestess sarcastically.

Sianna flushed, sensing the rebuke without understanding it, and in her defense Gawen felt a quick spurt of anger.

"The tail of the Great Bear points to its Keeper, the brightest star in the northern sky. The star which is our Tor is at the center of the heavens. This is what the ancient wisemen saw as they looked at the skies, and set shrines upon the earth so that we should not forget to honor the Power who protects this land."

Gawen could feel her gaze upon him, but he continued to stare out over the marsh. Suddenly he felt cold.

When the High Priestess dismissed them, he hung back and waited in the shadow of the willows, hoping for a word with Sianna.

"Do not presume to take over the teaching again!" Caillean spoke sharply, and Gawen peered through the leaves. Sianna was staring up at the older woman, her face showing her bewilderment.

"But you were asking us questions—"

"I was using questions to lead them to consider the mysteries of the heavens, not children's games!"

"You asked. I answered," Sianna muttered, staring at the ground. "Why take me for training if you don't value what I have to give?"

"You knew more of the ancient lore than most who make their final vows when you first entered here. You could be so much more than they—" Caillean broke off, as if she had said more than she meant to. "I must teach you the things you do not know!" she added repressively. Then she turned and stalked away.

When the priestess was gone, Gawen slipped from his hiding place and put his arm around the girl, who was weeping soundlessly. He felt anger and pity, but he could not help also being aware of the softness of her body, and the sweet scent of her bright hair.

"Why?" exclaimed Sianna when she could speak again. "Why doesn't she like me? And if she doesn't want me here, why won't she let me go?"

"*I* want you here!" he muttered fiercely. "Don't mind Caillean—she has many worries, and is sometimes rougher than she means to be. Try to avoid her."

"I do try, but it is a small place, and I cannot always be out of her way." Sianna sighed and patted his hand. "But I thank you. Without your friendship I would run away, no matter what my mother might say!"

"In another year or two you'll be sworn as a priestess," he said cheerfully. "She'll have to respect you as an adult then."

"And you will pass the first rank of your Druid training. . . ." For a moment longer she held his hand. Hers had been cool when he took it, but now a warmth was growing between them. Suddenly he remembered the other initiation that came with adulthood and saw from her blush that she was thinking of it too. Abruptly she pulled away.

But that night, as he reviewed his day before sleep came, it seemed to him that surely what was between them was more than friendship, and that a promise had been made.

⚛ ⚛ ⚛

A year passed, and then another winter, so wet that the whole Vale of Avalon became a muddy sea and the waters lapped at the floors of the marsh men's stilt-houses. Gawen, going down to visit Father Joseph, suppressed an oath as he slipped in the mud and almost fell. Since his voice had broken, he did not sing so often in their ceremonies, but Father Joseph had traveled widely in his youth, and knew not only the Jewish musical tradition but the theories of the Greek philosophers, and both he and the boy found pleasure in comparing them with the Druid lore.

But when Gawen went to the little church, Father Joseph was not there.

"He is praying in his hut," said Brother Paulus, his long face lengthening with disapproval. "God has sent him a fever to mortify the flesh, but with prayer and fasting he will be purified."

"Can I see him?" asked Gawen, his throat aching with the beginnings of concern.

"He needs nothing from an unbeliever," said the monk. "Come to him as a son in Christ and you will be welcome."

Gawen shook his head. If Father Josephus himself had not insisted he become a Nazarene, he was not likely to be persuaded by Brother Paulus.

"I suppose you would not convey to him the blessing of an 'unbeliever,'" he said tightly, "but I hope you have enough compassion to tell him I am sorry he is sick, and give him my love."

After such a hard winter, all the folk of Avalon were thin, but nothing short of sheer starvation would have stopped a boy of Gawen's age from growing, thought Caillean as she watched him at the ceremonies that marked the Turning of Spring. He was seventeen now, tall, like his mother's kindred. But his hair, after a winter without the sun, had darkened to Roman brown. His jaw had grown so that his teeth were no longer disproportionate, and there was a suggestion of the eagle as well in the forceful nose and chin.

In body, Gawen was a man, and a handsome one, though he did not yet seem to realize it. He played the harp for the ceremonies, his long fingers flickering with practiced certainty across the strings. But his eyes were watchful, as if he feared to do something wrong.

Is this part of being his age, wondered the priestess, *or something I have done to him, expecting too much of the child?*

Afterward, she called him to her.

"You have grown," she said, feeling unexpectedly awkward as she met his clear gaze. "You have gained great skill on the harp. Do you still study music with Father Joseph as well?"

Gawen shook his head. "He fell sick shortly after Midwinter. I have been down there several times, but they will not let me inside to see him. They say he no longer leaves his bed at all."

"They will not deny *me!*" she exclaimed. "I will go now, and you will attend me."

"Why did you not tell me Father Joseph was ill?" she asked as they made their way down the hill.

"You are so busy—" He stopped himself when he saw her face. "I thought you must know."

Caillean sighed. "Forgive me—it is not fair for me to take out my anxieties on you. Or to blame you for speaking the truth to me ..." she went on. "Sometimes it seems there is someone wanting my attention every moment of the day, but I hope I will always find time for those who are truly in need. I know it is a long time since I have spoken with you, and now it is almost time for you to take your vows among the Druids. How quickly time goes by!"

They passed the round hut that had been built for the priestesses who watched over the Blood Well and the orchard they had planted there, and continued along the path that followed the high ground. The chapel the Christians had built, thatched like the others but with a second cone-shaped tier above the first, so that it appeared to have two stories, sat like a mother hen among her chicks with the huts of the brothers surrounding it. One of the younger monks was sweeping away the leaves that last night's wind had brought down across the path. He looked up as they approached and came to meet them.

"I have brought some preserved fruit and sweet cakes for Father Joseph." Caillean indicated her basket. "Will you take me to him?"

"Brother Paulus might not like—" the man began, frowning, then shook his head. "Never mind. Perhaps your delicacies will tempt

Father Joseph as our rough food can no longer do. If you can persuade him to eat you will have our gratitude, for I tell you that since the festival of Christ's birth he has taken scarcely enough to keep a bird alive."

He led them to one of the round huts, no larger than the others, though the path was edged with whitewashed stones, and pulled the hide doorcover aside.

"Father, here is the Lady of Avalon come to see you. Will you welcome her?"

Caillean blinked, straining to adjust to the shadows after the brightness of the spring day. Father Joseph lay on a pallet on the floor, a rushlight flickering beside him. The other monk set some cushions behind the old man's back to raise him, and brought a little three-legged stool for Caillean.

He was like a bird indeed, thought the priestess as she reached out to take the old man's hand. His thin chest scarcely stirred; all the life left to him glowed in his eyes.

"My old friend!" she said in a low voice. "How is it with you?"

Something that might have been a laugh whispered in the air. "Surely you, Lady, have the training to see!" Father Joseph read in her eyes the words she would not say, and smiled. "Is it not also given to those of your order to know their time? Mine comes soon, and I am content. I will see my Master once more. . . ." For a little while he was silent, gazing inward and smiling at what he saw there.

Then he sighed and his eyes focused on Caillean. "But I shall miss our conversations. Unless an old man on his deathbed can convince you to accept the Christos, only at the end of all things will we meet again."

"I will miss talking with you as well," said Caillean, blinking back tears. "And perhaps in another lifetime I may follow your path. But for this one, my oaths are given elsewhere."

"It is true that no man knows his road until he reaches its ending . . ." Father Joseph whispered. "When my life changed I was not much younger than you. . . . It would give me comfort to tell you the tale, if you are willing to hear."

Caillean smiled and took his outstretched hand in her own. It was so frail, the light seemed to shine through it. Eiluned and Riannon would be expecting her back to discuss the girls who were applying to join their community, but they could wait. There was always something to be learned when men spoke of how they came to the Light, and Father Joseph had very little time.

"I was a merchant of Judea, from a town called Arimathea, in the eastern part of the Empire. My ships went everywhere, even to Dumnonia to trade for tin, and great wealth came to me." His voice gathered strength as he went on. "In those days I never thought beyond the next day's accounting, and if in my dreams I sometimes remembered the land that is now sunk beneath the waves and yearned for its wisdom, I forgot it with the dawn. I brought those who were notable in every craft to my table, and when the new teacher from Galilee whom men called Yeshua began to be widely talked of, I invited him as well."

"Did you know then that he was one of the Sons of Light?" asked Caillean. The gods were always speaking, in tree and hill and the silence of men's hearts, but in each age, it was said, they sent an Enlightened One to speak in human words to the world. But in any age, as she had also heard, never more than a few could hear.

Father Joseph shook his head. "I listened to the Master's words, and found Him pleasant, but I did not know Him well. The old teachings were still hidden from me. But I saw that He brought hope to the people, and I gave money when His followers needed it, and allowed them to celebrate the Paschal feast in a house that I owned. I was away from Jerusalem when He was arrested. By the time I returned, He was already on the cross. I went out to the hill of execution, for I had heard that His mother was there and I wished to offer my assistance."

He stopped, remembering, and she saw his eyes grow luminous with tears. It was Gawen, sensing the weight of emotion without understanding it, who broke the silence.

"What was she like—his mother?"

Joseph focused on the boy. "She was like your goddess, when she weeps at harvest for the death of the god. She was young and old, fragile and enduring as stone. I saw her tears and I began to remember my dreams. And then I stood at the foot of the cross and looked up at her Son.

"By then, His agony had burned most of the human guise away. The knowledge of His true nature came and went—at times He cried out in despair, and at others He would speak words of comfort to those who waited below. But when He looked at me, I was dazzled by His Light, and in that moment I remembered who I myself had been, in times past, and the oaths that I had sworn." The old man took a deep breath. It was clear that he was tiring, but no one would have tried to stop him now.

"They say the earth shook when He died. I do not know, for I had been shaken to my core. Afterward, when they speared Him to make sure He was dead, I caught some of His blood in a flask I had by me. And I used my influence with the Romans to get His body, and laid it in my own family tomb."

"But he didn't stay there . . ." said Gawen. Caillean looked at him and remembered how long he had studied music with the Nazarenes. He must know their legends well.

"*He* was never there," Father Joseph said with a little smile. "Only the flesh He had worn . . . The Master took it back again to show the power of the spirit to those who think that the life of the body is all there is, but I did not need to see Him. I *knew.*"

"But why did you come here, to Britannia?" Gawen asked then.

Joseph's gaze grew sorrowful; he spoke more slowly now. "The followers the Master had left began to fight over who should lead, and who should interpret the meaning of His words. They would not listen to me, and I refused to be drawn into their quarrels. . . . I remembered then this green land beyond the waves where there were those who still, in a fashion, followed the ancient wisdom. . . . And so I sought refuge here, and your Druids welcomed me as a fellow seeker of the Truth behind all mysteries."

He coughed, and his eyes closed as he fought for breath. Caillean murmured soothingly, willing her own energy through their linked hands.

"Don't try to talk," she said as he opened his lips and coughed once more.

"I ... must ... tell you." He forced himself to take a deeper breath, and gradually grew calm, though he was perceptibly weaker now. "The flask with the holy blood—"

"Do not your brothers here have charge of it?" Caillean asked.

He shook his head. "His mother told me ... a woman must guard it. I bound it to the old ring, in the niche ... in the holy well."

Caillean's eyes widened. The iron-rich water of the well left a stain like blood, though it was icy cold and pure. The wise ones of ancient times had by their arts built a well house around it, cut from a single massive stone. That much, anyone could see. But the existence of the niche in the well shaft, just tall enough to hold a man, was a secret known only to the initiates. A fitting place to shelter the blood of sacrifice, she thought then, for it had undoubtedly been used for that purpose in ancient days.

"I understand ..." she said slowly, "and I will guard it well...."

"Ah ..." Father Joseph settled back. Her promise seemed to ease him. "And you—" His gaze turned to Gawen. "Will you join my brethren, and link the old wisdom with the new?"

The boy sat back, his eyes widening like those of a startled deer. For a moment he looked at Caillean—not in appeal, as she had expected, but in apprehension. The priestess blinked. Did the boy *want* to join the Nazarenes?

"Child, child," said Joseph, understanding, "I did not mean to press you. When the time is right, you will choose...."

A hundred replies surged in Caillean's mind, but she said nothing. She would not debate religion with a man so near to death, but she could not believe that the arid existence of a monk was what the gods wanted for this child, whom the Lady of Faerie herself had called "Son of a Hundred Kings"!

Father Joseph's eyes had closed. Caillean felt him drifting into sleep and let go of his hand.

When they emerged from the hut, she looked around for the brother who had shown them in. But it was Brother Paulus who was waiting, and from the outrage in his eyes she knew that only respect for the dying man prevented him from railing at her.

His gaze softened a little as Gawen approached behind her. "Brother Alanus has written a new hymn. Will you come tomorrow, when we are to learn it?"

Gawen nodded, and Paulus stalked away, the ragged hem of his grey robe hissing across the stones.

◁ ◁ ◁

In the days following their visit to Father Joseph, Gawen waited fearfully to hear that the old man had died. But, astonishingly, the word did not come. Father Joseph struggled on, and as the festival of Beltane approached, other matters distracted Gawen from his concern. He and two of the other boys were being prepared for initiation on the eve of the festival, and he was afraid.

But he did not know how to voice his feelings. No one had ever really asked him if he wanted to become a Druid; they simply assumed that, because he had completed the first stage of training, he would continue. Only Father Joseph had even suggested there might be another choice, and although Gawen admired the purity of the Nazarenes' devotion and found much good in their teachings, their lives seemed even narrower than those of the Druids on the Tor. The Druids, at least, were not completely cut off from womankind.

The community of Avalon had inherited the traditions of the Forest House, but Caillean did not make them keep those rules which had been imposed in deference to Roman prejudices. For the most part, the priests and priestesses of the Tor lived chastely, but the rule was relaxed at Beltane and Midsummer, when the power raised by the joining of man and woman gave life to the land. But only those who had made their vows could participate in these rites.

Sianna had been made a priestess the preceding autumn. This would be her first Beltane ritual. In his dreams Gawen saw her body glowing in the light of the holy fires and would wake, groaning with frustration at the unmistakable response of his own.

There had been a time, before the demands of his flesh had

become so distracting, when he had wanted the wisdom at the end of the Druids' road. He could hardly remember that pure longing now. The Nazarenes said that to lie with a woman was the blackest sin. Would the gods strike him down for impiety if it was desire for Sianna that motivated him to take the Druidic vows? It was not only lust that drove him, he told himself. Surely what he felt for her was love. But since her initiation he had not been alone with her. Was the friendship she had always shown him only a sisterly affection, or did she feel the same as he?

His feelings in turmoil, he gazed across the marshes to the distant line of the hills as a captive bird looks out through the meshes of its cage. Surely, he thought, becoming a man must be simpler in the Roman lands. What would his life have been like if he had been fostered by his grandfather Macellius instead of by Caillean? At times the peace of Avalon was a prison, and he grew so tired of seeing the same faces every day he could have screamed. But a Roman was a citizen of the whole world.

Gawen thought that if he had gone to Macellius he might have become a soldier like his father. Soldiers only had to take orders, not make decisions like these. Sometimes that seemed very attractive. But at other times it seemed as if everyone he knew was trying to give him commands, and all of them different, and all he wanted was to be free.

Then, one morning, he went out to join the sunrise procession and heard from below the sound of lamentation. He started down the hill, but he knew, even before he saw the monks standing about like lost children, what was wrong.

"Alas," said Brother Alanus, his pale cheeks tear-streaked, "our Father Joseph is gone from us. When Brother Paulus went to his quarters this morning he found him already stiff and cold. I should not weep," he went on, "for I know he is with our Master in heaven. But it is hard that he should have gone alone, in the dark, without the comfort of his sons around him, and harder still that we did not have his last farewell. Even when he was sick, it was a comfort to know he was there. He was our father. I do not know what we shall do now!"

Gawen nodded, his throat aching as he remembered that strange afternoon when the old man had told them how he came to Avalon. He had not seen the Light Father Joseph spoke of, but he had seen its reflection in the old man's eyes, and he did not think the old man had died alone.

"He was a father to me as well. I must go back up the hill and tell them." But it was Caillean he was thinking of as he hurried back up the path.

⊲ ⊲ ⊲

That afternoon, the Lady of Avalon came down from the Tor to express her condolences, drafting Gawen to join her escort as she had before. The confusion of the morning had ended. From inside the round church came the sound of chanting. The Druidic procession came to a ragged halt outside, and Gawen went to the door.

The old man's body lay on a bier before the altar with lamps burning around it. Incense swirled in thick clouds, obscuring the shadowy forms of the monks, but for a moment Gawen seemed to glimpse shining forms hovering above them, as if the angels of which Father Joseph had often spoken were watching over him. Then, as if aware of the touch of pagan eyes, one of the shadows rose and Father Paulus came toward him.

Gawen backed away as the Nazarene came through the door. Paulus' eyes were rimmed red with weeping, but his expression had grown no gentler with sorrow. His gaze fixed with disfavor on Caillean.

"What are you doing here?"

"We have come to share your sorrow," said the High Priestess gently, "and to honor a good man's passing, for, truly, Joseph was like a father to us all."

"Then he was not so good a man as he seemed, or not so good a Christian, or you heathen would be rejoicing," Paulus said stiffly. "But I am the leader here now, and I will enforce a purer faith upon my brethren. And my first act will be to put an end to the coming and going between our brotherhood and your accursed priesthood.

Woman, begone. Neither your sympathy nor your presence is welcome here."

Gawen took an instinctive step forward as if to place himself between them. Some of the Druids were muttering angrily, but Caillean looked simultaneously astonished and amused.

"Not welcome? But was it not we who gave your people permission to build your church here?"

"It is so," Father Paulus answered sourly, "but the land was God's, not yours, to give. We recognize no debt to worshippers of demons and false gods."

Caillean shook her head in sorrow. "Do you betray Father Joseph before he is even buried? He said that true religion would forbid blaspheming the name by which any man called his god, for they are all names for the One."

Father Paulus crossed himself. "Abomination! I never heard him speak such heresy! Get you gone or I will summon my brothers to drive you away!" His face had gone alarmingly red, and flakes of foam caught in his beard.

Caillean's face set like stone. She motioned to the Druids to move away. As Gawen turned to follow them, Paulus reached out and gripped his sleeve.

"My son, do not go with them! Father Joseph loved you—do not give over your soul to idolatry and your body to shame! They will summon the Great Whore whom they call Goddess up there in that ring of stones. You are a Nazarene in all but name! You have knelt at the altar and lifted your voice in holy chants of praise. Stay, Gawen, stay!"

For a moment amazement held Gawen still. Then it was replaced by rage. He jerked free, looking from Paulus to Caillean, who had stretched out her hand as if to pull him after her.

"No!" he gasped. "I will not be squabbled over like a bone among dogs!"

"Come, then," said Caillean, but Gawen shook his head. He could not join Father Paulus, but the priest's words had tainted the Druid ways as well. His heart ached for Sianna, but how dare he touch her now? All his confusion and longing settled suddenly into certainty. There was no way he could stay here at all.

One step at a time he began to back away.

"You both want to possess me, but my soul is my own! Fight over Avalon if you will, but not over me! I am leaving"—decision came to him with the words—"to seek my kin of Rome!"

Chapter Five

Gawen moved through the marshes swiftly, using the skills he had learned from the Lady of Faerie. Indeed, she was the only one who could have stopped him once he was on his way, and for the first day of his journey he walked in fear that Caillean would send her after him. But whether the Lady had refused, or his foster-mother had not thought of asking her help, or else, as he thought now, she simply did not care, he saw nothing but the clamoring water birds, a family of otters, and the shy red deer.

For seven years he had not left the Vale of Avalon, but his education had included the boundaries of Britannia's tribal territories and the location of the Roman forts and towns, as well as a map of the network of lines along which power flowed through the land. He knew enough to find the road north, and his woodscraft kept him from starving along the way. Two weeks of travel brought him to the gates of Deva.

His first thought was that he had never seen so many people in one place, doing so many things. Great ox-drawn wains laden with red sandstone were groaning along the road toward the fortress beyond the town. Parts of the earthen rampart with its palisade had been taken down and in its stead a wall of stone was rising. There was no sense of urgency—this land was completely pacified—but just as clearly the Romans meant it to stay that way.

It made him shiver. The Druids had scoffed at the Roman preoccupation with temporal power. But there was a spirit here as well, and the red stone fortress was its sanctuary. There was no turning back now. Gawen braced his shoulders, trying to remember the Latin he had never thought to have a use for, and followed a string of donkeys laden with net bags full of crockery beneath the arch of the gatehouse and into the world of Rome.

◁ ◁ ◁

"You are like your father—and yet you are a stranger. . . ." Macellius Severus looked at Gawen and then away. The old man had been doing that, thought the boy, since he arrived, as if he did not know whether to be glad or dismayed that he had a grandson after all. *That is how I felt,* thought Gawen, *when I found out who my parents were. . . .*

"I don't expect you to acknowledge me," he said aloud. "I have some skills—I can make my way."

Macellius straightened, and for the first time Gawen glimpsed the Roman officer he had been. His big frame was stooped now with age, and his hair had thinned to a few wisps of white, but he must have been a powerful man. Sorrow had marked his face, but he seemed to have his wits about him, for which Gawen was thankful.

"Do you fear to embarrass me?" Macellius shook his head. "I am too old for it to matter, and all your half-sisters are married or promised, so it will not affect their future. Still, adoption would be the simplest way to give you my name, if that is what you want. But first you must tell me why, after all these years, you have come to me."

Gawen found himself fixed by the eagle gaze that had undoubtedly made many a recruit tremble, and looked at his clasped hands.

"The Lady Caillean said that you had asked about me. . . . She didn't lie to you," the boy added quickly. "When you met, she did not yet know where I was."

"And where were you?" The question came very softly, and Gawen felt a breath of danger. But it was all in the past—what harm could it do the old man to know?

"One of the older girls who helped care for the children at the Forest House hid me when my other grandfather, the Arch-Druid, took my mother and father prisoner. And then—when it was all over—Caillean took me with her to Avalon."

"They are all gone now, the Druids of the Forest House..."
Macellius said absently. "Bendeigid, your 'other grandfather,' died
last year—they say, still babbling of sacred kings. I did not know that
any Druids remained in southern Britannia.... Where is 'Avalon'?"

The question came so suddenly, Gawen had answered before he
wondered why the old man wanted to know.

"It is only a small place," he stammered then, "a house of women
and a few old men, and a community of Nazarenes at the bottom of
the hill."

"I can see, then, why a strong young man like you might want to
get away...." Macellius roused himself, and Gawen began to relax.
"Can you read?"

"I can read and write in Latin, about as well as I speak it, which is
not very well," Gawen answered. This was not the time to boast that
the Druids had trained him to memorize vast quantities of lore. "I
can play on the harp. But in truth," he added, remembering the
training he had received from the Lady of Faerie, "hunting and
woodscraft are probably my most useful skills."

"I suppose so. It is something to build on. The Macellii have
always been in the Army," Macellius added with sudden diffidence.
"Would you like to be a soldier?"

Seeing the hope in the old man's eyes, Gawen tried to smile. *Until
half a moon ago,* he thought, *I was going to be a Druid priest.* To join the
Army would be a total rejection of that part of his heritage.

Macellius continued, "I will look about for a place for you. It is
an interesting life, and an intelligent man can rise from the ranks to a
position of some authority. Of course, promotion is not so easy in a
peaceful country such as Britannia has become, but perhaps when you
have some experience you can do a tour of duty on one of the fron-
tiers. In the meantime, we shall see if we can get you to sounding
more like a Roman."

Gawen nodded, and his grandfather smiled.

He spent the next month with Macellius, escorting the old man
around the town by day, and in the evening reading aloud to him
from the speeches of Cicero or the account Tacitus had written of

Agricola's wars. His adoption was duly witnessed before the magistrates, and he received his first lessons in the wearing of the toga, a garment whose draping made the robes of the Druids seem models of simplicity.

During his waking hours, the world of Rome absorbed him. It was only in sleep that his spirit yearned toward Avalon. In his dreams he saw Caillean teaching the maidens. There were new furrows in her brow, and from time to time she would gaze northward. He wanted to tell her that he was well, but when he woke, he knew there was no way to send word that would not compromise Avalon.

On the Eve of Beltane, he fell into an uneasy doze in which he saw the Tor ablaze with the light of the holy fires. But he could not see Sianna at all. His spirit ranged more widely, swinging like a lodestone as he sought hers. It was not on the Tor, but on the stone bench beside the sacred well, that he found her.

"Without you, I had no desire to dance around the fires. Why did you leave me? Do not you love me?" asked her dream image sorrowfully.

"I love you," he answered, *"but everyone serves the Lord and the Lady at Beltane. . . ."*

"Not the maiden who guards the well," she answered with a certain bitter pride. *"Father Paulus rules the Nazarenes now, and will allow them no communication with Avalon. But they have no holy women of their own, and even he cannot deny the will of Father Josephus in this, and so the sacred spring is warded by a maiden of Avalon. So long as I keep this trust, I may remain a maid and wait for you. . . ."* She smiled at him. *"If you remember nothing else of this night's dreaming, let your heart remember my love. . . ."*

When Gawen awoke, his cheeks were wet with tears. He longed for Sianna, but nothing had changed. He had cut himself off from the Druids, and it was only as a priest that he could have come to her.

About the time of Midsummer, the Romans celebrated the festival of Jupiter. Macellius, as a magistrate, had borne part of the cost of the festivities. He sat with the other notables on a platform that overlooked the playing field, with Gawen beside him. One day, he said proudly, they would build an arena, and the city fathers would view the games from a box, like the Emperor in Rome.

Gawen nodded. His Latin had improved rapidly, and was now quite grammatical, though spoken with the inflection of Britannia. But he still had to think before he said anything, and no matter how much he studied Tacitus and Cicero, he could not join in the light chatter of the other young men who had accompanied their fathers today.

Most of them were much younger. He could see those who did not know him wondering why he was not in the Army at his age, and those who did know him telling the others about the half-blood bastard Macellius had adopted so unexpectedly. When they thought no one could hear, they laughed, but Gawen's hunt-trained ears caught the sound.

But he would have found no friends among them, Gawen thought grimly, even if they had not despised him. He did not understand most of their jokes, and those he did, he did not consider very funny. He had chosen Rome, but he could not despise the British folk from whom he had come.

He watched the gladiators who battled below and mourned for their wasted lives even as he admired their skill. *I do not belong here . . . ,* he thought unhappily, *any more than I belonged at Avalon. Eiluned was right. I should never have been born!*

But at least the Druid training gave him the self-control not to show his despair, and when he and Macellius returned home, the older man, pleased with the success of the celebration, never guessed. Macellius, going over the events of the day, was beaming.

"That, my boy, is how the festival ought to be done! It will be a long time before Junius Varo or one of the other windbags can equal this day." He shuffled through a pile of messages on his worktable, stopped at one of them, and unrolled it. "I'm glad you were here, lad, to see—"

Gawen, who had shed the stifling folds of his toga with a sigh, looked up, sensing a change in tone.

"What is it?" he asked.

"Good news, at least I trust you will think so—I've found a place for you in the Army. The message must have arrived while we were at the games. You're to report to the Ninth Legion, the Hispanica, at Eburacum."

A legion! Now that it had come, Gawen did not know whether to be eager or afraid. At least it would get him away from the arrogant cubs who sneered at him here, and perhaps the Army would keep him too busy to long for Avalon.

"Ah, lad, this is the right thing for you—all the Macellii are soldiers—but the gods know how I'll miss you!" Macellius' face showed his own mixed feelings clearly. He held out his arms.

As Gawen hugged him, through his own confusion one thought came clearly—he would miss the old man too.

The Roman word for the Army was derived from the term for a training exercise, *exercitio,* and as Gawen discovered in his first days of service, that was apparently what everyone had joined the Army to do. The recruits were all young men, selected for their fitness and intelligence, but to march twenty Roman miles in five hours with a full pack took working up to. When they were not marching, they practiced fighting in doubly weighted armor, with sword or *pilum,* or drilling, or putting up temporary fortifications.

Gawen was vaguely aware that the country around Eburacum was harsher than his own hills, but beyond that knowledge, which came as much from his sore feet and aching thighs as from his eyes, his surroundings were a blur. The recruits saw little of the regular troops, except when some bronzed veteran would jeer as their sweating line trotted by. It was hard, but no stranger than his first introduction to Roman life in Deva. Oddly enough, it was his Druid training that gave him the self-control to endure Army discipline while boys from good Roman families collapsed and were sent home.

As their military education progressed, the recruits were given an occasional day off, when they could rest, repair their gear, or even visit the town that was growing outside the fortress walls. To hear the lilting British speech after so many weeks of camp Latin was a shock, reminding him that he was still Gawen, and "Gaius Macellius Severus" his name only by adoption. But the British shopkeepers and mule drivers who gossiped so freely in front of him never guessed that the tall young man with his Roman features and legionary tunic understood every word.

The marketplace of Eburacum did a lively trade in rumors. The local farm folk thronged to the town to sell their produce, and traders hawked wares from every part of the Empire, but the young men of the Brigantes, who in other times had come to gawk at the soldiers, were conspicuous by their absence. There were whispers of dissent, speculation about an alliance with the northern tribes.

It made Gawen uneasy, but he kept silent, for the gossip from inside the fortress was even more disturbing than what he heard outside its walls. Quintus Macrinius Donatus, their *legatus legionis,* owed his command to the patronage of the governor, who was his cousin, and the senatorial tribune who was his second was generally thought to be a frivolous puppy who should never have left Rome. Normally this should not have mattered, but although Lucius Rufinus, the centurion in charge of the recruits, was a decent fellow, word ran that the officers commanding the cohorts included more than the usual number of cruel and vicious men. Gawen suspected that it was just because of his decency that Rufinus had been given the unenviable job of turning a lot of country louts into the backbone of the Empire.

◁ ◁ ◁

"Only a week to go," said Arius, offering the dipper to Gawen. At the end of the summer even the north of Britannia was warm, and after a morning's march the water of the well where they had halted tasted better than wine. The well was only a few stones set around a spring that trickled from a hole in the hillside. Above them the road wound up through heather that bloomed purple against the dry grass. Below, the land fell away to a tangle of field and pasture, veiled by August haze.

"I'll be glad to take my oath at last," said Arius. "Regular armor will feel like a summer tunic after this, and I'm tired of listening to the regulars giving us catcalls when we go by!"

Gawen wiped his mouth and handed the dipper back to the other man. Arius was from Londinium, wiry and quick and incurably sociable. To Gawen, unskilled in making friends, he had been a gift from the gods.

"Wonder if we'll be assigned to the same cohort?" As they neared the end of their training, Gawen was beginning to worry about what came after. If the tales the older men traded in the wineshops were not told just to scare them, regular Army life might be worse than training. But that was not what kept him wakeful.

He had spent half his life preparing to pledge himself as a Druid, and then he had run away. How could a single summer commit him to an oath which might be less sacred but would be just as binding?

"I've vowed a red cockerel to Mars if he will put me in the fifth, with old Hanno," Arius replied. "He's a wily old fox, they say, who always gets the best for his men!"

"I've heard that too," said Gawen, taking another sip. He, who had deserted his own gods, had not dared to pray to the gods of Rome.

The next file came down to drink. Gawen handed over the dipper and clambered back up to the line. As the men formed up again, he gazed northward, where the white road snaked across the hills. It seemed a fragile barrier; even the milefort he could see in the distance looked as puny as a child's toy in the midst of that expanse of rolling hills. But the road, with the deep ditch of the *vallum* behind it, marked the *limes*, the limit of Empire. Some dreamers among the Army Engineers said it was not enough, that the only way to keep southern Britannia safe would be to build an actual wall. But so far it had worked. It was an idea, like the Empire itself, thought Gawen suddenly, a magic line which the wild tribes were forbidden to cross.

"One side doesn't look much different from the other," said Arius, echoing his thought. "What's out there?"

"We have a few observation posts up there still, and there are some native villages," said one of the other men.

"That'll be it, then," Arius answered.

"What do you mean?"

"See that smoke? The tribesmen must be burning off the stubble from their fields."

"We had better report it, though. The Commander will want to send out a patrol," said Gawen. But the centurion was giving the command to form up. No doubt Rufinus had seen the smoke as well and would know what to do about it. Gawen shouldered his pack and took his place in the line.

⊗ ⊗ ⊗

That night the fort buzzed with tales. Smoke had been sighted elsewhere along the border, and some folk said the war arrow had been seen among the tribes. But the legionary command did no more than send out a cohort to strengthen the auxiliary forts along the *limes*. They were entertaining brother officers from Deva who had come up for the hunting. Rumors were rife on the border—no need to put everyone on alert just because a few farmers were burning their fields.

Gawen, remembering Tacitus' account of the rebellion of Boudicca, wondered. But there had been no recent incident to set off the tribes—only, he thought, the ever-present tramp of hobnailed sandals on the Roman road.

Two nights later, when the hunting party was well on its way, fire blossomed suddenly in the hills above the town. The men in the fortress were ordered to arm up, but the legionary second-in-command was away with the Commander, and the camp prefect had no authority to order the troops to march. After a sleepless night the troops were told to stand down, leaving only those on guard duty to watch the plumes of smoke drifting across the dawn sky.

The recruits in Gawen's cohort found it hard to sleep, but even the veterans were not allowed to sleep long. The scouts that the prefect had sent out were returning, and the news was bad. The "idea" of a barrier had not been enough after all. The Novantae and Selgovae warriors had broken the border, and their Brigante cousins were rising to join them. By noon, the sun rode bloody through a smoke-palled sky.

Quintus Macrinius Donatus rode in late that night, covered with dust and flushed with excitement, or perhaps with anger at having missed his hunting. Man was a nobler prey, thought Gawen, who was on guard duty when the Commander came in. But, considering the numbers of tribesmen who were said to be out there, perhaps the hunters would become the hunted soon.

"Now," said the men, "we'll see some action. Those blue-painted fellows will never know what hit them. The Legion will send them scampering like scared rabbits back to their holes in the hills!"

But for another day nothing happened. The Commander was waiting for more intelligence, ran the rumors. Some said he was waiting for orders from Londinium, but that was hard to believe. If the Ninth was not here to guard the border, why was it stationed at Eburacum?

On the third day after the breaking of the border, the legionary trumpets sounded at last. Even though they had not yet taken their oaths to the Army, the recruits' cohort was divided up among the veterans. Gawen, because of his woodscraft, and Arius, for some reason known only to the gods of the Army, were attached as scouts to the cohort of Salvius Bufo. Even if there had been time for it, neither of them was complaining. Bufo was neither the best nor the worst of the centurions, and he had served for a number of years in Germania. Whatever protection might come from his experience, they would have.

There were a few groans from the regulars when the recruits joined them, but to Gawen's relief, Bufo's sharp order to "save it for the enemy" quieted them down. By noon they were moving out, and Gawen began to bless the long training marches that had hardened him to the weight of his pack and the steady tramp up the Roman road.

That night they built a fortified camp at the edge of the moors.

After three months in barracks, Gawen found sleeping out oddly disturbing. This marching camp was ditched and palisaded, and he lay in a leather tent crammed with men, but he could hear the night sounds above their snoring, and the draft that crept under the side of the tent carried the scent of the moors.

Perhaps that was why he dreamed of Avalon.

In his dream, the Druids, priests and priestesses together, had gathered in the stone circle on top of the Tor. Torches had been set on poles outside the circle; black shadows flitted across the stones. On the altar a small fire was burning. As he watched, Caillean cast herbs onto the flames. Smoke billowed upward, swirling northward, and the Druids lifted their arms in salutation. He could see their lips moving, but he could not make out their words.

The smoke from the fire grew more dense, glowing red in the torchlight, and his wonder deepened as it shaped itself into the figure of a woman armed with sword and spear. Face and body shifted from hag to goddess and back again, but always the smoke that swirled upward was her flowing hair. Swiftly the figure grew; the priests threw up their hands with a final shout, and a gust of wind carried it out of the circle and away to the north, followed by a host of winged shadows as the torches flared and went out. In the last moment of illumination, Gawen glimpsed Caillean's face. Her arms were outstretched, and he thought she was calling his name.

Gawen woke, shivering. A glimmer of pale light showed around the edges of the doorflap. He got up, picked his way across the legs of his tentmates, and slipped through the doorway. Mist lay heavy on the moors, but the growing light was filling the sky. It was very still. A sentry turned, one eyebrow raised in inquiry, and he pointed toward the privy trench. Wet grass soaked his bare feet as he made his way across the enclosure.

As he returned, a harsh cawing tore the silence. In another moment the mist was darkened by black wings. Ravens—more than he had ever seen together at one time—flapped up from the south to circle the hill. Three times the black birds flew over the Roman encampment; then they winged off to the west, but he could still hear them crying even after they had disappeared.

The sentry had his fingers splayed in the sign against evil, and Gawen felt no need to apologize for trembling. He knew now the name of the Raven Goddess to whom the priests of Avalon had prayed, and he needed no Druid training to interpret the omen. They would face the warriors of the tribes in battle that day.

◁ ◁ ◁

The sharp crack of a breaking branch behind him brought Gawen around, heart pounding. Arius looked up, his face flaming, and gestured an apology. Gawen nodded and, still without words, tried once more to demonstrate how to pass through the tangle of juniper and bracken without a sound. Until now he had never realized how much he had learned from the Lady of Faerie. Reason told him that a few moments of instruction could do little for a city-bred lad like his friend, and if the Brigantes were out in force, the Roman scouts would hear them before they were heard. But he still jumped every time Arius made a sound.

So far, they had tracked a tangle of hoofprints to the smoking ruins of an isolated farmstead. It had been a prosperous place; among the ashes they found fragments of red clay Samian dinnerware and stray beads. There were also several bodies, one of them headless. Turning a corner, they flinched from the glassy stare of the head, which had been hung by the hair from a dagger stuck into the door. The farmer had obviously done well under Roman rule, and had consequently been treated as an enemy.

Arius looked a little green, disturbed as much by Gawen's ability to interpret the scene so swiftly as he was by the evidence. But the Brigantes had gone on, and so must they. The enemy had risen first near Luguvalium and were moving toward Eburacum along the *limes*. If they turned southward, the scouts who had been sent out in the other direction would sound the alarm.

Bufo's orders had been clear. If Gawen and Arius did not sight the enemy before midmorning, they must assume the Brigantes were heading eastward, along the natural route toward Eburacum. What they needed now was a vantage point from which they could see them coming, and warn the Romans who were taking up position to defend the town. Gawen cast an experienced eye over the terrain and led the way uphill, where some ancient torment of the earth had thrust the soil upward. Rock jutted out from the cliffs like bared bones.

When they reached the gnarled pines at the top of the crag, they mopped the sweat from their faces with their legionary scarves, for the day had grown warm, and began to gather wood for a signal fire. Behind them, a grassy vale made a natural highway for anyone seeking the rich lands nearer the sea. It was very quiet. Too quiet, thought Gawen as he gazed across the valley. His skin twitched. Whether the rebels continued their raiding or headed homeward, they had to come this way. Maybe they had scouts out too, he thought, pulling back behind a tree. Maybe they were laughing already, planning how to pick off these Romans who had so foolishly ventured away from the safety of their walls.

Beyond, the land fell away to the north in long swales, veiled in smoky haze. It reminded Gawen of the way the land beyond would sometimes be hidden by the mists that surrounded Avalon, as if the isle had withdrawn from the world. Borderlands could be like that too. For half a year he had lived entirely in his father's world, but in this place, which belonged wholly neither to Britannia nor to Rome, he was becoming uncomfortably aware of his own mixed allegiances, and questioning whether there were any place where he truly belonged.

"I wonder if the new Emperor will do anything about the rebellion," the voice of Arius came from behind him. "This Spaniard, Hadrianus . . ."

"No emperor has visited Britannia since Claudius," answered Gawen, still gazing over the countryside. Was that a dustcloud, or smoke from a dying fire? For a moment he half rose, squinting, then settled back again. "The Brigantes would have to make a pretty good showing to merit his attention. . . ."

"That's true. The British can't coordinate worth a damn—even when they had a leader, at the battle of Mons Graupius, they lost. That was the last stand of the tribes."

"That's what my father thought," said Gawen, remembering the pride with which his grandfather had talked about his son's military career. "He was there."

"You never told me that!" Arius turned to him.

Gawen shrugged. He found it hard to think of the elder Gaius as his father, even though he had only to compare the portrait that Macellius kept in his study with a bronze mirror to know it must be true. At Mons Graupius his father had fought bravely. Despite his training, when it came to his own challenge Gawen wondered how he would fare.

"Unless they have found a new leader of the caliber of Calgacus, I don't think they will be dangerous for long," he said aloud.

Arius sighed. "No doubt it will be all over as soon as the Ninth catch up with the Brigantes. It will be reported to Hadrianus as no more than a border skirmish, if at all. The battle won't even have a name."

No doubt . . ., thought Gawen. In the past three months he had become intimately acquainted with the discipline and strength of the Roman Army. Despite their individual courage, for the tribesmen to stand against them would take a miracle. For a moment his dream of the Lady of the Ravens flickered into memory, but surely that had only been a night fancy. The iron tread of the Legions was the reality of the daylight.

"And then it will be back to barracks for us all," Arius went on. "And *exercises* . . . What a bore!"

"They made a desert, and called it peace . . ." Gawen quoted softly. "Tacitus said that about the pacification of the north after Mons Graupius. After this, we may be glad to be bored."

"You're twitchy because of the waiting." Arius grinned suddenly. "I know—I'm nervous too."

That must be it. His doubts were the thoughts a man has before a battle, that was all. Gawen managed a laugh, suddenly very glad that Arius was with him, and returned to his survey of the northern hills.

◁ ◁ ◁

It was Arius who first sighted the enemy. He came running back up from the thicket where he had gone to relieve himself, waving his arms in excitement, and Gawen, slipping back through the tangle of pines, saw the dustcloud to the west, where the sun was already sliding toward the hills, resolving into a moving mass of men and horses.

The Brigante advance was slowed by captured oxcarts laden with spoils. A mistake, thought Gaius. One of the greatest strengths of the tribes was mobility. But there were more than he had expected—thousands of them. He looked southward, where the Legion should be waiting, calculating time and distance.

"We'll watch until the main body of the enemy has passed and then light the fire."

"And then what?" asked Arius. "If we get cut off from our own lines, we'll miss all the fun."

"If we wait, the battle will come to us." Gawen did not know whether to hope or to fear that was true. The danger, it occurred to him then, was going to be in the moments between the lighting of the fire and the appearance—*if* they had reached their position and seen his signal—of the Roman Army.

The enemy was almost below them now, Brigantes by their gear, though he could see some of the wilder tribesmen from the north riding in the van. Arius caught his eye, and then, frowning grimly, pulled out his flints and steel. It took several tries to get a spark, but soon a wisp of smoke curled up from the tinder, which strengthened as they added kindling, and then burst into vigorous flame. A judicious application of green stuff turned the white smoke to grey; the plume wavered, then strengthened, staining the sky.

Could the Romans see it? Gawen tensed, staring. Light sparkled suddenly across the rim of the far hill. He recognized the silver shimmer of lance points, and one flare of gold. *The Eagle* ... Wordless, he pointed at the legionary standard, and Arius nodded. A blur of shadow grew beneath it, deepened, spilled down the slope, inexorable as the tide. Sweet with distance, trumpets blared, and the moving mass became three columns, the center slowing while the two flanks advanced along the higher ground to either side.

The Brigantes had seen them too. For a moment they faltered; then a discordant bawling came from their cowhorns. A ripple of movement passed through the crowd of men as shields were shrugged from back to arm and lances swung forward. Gawen and Arius, making their way down the far side of the crag, paused as the yelling intensified, pulling at a screen of junipers to see.

The Roman formation advanced with the remorseless regularity of one of their war machines, blocs of men moving in straight lines at a steady pace, flanks curving out to protect the center. The Celtic rush pulsed with the wild energy of a wildfire, roaring toward the foe.

The British could see the Roman plan, but no one, not even their own leaders, could ever be sure what the Celtic warriors would do. And in the moment when it seemed that the entire Brigante force would be surrounded and crushed by the Roman foundation, several bands from the wilder tribes who rode with them broke away suddenly.

"They're running!" exclaimed Arius, but Gawen said nothing.

They did not look panicked, but furious, and in another moment it was clear that they were swinging around to charge down upon the Roman flank, not running away. Suddenly the high ground, which had allowed the Romans to get beyond the center of the enemy, became a disadvantage, for the Celtic horsemen were higher still. Screaming, they sent their surefooted ponies hurtling down the hill.

On that ground, no infantry could stand against them. The legionaries went sprawling, trampled by the horses or by each other as they tried to get out of the way. The confusion spread through the ranks. From above they could see the orderly pattern unraveling, the flanks recoiling upon the center just as its front line encountered the main group of the unmounted Brigante warriors.

The two scouts watched the seething mass of men with horrified fascination. Gawen remembered suddenly how once, when he had dropped a squirrel with a thrown stone, it had fallen into a nest of bees. In moments the poor beast had disappeared beneath hordes of attackers. Unbelievably, that was what he was seeing now. Watching, he winced at every blow. Was it more horrible to be in the thick of battle, he wondered, or here, where he could die a thousand deaths in sympathy?

But the Romans, better armored against the stings of these enemies, were not entirely overwhelmed. Many died where they stood, but those who could do so broke and ran. The Commander and his staff had stationed themselves on a small rise. The bright cloaks began to move as the first wave of retreating soldiers reached them. Could Donatus rally them?

Gawen never knew if the Commander had even tried. He saw the red cloaks retreating, saw them engulfed by the rout, and then the flash of bloody swords as the British caught up with them. The Legionary Eagle tossed above the fray for a few desperate moments longer, then went down.

"Jupiter Fides," whispered Arius, his face the color of cheese. But Gawen, seeing the flock of crows that whirled above the battle, knew that the deity who ruled here was no god of Rome but the Great Queen, the Lady of Ravens, Cathubodva.

"Come on," he whispered. "We can't help them now."

Arius staggered as they picked their way down the far side of the hill. But Gawen, who felt none too steady himself, had no time for sympathy. His senses were strained to the limit, seeking for danger, and when he heard, above the tumult of the battlefield, the clank of metal against stone, he shoved the other man down into the bracken beside a little stream, hissing at him to be still.

They lay like hunted rabbits as the sounds grew louder. Gawen thought of the severed head they had seen at the farmstead. The tribesmen took heads sometimes as trophies. For a moment he had an awful vision of his own head and that of Arius grinning from poles outside some northern warrior's door. His gorge rose and he swallowed, afraid that if he was sick he would be heard.

Through the ferns Gawen saw scratched bare legs, and heard men singing. They were laughing, chanting in disjointed phrases that would become a song of victory. He listened to the blurred speech of the north and tried to make out words.

He was startled into looking up by a convulsive movement at his side. Above the heads of the tribesmen swayed the Legionary Eagle. He felt Arius rising and reached out to stop him, but his friend was already on his feet, drawing his *gladius*. The flash of sun on steel stopped the singing. Gawen rolled to a crouch, his own blade ready, as the Brigantes began to laugh. In alarm he realized there were nearly two dozen.

"Give me the Eagle!" Arius said hoarsely.

"Give me your sword!" said the tallest in accented Latin. "And maybe we will let you live."

"As a slave among the women—" said one of the others, a big man with red hair.

"Oh, leave him for their amusement!"

"They'll just love those curls—maybe he's really a girl, following her man to war!"

From his companions came a spate of lewd speculation in the British tongue regarding what the women would do to him. For a moment, Gawen, caught between fear for his friend and a gibbering panic that urged him to run away, could not move. Then he found himself rising to his feet.

"This is a madman," Gawen replied in the same tongue, grabbing the tail of Arius' tunic to halt him. "The gods protect him."

"We are all madmen." The Brigante chieftain eyed him warily, trying to reconcile the British speech and the Roman gear. "And the gods have given us the victory."

True enough, thought Gawen, *and I am the craziest of all.* But he could not stand by and let his friend be killed. That memory would have sent him mad indeed.

"The gods of our people have been kind," answered Gawen, babbling, "and they will not care to see you dishonor the gods of your beaten foe. This one is their priest. Give him the Eagle and let him go."

"And who are you to give us orders?" asked the chieftain, his face darkening.

"I am a Son of Avalon," answered Gawen, "and I have seen Cathubodva riding the wind!"

From the tribesmen came an uneasy mutter, and for a moment Gawen hoped he was going to get away with this. Then the redheaded man spat and lifted his spear.

"Then you are a traitor and a fool traveling together!"

At the movement, Arius jerked free. Gawen was just a moment too late to catch him as he charged, but he could see, with excruciating clarity, the arc the Brigante spear cut through the sky.

A breastplate might have repelled it, but scouts wore only a heavy tunic of hide. Arius staggered as the blade pierced his breast, his eyes widening in surprise. Even as his friend fell, Gawen knew the wound was fatal. But that was the last coherent thought he had for some time. The face of Cathubodva rose before him and, screaming, he charged.

He felt the impact as his blade struck flesh. Without thinking, he parried a blow and ducked under the man's arm. At close quarters the Celts could not swing their longer blades. His shorter sword stabbed upward, biting into flesh, scraping on bone. The long hours spent in sword drill directed his blows, but it was Druid curses that he was shouting, and to his enemies they were more deadly than his sword.

Gawen sensed first a faltering, and then, suddenly, no one was attacking him. He blinked, gasping like an overdriven horse.

He saw Brigante warriors disappearing over the rise. Eight bodies lay sprawled on the bloody ground. Staggering a little as the spirit that had filled him drained away, Gawen made his way back to Arius. His friend lay still, staring emptily at the sky. But nearby, where one of the fleeing Brigantes had tossed it, lay the Eagle of the Ninth.

He should bury his friend, Gawen thought dimly. He should lay Arius in a hero's mound with his enemies around him and the Eagle for a monument. But he knew he did not have the strength, and it would make no difference. Arius would still be dead, like all the others. Even the Eagle was nothing to him now except a reason for men to kill.

I don't belong here . . ., he thought hazily. The sword slipped from his hand. With clumsy fingers he pulled at the lacings of his leather tunic. It was better without the heavy gear, but he still stank of blood. In the silence, the trickling of water from the little burn called him. He stumbled back through the bracken and plunged his face into the chill water where the stream had hollowed out a deep pool, washed the blood from his arms and legs, and drank again. To his amazement, only a little of the blood was his own. The water made him feel better, but the stain of blood, the blood of his own people, was still on his soul.

I have not taken oath to the Emperor, he thought. *I don't have to stay in the Army to be a butcher!* Could they keep him if he went back to Eburacum? He did not know, and surely the disgrace would kill his grandfather. Better the old man should think him dead than believe that the horror of battle had made him run away. It was being a killer that he was afraid of, he thought, looking at the men who lay on the ground, not of being slain.

Finally he got up. Among the bodies, the gilded wings of the Eagle glinted balefully in the light of the setting sun.

"You, at least, shall destroy no more men!" he muttered, lifting it, and bore it back to the stream. The waters of the pool closed over its brightness, as water had hidden the gleam of many another treasure offered by his mother's people to the gods.

On the other side of the ridge men might still be fighting and dying, but here it was silent. Gawen tried to think what to do. He could not go back to the Legions, but his Roman features would damn him among the tribes. There was just one place, really, where they had not cared whether he was Roman or British, but only about what was in his soul. Suddenly, with an aching intensity, he wanted to go home, to Avalon.

Chapter Six

The Vale of Avalon lay wrapped in harvest peace. Golden light filtered through the leaves of the apple tree, glowing in the scented smoke that twined from the firepot, and lending a soft illumination to the veils of the priestesses and the bright hair of the girl who sat between them. In the silver basin before her, water trembled at the touch of breath, then stilled. Caillean, resting her fingers on Sianna's shoulders, felt the tension draining out of them as the girl's trance deepened, and nodded. She had waited a long time for this day.

"Let it go, that's right," she murmured. "Breathe in . . . and out . . . and look at the surface of the pool." She felt her own vision flickering as she breathed in the magic of the burning herbs, and looked quickly away, anchoring her awareness firmly in the present.

Sianna sighed and swayed forward, and Caillean steadied her. She had been certain the girl would have an aptitude for Seeing, but until Sianna had been sworn as a priestess it was not right to use her so. Then Gawen had run away, and the girl had moped and grown so thin Caillean had forbidden her to work any kind of magic. Only in the past month had she begun to recover her spirits. It was a relief to Caillean to see it. The daughter of the Faerie Queen was the most talented of the young girls who had come to them for training, and no wonder, with her heritage. The High Priestess had been harder on her than on the others, and she had not broken. This, if anyone, was the maiden who would be able to learn all of the ancient magics and wield them when she herself was gone.

"The water is a mirror," Caillean said softly, "in which you can see things far off in distance and time. Seek now the summit of the Tor, and tell me what you see. . . ."

Sianna's breathing grew deeper. Caillean matched it, relaxing a little of her own control in order to share the vision while retaining her connection to the outer world.

"I see . . . the ring stones shining in the sun. . . . The Vale is laid out below. . . . I see patterns . . . glowing paths that pass through the isles, the shining road that comes up from Dumnonia and passes toward the eastern sea. . . ."

Through half-closed lids, Caillean glimpsed the surface pattern of hill and wood and field, and beneath it, the bright lines of power. As she had hoped, Sianna could see the inner world as well as the outer.

"That is well, very well," she began, but Sianna was continuing—

"I follow the shining path; northward it leads toward Alba. Smoke rises; the borders are soaked in blood. There has been battle, and the ravens feast on the slain. . . ."

"The Romans," breathed Caillean. When word of the uprising had come to them, the Druids had agreed to lend their power to help, and the priestesses, fired by their enthusiasm, were eager to join with them. Caillean remembered the first surge of exultation at the prospect of driving out the hated Romans at last, and then the doubt—was this the right way to use the power of Avalon?

"I see Romans and Britons, their bodies tangled together on the battlefield—" Sianna's voice shook.

"Who won the battle?" Caillean asked. They had sent forth their power; they had heard there was fighting. And then nothing. If the Romans themselves knew what was happening, they had not allowed the news to travel far.

"The ravens feast on both friend and foe. Homes lie in ruins, bands of fugitives wander the land."

The High Priestess straightened, frowning. If the rebels had been beaten easily, Rome would think no more of these troubles than of any other flare-up. If the tribesmen had destroyed the Roman force completely, the Empire might give up Britannia. But this halfway disaster would only enrage them.

"Gawen, where are you?" Sianna whispered, shaking.

Caillean stiffened. She still had some connections in Deva. She knew that the boy had gone to his grandfather, and then been sent to the Ninth Legion in Eburacum. Since then she had lived in fear that Gawen might have been in the battle. But how could the girl know? She had not intended to have Sianna search for him, but she knew the strength of the link between them, and she could not resist the opportunity to use it to learn what she, too, desperately desired to know.

"Let your vision expand," she said softly. "Let your heart lead you where you must go."

Sianna grew, if possible, even more still, her eyes fixed on the swirl of light and color in the bowl.

"He is fleeing . . ." she said at last, "trying to find his way home. But the land is full of enemies. Lady, use your magic to protect him!"

"I cannot," Caillean replied. "My own strength can ward no more than this Vale. We must pray to the gods."

"If you cannot help him, then there is only one who can, nearer than the Goddess, if not so powerful." Sianna straightened with a shuddering sigh, and the surface of the water went abruptly blank. "Mother!" she cried. "Your fosterling is in danger! Mother—I love him! Bring Gawen home!"

⊲ ⊲ ⊲

Gawen jerked upright, listening, as a whisper of sound swept through the heather. It grew louder. On his cheek he felt the chill brush of cold air and settled back again. It was only the wind, rising as it always did at sunset. It was only the wind, this time. In the three days since the battle, it seemed to him, he had done nothing but run and hide. The bands of marauding Brigantes and disorganized units of legionaries were equally a danger to him, and any herder might betray him. He could survive by trapping small game and stealing from farmers' store sheds, but the weather was getting colder. In the north he was one of many who had fled the battle, in danger from both sides. But when he moved south he would be an obvious fugitive. Technically he was not a deserter, but the Romans, still smarting from their defeat, must be looking for scapegoats.

He shivered and pulled his cloak around him more tightly. Where could he go? Was there anywhere, even Avalon, where a man with his divided heritage could be at home? He watched the last of the light fade in the west and felt hope dying in his soul.

That night he dreamed of Avalon. It was night there as well, and on the Tor the maidens were dancing, weaving among the stones. There were more of them than he remembered; he searched for Sianna's bright hair. Through shadow and moonlight the figures wove their pattern, and as they moved the grass of the Tor seemed to glimmer with an answering glow, as if their dance had awakened a power that slept within the hill.

"*Sianna!*" he cried, knowing she could not hear him. And yet, as her name left his lips, one of the figures paused, turned, extended her arms. It was Sianna; he recognized the lithe poise of her body, the tilt of her head, the radiance of her hair. And behind her, like a shadow, he saw the figure of her mother, the Faerie Queen. As he watched, the shadow grew, until it was a door into darkness. He shrank back, fearing to be engulfed by it, and some sense beyond hearing perceived her words—"*The way to all that you love is through Me. . . .*"

Gawen woke in the dawning, cold, stiff, but, oddly, a little more hopeful. His snares had caught a young hare, whose meat eased his hunger. It was at midday, when he had ventured down to drink at a small spring, that his luck turned evil once more. He should have moved on as soon as he had eased his thirst, but the afternoon had turned warm and he was very tired. Sitting with his back against a willow, he allowed his eyes to close.

He woke suddenly, aware of a sound that was not the wind in the trees or the gurgling of the stream. He heard men's voices and the tramp of hobnailed sandals—now he could see them through the screen of leaves—Roman soldiers, and not the demoralized stragglers he had been encountering. This was a regular detachment under the command of a centurion.

They would recognize his tunic as legionary issue, he thought, instinctively looking around him for cover. Behind him was a hill, its slopes covered with tangled trees. Crouching, he moved toward it, pushing aside the branches of the willow tree. He was on the lower slope when they saw him.

"Halt!"

For a moment the authority in that voice stopped him. Then he pushed on, and a thrown *pilum* slashed through the brush beside him and rattled over stone. Gawen snatched it up and automatically flung it back again. He heard someone swear and scrambled onward, realizing too late that, if they had not intended to follow before, they certainly would now.

He had begun to believe he would get away when the slope ended abruptly where some ancient convulsion of the earth had wrenched apart the stones. He teetered at the edge of the gorge, looking from the sharp-edged rocks below to the weapons of those who pursued him. Better to go down fighting, he thought desperately, than to be dragged back in chains to be tried for desertion.

Gawen could see their faces now, red with exertion but dreadfully determined. He drew his long dagger, regretting that he had thrown back the spear. And then someone called his name.

He stiffened, but the legionaries had no breath for calling, even if they had known who he was. It must be the rush of blood in his ears that was deceiving him, or the wind in the stones.

"Gawen—come to me!" It was a woman's voice. Involuntarily he turned. Shadow veiled the depths below, deepening even as he looked at it. *"Remember, the way to safety is through Me. . . ."*

Desperation has driven me mad, he thought, but now it seemed to him he saw dark eyes luminous in an angular face framed by waves of dark hair. The fear went out of him in a little sigh. As the first of the legionaries reached the ledge on which he stood, Gawen smiled and stepped out into the void.

⊲ ⊲ ⊲

To the Romans, he seemed to fall into darkness. A chill wind came up then, like the breath of winter upon their souls, and not even the bravest cared to search down into the chasm for the body of the man they had pursued. If he had been an enemy he was dead, and if a friend, a fool. They climbed back down the hill, curiously unwilling to discuss what they had seen, and by the time they rejoined the rest of the troop, the incident was receding into that part of the soul where one remembers evil dreams. Not even the centurion thought to include it in the report he made.

Certainly they had other, more pressing matters to concern them. The remnants of the shattered Ninth Legion slowly made their way back to Eburacum, where the Sixth, posted up from Deva, received them with barely restrained contempt. The new Emperor Hadrianus was said to be furious, and there was talk that he might actually come to Britannia himself to take matters in hand. The survivors of the Ninth were to be transferred to other units, elsewhere in the Empire. It was not surprising if they responded with a sullen silence to any questioning.

Only the centurion Rufinus, who had actually cared about the recruits under his command, had a word to spare for the soldierly old gentleman who had also come up from Deva. Indeed, he remembered young Macellius. The boy had been sent off as a scout and might well have missed the great battle. But no one had seen him since that day.

Then the Sixth marched out to begin the long, brutal task of re-pacifying the north, and Macellius went home to Deva, still wondering about the fate of the boy whom he had learned in a few short months to love.

That year winter came hard and wet. Storms blasted the north, and heavy rains made the whole Vale of Avalon a grey sea that turned its hills into true islands on which folk huddled and prayed for spring.

On the morning of the equinox, Caillean awakened early, shivering. She lay swaddled in wool blankets, and the straw pallet on which she lay was covered by sheepskin, but the damp chill of the winter had gotten into everything, including her bones. Since her moon blood had ceased to flow, she had been healthy and vigorous, but this morning, remembering how her joints had pained her throughout the winter, she felt ancient. Her heart pounded with sudden panic. She could not afford to grow old! Avalon was thriving, even after a season like this one, but there were so few trained priestesses that she could depend on. Avalon could not survive if she were gone!

She took a deep breath, willing her heart to steady, forcing taut muscles to relax again. *Are you a priestess? What has become of your faith?* Caillean smiled, realizing she was scolding herself as if she had been one of her own maidens. *Cannot you trust in the Goddess to take care of Her own?*

The thought eased her, but in her experience the Lady was most disposed to help those who had already tried to help themselves. It was still her duty to train a successor. Without Gawen, the sacred bloodlines which Eilan had given her life to continue were lost, but that was all the more reason for Avalon, which preserved her work and teachings, to endure.

Sianna . . . , she thought then. *It is she who must follow me.*

The girl had sworn the vows of a priestess, but she had been ill at the feast of Beltane and had not gone to the fires. And then she had become the guardian of the well. But that could be done by one of the younger girls. It had been hard for some of the priestesses who had known the enforced chastity of the Forest House to see the value in allowing the priests and priestesses to lie down together in the ritual. Those who did so were not making love for their own pleasure, or not entirely, but as representatives of the mighty masculine and feminine forces that men called gods. The future High Priestess of Avalon must make that offering.

This year, I will accept no excuses. She must complete her consecration, and give herself to the god.

Someone scratched at her door and she sat up, wincing at the chill.

"Lady!" It was Lunet's voice, breathless with excitement. "Waterwalker's boat is pulling in at the landing. Someone is with him. It looks like Gawen! Lady, you must come!

But Caillean was already in motion, stepping into her sheepskin boots with the fleece still inside and pulling on her warm cloak. When she opened the door she blinked at the brightness of the day, but the air, which a moment ago had felt so cold, seemed now as invigorating as wine.

They met on the path. Below, Waterwalker was already pushing his craft away from the muddy shore. Lunet and the other priestesses who had been awakened by her shouts hung back, staring at Gawen as if he were returning from the dead.

Examining him, Caillean understood their uncertainty. Gawen had changed. He seemed taller, and thinner, but there was hard muscle on that long frame, and the strong-boned face he turned to her was unmistakably that of a man. But wonder filled his eyes.

She shook her head and waved the others away. "Silly girls, this is not Samhain, when the dead return, and he is no ghost but a living man. Go get him something hot to drink and dry clothing if you can think of nothing else more useful—go on!"

Gawen stopped, looking around him. Softly, Caillean spoke his name.

"What has happened?" he asked, focusing on her at last. "There is so much water, but I saw no rain, and how can buds be coming on branches that were just losing their leaves?"

"It is the equinox," she said, not understanding.

He nodded. "The battle was a moon before it, and then for some days I wandered. . . ."

"Gawen," she interrupted, "the great battle in the north was fought last harvest tide, half a year ago!"

He swayed, and for a moment she thought he would fall. "Over six moons? But since the Lady of Faerie saved me only six days have passed!"

Caillean took his arm, beginning to understand. "Time runs differently in the Otherworld. We knew you were in danger, but not what became of you. I see that we must thank the Lady of Faerie for preserving you. Don't complain, child—you have missed the winter, and it was a hard one. But you are home now, and we must decide what is to be done with you!"

A little shakily, Gawen sighed, and then managed a smile.

"Home ... It was only after the battle that I understood I have no place in either Roman or British lands. Only here, on this isle that is not wholly in the world of men."

"I will not force a choice upon you," Caillean said carefully, suppressing her excitement. What a leader for the Druids he could be! "But if you have taken no other vows, the dedication you were going to make before you left us is still open to you."

"In another week I would have made my oath of allegiance to the Emperor, but the Brigantes came, and we were sent out unsworn," answered Gawen. "Brother Paulus will be livid." He grinned suddenly. "I met him as I was coming up the hill and he begged me to join his brethren. I refused, and he shouted something—What has happened to the Nazarenes since Father Joseph died? Paulus seems even crazier than he was before!"

"He is Father Paulus now," answered Caillean. "They have chosen him as their leader, and he seems determined to make the rest of them as fanatical as he. It is a pity, after the many years in which we lived side by side in peace upon this hill, but he will have nothing to do with a community where a woman rules. None of our folk have spoken to theirs for many moons. But he does not matter," she went on. "It is you who must decide what you will do now."

Gawen nodded. "I seem to have done six moons of thinking in the Otherworld, for all that the time seemed so short. I am ready"— he paused, gazing around him at the weathered huts and then up at the stone-crowned Tor—"to face whatever fate the gods will give me now."

Caillean blinked. For a moment she had seen him ablaze with gold like a king, or was it fire?

"Your destiny may be greater than you suppose ..." she said in a voice that was not her own.

Then the moment of vision passed. She looked up to see his reaction, but he was staring past her, and from his face all the weariness had fallen away. Caillean did not need to turn to know that Sianna was standing there.

& & &

The new moon was setting. Through the entry to the low brush hut in which they had put him, Gawen could just see her fragile sickle brushing the edge of the hill. Poor baby moon, hurrying to her bed; in a few moments she would leave him in darkness. He shifted position uncomfortably and settled himself once more. It was the night before the Eve of Beltane. Since the setting of the sun, when the new moon was already high, he had been here. It was a time for him to meditate, they had told him, to prepare his soul. It was uncomfortably like those long hours when he and Arius had waited for the battle between the Romans and the Brigantes to begin.

Nothing but his own will held him here. It would be easy enough to slip away through the darkness. Not that the folk of Avalon would have cast him out if he changed his mind—they had asked if he sought initiation of his own will again and again. But if he had refused this, and stayed, he would always have seen the disappointment in Caillean's eyes, and as for Sianna—he would have faced far more than whatever they planned to do to him for the right to claim her love.

He looked out again. The moon had disappeared. A practiced glance at the positions of the stars told him that midnight was near. *Soon they will come, and I will be waiting. Why?* Was it only his desire for Sianna that had held him, or some deeper compulsion of the soul?

Gawen had tried to run away, and found he could not evade his own divided nature. It seemed to him now that to choose something to serve, and give himself to it completely, was the only way to unity.

Something rustled outside; he looked up and saw that the stars had moved. The Druids, their white robes ghostly in the starshine, were gathering.

"Gawen, son of Eilan, I call you now, at the hour of night's high noon. Is it still your desire to be admitted to the sacred mysteries?" The voice was that of Brannos, and it warmed Gawen's heart to hear it. The old man seemed ancient as the hills, his fingers were now so twisted by joint ache that he could no longer play the harp at all, but at need he could still act with the power of a priest at the rituals.

"It is." His own voice was hoarse in his ears.

"Then come forth, and let the testing begin."

They took him, still in darkness, to the sacred well. There was something different in the sound of the water. Peering down, Gawen realized that the flow had been diverted. He could see steps leading down into the well shaft, and the niche in its side.

"To be reborn in the spirit, you must first be purified," said Brannos. "Go down into the well."

Shivering, Gawen stripped off his robe and clambered downward. Tuarim, who had taken his vows the previous year, followed him. He started as the young man knelt and snapped a pair of iron manacles around his ankles. He had been told to expect this, and knew that he could release himself if his courage failed him, but the cold weight of metal on his flesh filled him with an unexpected fear. Yet he said nothing as he heard the rush of water, released, beginning once more to fill the well.

The water rose swiftly. It was bitterly cold, and for a time he could think of nothing else. But every one of those priests whom he had remembered with scorn when he was being trained as a soldier must have been through this; he would not flee what they had endured. He tried to distract himself by wondering if the sacred vessel Father Joseph had spoken of was still here, or whether Caillean had taken it for safekeeping. If he tried, he thought he could sense something, an echo of joy beyond pain, but the waters were rising.

By the time the water reached his chest, Gawen could hardly feel the lower parts of his body at all. He wondered if his muscles would obey him well enough to escape if he tried. Had this all been a trick to make him go to his death unprotesting? *Remember!* he told himself. *Remember what Caillean taught you! Summon the inner fire!*

Cold water embraced his neck; his teeth were chattering. Desperately he grasped for a memory of flame—a spark in the mind's darkness that flared as he sucked in air and then exploded through every vein. Light! He refused to know anything other than that radiance. For a moment then, he seemed to see a tumult of shadow split by a single lightning stroke that divided light from darkness and in a chain reaction sent pattern, order, meaning, into the world.

Awareness of his body returned, but it was at a new level. Gawen found that he could see, for the darkness around him was lit by a radiance that shone from within. He was no longer cold—in another moment, he thought, his inner heat would turn the water to steam. When it touched his lips he laughed.

It was at that moment that the level of the water began to sink once more. It did not take long for the well, its inflow blocked and exits freed, to draw in enough for the Druids to release him. Gawen hardly noticed. He was light! That new knowledge was the only thing that he could think of now.

Below the well a great fire had been kindled; if he had failed, perhaps it would have warmed him. They told him that he must go through it in order to continue, and Gawen laughed once more. He was fire—why should he fear the flame? And, naked as he was, he walked across the coals, and though the heat dried the water from his body, not a single toe of his foot was burned.

Brannos was waiting for him on the other side.

"Through fire and water you have passed, two of the elements from which, as we are taught by the ancient men of wisdom, the world is made. There remain earth and air. To complete your testing, you must find your way to the summit of the Tor—if you can...."

While the old man was speaking, others had brought up earthen pots in which herbs were smoking, and set them around him. Smoke billowed upward, sweet and choking; he recognized the acrid-sweet scent of the herbs they used to bring visions, but he had never encountered it in such concentration. He took an involuntary breath, coughed, and forced himself to breathe again, bracing himself against the wave of vertigo that came with it.

Accept it, ride it, he reminded himself of old lessons. The smoke could be a great aid in detaching the mind from the body, but without discipline the spirit could be lost in evil dreams. But he, coming to it already filled with sacred fire, needed no help to transcend ordinary awareness. With each breath he felt the smoke pushing him further from ordinary consciousness; he looked at the Druids, and saw them haloed with light.

"Ascend the holy hill and receive the blessing of the gods. . . ."
Brannos' voice resonated through all the worlds.

Gawen blinked at the slope above him. That should be easy
enough, even when his spirit was flying. In seven years he had climbed
the Tor so often, his feet must know the way by now. He took a step
and felt his feet sinking into the soil. Another—it was like wading
through deep water. He peered ahead of him; what he had thought
was firelight on the ground mist seemed now to be a glow that was
coming from the earth itself, and the hill had the luminous trans-
parency of Roman glass. The stone that marked the beginning of the
path was a pillar of fire

It was like the light he had seen coming from his own body—
like the auras that he saw surrounding the others. *It is not just me!* he
knew then. *Everything is made of Light!*

But the things revealed by that illumination were not the same as
they appeared in the light of everyday. It was clear now that the
labyrinthine path he knew so well led not around the Tor but *into* it.
He felt a moment's fear—what if his vision deserted him and he
found himself trapped beneath the earth? But this new perception
was so *interesting;* he could not resist the desire to learn what lay within
the holy hill.

Gawen took a deep breath, and this time the smoke, instead of
disorienting him, only made his vision sharper. The way was clear.
He strode boldly forward.

From the westernmost point of the Tor, the passageway led
directly into the hill. He found himself moving in a long curve
through some transparent medium that resisted like water and tingled
like fire but was neither. It felt, he realized as he rounded the far curve
and started back again, as if the substance of his body had become
less solid; he flowed, rather than pushed, through the soil, and only
his hold on his body of light allowed him to retain his identity.

Now he was nearing the point of entry, but rather than spiraling
around, the way doubled back upon itself. Once more he swung back
and around the hill. This curve was longer; he sensed that he was
moving away from the center rather than closer to it. But the same

compulsion drew him around once more, so close to the surface that he could see the outside world as if through a crystal haze. Around and back again he passed, and now at last the way led straight into the hill.

He was very deep now. Power throbbed from the heart of the hill so strongly that he could hardly stand. He pushed against the passageway, trying to reach it, and felt the first ecstatic disintegration of his being begin as he touched the barriers. *The way is barred*, came a voice from deep within; *you have not yet completed your transformation.*

Gawen drew back. He could see that the only way out was to go forward, but the pain of moving away from the center was almost more than he could bear. But this turn of labyrinth was more tight than the others, and presently he rounded a sharp curve and staggered as the current of power that flowed through the Tor caught and swept him toward the heart of the hill.

From somewhere beyond the circles of the world a voice proclaimed, *"The Pendragon walks the Dragon Path. . . ."*

It was like sunlight coruscating from the ice-sheathed branches of a winter wood; it was like the blaring of trumpets, a shimmer of notes from all the harps in the world; it was all bliss and all beauty. He was the Head of the Dragon, and he floated at that incandescent point which was the center of the world.

But, after an eternity beyond time, it seemed to him that someone was calling him by his earthly name.

"Gawen . . ." The call was faint with distance, a woman's voice he ought to know. "Gawen, son of Eilan, return to us! Come forth from the crystal cave!"

Why should he, he wondered, when here was the end of all desire?

Could he? he wondered, immersed in this blaze of beauty which had neither beginning nor end.

But the voice insisted, separating into three voices sometimes, then joining once more in a single cry. He could not ignore it. Images came to him of a beauty which was less perfect but more real. He remembered the taste of an apple, the flex of muscles as he ran, and the simple human sweetness of a girl's hand touching his own.

And with that memory came her face. *Sianna* . . .

I must go to her, he thought, reaching out into the radiance. But he could not leave when he could see nowhere to go.

"This is the test of Air," came another memory. *"You must speak the Word of Power."*

But they had not told him what that word might be.

Fragments of old tales shimmered in his awareness—the stories old Brannos had told him, bits of bardic lore. Names were magic, he remembered, but before you could name another, you first must name yourself.

"I am the son of Eilan, daughter of Bendeigid . . ." he whispered, and more reluctantly. "I am the son of Gaius Macellius Severus." There was a sense of anticipation in the presence that surrounded him. "I am a bard and a warrior and a Druid trained in magic. I am a child of the holy isle." What else could he say? "I am a Briton and I am a Roman, and . . ." Another memory came to him: "I am the Son of a Hundred Kings. . . ." That seemed to mean something here, for the radiance flickered, and for a moment he glimpsed the way. But still he could not move. He groaned, dredging his mind for another name. Who was he? Who was he *here?*

"I am Gawen," he answered, and then, remembering the force that had swept him inward, "the Pendragon. . . ."

And with that word, he felt himself lifted, rushed through a tunnel of light by some force beyond comprehension that thrust him to the top of the Tor and flung him, gasping, onto the moist turf inside the circle of stones.

For several moments, Gawen lay panting. His ears were ringing; only gradually did he become aware that somewhere in the distance birds were beginning the first tentative chirps that would greet the coming day. The grass beneath him was wet. He had fingers. . . . He clutched at the grass, feeling its strength, drawing in the rich scent of damp earth. He realized with a pang of loss that he was merely human once more.

There seemed to be a great many people gathered around him. He pushed himself upright, rubbing his eyes, and found that not everything was back to normal, for, although the sun had not yet risen, everyone he looked at was haloed in light. The greatest radiance came from the three figures before him—three women, robed and veiled with the ornaments of the Goddess on breast and brow.

"Gawen, son of Eilan, to this sacred circle I have called you. . . ."

They spoke in unison, and the hair lifted on his neck and arms. He managed to stand up, only momentarily embarrassed to find he was still naked. Before *them*—before *Her*—he thought he would have been naked even if he had been wearing clothes.

"Lady," he said in a hoarse voice, "I am here."

"You have passed the tests the Druids set you, and endured the ordeals. Are you ready to take oath to Me?"

Gawen managed some sound of assent, and one of the figures moved forward. She seemed taller than the others, and slender, though a moment ago they had all been equal. Above her white veil a garland of hawthorn made for her a starry crown.

"I am the Maiden, forever Virgin, the holy Bride. . . ." Her voice was soft, sweet.

Gawen strained to make out the features beneath the veil. Surely this was Sianna, whom he loved, and yet her face and form kept changing, and the love he felt for her was sometimes that of a father, and sometimes a brother's fierce affection, and sometimes that of the lover he would like to be. Only one thing was clear to him—he had loved this girl many times before, in many ways.

"I am all beginnings," she went on. "I am the renewal of the soul. I am Truth, which cannot be soiled or compromised. Will you forever swear to help what is good come to Birth? Gawen, will you swear this to me?"

He drew in a deep breath of the sweet dawn air. "I swear."

She came to him, lifting her veil. It was Sianna he saw as he bent to kiss her lips, Sianna and something more, whose touch was like white fire.

Then she was moving away from him. Trembling, he straightened as the middle figure came toward him. A wreath of wheat ears crowned her crimson veil. Who, he wondered, had they found to play this role in the ritual? Alone, she seemed in one moment smaller, and in the next gigantic, a massive figure whose throne was the whole world.

"I am the Mother, forever fertile, Lady of the Land. I am growth and strength, nourishing all that lives. I change, but I never die. Will you serve the cause of Life? Gawen, will you swear to me?"

Surely he knew that voice! Gawen peered through the veil, and flinched from the flash of dark eyes. But he recognized, with a sense other than sight, the Lady of Faerie, who had rescued him.

"You are the Door to all I desire," he said in a low voice. "I do not understand you, but I will serve you."

She laughed. "Does the seed understand the power that makes it burst from the darkness into day, or the child the force that thrusts it forth from the safety of the womb? That you should be willing is all I require. . . ."

She opened her arms, and he stumbled into them. When he knew her as the Lady of Faerie there had always been a distance between them. But in the softness of the breast against which he lay there was a totality of welcome that made him weep. He felt himself a tiny child, cradled in soft arms, soothed by an ancient lullaby. His real mother was holding him. A memory he had repressed since infancy now recalled her white skin and bright hair, and for the first time in his conscious life he knew that she loved him. . . .

And then he was standing once more, facing the Goddess, and Her third shape moved painfully forward to confront him. Her crown was made of bones.

"I am the Crone," she said harshly, "the Ancient One, the Lady of Wisdom. I have seen everything, endured everything, given everything. I am Death, Gawen, without which nothing can be transformed. Will you take oath to me?"

I know about Death, thought Gawen, remembering the empty, accusing stares of the men he had slain. Death had struck men down as a reaper scythes the harvest that day. What good could come from that? But even as he remembered, the image of sheaves of grain in the cornfields came to mind.

"If it has some meaning," he said slowly, "even Death I will serve."

"Embrace me . . ." said the Crone, as he stood staring.

Nothing in that bent figure attracted him. But he had sworn, and so he forced leaden feet to carry him toward her, to stand as her black veils stole vision, and her bony arms locked around him.

And then he felt nothing, only floated in a darkness in which, presently, he began to see stars. He stood in the void, and facing him he saw the woman, her veils floating around her, a beauty beyond youth in her eyes. It was Caillean, and it was someone else, whom, in ages past, he had served and loved. Bowing deeply, he saluted her.

And then, as before, he was himself again, trembling with reaction as he gazed at the priestesses, black and white and red. In the east, the sky was beginning to glow with the first blush of the coming dawn.

"You have sworn, and your oath has been accepted." Once more, they spoke in unison. "One thing only remains, to call down the spirit of the Merlin, that he may make you priest and Druid, servant of the Mysteries."

Gawen knelt with bowed head as they began to sing, waiting. It was at first a wordless music, note building on note until he felt his flesh tingling with the vibrations of that sound. Then came words, though they were not in any tongue he knew. But the need, the supplication, was clear.

Wise One, he prayed, *come to us, if you will, come through me. For we badly need your wisdom here!*

A choked sound from someone in the circle brought him upright, blinking at the blaze of light. At first he thought that the sun had risen and the Master of Wisdom had not come. But it was not the sun.

A pillar of radiance shimmered in the center of the circle. Gawen called forth his own light to protect him, and with altered vision saw the Spirit they had summoned, ancient and yet in his prime, leaning on the staff of his office, with the white beard of wisdom spilling across his breast and a circlet set with a shining stone upon his brow.

"Master, he has sworn," cried Brannos. "Will you not accept him?"

The Merlin looked around the circle. "Accept him I shall, but it is not yet time for me to come among you." His gaze came back to Gawen, and he smiled. "You have sworn, and taken the priesthood upon you, and yet you are no mage. In the crystal cave you Named yourself. Say, then, my son, by what Words you were freed?"

Gawen stared at him. He had always been told that what happened at such moments must be forever a secret between a man and his gods. But as he remembered what he had said, he began to see why these names, unlike all others, must be proclaimed.

"I am the Pendragon . . ." he whispered. "I am the Son of a Hundred Kings. . . ."

A murmur of wonder rippled around the circle. The air grew brighter. The eastern sky was ablaze with golden banners and sunfire rimmed the hills. But that was not what they were looking at. Gawen felt upon his brow the shining weight of a golden diadem, and saw his body enveloped in a royal robe, embroidered and gemmed as no artist now living in the world could do.

"Pendragon! Pendragon!" the Druids cried, giving him the title of the Sacred King, who rules by the spirit, not the sword, the living link between the people and the land in which they dwell.

Gawen lifted his arms in acceptance and in salutation, and the sun rose before him, and glory filled the world.

Chapter Seven

The dragons tattooed on Gawen's forearms prickled in the warmth of the afternoon sun. He looked down at them with the wonder that had not left him since the Merlin appeared. The sinuous serpentine lines curved across the hard muscle and back again. They had been pricked into his skin by thorns and stained blue with woad by an old man of the little dark folk of the marshes. Gawen had still been half tranced when the work was begun, and when he started to feel the pain he pushed awareness away again. The tattooing had smarted at first, but now only an occasional prickle reminded him of it.

They had told him to rest, but to lie on a bed of sheepskins, bathed and dressed in a tunic of embroidered linen, seemed scarcely more real than the ordeal he had endured. Gawen could not deny what had happened to him, but he did not begin to understand it. The Druids called him Pendragon, hailing him as a priest-king, like those who had ruled in the lands now drowned beneath the sea. But it seemed to him that the Vale of Avalon was a very small kingdom. Was he, like the Christos whom Father Joseph had called a king, to have a kingdom which was not of this world?

Perhaps, he thought as he sipped watered wine from the goblet they had set by his side, when this night was over he and Sianna would reign as king and queen in Faerie. The thought made his heart pound. He had not seen her since the ritual in the dawning. But tonight she would dance around the Beltane fire. And as a king he would walk among the revelers, with the power to choose any woman who might catch his eye. He knew already which one he wanted. Despite his time in the Army, since first he had seen Sianna there had never been any other girl he would have chosen for his first experience of a woman's love.

He found himself growing ready even thinking about it. If things had gone according to plan they would have come together a year ago, but he had deserted her. Had she waited? He had dreamed that she had, but he knew the pressures upon the priestesses to participate in the rites, and had not dared to ask. It did not matter. In spirit she was his. From across the waters of the marshes drifted a faint tremor of drums. Gawen felt his heart beating with them, and smiled even as his eyelids closed once more. Soon, it would be soon.

⊗ ⊗ ⊗

Next year, thought Caillean as she surveyed the dancers, they might have to move the celebration to the meadow at the foot of the Tor. In the open space beyond the stone circle there was hardly room for the Druids and the young priestesses, and marsh folk were still arriving, watching from the edge of the firelight with wondering dark eyes. It was amazing, really, how fast the word had been carried, but of course the old hunter who had been summoned to tattoo Gawen's dragons would have told them.

The priestesses, of course, had known what had happened since this morning, when the Druids had come back down the hill with glory in their eyes. She thought she sensed a certain edge to the anticipation natural to the holiday, an intensity that had not been there before. Certainly they had taken extra pains with their hair and ornaments. Tonight the King would walk among them. Whom would he choose?

Caillean did not need to look into a silver bowl of water to know the answer. Even if he had not loved Sianna since they were children, since he had seen her as the Maiden Bride that morning, his heart would be full of her grace and beauty. The priests and priestesses of Avalon did not marry in the human way, but when they came together in the Great Rite they were the vehicles by which the Lord and the Lady were united. What was going to happen here tonight would be a royal wedding, and Gawen's joining with Sianna would bless the land.

She had known that Gawen had been born to some great destiny, but who could have imagined this? Caillean smiled at her own enthusiasm. In her own way, she was as dazzled as any of the young priestesses, dreaming of Gawen and Sianna as sacred king and queen, who would rule the soul of Britannia from Avalon with herself behind them.

Two oxen had been purchased for the festival and roasted on spits at the bottom of the hill. Their meat was being carried up to the top in baskets, and the folk of the marshes had brought venison and waterfowl and dried fish as well. Heather beer in skin bags, and mead in jars of earthenware, made their own contribution to the merriment. And in the space between the crescent of feasters and the stone circle blazed the Beltane fire.

If she sighted southwest she could see the glow of the fire that had been lighted on the Dragon Hill there. She knew that from that place another fire would be visible, and another, all the way to Land's End, just as the ley that led northeastward to the great circle of stones by the sacred hill was on this night marked by fire.

On this night, she told herself with satisfaction, *on this night, all of Britannia is webbed with light that even the once-born without spirit sight can see!*

A maiden of the marsh folk, her cloud of black hair bound back with a wreath of eglantine, knelt before the priestess with shy grace, offering a basket of dried berries preserved in honey. Caillean pushed back the blue veil from her brow and took some, smiling. The girl, glimpsing the silver crescent that gleamed above the smaller half-moon tattooed on the priestess's brow, made a sign of reverence and looked quickly away.

When she had gone, the High Priestess left her face uncovered. This was a night of festival, when the doors opened between the worlds and the spirit swung free. There was no need for mystery. The veil was only a symbol anyhow—Caillean knew how to draw an illusion of shadow across her features when there was need. The maidens they were training were convinced that she, like the Faerie Queen, could appear out of thin air.

To the sound of the drum that had pulsed like a heartbeat beneath the sounds of celebration was added suddenly a ripple of harpsong. One of the young Druids had carried his lap harp to the top of the Tor. Now he sat cross-legged beside the little dark drummer, fair head cocked to one side as he listened for the rhythm. In another moment the bittersweet bray of a cowhorn pipe joined the music, leaping about the chiming chords of the harp like a young calf in a field of flowers.

The girl with the eglantine wreath began to move to the music, arms twining, slim hips shifting beneath the doeskin garment she wore. Hesitantly at first, and then with more abandon, Dica and Lysanda joined her. The drumming quickened, and soon their brows shone with perspiration and the thin blue stuff of their tunicas began to cling. How beautiful they were, thought Caillean, watching. Even she found herself swaying to the music, and it had been many years since she had danced at a festival.

It was a change in the pattern of the dancing that alerted her, a ripple of motion like the shift in the current when a man steps into a stream. Dancers swayed aside, turning, and Caillean glimpsed Gawen. He wore the white kilt of a king, belted in gold. A royal medallion of ancient workmanship lay on his breast, and green oak leaves formed his crown.

Besides those, only the blue serpents etched into his forearms adorned him. But he needed nothing else. Those months of Roman training had sculpted his upper body and put hard muscle on his calves and thighs. More than that, the last youthful softness had been honed from his features; the good bones defined his face, everything in balance now. The boy whom she had loved and feared for was gone. This was a man.

And, she thought, seeing the radiance that glimmered about him, this was a king. Did she want him? Caillean knew that she still had the power to wrap herself in a glamour beside which even Sianna's radiant youth would pale. But if, as she suspected, the tie between them was a thing of the soul forged in ages past, Gawen would choose his true mate even if she appeared a hag. In any case, Sianna was young, and she could give Gawen a child, as Caillean, for all her wisdom and all her magic, could never do now.

He is not the beloved of my soul, she thought with a touch of sorrow. *The soul of the man who should be my mate is not incarnate in a body now.* Her attraction was only a natural response to the overwhelming male magnetism of the King and the power of the Beltane fires. On this night Gawen was everyone's beloved—male or female, old or young.

Was this how Eilan had seen the boy's father when he came to her beside the Beltane fire? Gawen was taller than Gaius had been, and though the proud arch of his nose was all Roman, it seemed to her he had something of Eilan in the set of his eyes. But in truth, at this moment Gawen did not really resemble either parent, but someone else whom she had known, in other lifetimes, long ago.

"The Year-King," ran the whisper as he moved among the dancers, and Caillean repressed a pang of foreboding. This boy's father had claimed that title before he died. But Gawen bore the sacred serpents. He was not merely the Year-King, who for one cycle of the seasons is honored and then, if the times require it, is sacrificed, but the Pendragon, who serves the land as long as he lives.

The maidens clustered around him and drew him into the dance. She saw him laughing, taking a girl by the hands and swinging her around, then leaving her breathless and laughing while he moved to another, clasping her in a brief embrace, and sending her spinning into the arms of one of the young men. They danced until everyone but Gawen, who seemed ready to go on all night, was gasping. Then he allowed them to lead him to a seat, covered with soft deerskins like the one on which Caillean was sitting, on the other side of the fire.

They brought him food and drink. The drumming ceased, and only the sweet trilling of a bone flute continued to ornament the babble of talk and laughter. Caillean drank watered wine and surveyed the gathering with a benign smile.

It was the return of the drum, soft and steady as a heartbeat, that made her turn.

The drummer, a man of the marshes himself, must have known what was coming, but Caillean frowned, wondering what Waterwalker and the ancient who walked with him were intending now. Nothing hostile—beyond the sheathed knives at their belts they were unarmed—but something more serious, or perhaps she meant solemn, than the playful abandon of the festival. Three younger men escorted them, watching Gawen with shining eyes. What were they carrying? She got to her feet and moved softly around the fire so that she could see.

"You are king." In Waterwalker's guttural tones it was a statement, not a question. His gaze flickered to the dragons on Gawen's arms. "Like the old ones who come from the sea. We remember." The elders nodded. "We remember the old tales."

"It is so," said Gawen, and Caillean knew that he was seeing former lives that his initiation had allowed him to remember. "I have come once more."

"Then we give you this," said the old man. "From a fallen star our first smiths forge it—oh, long ago. And when it is broken, a sorcerer of your people made it whole. In that time, lord, you use it to protect us, and when you die, we hid it away." He held out the bundle he had been carrying, a long shape swathed in wrappings of painted hide.

A silence fell as Gawen accepted it. Caillean could hear the pounding of her heart, heavy and slow. Within the wrappings, as her own returning memories had told her it must be, lay a sword.

It was a long, dark blade, about the size of a Roman cavalry sword, with the leaf shape she remembered from the bronze blades the Druids used in ritual. But no bronze ever had that mirror sheen. *Star metal* ... She had heard of such blades but never seen one. Who would have thought the marsh folk had such a treasure in their keeping? It did not do to forget that, though they might be humble, their tribe was very old.

"I remember ..." Gawen said softly. The hilt fitted his hand as if it had been tailored to his palm. He lifted the sword, and flickers of reflected firelight danced across the faces of those gathered around him.

"Then you take it, to defend us," said Waterwalker. "Swear!"

The sword swung upward with weightless ease. The boy Gawen had been would have dropped it. A deft twist of the wrist sent it slicing the air. How strange, thought Caillean, that it was the Romans who had trained him to become a protector of those whom they themselves oppressed.

"I have sworn to serve the Lady," Gawen said softly. "Now I swear to you also, and to the Land." He turned the blade and drew the edge across the fleshy part of his hand. It did not take much pressure—the thing was serpent-sharp—and in a moment dark blood welled along the cut and began to drip onto the ground. "For this life, and this body," he went on. "And as for my spirit, I renew the oath I swore before . . ."

Caillean shivered. What memories *had* the lad recovered when he was in the hill? With luck, they would wear away as time went on. It could be hard to live normally if one remembered one's past lives too well.

"In life and death, lord, we serve you." Waterwalker touched his finger to the blood on the ground and then brought it to his forehead, leaving a red smear on his brow. The other young men did the same, then ranged themselves around Gawen like a guard of honor, two to either side. The young Druids who were watching looked rather bemused, as well they might, trying to understand this transformation of one who had been a boy among them until the year before.

Caillean glanced upward. The stars were wheeling toward midnight, and the fire was beginning to burn low. The astral tides were turning; the time for the working of the deepest magics was near.

"Where is Sianna?" Gawen asked softly. Caillean realized that even before they brought him the sword he had been scanning the crowd.

"Go into the circle. Call your bride, and she will come."

His eyes glowed suddenly with a light that did not come from the fire. Without another word he strode toward the circle of stones. His escort followed, but when he passed the two pillars that flanked the entrance they took up position before it. For a moment Gawen faced the altar, then lifted the sword and placed it like an offering before the stone. Empty-handed, he turned to look back the way he had come.

"Sianna! Sianna! Sianna!" he cried, and the longing in that call carried it through all the worlds.

For a moment all the Tor was silent, waiting.

And then, from the far distance, they heard a sound like silver bells. With it came drumming, a swift and dancing beat that set the heart to skipping with joy. Caillean peered down the hill and saw lights bobbing up from below. Soon she could glimpse faces—the rest of the marsh folk, and others, who were not quite human, able to walk among men on this night when the gateways opened between the worlds.

A shimmer of white moved in the midst of them—a length of some gauzy material held like a canopy over the one they were escorting. The music grew loud, voices soared in the bridal song, the feasters drew back to either side as the procession came over the rim of the hill.

A king at his crowning, a groom at his wedding, a priest at his initiation—all these were in their moment of glory divine. And Gawen, watching as they brought his bride to him, was all three.

But Sianna—however great the beauty of the God, that of the Goddess surpassed it. As they lifted the canopy and the maiden passed between the pillars to meet him, hawthorn-crowned, Caillean recognized that even with all her magic she could never have matched her. For, while Gawen had slept, Sianna had gone back to her mother's realm, and it was the jewels of the Otherworld that adorned the daughter of the Faerie Queen.

Gawen's whole body shook along with the pounding of his heart. He was glad he had put down the sword; the way he was trembling, he would have cut himself for sure. The torchbearers who had escorted Sianna stood now around the circle. As Sianna passed between the pillars and came toward him, their light seemed to thicken, and the world outside the circle disappeared.

In that moment he could not have said if she was beautiful. That was a human word, and, bard-trained though he was, no words he could command would have expressed what he was feeling now. He wanted to bow down and kiss the ground upon which she was walking, and yet something equally divine within him was rising up to meet her. He saw its reflection in her eyes.

"You called me, my beloved, and I am here...." Her voice was soft; in her eyes he saw a gleam that recalled the human girl with whom he had hunted birds' nests so long ago. It made it easier to bear the god-power that beat within him.

"Our joining," he said with difficulty, "will serve the land and the people. But I ask you, Sianna, if to lie with me now will serve *you?*"

"And what will you do if I say no?" There was a gentle mockery in her smile.

"I would take another—no matter who—and try to do my duty. But it would be my body only that acted, not my heart or soul. You are a priestess. I want you to know that I understand if you—" He stared at her, willing her to understand what he could not say aloud.

"But I have not," she answered him, "and neither will you."

Sianna moved closer and set her hands upon his shoulders, tipping back her head to receive his kiss, and Gawen, his hands still open at his sides, bent to take what she offered him. And as his lips touched hers, he felt the God enter fully in.

It was like the fire that had filled him the night before, but gentler, more golden. He knew himself, Gawen, but he was conscious also of that Other who knew, as he did not, just how to untie the complicated knot of the Maiden cincture, and unpin the brooches that held her gown. In a few moments she stood before him, the sweet curves of her body more beautiful than the jewels she still wore.

She moved then, unhooking his gilded belt and tugging at the ties of his kilt until he too was freed. In wonder he touched her breasts, and then, straining together as if they could become one being, they kissed once more.

"Where shall we lie, my love?" he whispered when he could breathe again.

Sianna moved back and eased down upon the stone. Gawen stood before her, feeling the great current that passed through the Tor surge upward from the core of the hill through the soles of his feet, rushing up his spine until he trembled with power. Carefully, as if at any sudden movement he would shatter, he bent over her, sinking between her opening thighs as he fitted his body to hers.

In the moment of their joining, he felt the barrier of her maidenhood, and knew she had not lied, but that no longer mattered. He was coming home, with a sweetness that the man in him had not expected, and a certainty that the god in him recognized with joy. For the space of a breath they lay without moving, but the power that had brought them together could not be denied.

As Sianna clasped him, Gawen found himself moving in the rhythms of the oldest dance of all, and knew that he was only a channel for the power that surged within him, that drove him to give all the strength that was in him to the woman in whose arms he lay. He felt her turn to fire beneath him, opening yet further, and strained against her as if through that human body he could reach something beyond humanity.

In the final moment, when he had imagined himself beyond conscious thinking, he heard her whisper, "I am the altar..." He answered, "... and I am the sacrifice," and, answering, found release at last for the passion of the man and the power of the god.

◁ ◁ ◁

The fountaining flow of energy, magnified by the union of God and Goddess, rushed back through the Tor. Too great for its main channel, it surged through every passage available, pulsing down the lesser leys that crossed at the Tor to bless all the land. Caillean, waiting outside the circle, felt it and sat back with a sigh. Others, sensing in their own ways what had happened, leaped to their feet, eyes brightening. The drums, which had continued their steady beat since Sianna joined Gawen within the circle, exploded with a sudden thunder of exultation, and first one voice, then another took up the shout until the entire hill resounded with their joy.

"The God has joined with the Goddess," Caillean proclaimed, "the Lord with the Land!"

The drummers, after their first tumult, settled into a lively dance beat. Laughing, the people got to their feet. Everyone, even the oldest Druids, had felt the release of tension. With it went fatigue and, as it seemed, inhibition. Those who had watched the earlier dancing from the sidelines began to sway. A young girl of the marsh folk pulled old Brannos into the space before the fire, and he bobbed and circled more nimbly than Caillean would have believed possible.

Though the fire was lower, the heat was greater than it had been before. Soon the dancers were streaming with perspiration. To Caillean's surprise, it was one of her priestesses, Lysanda, who first pulled off her tunica, but others swiftly followed her example. A young man and woman of the marsh folk, freed from the danger of fluttering clothing, joined hands and leaped for luck across the fire.

Watching them, Caillean thought that it had been years since she had seen such joy at the Beltane reveling. Perhaps never, for the rites at Vernemeton had been inhibited by the fear of Roman disapproval, and they were still learning the ways of the land at Avalon. But that had been remedied by the joining of a son of the Druid line with a daughter of the Folk of Faerie. They could all, she thought as she surveyed the leaping dancers, take satisfaction from this night's ceremonies.

But no night, however joyous, could last forever. Two by two, men and women moved off to celebrate their own rites on the hillside. Others wrapped themselves in their mantles and lay down to sleep off the heather beer beside the fire. The torches of those who guarded the circle had long ago burned out, but the stones themselves cast a barrier of shadow which assured the privacy of those who lay within.

A little before dawn, some of the younger folk went off to cut the Beltane tree and gather greenery with which to deck the buildings at the foot of the Tor. The dancing that honored the tree during the daylight, though just as joyous, was more decorous than the night-time celebrations at the fires, and would give the uninitiated maidens and younger children who had stayed below a chance to share in the festival.

Caillean, who had danced less and drunk less than the others, and who was accustomed to keeping vigil, watched out the night, still sitting in her great chair by the fire. But even she fell into an exhausted sleep once the shadows of night had been banished by the dawn.

It was a beautiful day. Through the screen of leafy branches with which they had built a bothy to provide some privacy, Gawen gazed out from the top of the Tor across the patchwork of water and wood and field that basked in the sunlight of Beltane morning. He was sure he would have thought so even if he had not been so happy. True, he ached in odd places, and the lines of his new tattoos had scabbed over and pulled when the muscles flexed beneath them, but those were only surface pains, scarcely to be noted when compared with the marvelous feeling of well-being that sang through every vein.

"Turn," said Ambios, "and I'll scrub your back." He poured water over the cloth. From the other side of the partition, where Sianna was being bathed, came the sweet sound of girlish laughter.

"Thank you," said Gawen. Any new initiate might expect to be coddled, but there was a deference to Ambios' service that surprised him. Was it going to be this way always? It was all very well to feel himself a king in the ecstasy of ritual, but he wondered how well it would wear from day to day.

A twinge from his forearms brought his gaze back to the dragons. Some things, at least, had forever changed. Those tattoos were not going to go away. And Sianna was his forever.

He finished bathing and pulled on the sleeveless tunic they had brought him, of linen dyed a living green and embroidered in gold. He had not imagined the Druids had such a splendid thing in their stores. He tied the cincture and then belted on the sword. Though the blade showed no sign of age, the leather of the sheath that had come with it was powdery, and some of the stitching had begun to give way. He would have to see, he thought as he came out from the leaf shelter, about having a new one made.

All thoughts of the sword were driven from his mind when he saw Sianna. She was robed, like himself, in spring-green, and was just settling a fresh crown of hawthorn upon her brow. In the sunlight her hair shone like red gold.

"Lady ..." He took the hand she held out to him and kissed it. *Are you as happy as I am?* asked his touch.

"My love ..." *Happier*, her eyes replied. Suddenly he longed for the night, when they could be alone once more. She was only a human woman now, but to him the Goddess who had come to him the night before had been no more beautiful.

"Gawen—my lord—" stammered Lysanda. "We have food for you."

"We had better eat," murmured Sianna. "The feast they are preparing down below won't be ready until after they dance around the tree at noon."

"I have fed," said Gawen, squeezing her hand, "but I will be hungry again soon...."

Sianna blushed, then laughed and pulled him toward the table where they were setting out cold meats and bread and ale.

They were about to sit down when they heard shouting from below.

"Do they want us to come down already?" Sianna began, but there was an urgency in those cries which did not sound right for a festival.

"Run!" The words came clearly now. "They are coming—you must get away!"

"It's Tuarim!" exclaimed Lysanda, looking down the hill. "Whatever can be wrong?"

The training that Gawen thought he had left behind him brought him to his feet, hand moving toward the hilt of his sword. Sianna started to speak, then, as she met his eyes, bit off the words and rose to stand at his side.

"Tell me." He strode forward as the young Druid staggered the last few steps to the flat top of the hill.

"Father Paulus and his monks," gasped Tuarim. "They have ropes and hammers. He says they're going to throw down the sacred stones on the Tor!"

"They're old men," said Gawen soothingly. "We'll stand between them and the circle. They won't be able to budge us, much less the stones, even if they have gone mad." He found it hard to believe that the gentle monks with whom he had made music could have become such fanatics, even after a year of listening to Father Paulus' fulminations.

"It's not that—" Tuarim gulped. "It's the soldiers. Gawen, we must get you away. Father Paulus has sent to Deva and called the Romans in!"

Gawen took a deep breath, his heart pounding in a way he hoped they could not see. He knew what the Romans did to deserters. For a moment then, he almost considered trying to flee. But he had done that once already, and if the shame of abandoning a war which was not his own and an army to which he was not sworn still burned in his belly, how could he live with himself if he deserted the folk who had hailed him as Pendragon on the Holy Tor?

"Good!" He forced himself to grin. "The Romans are reasonable men, and their orders are to protect all religions. I'll explain matters to them, and they will keep the Nazarenes from harming the stones."

Tuarim's expression began to clear and Gawen let his breath out, hoping that what he had said was true. And then it was too late to change his mind, for Father Paulus himself, his face crimson with exertion and fury, was clambering over the edge of the hill.

"Gawen! My son, my son, what have they done to you?" The priest took a step forward, wringing his hands, and three of his brethren appeared behind him. "Have they forced you to bow down to their idols? Has this whore seduced you into shame and sin?"

Gawen's amusement changed abruptly to anger, and he stepped between Sianna and the old man.

"I have been 'forced' to do nothing, nor will I be! And this woman is my bride, so keep your foul tongue between your teeth regarding her!" Now the rest of the Nazarenes had reached the top of the Tor, and they did indeed have mallets and rawhide ropes. He gestured to Tuarim to get Sianna out of the way.

"She is a demon, a snare of that great Seducer who through the temptress Eve betrayed all mankind to sin!" Father Paulus replied. "But it is not too late, boy. Even the blessed Augustine was able to repent, and he had spent all his youth in sin. If you do penance, this single failure will not be counted against you. Come away from her, Gawen." He held out his hand. "Come with me now!"

Gawen gazed at him in astonishment. "Father Joseph was a holy man, a blessed spirit who preached a gospel of love. To him I might have listened, but he would never have spoken such words. You, old man, have gone entirely mad!" He glared at the others, and there was something in his expression that made them step back.

"Now it is my turn to give orders!" he said, and felt the astral presence of a royal mantle enfolding him. "You came to us as suppliants and we gave you sanctuary, and let you build your church beside our holy hill. But this Tor belongs to the old gods that protect this land. You have no right to be here; your feet profane this holy ground. And so I say to you, begone, lest the mighty powers you have called demons strike you where you stand!"

He raised his hand, and though it was empty, the monks recoiled as if he had brandished the sword. Gawen smiled grimly. In another moment they would take to their heels. Then he heard the clatter of hobnailed sandals against stone. The Romans had arrived.

There were ten of them, under the command of a sweating decurion, the short thrusting spear they called the *pilum* in each hand. Barely winded, they surveyed the angry Nazarenes and the outraged Druids with an equally jaundiced eye.

The decurion considered Gawen's gold embroidery, apparently decided it was a mark of rank, and addressed him. "I'm looking for Gaius Macellius Severus. These monks sent word that you might be holding him."

Someone behind Gawen gasped, then stilled. He shook his head, hoping the man had not been in Britannia long enough to realize how clearly his own features bore the stamp of Rome.

"We are celebrating a ritual of our religion," he said quietly. "We constrain no one."

"And who are you to say so?" The Decurion frowned from under his helm.

"My name is Gawen, son of Eilan—"

"Fool!" cried Father Paulus. "That's Gaius himself who is talking to you!"

The Roman's eyes widened. "Sir," he began, "your grandfather sent us—"

"Seize him!" Paulus interrupted once more. "He's a deserter from your Army!"

A convulsive movement rippled through the file of soldiers, and while the Druids watched them, Father Paulus shoved one of his brethren toward the circle of stones.

"Are you young Macellius?" The decurion eyed him uncertainly.

Gawen let out his breath. If his grandfather in Deva were willing to speak for him, he might get out of this after all.

"That's my Roman name, but—"

"Were you in the Army?" snapped the Roman.

Gawen jerked around as he heard the sound of a hammer striking stone. Two of the monks had ropes around one of the pillar stones and were tugging at it, while a third was swinging at the other one.

"Straighten up, soldier, and answer me!"

For three long months Gawen had been conditioned to respond to that tone. Before he could think, his body had snapped to that pose of rigid attention that only legionary training could produce. In the next moment he tried to relax, but the damage had been done.

"I never swore the oath!" he cried.

"Others will be the judge of that," said the decurion. "You'll have to come with us now."

From the circle came a *crack* and the tortured shriek of rending rock as the mallet struck a fault in the stone. One of the women screamed, and Gawen turned to see the pillar stone falling in two pieces to the ground.

"Sir, stop them!" he cried. "It's forbidden to desecrate a temple, and this is sacred ground!"

"These are Druids, soldier!" spat the Nazarene. "Did you think that Paulinus and Agricola had got them all? Rome does not tolerate those who use magic against her. The Druids and their rites are forbidden—your duty is to destroy any who remain!" He darted toward the second pillar, which was beginning to rock alarmingly, and started to shove. The monks with the hammers, emboldened by success, had begun to batter at another stone.

Gawen stared at him, all memories of Rome and his own danger whirled away by a tide of royal rage. Ignoring the decurion's commands, he strode toward the circle.

"Paulus, this place belongs to my gods, not yours. Get away from that stone!" The voice was not his; it vibrated in the stones. The other monks blanched and stepped back, but Paulus began to laugh.

"Demons, I deny you! *Satanas, retro me!*" He heaved at the stone.

Gawen's hands closed on the bony shoulders; he wrenched the man away and sent him sprawling to the ground. As he straightened, he heard the unmistakable scrape of a *gladius* being drawn from its sheath and turned, his hand going to the hilt of his own blade.

The legionaries had their spears poised, but Gawen forced his fingers to unclose. Thoughts whirled madly. *I will not shed blood on this holy ground! They did not consecrate me as a war-leader, but as a sacred king.*

"Gaius Macellius Severus, in the name of the Emperor I arrest you. Lay down your arms!" The voice of the decurion boomed across the space between them as he gestured with his sword.

"Only if you will also arrest *them.*" He motioned toward the monks.

"Your religion is outlawed, and you are a renegade," snarled the officer. "Take off that sword or I will order my men to spear you where you stand."

It is my fault, thought Gawen numbly. *If I had not sought out Rome, they would never have known that Avalon was here!*

But they know now, some rebellious part of his own soul answered him. *Why waste your life for the sake of a few stones?*

Gawen looked at the boulders. Where was the magic that had flared from stone to stone when the Merlin appeared? They were only rocks, looking oddly naked in the full light of day, and he had been a fool to fancy himself a king. But, whatever else might be true, on that stone altar Sianna had given him her love, and he could not allow it to be soiled by Father Paulus' unconsecrated hands. Beyond the line of soldiers he saw Sianna and tried to smile, then, lest her despair should unman him, looked quickly away.

"I never took oath to the Emperor, but I am sworn to protect this holy hill!" he said quietly, and the ancient sword that the marsh men had given him—only last night—came sweetly into his hand.

The decurion gestured. The wicked sharp point of a lifting *pilum* caught the sun. Then, suddenly, a thrown stone clanged against an iron helmet, and the *pilum,* released too soon, went wide.

The other Druids were unarmed, but on the top of the Tor there were plenty of stones. A hail of missiles bombarded the legionaries. They responded. Gawen saw Tuarim pierced by a thrown *pilum* and go down. The other priestesses, thank the gods, were pulling Sianna away.

Three of the soldiers trotted toward him, shields up and swords poised. Gawen dropped into a defensive crouch, batting aside the first thrust with the neat parry Rufinus had drilled into him, and continuing with a stroke that sliced through the straps holding the front and back of the body armor together and into the man's side. The soldier yelled and fell back, and Gawen whirled to thrust at the next man, the superb steel of his sword piercing *through* the breastplate. The look of surprise on his face would been comical if Gawen had had time to appreciate it, but the third man was bearing down on him. He leaped inside the fellow's guard, and as the enemy blade, descending, scraped along his back, jabbed his own up beneath the armor all the way to the heart.

The falling body almost took the sword with it, but Gawen managed to wrench the weapon free. Four of the young Druids lay on the ground. Some of the marsh men had come up to help, but their darts and arrows were little use against Roman armor.

"Run—" He waved at them. Why would the fools not flee while there was time? But the remaining Druids were trying to reach his side, yelling his name.

Gawen's charge took the Romans by surprise. One went down to his first stroke; the second got his shield up in time and slashed back at him. The blow sliced across Gawen's upper arm, but he felt no pain. A stroke to his back made him stumble, but in the next moment he recovered, and his return blow took off the fellow's hand. Five of them remained, plus the decurion, and they were beginning to learn caution. He might do it after all. Grinning savagely, he drove the next man who came at him back with swift strokes that whittled pieces from his shield.

The blue dragons on Gawen's arms were crimson now, and though he still felt nothing, much of the blood was his own. He blinked as a wave of shadow passed over him, then danced aside, a little more slowly, from another blow. It was not blood loss, he decided, risking a glance upward, where a dark mist was spreading rapidly across what had been a clear sky.

Caillean and Sianna, he thought grimly. *They'll rout them. I have only to hang on.*

But he still had five enemies. His sword flared as he swung it around. The legionary he was facing jumped backward, and Gawen laughed. Then, like a bolt from the heavens, something struck him between the shoulder blades. Gawen lurched forward and fell to his knees, wondering what was dragging him down, why it was suddenly so hard to breathe.

Then he looked down and saw the evil head of the *pilum* protruding from his chest. He shook his head, still not believing it. It was growing dark quickly now, but not quickly enough to stop the Roman swords from stabbing into back and legs and shoulders.

And now Gawen could see nothing. The star sword slipped from a nerveless hand. "Sianna—" he whispered, and sank down upon the holy soil of Avalon, sighing as he had the night before, when he had poured out his life in her arms.

Chapter Eight

"Is he dead?"

Very gently, Caillean laid Gawen's hand back down. Her inner senses, seeking the life force, could find only a flicker. She had had to search for a pulse to be sure.

"He lives"—her voice cracked—"though only the gods know why." There was so much blood! The holy earth of the Tor was soaked with it. How many years of rain, she wondered, would be needed to wash it away?

"It is the power of the King that is keeping him alive," said Riannon.

"Even the courage of a king could not overcome such odds as these," answered Ambios. He was wounded too, but not badly. Several of his fellows had died. But the Romans had died too, when the sorcerous darkness came and only those with spirit sight could tell friend from foe.

"I should have been here," whispered Caillean.

"You saved us. You called the shadow . . ." said Riannon.

"Too late . . ." Her breath caught. The darkness was gone now. If she could not see it, it was because her eyes were dimmed by tears. "Too late to save *him* . . ." She had been in her own home when the Romans came, resting to be ready for the celebrations later in the day. There was no guilt in that, they all said so. How could she have known?

But no excuses could change the fact that Eilan had died because Caillean had failed to reach Vernemeton ten years ago. And now

Eilan's son, whom she had learned to love, lay dying because she had not been there when he most needed her.

"Can he be moved?" asked Riannon.

"Perhaps," answered Marged, the closest thing they had to a healer. "But not far. It would be better to build a shelter above him. If we cut through the spearshaft we can lay him on his back. He will be easier then."

"Can't you pull it out?" Ambios said thinly.

"If we do, he will die now."

Swiftly, and without knowing what is happening to him, thought Caillean, *instead of later, with greater pain.* She knew how men struck through the lungs died. It would be far kinder to draw out the *pilum* immediately. But, however short the time, Gawen had been the Pendragon, and the deaths of kings, like those of High Priestesses, are not like those of other men.

Sianna must be allowed to say farewell, she told herself, but in her heart Caillean knew that it was her own need for one last word from her fosterling that compelled her decision.

"Lift the shelter of branches you built for him this morning and bring it here. We will cut the shaft of the *pilum* and tend him as best we can."

Slowly, Caillean walked around the circle. While Gawen fought the Romans, the Nazarene monks had continued their work of destruction. Both pillars were cast down, along with three of the lesser stones, and there was a great crack in the altar stone. Out of long habit she moved sunwise, but the power which should have awakened as she passed, flowing smoothly from stone to stone, now welled sluggishly without force or direction. Like Gawen, the Tor had been wounded, and its power was bleeding away through the shattered stones.

Caillean's steps slowed, as if her heart no longer had the strength to pump the blood through her veins. She could feel its erratic fluttering. *Perhaps I will die too.* At the moment, the thought was welcome.

Outside the circle, Gawen lay cleansed and bandaged on his

makeshift bed, with Sianna watching beside him. They had stopped his other wounds from bleeding, but the spearhead was still in his chest, and his spirit still wandered in the borderland between death and dream. Caillean forbade herself to turn to see if anything had changed. If he woke, someone would call her; she would not take from Sianna whatever comfort the girl might find in being alone with him now.

The last of the daylight veiled the land in gold, glowing in the mists that were beginning to gather around the lower hills. Caillean could see no movement in the reeds or open water, or on the wooden trackways that crossed them. Nothing stirred in the water meadows or on the tree-clad island hills. Everywhere she looked, the country-side was peaceful. *It is an illusion,* she told herself. *The land should be erupting in storm and fire on such a day!*

The surge of hatred that shook her as her gaze moved to the wattled huts that circled Father Joseph's beehive church took her by surprise. Paulus had killed the old man's dream of two communities living side by side, following their separate paths toward the goal that she and Joseph had shared. But even there, she could see no one. The marsh folk said that they had run away when the darkness came, praying desperately for deliverance from the demons that they them-selves had raised.

Beyond the church, the Aquae Sulis road ran away to the north. It was white and empty now, but how long would it be, she won-dered, before old Macellius would begin to worry about his sol-diers and send another detachment to find out what had become of them?

Gawen had killed five, and when the darkness fell, the wicked little knives of the marsh men had disposed of the remainder. After-ward they had dragged the bodies away and sunk them in the bogs, lest they further pollute the Tor. But the monks were no doubt even now on their way to tell the Romans that the soldiers had come here, and the Army would exact a heavy reckoning.

They will come, and they will finish what was begun with the massacre on the Isle of Mona when I was a child. The Order of Druids and the service of our

Goddess will be obliterated at last . . ., Caillean thought grimly. At this moment she found it hard to care. She stayed where she was, gazing out across the land as the sun set and the light ebbed out of the world.

⊲ ⊲ ⊲

It was full dark when a touch on her arm brought Caillean back to awareness. She was no more hopeful, but her abstraction had at least given her a little peace.

"What is it? Is Gawen—"

Riannon shook her head. "He still sleeps. It is the rest of us who need you. Lady, all of the Druids and the initiated priestesses are here. They are frightened; some want to flee before the Romans come again, others to stay and fight. Speak to them—tell us what we must do!"

"Tell you?" Caillean shook her head. "Do you think my magic so great that I have only to whisper an invocation and all will be well? I could not save Gawen—what makes you think I can save you?" In the dim light she saw the hurt in Riannon's face and bit off any further words.

"You are the Lady of Avalon! You cannot simply withdraw because you have lost hope. We feel the same despair you do, but you have always taught us that we must not allow our feelings to determine our actions, but to seek calm and allow the eternal spirit within us to decide. . . ."

Caillean sighed. She felt as if her own spirit had died when Paulus thrust down the sacred stones, but the actions of the woman she had been still bound her. *It is true*, she thought, *that the strongest chains are those we forge for ourselves.*

"Very well," she said at last. "This decision will affect all our lives. I cannot make it for you, but I will come, and we will talk about what to do."

One by one, the Druids limped into the shattered circle. Ambios brought Caillean's chair, and she sank into it, realizing painfully just how long she had been standing. She had learned to ignore the body's demands, but now she felt every one of her sixty years.

Several oil lamps had been set on the ground. In the flickering light, Caillean saw a reflection of her own anguish and fear.

"We cannot stay here. I do not know much of the Romans," said Ambios, "but everyone has heard how they punish those who attack their soldiers. If it is in war, their prisoners are sold as slaves, but when members of the civilian population rebel and strike back at their masters, they are crucified. . . ."

"We Britons are not allowed to bear arms, lest they be used against them," said another.

"Are you surprised?" Riannon asked with bitter pride. "Look how much damage Gawen did with his!" They all turned to gaze for a moment at the still figures in the leafy shelter.

"It is certain that on us they will have no mercy, in any case," said Eiluned. "I heard the tales of what they did to the women of Mona. The Forest House was founded to protect those who remained. We should never have left it."

"Vernemeton is in ruins," said Caillean wearily. "It was only because the old Arch-Druid, Ardanos, had become a personal friend to several prominent Romans that it lasted as long as it did. We have lived in peace since then because the authorities did not realize we were here."

"If we stay here we will be massacred, or worse. But where can we go?" asked Marged. "Even the mountains of Demetia would not hide us. Shall we ask the folk of the marshes to build us coracles and set sail for the isles beyond the western sea?"

"Alas," said Riannon, "poor Gawen is likely to reach those isles before we do."

"We could flee to the north," said Ambios. "The Caledonians do not bow to Rome."

"They did in Agricola's day," answered Brannos. "Who's to say that some ambitious emperor might not try it again? And the folk of the north have their own priests. They might not welcome us."

"Then the Order of Druids in Britannia is ended," said Riannon heavily. "We must send the children we have taken for training back to their families, and we ourselves must flee separately to make our way as best we can."

Brannos shook his head. "I am too old for such jaunterings. I will stay here. The Romans are welcome to such sport as they may get from my old bones."

"And I will stay as well," said Caillean. "The Lady Eilan set me to serve the Goddess on this holy hill, and I will not betray my oath to her."

"Mother Caillean!" Lysanda began. "We cannot leave—" But another sound interrupted her. Sianna had half risen and was calling to them.

"Gawen is awake!" she cried. "You must come!"

Strange, thought Caillean, how her weariness had suddenly not gone but become unimportant. She was the first to reach Gawen, kneeling on his other side, moving her hands above his body to sense the life force there. It was steadier than she expected, and she remembered that he had been in the prime of his youth and in good physical condition as well. This body would not easily relinquish the spirit it bore.

"I have told him what happened after he lost consciousness," Sianna said softly as the others joined them. "But what have you decided to do?"

"There is no refuge for the order," said Ambios. He looked at Gawen's white face and quickly away. "We must scatter and hope the Romans will not think us all worth the trouble to hunt down."

"Gawen cannot be moved and I will not leave him!" Sianna exclaimed.

Caillean saw his convulsive movement and laid her hand over his. "Be still! You must save your strength!"

"For what?" Gawen mouthed the words. Amazingly, there was a spark of humor in his eye. Then his gaze moved to Sianna. "She must not risk danger . . . for me. . . ."

"You did not desert the sacred stones," said Caillean.

He tried to take a deep breath and winced. "Then there was something . . . to defend. Now I . . . am done."

"And what will this world hold for me if you are not in it?" cried Sianna, bending over him again. Her bright hair veiled his wounded body and her shoulders shook with the force of her weeping. Gawen's face contorted as he realized he had not even the strength to lift his unhurt arm and comfort her.

Caillean, her eyes stinging with tears, lifted his hand and laid it on Sianna's shoulder. Suddenly she felt her flesh prickle. She looked up and saw the shimmer of displaced air and within it the slim shape of the Faerie Queen.

"If the priestesses cannot protect you, my daughter, then you must return to Faerie, and the man also. He will not die if he is in my keeping in the Otherworld."

Sianna sat up, hope and despair warring in her eyes. "And will he be healed?"

The fairy woman's dark gaze turned to Gawen, with an infinite compassion and an infinite sorrow. "I do not know. Perhaps in time—a very long time, as you count such things among men."

"Ah, Lady," whispered Gawen, "you have been good to me, but you do not understand what it is you ask. You would offer me the immortality of the Elder kin, but what would it bring me? Unending suffering for my broken body, and suffering for my spirit when I thought of the people of Avalon and the desecrated stones. Sianna, my dear one, our love is great, but it would not survive that. Would you ask it of me?" He coughed, and on the bandaging around his chest the red stain deepened.

Sobbing, she shook her head.

"I could take from you even those memories," her mother said then.

Gawen stretched out his arm, where the royal dragon spiraled, its sinuous lines shockingly dark against his bloodless skin. "Could you take these?" he asked. "Then I would be dead, for what you would have would no longer be me. I will accept no rescue that does not include the Druids and the sacred stones."

Did his father have this wisdom at the end? wondered Caillean. *If so, then Eilan saw more clearly than I did, and I have wronged her judgment all these years.* It was ironic that she should only come to this understanding now.

The Queen surveyed them with a rueful sorrow. "Since before the tall folk came over the sea, I have watched and studied humankind. But still I do not understand you. I sent my daughter to learn your wisdom, and with it she has assumed your frailties. But I see that you are determined, and so I will tell you of a way in which the priestesses and Druids of Avalon might be saved. It will be difficult, even dangerous, and I cannot guarantee what will happen, for I have only ever heard of such a thing being attempted once or twice in my long existence, and then it was not always successful."

"One other way to do what? Mother, what do you mean?"

Caillean sat back on her heels, eyes narrowing, for it seemed to her that this was something of which she too had once heard tales.

"A way to separate this Avalon in which you dwell from the rest of the human world. The Romans will see only the isle of Inis Witrin, where the Nazarenes have their church. But for you there will be a second Avalon, shifted just sufficiently so that its time will move along a different track, neither wholly in Faerie nor in the human world. To mortal sight, a mist will enfold it, which can only be passed by those who have been trained to shape the power." Her shadowed gaze moved to Caillean. "Do you understand, Lady of Avalon? Are you willing to dare this working for the sake of those you love?"

"I am," she said hoarsely, "even if it consumes me. I would dare more than this for the sake of the trust to which I am sworn."

"This can only be done when the tides of power are cresting. If you wait until Midsummer, your enemies may come upon you, and I do not think that Gawen can last so long."

"But the tides of Beltane are just beginning to ebb, and the rite that was celebrated here last night raised great power," Caillean said swiftly. "We will do it now."

It was very late before they were ready to begin. It would not be possible for them to transport the entire Vale of Avalon; even to affect the seven sacred islands was a task almost beyond imagining. Caillean had sent her people out in pairs, priest and priestess, to mark the points with fires kindled from the embers of the Beltane blaze. The others were gathered on the Tor.

At the moment when the stars stood still for midnight, Brannos stepped to the brow of the Tor, set his horn to his lips, and blew. His fingers might be too gnarled for the harp, but there was nothing wrong with his lungs. Softly at first, the horncall drifted out upon the shadowed air, gathering volume as if it were drawing strength from the night itself, filling the darkness with a music so profound that she thought an answering vibration must be echoing from the stars. Caillean felt her skin shiver with the chill of impending trance, and knew that what she was hearing was not entirely physical, for what sound produced by a human frame could fill the world? And by what senses of the flesh could it be perceived? What her spirit heard was the manifestation of the old Druid's trained will.

She looked around the circle. They had repaired it as best they might, propping up the stones that were fallen and binding shattered pieces together, but tonight the real circle was built from human flesh and human spirit. The people of Avalon had been positioned around it, one circle inside and the other out, living extensions of the points of power that were the stones. The dance they had not had time for in the afternoon they would do now. Caillean signaled to Riannon to begin the music.

What she played was a stately, sprightly air, like a heron stalking through reeds, that had been old when the Druids came to this isle. The two lines of dancers began to move sunwise around the circle, separating to pass the stones, crossing between them, and, separating around the next, so that the stones were framed in meanders of light. Inward and out again, outward and in wove the dancers, the melody quickening with each circuit.

Caillean felt the flow of energy growing stronger, the visible light a manifestation of the power that was swirling around the perimeter of the circle. It wavered a little when it touched the broken stones, like water meeting a blockage in the bed of a stream. But water was mindless, following the path of least resistance. The determination of the dancers would carry this flow of force through.

As the dance moved faster, energy spun off from the circumference, thinning as it radiated outward. But the power that moved inward was contained, borne on by its own momentum in its own, slower swirl, a little uneven where the stones had been damaged, but strong. The High Priestess sent a tendril of spirit downward, anchoring herself in the earth of the Tor. As many times as she had done this, there was always a moment of surprise when the power began to really flow.

The air within the circle was thickening. She blinked; stones and dancers were veiled by a rippling golden haze. Caillean lifted her hands to gather the light in. In a dimension just a breath away from this one, the Faerie Queen was waiting. If the Druids could raise enough power, and if Caillean was strong enough to focus it, the fairy woman could use it to draw Avalon between the worlds.

The energy rose in dizzying waves, the distortion from the broken stones increasing as it grew. Caillean struggled for balance, remembering a night when she had returned to the Tor across the waters during a storm, the boat leaping beneath them as Waterwalker struggled to bring her in. Friendly hands were waiting to pull them to shelter if only Caillean could toss the rope to shore. She had strained to do so, heaving the rope until she almost went over the side. But it had been a momentary easing of the wind that had saved them.

It was like that now. She staggered, buffeted by the surging energy, and could not regain her balance; she could gather the power, but she could not direct it away.

"Let go!"

Caillean did not know if the voice came from without or within. But she could not in any case have continued much longer. As the will that had sustained her faltered, the energy burst outward, and she fell.

☙ ☙ ☙

"I'm sorry. . . . I wasn't strong enough. . . ." Caillean knew she was babbling. She blinked, unsure whether she was conscious or this was all some dream. Gradually the world steadied. She was sitting with her back to the altar stone, pale faces swimming in and out of focus around her. "I'm sorry," she said again, more strongly. "I didn't mean to frighten you. Help me to stand."

At least, she thought grimly as she looked around her, she had retained enough of her old discipline to ground the backlash of power herself instead of allowing it to devastate the circle. The others looked shaken, but they were all on their feet. She herself felt rather as if she had been trampled by a herd of horses, but the painful thumping of her heart was beginning to ease.

A stir from beyond the circle caught her attention. What were they doing? Four of the younger folk had gotten Gawen up on a litter and were bringing him into the circle of stones.

"It was his will, Lady," said Ambios, with an intonation that added, *Even dying, he is the King....* They brought benches and laid the litter across them. The taut muscles of Gawen's cheeks unclenched as the jolting stopped, and after a moment he opened his eyes.

Caillean looked down at him. "Why ...?"

"To give you what help I may when you try again..." Gawen replied.

"Again?" Caillean shook her head. "I did all I knew...."

"We must try another way," Sianna said then. "Did you not teach us the power of a triad in working such as this one? Three points are always much better balanced than one alone."

"Do you mean myself and Gawen and you? Even to remain within the circle would be a danger to him. It would kill him to channel such power!"

"I will die anyway, of my wounds, or when the Romans come," Gawen said quietly. "I have heard there is great magic in the death of a king. I think that, dying, I will yet have more power than I would have had in full health a week ago. You see, I now *remember* what I am, and who I have been. What life remains to me is a small price to pay for such a victory."

"Does Sianna think so?" Caillean asked bitterly.

"This is the man I love...." Sianna's voice wavered only a little. "How can I deny him? He has always been a king to me."

"We will find each other again." He looked up at her, and then at Caillean. "Did you yourself not teach us that this life is not all?"

Caillean met his gaze, feeling as if her very heart would crack. In this moment it was not only Gawen whom she was seeing clearly, but Sianna as well, and she knew that the spirit that shone through the girl's eyes was one that she had sometimes loved, and sometimes fought, before.

"Be it so," she said heavily. "We will take our risks together, then, for I think that we are all three bound into the same chain." She straightened and looked at the others.

"If you also are still determined to dare this, then you must resume your places and stand with linked hands around the stones. But we will not dance this time. The damaged stones cannot anchor the energy. You must send it sunwise through your linked hands as we sing...."

Once more, silence fell upon the Tor. Taking a deep breath, Caillean rooted her being in the earth and began to vibrate the first note in the sacred chord. Softly at first it began, intensifying as more and more voices joined in, until Caillean began to *see* the vibrations as a haze in the air. After the note was established, she ceased to sing. Sianna and Gawen were silent also, but she could feel them using the sound to center and focus their energy.

That was encouraging, or perhaps it was only that she herself was now beginning to slide into a deeper state in which she could view all that occurred with a dispassionate eye. She deepened her focus, and began the second note in the chord.

As the harmony grew more complex, the hazy luminescence grew brighter. If the energy raised by the dancing had been more vigorous, this light appeared more stable. The more experienced Druids had taken their positions by the damaged stones, and their strength was balancing that of the others.

Once more Caillean gathered her own forces, and released the third note into the heavy air.

Surely, she thought as the higher voices of the younger women completed the chord, it must be working, for now she could discern in the glow a rainbow shimmer, which was gradually beginning its sunwise swirl. This was a power not to control but to ride, lifted gently by its strengthening flow. It only needed direction now.

"I sing the sacred stones of Avalon," she intoned on a fourth note that was supported by the chord.

"I sing the circle of light and song . . ." Sianna echoed her.

"I sing the spirit that past pain is soaring. . . ." Gawen's voice was surprisingly strong.

"Holy the high place that holds us—"

"Grass on its slopes green growing—"

"Blossoms that blow on the wind—"

Voices chiming in sequence, they continued the incantation. In the rainbow light Caillean saw images of Avalon: mist veiling the pink gleam of the lake at sunrise, the silver-bright glitter of light at noon, shards of flame among the reedbeds at the close of day. They invoked the beauty of the Tor in the springtime, garlanded with apple blossom, in the green strength of summer, and veiled in the quiet grey mists of the fall. The song turned to green islands, to oak trees reaching skyward and the sweetness of berries guarded by briars.

There was none of the excitement of the first attempt, only a growing certainty that they were being lifted by the music. Steadily the power contained within the circle intensified, raying outward gradually to the perimeter of the territory the Druids had claimed. But the axis of the entire great and slowly turning wheel was the triad stationed at the altar stone. Caillean was aware of Sianna's loving heart and Gawen's brave soul, and of herself, moving beyond male or female to a wisdom that was both and neither, passing the focus from one to another as they sang.

And presently it began to seem to her that she could hear another voice, sweet with distance, a voice from the Otherworld. Its song was also of Avalon, but the beauties of which it sang were transcendent and eternal, belonging to that Avalon of the heart which exists between the worlds.

Nothing mortal could have resisted that calling. Caillean's spirit fluttered like a fledgling seeking the skies. A tremor shook the ground; she swayed forward, clutching at the altar stone. The earth beneath her feet was no longer stable, but her link to the other two was a lifeline to which she clung as waves of vibration lifted her farther and farther from ordinary reality.

She could no longer see the stone or the circle, only her two companions, floating in a haze of light. She knew then that they were no longer in the body, for Gawen stood radiantly whole as he had been the night before, with Sianna by his side. Caillean reached out and they joined hands, and at the contact felt a momentary searing flare of power and then a great peace.

"It is accomplished . . ." said a voice above them. They looked up, and saw the Queen of Faerie as she is on the other side, shining with a splendor for which the beauty she sometimes wears among men is only a hint and a disguise.

"You have done well. There remains only the task of calling the clouds to hide the Isle of Avalon from the world. You, my children, should return to your bodies. It will be sufficient for the Lady of Avalon, who is accustomed to faring out of her body for longer, to bear witness, and learn the spell by which one may pass through those mists to the outer world."

Caillean stepped away from the others. Sianna, smiling, began to turn, but Gawen shook his head.

"The cord that bound me to that form is broken."

Sianna's eyes widened. "You're dead?"

Surprisingly, Gawen grinned. "Do I look dead? It's only my body that has given up. Now I am free."

And lost to me . . . , thought Caillean. Oh, my sweet boy, my son! She started to reach out to him, then let her hands fall. He had gone beyond her now.

"Then I will stay here with you!" Sianna gripped him fiercely.

"This place is only a threshold," said her mother; "soon it will disappear. Gawen must go on, and you must return to the human world."

"Avalon is safe," she exclaimed. "Why should I go back now?"

"If you have no care for the life you have not yet lived, then go back for the sake of the child you bear...."

Sianna's eyes widened, and Caillean felt her own spirit leap with a hope she had not known she had lost. But it was Gawen whose radiance was growing, as if with each moment the conventions of the flesh became of less importance.

"Live, my beloved, live, and raise our child, so that something of me will remain in the world."

"Live, Sianna," cried Caillean, "for you are young and strong, and I will need your help badly in the time to come."

Gawen took her in his arms, so bright now that his light shone through Sianna as well. "It will not seem so long. And when your time is done, we will walk together once more!"

"Do you promise?"

Gawen laughed. "Only truth can be spoken here...." And with those words, the light became blinding.

Caillean shut her eyes, but she heard him say, *"I love you...."* And though those words might have been said to Sianna, it was her soul that heard them, and she realized that they had been meant for her as well.

◁ ◁ ◁

When she opened her eyes, she was standing at the broad, muddy shore of the wetlands where the waters of the Sabrina were returned in a brackish backflow by the tide. Beside her stood the Faerie Queen, arrayed once more in her woodland guise, though a hint of the glamour of the Overworld clung about her still. Night was done, and from moment to moment the air was brightening. About their heads gulls swooped, calling, and the damp air was heavy with the tang of the distant sea.

"Is it done?" Caillean whispered.

"Look behind you," came the answer. Caillean turned. For a moment she thought that nothing had changed. Then she saw that the ringstones on the Tor were whole and straight, as if they had never been desecrated, and the slope beyond the holy well where the beehive huts of Father Josephus and his monks had stood was empty and green.

"The mists will protect you—call them now. . . ."

Once more Caillean looked westward. A faint mist swirled off the waters, deepening the farther she looked until it merged into the solid wall of sea-fog that had come in with the dawn.

"By what spell shall I summon them?"

The Lady took from her belt pouch something wrapped in yellowed linen. It was a small golden tablet inscribed with strange characters, and at the sight of them far-memory awakened and Caillean knew that they had been written by the men who came from the mighty lands that now lie drowned beneath the sea. And when she touched it, though she had never heard that language with her mortal ears, she knew what words she must say.

In the distance the thick mists curdled and began to flow. As she continued to call they came billowing in, rolling across tree and reed and water to the mud flats on the shore, swirling around her in a cool embrace that soothed away the last of her pain.

She gestured, sending the mist away to either side. *Enfold us, surround us, draw us farther into the mist where no fanatic can shout his curses or cast his spells and only the gods can find us. Surround Avalon with mist where we will be forever and eternally secure!*

Presently she began to feel cold. At the edge of vision, mist hung heavy above the water, and she sensed that the familiar landscape through which she had once traveled from Deva no longer lay beyond it but, rather, a strangeness, something uncanny and only partly visible to mortal eyes.

Had she been here for minutes, or hours? She felt cramped and stiff, as if she had carried all Avalon upon her back and shoulders for a long and weary way.

"It is done." The Queen's voice wavered. She seemed smaller, as if she too had exhausted herself in this night's working. "Your isle lies between the world of men and Faerie. If any would now seek Avalon, it will be the holy isle of the Nazarenes they will find, unless they have been taught the ancient magic. You may teach the spell to some of the marsh folk, if they are worthy, but otherwise the way can be passed only by your initiates."

Caillean nodded. The damp air felt fresh and new. Henceforth they would dwell in a clean land, owing no service to prince or emperor, guided only by the gods. . . .

Caillean speaks:

*From the moment when the fairy mists first swirled around us, the time of
Avalon began to run on a different track from that of the outer world. From
Beltane to Samhain, and from Samhain to Beltane again, the years have circled
round, and from that day to this no unhallowed foot has trod the Tor. As I look
back, it seems so short a time ago. But the daughter that Sianna bore to Gawen is
now a woman grown and sworn to the Goddess in her turn. And Sianna herself
is Lady of Avalon in all but name.*

*As I grow older, I find my thoughts turning inward. The maidens tend me
carefully, and pretend not to notice when I call one of them by her mother's
name. I am not in pain, but it is true that things past are often more vivid to me
than those of the present day. They say that it is given to a high priestess to know
her time, and I think that I will not remain in this body long.*

*From time to time new girls come to us for training, brought by the marsh
men, who know the spell, or found by our priestesses when they go out into the
world. Some stay for a year or two, and others remain and take vows as priestesses. Still, the changes here are slight, compared with events beyond our Vale.
Three years after Gawen died, the Emperor Hadrianus himself came to Britannia and set his armies to building a great wall across the northlands. But will
it keep the wild tribes penned in their moors and mountains forever more?*

I wonder. Walls are only as strong as the men who man them.

Of course, the same is true of Avalon.

*By day I think of the past, but last night I dreamed I was leading the full-
moon rites atop the Tor. I looked into the silver bowl, and saw visions of the*

future reflected there. I saw an emperor they called Antoninus marching north from Hadrian's Wall to build another in Alba. But the Romans could not hold it, and only a few years later they pulled down their forts and marched back. In the future I saw in the bowl, times of peace were succeeded by seasons of war. A new confederation of northern tribes overran the Wall, and another emperor, Severus, came to Britannia to quell them and returned to Eburacum to die.

In my visions, almost two hundred years passed, and in all that time, the mists guarded Avalon. In southern Britannia, British and Roman were becoming one people. A new emperor arose, called Diocletian, and set about healing the Empire from its latest civil wars.

Mixed with the glimpses of Roman conflicts I saw my priestesses, generation after generation worshipping the Goddess on the Holy Tor or going out to become the wives of princes and keep a little of the old wisdom alive in the world. And sometimes it seemed to me that one had the look of Gawen, and at others there would be a maiden with the beauty of Eilan, or a little dark girl who looked like the Faerie Queen.

But I did not see myself reborn in Avalon. According to the Druid teachings, there are some whose holiness is such that when death releases them from the body they go forever beyond the circles of the world. I do not think that I am such a shining soul. Perhaps, if the Goddess is merciful, She will allow my spirit to watch over my children until it is needful for me to live in the flesh once more.

And when I do, it may be that Gawen and Sianna will also come again. Will we know each other? I wonder. Perhaps not, but I think we will carry into those new lives some memory of our former love. Perhaps it will be Sianna's turn to be the teacher next time, and mine to learn. But as for Gawen, he will always be the Sacred King.

PART II

The High Priestess

A.D. 285–293

Chapter Nine

Since midmorning it had been raining, a thin, soaking drizzle that weighted the cloaks of the travelers and drew fine veils of mist across the hills. The four freedmen who had been hired to escort the Lady of Avalon to Durnovaria rode hunched in the saddle, water dripping from the stout oaken cudgels at their sides. Even the young priestess and the two Druids who attended her had pulled the hoods of their hairy wool cloaks down over their eyes.

Dierna sighed, wishing she could do the same, but her grandmother had told her too many times that the High Priestess of Avalon must set an example, and had herself ridden straight-backed till the day she died. Even had she wished to, Dierna could not have ignored that discipline. There were times, she thought, when being able to trace her descent through seven generations, most of them priestesses, from the Lady Sianna was an honor she did not need. But she would not have to endure the weather much longer. Already the ground was rising, and there was more traffic on the road. They would be in Durnovaria before night fell. She hoped that the maiden they had come here to fetch would be worth the ride.

Conec, the younger of the Druids, pointed, and she saw the graceful curve of the aqueduct cutting through the trees.

"Indeed, it is a wonder," she agreed, "especially when there is no reason the people of Durnovaria could not get their water from wells in the town. The Roman magnates win fame by building magnificent structures for their towns. I suppose the Durotrige princes wanted to imitate them."

"Prince Eiddin Mynoc is more interested in improving the defenses," said Lewal, the older Druid, a stocky, sandy-haired man who was their Healer, and had come along to buy herbs they could not grow on Avalon.

"Well, he has need to be," put in one of the freedmen. "With the Channel pirates hitting us more often every year."

"The Navy should do something," said the other. "Or why do we pay those taxes to Rome every year?"

Young Erdufylla nudged her horse closer to Dierna's, as if she expected a band of pirates to jump out from the next clump of trees.

As they came up over the rise, Dierna could see the town, set on a chalk headland above the river. The ditch and rampart were as she remembered, but now they were partially fronted by a new masonry wall. The river ran brown and silent below the bluff, edged with black mud. The tide must be out, she thought then, peering through the drizzle toward the deeper greyness where sky merged into sea. Gulls yammered a greeting, sweeping over their heads and then away. The Druids straightened, and even the horses, sensing the end of the journey, began to step out more briskly.

Dierna let her breath out on a sigh, only then admitting her own anxiety. Tonight, at least, they would be safe and warm within Eiddin Mynoc's new walls. Now she could allow herself to wonder about the girl who was the reason for this journey through the rain.

⊲ ⊲ ⊲

"Teleri, are you listening? The High Priestess will dine with us this evening." Eiddin Mynoc's voice rumbled like distant thunder.

Teleri blinked, wrenching her mind back from that rapidly approaching future in which the priestesses were already bearing her away with them to Avalon. The present was her father's study in Durnovaria, where she was twitching her gown straight like a nervous child.

"Yes, father," she answered in the cultivated Latin which the Prince had required all his children to learn.

"Lady Dierna is coming all this way to see you, daughter. Is your mind still set on going with her? I will not press you to this decision, but there is no going back once it is made."

"Yes, father," Teleri said again, and then, seeing he expected some elaboration, "Yes, I want to go."

No wonder if he thought her fearful, standing before him tongue-tied as a kitchen slave. The Prince was an indulgent father—most girls her age had already been married off without anyone's considering their wishes at all. But the priestesses did not marry. If they wished they took lovers in the holy rites and bore children, but they answered to no man. The priestesses of Avalon had powerful magic. It was not fear that held Teleri silent, but the strength of the wild joy that surged through her at the thought of the holy hill.

She wanted it too much—she would sing, shout, whirl about her father's study like a madwoman if she once began telling him how she really felt today. And so she cast down her eyes as a modest maiden should and murmured monosyllabic answers to his exasperated questioning.

They will be here tonight! she thought when the Prince dismissed her at last and she was free to return to her rooms. The house, Roman in structure, looked inward to the atrium, its potted flowers glowing in the falling rain. Her whole life had been like that, she thought as she leaned against one of the pillars of the colonnade, protected and nurtured, but turned inward.

But there was a ladder that led to the rooftop. Her father had set it there so that he could watch the building of his new walls. Hitching up her skirts, Teleri climbed it, opened the trapdoor, and turned to face the wind. Rain stung her cheeks; in a few moments her hair was wet and water was running down her neck to soak her gown. She did not care. Her father's walls gleamed pale through the rain, but above them she could see the grey blur of the hills.

"Soon I will see what lies beyond you," she whispered. "And then I will be free!"

◁ ◁ ◁

The town house in which the Prince of the Durotriges stayed when he was in his tribal city was Roman in design, decorated by native craftsmen who had attempted to interpret their own mythology in a Roman style, and furnished with a careless disregard for consistency and an eye to comfort. Thick native rugs of striped wool covered the cold tiles; a coverlet of pieced fox pelts lay across the couch. Dierna eyed it wistfully, but she knew that if she once sank into its softness she would find it hard to get up again.

At least the Prince's slaves had brought warm water for them to wash in, and she had gratefully stripped off the breeches and tunic in which she had made the journey and put on the loose-sleeved blue robe of a priestess of Avalon. She wore no ornaments, but her garments were of finely woven wool dyed that particularly rich and subtle blue whose production was a secret of the holy isle.

She picked up the bronze mirror and twitched a stray tendril back under the coronet of braids into which she had twisted her abundant hair, then pulled the edge of the stola up over her head and drew its folds across her breast so that the free end hung down her back. Both garb and hairstyle were severe, but the soft wool molded itself to the generous curve of her breasts and hips, and against the deep blue her hair, curling ever more rebelliously in the damp air, blazed like fire.

She looked at Erdufylla, who was still trying to adjust the folds of her own stola, and smiled.

"We had best go. The Prince will not be happy if we keep him waiting for his dinner. . . ."

The younger priestess sighed. "I know. But the other women will be wearing embroidered tunicas and golden necklaces, and I feel so *plain* in this garb."

"I understand—when I first attended my grandmother on her journeys away from Avalon, I felt the same. She told me not to envy them—their finery signifies only that they have menfolk who can indulge them. You yourself have earned the garb you wear. When you go among them, carry yourself with such pride that it is they who will feel overdressed, and envy you."

With her narrow features and mouse-fair hair, Erdufylla would never be beautiful, but as Dierna spoke the younger woman straightened, and when the High Priestess moved toward the door she followed with the graceful, gliding gait that was the gift of Avalon.

The town house was a large one, with four wings surrounding a courtyard. The Prince and his guests had gathered in a large room in the wing farthest from the road. One wall was painted with scenes of the marriage of the Young God with the Flower Maiden against a burnt-orange background, and a mosaic patterned with knotwork covered the floor. But shields and spears were mounted on the other walls, and a wolfskin covered the chair on which Prince Eiddin Mynoc awaited them.

He was a man of middle years, with a great deal of silver in his dark hair and beard. What had been a powerful physique was going to fat, and only an occasional gleam in his eye revealed the wit he had inherited from his mother, who had been a daughter of Avalon. None of his sisters had shown any talent worth training, but according to Eiddin Mynoc's message, his youngest girl, though pretty enough, was "so filled with odd fits and fancies she might as well go to Avalon."

Dierna looked around the room, acknowledging the Prince's welcome with a gracious, and precisely equivalent, nod. That was another thing her grandmother had taught her. In her own sphere, the Lady of Avalon was the equal of an emperor. The other guests— several matrons dressed in the Roman style, a portly man wearing the toga of the equestrian class, and three beefy young men who she supposed were Eiddin Mynoc's sons—eyed her with mingled respect and curiosity. Was the girl she had come here to meet still primping, or too shy to face the company?

One of the women rather pointedly avoided her gaze. When the priestess saw that she wore a silver fish on a slender chain, she realized the woman must be a Christian. Dierna had heard there were many of them in the eastern parts of the Empire, but although a company of monks lived on the isle of Inis Witrin, the counterpart of Avalon that still remained part of the world, in the rest of the province their numbers were relatively few. They seemed to be so given to quarrels and disputations that they were likely to destroy themselves soon enough without any assistance from the Emperor.

"Your walls, lord, are rising quickly," said the man in the toga. "They have grown halfway around the city since I was here last."

"By the next time you come here they will be finished," Eiddin Mynoc said proudly. "Let those sea wolves howl elsewhere for their dinners, they'll get nothing in Durotrige lands."

"They are a magnificent gift to your people," said the man in the toga, ignoring him. Dierna realized that she had met him once before—he was Gnaeus Claudius Pollio, one of the senior magistrates here.

"It is the only gift the Romans will allow us to give," muttered one of the sons. "They do not let us arm our people, and they take the troops that should protect us back across the Channel to fight their wars."

His brother nodded vigorously. "It is not justice, to take our taxes and give us nothing. Before the Romans came at least we could defend ourselves!"

"If the Emperor Maximian will not help us, we need an emperor of our own!" said the third boy.

He had not spoken loudly, but Pollio fixed him with a disapproving glare. "And who would you elect, cockerel? Yourself?"

"Nay, nay," his father put in quickly, "we speak no treason here. It is only the blood of his ancestors, who have defended the Durotriges since before Julius Caesar came over from Gallia, that burns in his veins. It's true that when the Empire is troubled Britannia sometimes seems the last province they care for, but we are still better off within its boundaries than squabbling among ourselves. . . ."

"The Navy ought to protect us. What are Maximian and Constantius doing with the money we send them? They swore they would put the pirates down," one of the older men muttered, shaking his head. "Have they no admirals who can command a fleet against such men?"

Dierna, who had been listening with interest, turned in annoyance at a pull on her sleeve. It was the most richly dressed of the women, Vitruvia, who was married to Pollio.

"Lady, I am told that you know much of herbs and medicines...." Her voice dropped to a whisper as she began to describe the palpitations of the heart that had frightened her. Dierna, looking beneath the careful cosmetics and the jewels, recognized the woman's very real anxiety and forced herself to listen.

"Has there been a change in your monthly courses?" she asked. The men, still arguing politics, did not notice as they moved aside.

"I am still fertile!" Vitruvia exclaimed, the color in her painted cheeks intensifying.

"For now," Dierna said gently, "but you are passing from the governance of the Mother to that of the Wise One. To complete that transformation will take some years. In the meantime, you must make a preparation of motherwort. Take a few drops when your heart troubles you, and you will be eased."

From the other room came an enticing scent of roasted meat, and she was suddenly acutely aware of how long it had been since the morning meal. She had thought the Prince's daughter would be joining them for dinner, but perhaps Eiddin Mynoc was an old-fashioned parent who believed that unmarried girls should be kept in seclusion. A slave appeared in the doorway to announce that dinner awaited them.

As they moved out into the corridor, Dierna felt something, a breath of air, perhaps, as if a door to the outside had been opened farther along the hall, and turned. In the shadows at the far end of the hallway something pale was moving; she saw a woman's figure, coming with a quick, light step as if blown by the wind. The High Priestess stopped so suddenly that Erdufylla bumped into her.

"What is it?"

Dierna could not answer. A part of her mind identified the newcomer as a woman just emerging from girlhood, tall and slender as a bending willow, with pale skin and dark hair and a hint of Eiddin Mynoc's strong bones in the line of cheek and brow. But it was another feeling that had silenced her, which she could only characterize as *recognition.*

Dierna's heart bounded like poor Vitruvia's; she blinked, for a moment seeing the girl fragile, with fine pale hair and robed as a priestess, and then again small, with auburn highlights in her dark curls, and golden bracelets curling like serpents around her arms.

Who is she? she asked herself, and then, *Or who was she, and who was I, that I greet her return with such anguished joy?* For a moment then she heard a name—"*Adsartha . . .*"

Then the girl was before her, dark eyes widening as she saw the blue robes. With a fluid grace she sank to her knees, seized the trailing corner of Dierna's stola, and kissed it. The High Priestess looked down at that bent head, unable to stir.

"Ah, there she is, my erring child!" came Eiddin Mynoc's voice from behind her. "Teleri, my dear, get up! What will the Lady think of you?"

She is called Teleri. . . . The other names and faces were banished by the living reality of the girl before her, and Dierna found that she could breathe once more.

"Indeed, my daughter, you do me honor," she said softly, "but this is not the time or the place for you to kneel to me."

"There will be another, then?" asked Teleri, taking Dierna's outstretched hand and rising. Already the awe in her face was giving way to a delighted laughter.

"Is that what you wish?" asked Dierna, still holding her hand. A power too deep to be called impulse brought new words to her lips. "We will say this again in the presence of the priestesses, but I ask you now. Is it of your own free will, without force or coercion by your father or anyone, that you seek to join the holy sisterhood that dwell in Avalon?"

She knew that Erdufylla was staring at her in amazement, but since she had been made High Priestess, there had rarely been anything of which she had been so sure.

"By moon and stars and the green earth I swear it," said Teleri eagerly.

"Then, in earnest of the greeting my sisters will give you when we return, I welcome you." Dierna took Teleri's face between her two hands, and kissed her on the brow.

◁ ◁ ◁

That night Teleri lay long wakeful. When dinner was done, Eiddin Mynoc, pointing out that the priestesses had had a weary day on the road, had bidden them good night and sent his daughter to bed. With her mind Teleri knew that he was right, and that she herself ought to have noticed their fatigue. She told herself that she could talk to them on the journey back to Avalon—she would have the rest of her life to talk to priestesses. But her heart cried out in frustration at having to leave them.

Teleri had expected to be impressed by the Lady of Avalon. Everyone had heard tales of the pointed Tor that was hidden, like Faerie, by mists through which only an initiate could pass. Some thought it a legend, for when the priestesses went out into the world it was usually in disguise. But in the old royal families of the tribes the truth was known, for many of their daughters had spent a season or two upon the holy isle, and at times, when the health of the land required it, one of the priestesses would be sent to make the Great Marriage with a chieftain at the Beltane fires. What she had not expected was to respond as if the High Priestess were someone dearly loved from long ago.

She must think me a fool! Teleri told herself, turning over yet again. *I suppose they all worship her.* In all the stories, the Lady of Avalon was an awesome figure, and it was true. Lady Dierna was like a beacon fire blazing against a midnight sky. Next to that radiance Teleri felt ghostly. Perhaps, she thought then, she was indeed the spirit of someone who had known Dierna in another lifetime.

At that, she began to laugh. Next she would be fancying herself Boudicca, or the Empress of Rome. *It is more likely,* she told herself, *I was Dierna's serving maid!* And, still smiling, she fell asleep.

Teleri would have happily ridden out the next morning, but as her father pointed out, it was hardly hospitable to send the folk of Avalon off without even a day to recuperate from their journey, and as it happened, they needed items from the markets of Durnovaria. Teleri made herself Dierna's shadow. The moment of astonishing intimacy which had occurred when they met was not repeated, but she found it surprisingly easy to be in the older woman's company.

And gradually Teleri realized there was not so great a difference in their ages as she had supposed. She herself was now eighteen, but the High Priestess was only ten years older. It was responsibility and experience that made the difference between them. Erdufylla had told her that Dierna's first child, a daughter, had been still in the womb when her mother became High Priestess at the age of twenty-three, and had been sent away for fostering before she was three. To think about Dierna's children made Teleri feel like a child herself. And it was with a child's anticipation that she fell asleep that night, eager for their departure the next morn.

They rode out from Durnovaria in the damp and rainy dawning, leaving the city still wrapped in sleep behind them. The High Priestess had wanted an early start, for the first stage of their journey would be long. The freedman who opened the gates had still been yawning and rubbing his eyes. Teleri wondered if he would even remember the travelers for whom he had opened them. Wrapped in their dark cloaks, the two priestesses passed like shadows, and even the men of their escort seemed to have absorbed some of their anonymity.

She herself was wide awake; she had always been an early riser, and anticipation had brought her from bed well before she was called. Even the glowering skies could not dampen her spirits. She twitched at the reins to make her mare step out and listened for the first birds to greet the dawning day.

They were just coming down the slope to the river when she heard a birdcall she did not recognize. It was autumn, when many birds passed through on their way southward. Teleri looked around her, wondering if the call had been made by a kind she had not seen before. They said that the wetlands around Avalon were a haven for waterfowl. No doubt she would find many new birds there. The call came again, and her mare's ears pricked. Teleri felt a flicker of unease and pushed back her hood to see.

Something moved among the willows. She reined her mare back and spoke to the nearest freedman, who straightened, reaching for his cudgel and looking where she had pointed. Then someone whistled, the willows shivered, and in the next moment the road filled with armed men.

"Look out!" screamed the younger of the two Druids, who rode in the lead. A spear jabbed; she saw his face change, and his pony bolted, whinnying, as he fell. Her own mare half reared as she started to pull her around; then Teleri realized that Dierna was unguarded, and reined back toward her.

The road was full of men. Spear points glinted in the early light, and she glimpsed the flare of a sword. The freedmen were laying about them with their cudgels, but those were poor weapons against sharp blades. One by one they were pulled off their horses; the air echoed to their screams. Teleri's own mount plunged at the scent of blood. A contorted face leered up at her and she felt a callused hand close around her ankle. She slashed at the man with her riding whip and he fell away.

Dierna had dropped her reins and lifted her arms, to draw strange signs in the air. Teleri felt her own ears hum as the High Priestess began to sing; the confusion around her slowed. From beyond her came a deep-voiced shout. She turned, saw a heavy spear flying toward Dierna, and kicked her mare forward. But she was too far away. It was Erdufylla, who had not dared to leave Dierna's side, who made the convulsive movement that put her body between the High Priestess and the spear.

Teleri saw the wicked point slam through the woman's breast, heard her scream as she was knocked backward into Dierna's arms. As their terrified horses reared, both women went down. Teleri lashed out with her whip again; a man swore, and her mare came to a plunging halt as he grabbed for the reins. When Teleri tried to pull back, the reins were wrenched from her hand. She fumbled beneath her cloak for her belt knife and struck at the first man who reached for her, but in another moment someone grabbed her from behind and dragged her from the saddle.

She yelled, still struggling, but a blow dazed her. When she could think again, she was lying in the woods and both her hands and feet were bound. Through the trees she saw their horses disappearing up the road. The raiders who rode them had pulled cloaks over their heads. She wondered if the gate guards would even notice that the riders had changed. But the two men who had been left to guard the prisoners had no need to hide their flaxen hair.

Pirates! she thought grimly. *Saxons, or perhaps renegade Frisians from Belgica.* The conversations which she had considered so boring at her father's dinner table abruptly acquired a brutal significance. Blinking back tears of rage, she turned her face away.

Dierna lay beside her. For a moment Teleri thought the High Priestess was dead; then she saw that, like herself, the older woman was bound. They would not have troubled to tie a corpse. But Dierna lay far too still. Her fair skin was pale, and Teleri could see an ugly bruise forming on her brow. In her throat a pulse was still beating, however, and ever so slowly, her breast rose and fell.

Beyond the priestess other bodies lay sprawled where they had fallen when they were dragged from the road. The young Druid was there, and the freedmen, and with a sinking heart Teleri recognized Erdufylla as well. She told herself that she should not be surprised— no one could survive such a wound. Besides herself and Dierna, of all their party only the Healer, Lewal, had survived.

Teleri whispered his name. For a moment she thought he had not heard; then his head turned.

"Did they hit her?" She nodded toward the priestess.

He shook his head. "I think one of the horses kicked her as she fell, but they wouldn't let me examine her."

"Will she live?" Teleri whispered more softly still.

For a moment Lewal closed his eyes. "If the gods are kind. With a blow to the head we can only wait. Even if I were free there would be little I could do except to keep her warm."

Teleri shivered. It was not raining, but the sky was still raw and grey.

"Roll this way, and I will do the same," she said softly. "Perhaps the heat of our bodies will help."

"I should have thought of that. . . ." A little light came back into his eyes. Carefully, pausing whenever one of their captors looked their way, they began to wriggle toward Dierna.

The time that followed seemed endless, but in fact scarcely two hours passed before they heard the main force of the raiders returning. Teleri remembered that it was the way of these animals to strike swiftly and then run, carrying off what booty they could, before their victims could gather enough force to resist them.

A warrior jerked Teleri to her feet and fingered the fine wool of her gown. When he began to squeeze the breast beneath, she spat at him; he laughed and let her go, saying something incomprehensible.

"I told them that you are rich and will bring a good ransom. I have learned some of their tongue so I can trade for herbs," he told Teleri.

One of the pirates bent over Dierna, clearly uncertain how to reconcile her white hands and rough traveling clothes. After a moment he shrugged and began to draw his dagger.

"No!" cried Teleri. "She is *sacerdos, opulenta.* A priestess! Very rich!" Some of these men must understand Latin. She looked desperately at Lewal.

"*Gytha! Rica!*" he echoed her.

The Saxon looked disbelieving, but he put away his blade, lifted Dierna's limp body, and heaved her over his shoulder. The men who held Teleri and Lewal shoved them along after, and in another moment all three of them were slung across the backs of stolen horses and tied.

By the time they finally came to a halt, Teleri was wishing herself as unconscious as the priestess.

The raiders' ships had been drawn up in a secluded inlet, and they had made a temporary camp on the shore. Rude tents sheltered the perishable booty; the rest of it lay heaped near the fires. The captives were dumped beside a pile of grain sacks and then apparently forgotten as men began to build up the fires and share out the foodstuffs they had captured, especially the wine.

"If we are lucky they will forget us," said Lewal when Teleri wondered if they would be fed, "at least until tomorrow, when they have slept off their wine." He squirmed upright and laid the back of his hand against Dierna's brow. She had moaned a little when she was taken off the horse, but though consciousness might be closer, the priestess had not yet opened her eyes.

Darkness fell. The camp began to assume a semblance of order as men settled beside the fires. Among the fair heads of the Saxons and Frisians were a goodly scattering of black and brown, snatches of rude Latin mixed with the gutturals of the Germanic tongues. Deserters from the Army and fugitive slaves had made common cause with the barbarians. The only requirement for acceptance here seemed to be brutality and a strong arm for an oar or a sword. The scent of roast pig made Teleri's mouth water; she turned her face away and tried to remember how to pray.

She had fallen into an uncomfortable doze when the crunch of a footstep nearby brought her to shuddering wakefulness. She was already beginning to turn over when a kick in the ribs brought her upright, glaring. The pirate who had kicked her laughed. He was no cleaner than the others, but the gold he was wearing above his fur vest suggested that he was a chieftain among them. He grasped Teleri's shoulders and pulled her up to face him and when she struggled held her hard against his chest with one arm, immobilizing her bound hands. His other hand closed in her hair. For a moment more he grinned down at her; then he set his mouth against hers.

When he straightened, some of the men were cheering while others frowned. Teleri gasped for air, not quite believing what he had done to her. Then his callused hand thrust beneath the neck of her gown, groping for her breast, and his intentions became quite clear.

"Please"—she could not pull away, but she could turn her head now—"if he harms me you'll get no ransom! Please make him let me go!"

Some of them at least had understood her Latin. Two or three stood up, and one of them took a step toward her captor. She did not understand what he said, but it was clearly a challenge, for the chieftain stopped what he was doing and reached for his sword. For a moment no one moved. Teleri saw how his pale glare moved from one man to another, saw the fight go out of them until no one would meet his gaze, and heard her own doom sealed as he began to laugh.

Teleri kicked and twisted as he picked her up, but her captor only gripped her more tightly. As he carried her toward the pile of bedding on the other side of the fire, she could hear the other men laugh.

For a long time Dierna had been wandering in a dream world of mist and shadow. She wondered if this was the marshlands below Avalon—cloud always clung to the borders between the protected sphere around the Holy Tor and the outer world. At the thought, the scene grew clearer. She stood on one of the many islets where a few willows clung to a hummock above the reeds. Feathers lay on the muddy ground; she nodded, knowing the mallard's nest must be near. And now she could see her own small bare feet and the soaked skirts of her gown. But there was something she ought to remember. She looked anxiously around her.

"D'rna . . . wait for me!"

The call came from behind her. She turned quickly, remembering now that she had forbidden her little sister to follow her when she went to gather birds' eggs, and the child had disobeyed.

"Becca! I'm coming—don't move!" At eleven, Dierna knew the wetlands well enough to make her way through them alone. She was looking for fresh eggs for one of the priestesses, who was ill. Becca was only six, too small to jump from one tussock to the next; Dierna had not wanted the child to slow her down. But since their mother died the year before, the younger girl had been Dierna's shadow. How had she gotten this far alone?

Dierna waded through the dark water, peering around her. A duck quacked in the distance, but here nothing moved.

"Becca—where are you? Splash the water and I'll follow the sound!" she called. And when she had gotten her sister safe, she told herself then, she would paddle Becca's bottom for disobeying her. It wasn't fair! Couldn't she have just these few hours to herself, without always having to be responsible for the child?

From the other side of the next hummock she heard a splash and stiffened, listening, until it came again. She tried to go faster, misjudged her step, and gasped as one foot sank into deep mud and continued to go down. She flailed wildly, grasped a trailing branch of willow, clung to it, bracing the foot that was on solid ground and working the other gently back and forth until the muck released its hold.

Dierna was wet to the waist now. Shivering, she called to her sister again. She heard a flurry of splashing from beyond the trees.

"D'rna, I can't move," came the reply. "Help me!"

Dierna had thought herself frightened before, but now terror shocked like ice through her veins. She grabbed at the reeds, not caring that they cut her hands, and pulled herself forward, clambered over tree roots, and, calling, pushed through the saw grass on the other side. The mist was heavy here, and she could see nothing. But she could hear Becca whimpering; she pushed off again, following the sound.

The way was blocked by a fallen willow. Dierna pulled herself into the branches, feet slipping on the rotting bark below. "Becca!" she shouted. "Where are you? Answer me!"

❧ ❧ ❧

"Help me!" The call came again.

Firelight danced against Dierna's closed eyelids, and she moaned. She had been in the marshes—why was there a fire? But that didn't matter; her sister was calling, and she must go to her. She sucked in breath. She couldn't move! Had the mud got her too? She twitched, struggling to remember her own body, and felt sensation returning with a rush of pain.

Someone was laughing. . . . Dierna stilled. Then her sister screamed.

Dierna sat up, her head spinning, and when she tried to steady herself found her hands bound and fell over again. Through slitted lids she saw the fire, leering faces, and the white body of the woman who was struggling with the man in the fur vest. His breeches were down; the muscles in his pink buttocks flexed as he tried to pin the girl against the ground.

The priestess stared. She did not know where she was, but she understood what was happening here, and in that moment it was her sister who was once more calling her to help. With a grunt of rage, she snapped the ropes on her wrists and sat up.

The reivers did not see her move. They were watching the struggle, making bets on how long it would last. Dierna took a deep breath, seeking not calm but the control that would let her channel her fury.

"Briga," she breathed, "Great Mother, give me your magic to save this child!" What could she use? There was no weapon in reach, even if she could have fought against so many, but there was the fire. With another breath she projected her will into those leaping flames. Heat seared her soul, but after the chill of the water in her memory, it was welcome. She embraced the torment, became part of it, rising until she stood at her full height in the midst of the fire.

To those who watched, it was as if the flames had been whipped to fury by an invisible wind, whirling upward until they could all see a woman formed of fire. For a moment she floated, sparks streaming from her hair; then she began to move. The reivers were on their feet now. Some, fingers flickering in signs of warding, began to edge away. One man threw his dagger; it passed through the fiery figure and clattered on the ground.

Only the man who was trying to rape Teleri failed to notice. He had the girl's legs pinned now and was tugging at her breeches.

"Do you desire love's fire? Receive my embrace, and burn!" the goddess cried.

Arms of flame reached forward; with a yell the chieftain jerked away from the girl. He yelled again as he saw what had burned him, and wrenched his body to one side. The fire hovered above him as he scrambled, hampered by his own unbelted breeches, to get away. But when he had rolled away from his victim it flared down again, pinning him as he had pinned the girl. In an instant his vest was smoldering and his hair was aflame. Then he began to scream in earnest, but his cries did even less good than had hers, for his men were crashing through the trees, tripping over their gear and each other in their haste to get away.

It made no difference to the fire. As long as he moved it continued to burn, and only when his last twitchings had ceased did the flame flare outward in a shower of sparks and disappear.

⊲ ⊲ ⊲

"Dierna . . ."

With a gasp, the priestess fell back into her body. She felt her unbound hands burning with the return of circulation, and bit her lip against the pain. Lewal was sawing at the ropes around her ankles; in another moment they too had been cut, and she shuddered as sensation prickled through her lower limbs.

"Dierna—look at me!" Another face swam into view, pale, framed by tangled dark hair.

"Becca, you're alive . . ." she whispered, then blinked, for this was a grown woman, her torn gown hanging off one shoulder, her eyes still dark with the memory of terror, her cheeks wet with tears.

"I'm Teleri, Lady—don't you know me?"

Dierna's gaze moved to the fire and the burned thing beyond it, then came back to Teleri's face.

"I remember now. I thought you were my sister. . . ." She shivered, seeing once more the ripples that had ridged the surface of the dark water, and something pale below. Dierna had jumped into the pool, reaching until her fingers closed on cloth, then on her sister's arm. Her breath came faster as she remembered pulling, going under, getting her sister's head up, and grabbing for a floating log. Her struggles had wedged it against a bank, and with that for purchase she could try to pull once more.

"She was caught in quicksand. I heard her screaming, but when I got there she had been pulled under, and I was not strong enough to drag her free." Dierna closed her eyes. Even knowing it was hopeless, she had stayed where she was, one hand holding on to Becca and the other to the log, until the searchers found her when they came searching through the marshes with torches.

"My Lady, don't weep!" Teleri bent over her. "You were in time to save me!"

"Yes—you must be my sister now." Dierna looked up at her and managed a smile. She held out her arms and Teleri came into them. It felt right, somehow. *This one I will keep safe*, she thought. *I will not lose her again!*

"Lady, can you ride? We must get away before those beasts return!" said Lewal. "Look for food and waterskins. I'll saddle three horses and set the others free."

"Beasts . . ." Dierna echoed as Teleri helped her to stand. "Not so—no animal is so vicious to its own kind. This evil belongs to men." Her head hurt, but she had long practice in conquering the body's complaints. "Help me get on the horse and I will stay there," she added, "but what about you, little one? How badly did he hurt you?"

Teleri glanced at the twisted lump of burned meat that had once been a man and swallowed. "I have bruises," she whispered, "but I am still a maiden."

In body, thought Dierna, *but that demon has raped her soul*. Holding on to Teleri's shoulder, she straightened, and stretched out her hand.

"This one will rape no more women, but he was only one of many. May the Lady's fire consume them all! By fire and water I curse them, by the winds of heaven and the holy earth on which we stand. Let the sea rise against them and no harbor give them shelter. As they have lived by the sword, may they find a foe whose sword shall strike them down!"

Dierna could feel power leaving her as the curse sped outward. With the certainty that came sometimes in magic, she knew that these words had been heard in the Otherworld, and though she might never know what happened to the raiders, their doom was sure. If the Goddess was kind, she would one day meet the hero who punished them, and clasp his hand. She swayed, and Teleri steadied her.

"Come now, my Lady," said Lewal. "I will help you to mount, and we will be gone."

Dierna nodded. "Let us go home, to Avalon. . . ."

Chapter Ten

Teleri pulled another handful of wool from the basket and added it to the wisp clinging to the distaff in her left hand. With her right hand she lifted the thread that led to it, taking up the tension; a swift twitch set the dangling spindle turning, and her fingers began once more to guide the yarn. The strengthening sunlight of early spring was warm on her back and shoulders. This corner of the apple orchard was out of the wind, a favorite place for sitting in winter, but even lovelier now, when the sun was beginning to coax the first buds into bloom.

"Your thread is so even," sighed little Lina, looking from the lumpy yarn twisted around her own spindle to Teleri's smooth strand.

"Well, I have had a great deal of practice," Teleri said, smiling back at her, "though I never expected to need that skill here. But I suppose that, so long as princes and priestesses both need clothing, someone will have to spin the thread for it as we are doing now. The women in my father's hall could talk of nothing but men and babies. At least what is spoken of over the spindles here has some meaning." She looked over at old Cigfolla, who had been telling them how the House of Priestesses had come to be established in Avalon.

Lina eyed her dubiously. "But some of the priestesses have babies. Dierna herself has had three. They are so sweet. I dream of having a child in my arms."

"I do not," answered Teleri. "That is the only thing the women I grew up with *could* do. Perhaps it is natural to dream of what you do not have."

"At least the choice is ours," said one of the other girls. "When our priestesses dwelt in the Forest House long ago, they were forbidden to lie with men. I am glad that custom was changed!" she added fervently, and everyone laughed. "The priestesses of Avalon may bear children, but they do not *have* to. Our babies come by the will of the Goddess and at our own, not to please any man!"

Then I will not bear any, thought Teleri, plucking another handful of wool.

Through the grace of the Goddess and Dierna's magic, she was still a virgin, and content to remain so. In any case, she was vowed to chastity until she had completed her training and taken her final vows. From being the youngest in her father's household she had become the oldest in the House of Maidens on Avalon. Even the royal daughters who were sent here for a little extra polish before marriage usually came at an earlier age. She had wondered if the other maidens would laugh at her ignorance—she had wasted so much time, and there was so much to learn! But after her journey with Dierna, some of the charisma of the High Priestess seemed to have rubbed off on her, and they treated her as an elder sister. In any case, she would not remain with the maidens for long. She had been here now for almost two years. In another year, perhaps she would take her vows and become the youngest of the priestesses.

Her only regret was that she saw so little of Dierna herself. As soon as they returned, the majesty, and the responsibilities, of the High Priestess of Avalon had enfolded her. Teleri told herself that she should be grateful to have had even so much of the Lady's company. The other girls envied her for having shared that journey; they did not know that even now, when so many moons had passed, she still woke whimpering from dreams in which the Saxon chieftain was attacking her.

The spindle was growing heavy with its weight of spun wool. Teleri let it down until the point was supported by a flat stone against which it could twirl, and lengthened the yarn between her fingers and the shaft. She would have to wind off the yarn into a skein as soon as she had spun out the last of this wool.

Old Cigfolla, who despite stiff joints could outspin any of them, drew out a fine thread of flax. The wool they spun came from their own sheep, but the flax was given in trade or tribute to Avalon. Some of it, thought Teleri, might have come from her own father's storerooms as part of the gifts he had sent after she came.

"We spin wool for warmth, and heavy linen for wear," said Cigfolla. "But what shall we do with such a thread as this?" The spindle twirled and the thread, so fine it was almost invisible, lengthened again.

"Weave it into veils for the priestesses to wear, because it is the most perfect?" asked Lina.

"Indeed, but not because it is better—only because the cloth it makes is so thin. That does not mean your own work should be less smooth or even," said the old woman sharply. "The apple tree is not more holy than the oak, nor wheat than barley. Each has its own purpose. Some of you will become priestesses, and some of you will return home to marry. In the eyes of the Goddess, all ways are equal in honor. You must strive to do whatever work She gives you as well as you can. Even if you are only spinning hemp for sacking, it should still be done as well as you know how. Do you understand?"

A dozen pairs of eyes met her rheumy gaze and flinched away. "You think that you are set to spinning here because we wish to keep you busy?" Cigfolla shook her head. "We could trade for cloth, as we do for other things. But there is a virtue in the cloth that is made on Avalon. Spinning is a mighty magic, did you not know? When we speak of holy things as we work, more than wool or flax goes into the thread. Look at your own work—see how the fibers twine. Singly they are no more than wisps on the wind, but together they grow strong. They are stronger still if you sing as you spin, if you whisper a spell into each strand."

"What spell, Wise One, do you sing into the linen that will veil the Lady of Avalon?" Teleri asked.

"Into this thread is bound all that we have spoken of," Cigfolla answered her. "Cycles and seasons, turning and returning as the spindle spirals round. Other things will be added in the weaving—

the past and the present, the world beyond the mists and this sacred soil, warp and woof interweaving a new destiny."

"And the dyeing?" asked Lina.

Cigfolla smiled. "That is the love of the Goddess, which permeates and colors all we do...."

"May She keep us safe here," whispered Lina.

"Indeed She has," said the old woman. "For most of my lifetime Britannia has been at peace within a united Empire. And we have prospered."

"The markets are full, but people do not have enough money to buy," objected Teleri. "Perhaps you do not see it, living here, but I spent too many years listening to those who came to plead in my father's hall not to see what is happening. The things we import from elsewhere in the Empire grow steadily more expensive, and our people demand higher wages so that they can buy them, and then our own people have to raise their prices as well."

"My father says it is all the fault of Postumus, who tried to split off the western half of the Empire," said Adwen, who would take her vows along with Teleri.

"But Postumus was defeated," objected Lina.

"Maybe so, but reuniting the Empire does not seem to have helped much. Prices are still going up, and our young men are taken away to fight at the other end of the world, but no one is sent to defend our own shores!" Teleri said hotly.

"That's true," chorused the others. "The pirates grow ever bolder."

Cigfolla added another handful of flax and set her spindle spinning once more. "The world turns like this spindle.... That good and ill shall follow one another is our only certainty. Without change, nothing new could grow. When the old patterns are repeated, it is in a new way—the face of the Lady changes, but Her power endures; the King who gives his life to the land is reborn to make the sacrifice anew. Sometimes I too grow fearful, but I have seen too many winters pass not to believe that spring will always come...." She lifted her face to the sun, and Teleri saw it filled with light.

To sit spinning with the other women was not the life of freedom she had imagined when she begged her father to let her come to Avalon. *Will I yearn always for a happiness that is beyond my grasp?* she wondered then. *Or will I learn in time to live contentedly within the mists that wall us round?*

◁ ◁ ◁

As the season advanced, the weather became warmer. Grass grew thick and green in the water meadows as the marshes dried. In the world beyond Avalon the roads were drying as well, and merchants and travelers began to move across the land, laden with goods and news. At times this spring, it seemed there was more of the latter, for the improving weather had signaled the start of the shipping season as well, and with the merchant ships, the pirates who preyed upon them also went to sea.

Though Dierna did not leave Avalon, news came to her. Messages came from women who had been trained on the holy isle or those who had at some point been helped by them, from wandering Druids, from a network of informants all over Britannia. Her communications were not so swift as those of the Roman Governor, but far more varied, and the conclusions to which she came were rather different.

As the moon moved toward the full just before Midsummer, the High Priestess withdrew to the enclosure on the isle of Briga to meditate. For three days she stayed there, eating nothing, drinking only water brought from the sacred well. All the information she had gathered must be understood and analyzed and then, perhaps, the Lady would teach her what must be done.

The first day was always the hardest. She would find herself wondering about all the tasks, and the people, she had left behind her. Old Cigfolla knew more about running the affairs of Avalon than she did, and Ildeg, who was only a little older than herself, could be depended on to keep the young women in the House of Maidens in line. Dierna had left them both in charge many times when she traveled away from Avalon.

The priestesses understood what she was doing, but what about her children? How could she explain why they must not try to see her even when they knew she was not far away? Their faces filled her vision: her first daughter, who was slim and dark, what they called a fairy child, and the red-haired, lively twins. She ached for the weight of them in her arms. She told herself that her daughters were born, like herself, to the service of Avalon, and this was not too early for them to learn its price. That first child, fathered by a Druid priest in the rites, was gone from her already, being fostered by a family of the blood of Avalon who had built their home from the scattered stones of the old Druid sanctuary of Mona. The twins, her children by a chieftain who had called on her to help him restore his blighted fields, must soon follow. Her heart hurt most for them, but at least they had each other for company.

Dierna shook her head, recognizing these thoughts for the pointless distractions with which the mind always tried to avoid its task. It did no good to deny them—each thought must be allowed to surface, and then eased on its way. She fixed her gaze on the flicker of the oil lamp once more.

When she awakened the next morning, the little marsh woman who served her had left a basket with a few of the powerful mushrooms her people found in the fens. Dierna smiled and, after cleaning them thoroughly, chopped them fine and cast them into her small cauldron with the other herbs she had brought along. Leaning over the cauldron, she began to chant and stir.

The act of preparation was itself a spell, and even before she drank any of the liquid, the acrid steam that swirled from its dark surface had begun to alter her perceptions. She strained the contents of the cauldron into a silver cup and carried it outside.

The hut in which she had kept vigil was surrounded by a thorn hedge. The moon was already a quarter of the way above the eastern horizon, her oval shape shining pale as shell, and homing birds soared and swooped in the golden sky. Dierna lifted the cup in salutation.

"To Thee, Lady of Life and Death, I offer this cup, but it is I myself who am the offering. If my death is required, I am in Thy hand, but if Thou wilt, grant me instead a blessing—a vision of what is and what must be, and the wisdom to understand it. . . ."

There was always that uncertainty, for the difference between a dose of the potion that was effective and one that was fatal was small, affected by the state of the mushrooms, by the health of the one who drank, and, as she had been taught, by the will of the gods. With only a little hesitation she set the cup to her lips and drained it, grimacing at the taste, and set the empty vessel on the ground. Then she wrapped her mantle of pale, undyed wool around her and lay down on the long, grey altar stone.

Dierna took a deep breath and let it out slowly, counting, and relaxed each limb in turn until she felt herself melting into the cold stone. Above her, the circle of sky was dimming from the luminous violet of sunset to grey. She gazed upward, and saw, between one blink of the eye and the next, the twinkle of the first star.

In the next moment a ripple of light seemed to pass across the sky. Her breath caught; then she forced her breathing to steady, responses trained by years of practice suppressing the instinct to fight or flee. She had seen one young priestess driven to madness because she had not the strength of will to give herself to the tumult of the senses that racked the body as the spirit of the mushroom took hold and yet retain control of the soul.

Now the starlight was pulsing in rainbows. She felt a moment of vertigo as the heavens seemed to turn themselves inside out, took another breath, and directed her awareness inward to the point of light in the center of her skull. The universe spiraled around her in swirls of multicolored light, but the observing "self" continued to throb steadily within. Monstrous shapes loomed from the shadows, but she banished them as she had banished the intruding thoughts before.

And presently the tumult began to lessen, her vision to focus until she was once more aware of herself lying upon the stone, gazing up at the night sky. She watched the heavens with a sustained attention that no one in a normal state of consciousness could have endured.

Moonlight brightened the eastern sky, but Dierna gazed straight up into a starry vastness into which one could fall upward forever. She was not here for her own pleasure, however. With an inner sigh she began to trace out the great constellations that rule the skies. Mortal sight could distinguish only the stars themselves, scattered in apparent confusion across the sky. But Dierna's tranced spirit saw also the spectral shapes that gave the constellations their names.

High above, the Great Bear lumbered around the pole. As the night progressed, she would circle around to the west and drop toward the horizon again. The Bear was the heavenly analogue of the isles in the Vale of Avalon—observation of the other stars with which she shared the sky would tell Dierna what powers ruled the future that was coming into being now.

Her gaze moved southward to the constellation called the Eagle—was that, perhaps, the Eagle of Rome? It was bright, but not so radiant as the Dragon that coiled across the center of the sky. Nearby, the Virgin sat in untouched majesty. Dierna turned her head, searching for the steadier blaze of the wandering stars, and saw toward the northern edge of the western horizon the liquid shimmer of the Lady of Love, with the ruddy gleam of the war god's planet close beside her.

Another ripple of color glimmered across the heavens; Dierna's breath caught and she made herself breathe out again, knowing the herbs were taking her to a level where image and meaning were the same. Radiance flared from those two lights until she saw the god pursuing, the goddess radiant with surrender that was also a victory.

The key is love, she thought; *love will be the magic that binds the warrior to our cause. . . .* Her gaze, moving southward along the horizon, found the planet of the heavenly king. *But sovereignty sits in the south. . . .* She blinked, her vision filled suddenly with images of marble columns, gilded porticoes, processions, and people—more people than she had ever seen gathered together at one time. Was this Rome? Her gaze swung wider; she saw the golden Eagles leading the Legions toward a white temple where a small figure draped in purple waited to welcome them.

It was magnificent, but alien. How should such folk as these care for the concerns of Britannia, away off at the end of the Empire?

Let the Eagle take care of his own! It is the Dragon we must summon to ward his people, as he has done before. . . . And even as she thought it, the starry Dragon became a rainbow serpent that uncoiled northward across the sky.

That opalescent splendor was overwhelming, and Dierna was swept, despite her discipline, into a maelstrom of visions that she could neither halt nor control. Colors became clouds, driving across a storm-scoured sea. Wind howled, so that hearing was as taxed as vision. The currents of force that guided her spirit when she journeyed over land were lost in this confusion of energies; it took all her strength to master the terror of the deeps, to force herself to stop fighting the storm and seek the rhythms underlying its dissonant harmonies.

Upon the surface of the sea ships tossed, even more vulnerable to the fury of the elements than she, for they were made of wooden planks and hempen ropes and crewed by creatures of flesh and bone. Her spirit sped on a gust of wind toward the largest, where she saw men heaving at oars. Tossed and turned as they were, they knew not where to seek a sheltering shore. Among that crew one man only stood unflinching, legs braced, swaying as the deck lurched and rolled. He was of middle height, round-headed and barrel-chested with fair hair plastered now to his skull by the rain. But, like the others, he peered anxiously across the waves.

Dierna willed her spirit upward, extending spirit-senses into the storm. She saw jutting sea cliffs at whose feet waves frothed among toothed stones. But beyond them was slack water. Through veils of rain she glimpsed the pale curve of a beach and the glimmer of lights on the shore.

Moved at first only by compassion, she sought the commander. But as she drew closer, she sensed the strength in him, and a spirit that would never be daunted. Was he the leader she was looking for?

She began to draw on the raw energy of the storm, building up a spirit-shape that even mortal eyes could see. Swathed in white, it walked upon the sea. One of the sailors shouted; in a moment they were all looking that way. Dierna willed a ghostly arm to move, pointing toward the land. . . .

⊲ ⊲ ⊲

"There—can't you see? There it goes—" The lookout shouted from his place at the prow. "A white lady, walking on the waves!"

Wind struck the water with a mighty hand, sweeping the waves and the fragile ships that rode them before it. The Dubris squadron had scattered. Marcus Aurelius Musaeus Carausius, their Admiral, braced himself against the sternpost of the *Hercules* and dashed spray from his eyes, trying to see.

"Hold fast," came the voice of Aelius, who captained her. "Watch out for rocks, not froth on the sea!"

A swell as high as a house rose to starboard, smooth slope gleaming as the moon broke for a moment through the clouds. The deck of the liburnian tilted sharply, oars waving like the legs of an overturned beetle, but from the port side came the ominous crack of overstressed wood as oars, driven deeply into the water, caught and broke beneath the strain.

"Neptunus!" exclaimed the captain as the ship, shuddering, began to right herself once more. "Another gust like that and we'll be under."

Carausius nodded. They had not expected such a storm at this season. They had put out from Gesoriacum at dawn, expecting to cross the Channel at its narrowest point and make Dubris by nightfall. But they had not reckoned with this Hades-born gale. They were far to the west of where they should be, and only the gods could bring them safe to harbor now. The gods, or the spirit the steersman had seen. He peered at the sea. Was that a figure in white or a gleam of moonlight on the wave?

"Sir." A dark shape staggered down the walkway, and Carausius recognized the hortator, the hammer he used to set the beat till clutched in his hand. "We've six oars smashed and two men with broken arms who cannot row." The sailors were muttering, the note of panic sharpening their voices as spray sluiced over the benches.

"The gods have abandoned us!"

"No, they've sent us a guide!"

"Silence!" Carausius' voice cut through the babble. He looked at the captain. Command of the squadron was his, if any of his ships survived, but the *Hercules* belonged to Aelius. "Captain," he said softly, "the oars are no use in this sea, but we'll need a balanced pull when it calms." Aelius blinked; then understanding came into his eyes.

"Tell the foreman to shift men from the starboard benches to even the numbers, and run in the oars."

Carausius looked once more at the sea. And for a moment then he saw what the officer at the prow had seen, the shape of a woman wrapped in white. She looked anguished, and surely it was not for herself, for her feet barely touched the waves. With a desperate entreaty, her eyes met his, and she motioned westward. Then a rising wave seemed to crash through her, and the image disappeared.

The Admiral blinked. If this were not some figment born of moonlight, he had seen a spirit, but not one that was evil, surely. In life, as in a dice game, a time came when a man had to chance all on a single throw. "Tell your helmsman to steer to port until we're running before the wind."

"We'll go on the shoals if we do," said the captain.

"Maybe, though I think we're too far to the west for that danger. Even so, better to go aground than capsize, as we surely will if we're struck by another such swell." Carausius had been raised among the mud banks at the mouth of the Rhenus. The shoals of Belgica seemed friendly compared with this maddened sea.

The ship still bucked beneath him, but the change in course had brought a certain predictability to her motion. Now the waves, driven by the wind, were carrying her forward. Each time her prow slid downward he wondered if this time they would go under, but before they could founder the next wave would bring the ship up again, with seawater cascading from the figurehead and the weathered bronze of the ram beneath it like a waterfall.

"Steer to port a little farther," he told the helmsman. The gods alone knew where they might be, but that glimpse of the moon had reoriented him to the directions, and if the apparition had not lied, they would find safety somewhere on the British shore.

The pitching grew a little less as they began to cut across the swells, though now and again a freak wave, cutting crosswise from the others, would break across the side. Half the sailors were bailing already. The ship would need the strength of her namesake to survive until dawn.

But, oddly enough, Carausius no longer felt afraid. When he was a child, an old wisewoman of his own people in the delta of the Rhenus had cast the sticks for him and pronounced him destined for greatness. To serve as admiral of a squadron had seemed achievement enough for a lad of the Menapii, who were one of the smaller German tribes. But if this vision brought them to safety, the implications could not be denied. Men whose birth was no better than his had risen to the purple, though never by command on the sea.

The Admiral stared over the waves. *Who are you? What do you want of me?* his spirit cried. But the white lady had disappeared. He saw only the wave crests, flattening at last as the storm passed them by.

◁ ◁ ◁

Dierna returned to knowledge of herself a little before dawn. The moon had set, and heavy clouds were coming in from the southeast, blotting out the stars. The storm! She had not dreamed it, then. The storm was real and it was coming to challenge the land. A damp wind stirred her hair, and muscles grown stiff with stillness complained. Dierna shivered, feeling very much alone. But before she spoke to any other, she had to bring from the depths of her vision the images that must guide her decisions in the months to come. The movements of the stars she remembered clearly. But of her final vision there were only fragments—there had been a ship, tossing upon a wind-whipped sea, and there had been a man. . . .

She turned to face the oncoming storm and lifted her hands.

"Goddess, keep him safe, whoever he may be," she whispered in invocation.

⊲ ⊲ ⊲

The sun was just beginning to spark through the clouds above the Channel, glinting from brown puddles ashore and the grey waves of the sea, when a fisher lad of Clausentum, watching for the driftwood tossed up by the storm, stiffened and stared past the dim bulk of the Isle of Vectis toward the sea.

"A sail!" His cry was taken up by others. Folk gathered, pointing across the waves, where a square of salt-stained canvas grew steadily larger. Even ashore they had felt the strength of last night's wind. How could any ship have lived in that sea?

"A liburnian," said one, seeing the two men who sat at each oar.

"With an admiral aboard!" exclaimed another as a pennon went fluttering up the mast.

"By the tits of Amphitrite, that's *Hercules!*" cried a trader, a big man who never let the rest of them forget that he was a naval twenty-year man. "I served as her helmsman the last two seasons out of Dubris before my enlistment ended. Carausius himself must be on board!"

"The one who outfought those two pirate keels a month ago?"

"The one who cares as much for keeping coin in our purses as for lining his own! I vow a lamb to whatever god has saved him," breathed the trader. "His loss would have hurt us indeed!"

Slowly, the liburnian came about and began to beat around the bend of the Ictis, toward the wharves of Clausentum.

Traders and fisherfolk streamed down to the shore, and the folk of the village, awakened by the shouting, came after them.

The *Hercules* stayed run up on shore for most of a week, while the carpenters swarmed about her, healing her wounds. Clausentum was a busy port; and if repairs were not up to fleet standard, nonetheless her artisans knew their trade. Carausius took advantage of the opportunity to confer with the magistrates and whatever traders were in port at the time, seeking to find a pattern in the pirates' raids. But it was noted that when he was not needed elsewhere he spent much of his time walking alone on the shore, and no man dared to ask him why he frowned.

Just before Midsummer, Carausius and the newly repaired *Hercules* set out, heading once more for Gesoriacum.

This time, the sea was as calm as glass.

☙ ☙ ☙

In Avalon, the rituals of Midsummer were ancient; these customs had been old when the Druids first came to these lands. At the base of the Tor cattle lowed, scenting the fire the Druids had built for their blessing. Teleri was glad she had been assigned to sing with the other maidens around the other fire, the holy flame that had been kindled atop the hill.

She smoothed her white gown, admiring the grace with which Dierna cast incense on the flames. Everything the High Priestess did had such certainty—perhaps the word she wanted was "authority"— it came, she supposed, from a lifetime of practice. She herself had come so late to the service of the Mysteries, she found it hard to believe that she would ever be able to move so that everything she did seemed part of a spell.

Below, the cattle were being driven between the fires while the people cried out to the gods for blessings. Above, the litany was a recognition that all things, both light and darkness, must pass. The full moon waned and was swallowed by the night, only to be reborn as a sliver of light. The cycle of the sun took longer, but she knew that this moment, the longest day, was the beginning of its decline. And yet in the midst of midwinter's darkness the sun would be reborn.

What else, she wondered then, followed this round? The Empire of the Romans covered half the earth. Many times it had been threatened, and always the Eagles had returned in even greater power. Was there a moment when Rome would reach the fullness of her power and begin to decline? And would her people recognize that moment when it came?

Dierna stepped back from the fire, bowing to Ceridachos, eldest of the Druids and Arch-Druid of Britannia, to begin the ritual. It was noon of the longest day, when the power of light was at its fullest, and it was right and proper that the priests should lead this ceremony. When darkness fell, the priestesses would come into their own. The old man gestured, wide sleeves fluttering.

"What existed in the beginning? Try to imagine—an emptiness, a gaping nothing? A teeming womb, pregnant with the world? If you can imagine it, already it existed in potential, and yet it was like nothing you can imagine, for it was the Force, it was the Void. It Was, it was Not. . . . An eternal, changeless Unity . . ."

He paused, and Teleri closed her eyes, swaying at the thought of that immensity. The Druid spoke again, and now his voice had the ring of incantation.

"But there came a moment of difference—a vibration stirred in stillness—

*"An indrawn breath in a silent shout,
And that which was contained flares out—
Divine Darkness and Supernal Light,
Time and Space appear in might,
Lord and Lady, Holy Pair—
Sisters, Brothers, call them here!"*

"We call Him Lugos!" cried the Druids. "Lord of Light!" Behind them, the younger men began to hum.

"We call Her Rigantona, Great Queen!" the priestesses replied from across the circle. Teleri opened her throat to support them with a note that was a third higher than the one the Druids sang.

More names followed. Teleri heard them as bursts of illumination, dazzling the senses. She sensed power building around the priests who stood on the other side of the altar stone, and felt an answering energy gathering among the priestesses.

Once more Dierna stepped forth, lifting her hands. As she spoke, Teleri felt the words resonating in her own throat, and knew the High Priestess spoke for them all.

"I am the Sea of Space and Primal Night,
I am the womb of Darkness and of Light;
I am the formless flux, eternal rest,
Matrix from which all matter manifests;
I am the Cosmic Mother, the Great Deep,
Whence life emerges and returns to sleep. . . ."

Ceridachos stepped forward to stand facing her, on the other side of the altar stone. Teleri blinked, for in the face of the old man she saw now a youth and a warrior, a father and a healer, radiant with power. And when he answered the priestess, she heard a multitude of voices resonating with his own.

"I am the Wind of Time, eternal Day,
I am the staff of life, I am the Way;
I am the Word of Power, the primal spark,
Igniting act and motion in its arc;
I am the Cosmic Father, radiant rod,
Source of energy, the seed of God!"

Dierna held out her hand above the kindling that had been laid upon the altar stone. "From my womb—"

"By my will—" said the Druid, reaching out so their hands were not quite touching. Teleri blinked, seeing a shimmer in the air between their palms.

"The Light of Life appears!" Priest and priestess spoke in unison, and the intricately crossed sticks burst suddenly into flame.

"So burns the Holy Fire!" cried the Druid. "Now is the triumph of the light—in this moment we claim its power. By the union of our forces we shall keep that light burning through the darkest hours, and so we shall have victory."

"This fire shall be a beacon, a light to be seen throughout the lands," said Dierna. "Let it summon to us a Defender, to keep Britannia in peace and safety!" From the fire she plucked a flaming brand.

"Let it be so!" responded the priest. He too took a burning stick and held it high.

One by one the Druids and priestesses took sticks from the fire, extending their lines to either side until the central blaze was surrounded by a circle of flame, as if the sun which blazed in glory overhead had sent down his rays to inflame those who stood below.

Teleri, gazing upward, shaded her eyes against the radiance of the sky. Then she rubbed them, for a black speck was moving across the blue. Others had seen it—they pointed, then fell silent in wonder as they realized it was an eagle, beating steadily up from the south and the sea. Closer and closer it drew, until she could see it clearly, as if the bird were being drawn by the flames.

Now it was overhead. The eagle dropped downward, circled three times above the altar, and then once more ascended, spiraling upward into the heavens until it became one with the light.

Blinded, Teleri shut her eyes, but behind her lids the image of the great bird still danced against the blaze of the sun. The eagle flew free—why did she feel as if it had escaped the compulsion of the fire only to be trapped by the sun? It must be her own fancy that made her think so, she told herself as she followed the other maidens down from the Tor, for if the freedom of the wild eagle of the heights was an illusion, what could be truly free?

For a moment then a memory from before this lifetime hinted at the paradox of a freedom that could exist only as part of a greater pattern, but the mind that knew itself as Teleri could not comprehend it, and, like the eagle, in another moment the insight had disappeared.

Chapter Eleven

"It is good to see you—we had almost given you up after that storm." Maximian Augustus looked up from his wax tablets and smiled.

Carausius stiffened to attention, his forearm slapping across his chest in salute. He had not expected to find the junior Emperor in Gesoriacum. Throughout the West, Maximian, stocky and grizzled and beginning to thicken in the belly, carried the imperium. Almost twenty years of service had conditioned Carausius to respond as if Diocletian himself were in the room.

"The gods favored me," he answered. "One of my ships was lost, but the other managed to return to Dubris. I myself was blown down-Channel and lucky to make Clausentum before I went onto the rocks or out to sea."

"You were indeed. But the gods love a man who will fight even when hope seems gone. You have luck, Carausius, and that is rarer even than skill. We would have been sorry to lose you."

Maximian waved at him to sit, and the other, younger man in the room relaxed as well. A glance was enough to identify him as regular Army—the erect posture, as if he were wearing an invisible breastplate over his tunic, was unmistakable. He was half a head taller than Carausius himself, with yellow hair that was beginning to thin.

"You know Constantius Chlorus, I assume?" the Emperor went on.

"Only by reputation," said Carausius.

Constantius had been popular when he served in Britannia.

Rumor had it that he had taken a native woman as his permanent concubine. Since then he had won several notable engagements on the German border. Carausius looked at the other man more carefully as Constantius smiled, his face for a moment open and unguarded as a boy's. Then the control snapped down again. *An idealist,* thought Carausius, *who has learned to hide his soul.* Such men could be useful friends—or dangerous enemies.

And how did he himself appear? With hair faded by years at sea, and skin weathered to brown, he supposed he must seem no different from many another sea-dog, unless some reflection of the vision he had seen during the storm still lingered in his eyes.

"You'll be happy to know that the cargoes from those raiders you captured last month have brought a good sum," said Maximian. "You keep telling me that we need another base on the southern coast. . . . A few more victories like this one will win the funds you need."

There was an odd expectance in his smile. Carausius frowned, aware of something strange in the wording. The gods knew he had argued for this long enough, but he had had little hope of being heard.

"Who will command it?" he asked carefully.

"Whom would you recommend?" said the Emperor. "The choice will be yours, Carausius—I'm giving you the Britannic fleet and the forts of the Saxon Shore."

He must have blinked then, for even Constantius began to grin. But Carausius scarcely saw him; abruptly his vision was filled by the image of the woman in white, walking upon the waves.

"Now, we will need to coordinate your dispositions on both sides of the Channel," Maximian said briskly. "What forces would you like, and how would you allot them? I can't promise you everything you ask for, but I will try—"

Carausius took a deep breath, forcing himself to focus on the man before him.

"First of all, we need the new base. There's a good harbor that could be fortified on the coast below Clausentum. The Island of

Vectis shelters it, and it could be supplied from Venta Belgarum." As he spoke, the image of the woman faded, to be replaced by dreams that had come as he paced the deck of a liburnian on the long Channel crossings.

⊲ ⊲ ⊲

Teleri had not wanted to leave Avalon. When Dierna had chosen her shortly after Midsummer as part of her escort for this journey, she had protested. But by the time their journey brought them to Venta Belgarum, she could no longer pretend a lack of interest. The old capital of the Belgae lay in a gentle valley with green water-meadows and noble stands of trees. After the marshes around the Tor, she found the rich earth beneath her feet solid and reassuring. There was a feeling of quiet assurance here, of permanence different in quality from the ancient echoes she sensed in Avalon, as if things had rarely changed. Despite the market-day bustle in the town, she found Venta relaxing.

The priestesses had been offered hospitality by the Duovir Quintus Julius Cerialis, most prominent of the local magistrates, who was in fact a descendant of the old royal house. Not that one would have known it by looking at him. Portly and complacent, Cerialis was more Roman than the Romans. He spoke Latin by preference, and Teleri, who had been brought up to speak it as well as the British tongue, was often asked to translate for the younger of the priestesses who had come with them, Adwen and Crida. Even Dierna sometimes requested her assistance, for, although the High Priestess understood the language of the Romans well, her command of its subtleties was not always sufficient for really formal occasions.

And yet the others could have managed without her. Certainly all the girls they were considering for training were fluent in British. At times, Teleri still found herself wondering why, before she had even taken her vows, she had been wrested from the peace of Avalon.

The weather continued fair and bright. This year would bring a good harvest of hay and grain, despite the earlier storms. Clearly, as Cerialis was fond of observing, the gods and goddesses were being kind. But the sheltering hills around Venta cut off the wind, and as the season grew warmer Teleri longed for the refreshing sea-breezes of Durnovaria. When Dierna announced that they were to go down to the coast for the groundbreaking rites of the new naval fortress, she was glad.

But this was more than a pleasant trip to the seaside. When some of the women questioned why the High Priestess should want to bless a Roman fort, Dierna reminded them of the eagle that had appeared at their Midsummer rite. "Once we were enemies, but our safety depends on the Romans now," she had told them, and Teleri, remembering the Saxons, agreed with her.

◁ ◁ ◁

"Ah, there's a breeze coming now!" exclaimed Cerialis. "That will cool your rosy cheeks, my dears!"

Teleri sighed. Despite his broad hat, Cerialis' face was flushed with heat. Perhaps the wind would cool him off as well.

As the road curved, she glimpsed blue water through the trees. The road, a new one, ran a little in from the shore southeastward from Clausentum, where they had stayed the night before. A good rider could have made the journey from Venta in a day, but Cerialis obviously believed that ladies needed pampering.

"Do you think this new fortress will discourage the Saxons?" She braced herself against the sway of the horse litter and looked up at him.

"Surely, surely!" He nodded emphatically. "Every wall and every ship are a message to those sea scum that Britannia stands fast." He straightened in the saddle, and for a moment she thought he was going to salute.

"I disagree," said his son Allectus, bringing his mare up beside them. "It is the soldiers and sailors who man them that will make the difference, father. Without men, ships are only rotting wood, and walls are only moldering stones."

The son was her own age or a little younger, thought Teleri, as angular and tense as his father was plump and placid, with a narrow face and intense dark eyes. He had the look of someone who has been ill a great deal in childhood. Perhaps that was why he had not gone into the Army himself.

"True—of course that is true—" Cerialis cast an uneasy glance at the boy.

Teleri suppressed a smile. The Duovir was a good man of business, but rumor had it that his son, though delicate in body, was something of a wizard with figures. It was his brilliance that had advanced the family fortunes sufficiently to fund the public works and entertainments a magistrate was expected to sponsor, and Cerialis knew it. Allectus was a cuckoo in the nest of a fat pigeon, or maybe something nobler, a sparrow hawk, she thought, eyeing the sharp profile. In any case, it was clear that the older man did not understand his son at all.

"Well, this new Admiral has persuaded the emperors to strengthen our defenses," she said brightly. "Surely that is a sign that this man, at least, is worthy of our trust."

"It is so. Unless the leaders are worthy, even the best of men will fail." Cerialis nodded sententiously.

In Allectus' glance she saw scorn, so swiftly hidden she could scarcely be sure it had been there.

"Or women," she said dryly. She doubted that the Roman Army, for all its tradition and discipline, could match the testing imposed on the priestesses of Avalon. Her gaze moved forward, where Dierna rode in another horse litter with little Adwen. She suppressed her envy, knowing it unworthy. Perhaps, she thought, the High Priestess would ask her to ride with her on the return.

The litter tilted as they descended toward the shore. Teleri sat up when they emerged from beneath the trees, looking around her. Certainly the new Admiral had a good eye for country. The ground that had been cleared for the fort lay at the northwestern corner of a fair-size harbor connected by a narrow channel to the sea. The site offered equal protection from storms and from pirates, though it was hard to believe in either on such a sparkling summer day.

Clearly it was going to be a noble fortress. Foundation trenches had been dug for the walls in a square several acres in extent, to be punctuated by U-shaped bastions. This was larger, Cerialis took care to inform them, than any of the other shore forts, even Rutupiae. As they drew closer, he surveyed the laborers with proprietary pride. Teleri had understood that such installations were always constructed by the military, but she could see that some of the men doing the digging were dressed differently.

"You are wise to notice that, very wise," said Cerialis, following her gaze. "They are slaves from my own estates, sent down to assist in the building. It seemed to me that a fortress to protect Venta would be a more useful tribute to my magistracy than a new amphitheatre for the town."

The curl of Allectus' thin lips was not quite a smile. Did he disapprove? No, thought Teleri, remembering how he had spoken before. More likely, it was he who had planted the idea in his father's mind.

"It was an excellent plan, and I am sure that this new commander will appreciate the assistance," she said warmly, and saw a faint betraying color stain the younger man's sallow cheeks.

But his eyes were fixed on the builders. Several men walked up and down, supervising the digging. Where, Teleri wondered, was the Admiral? She saw Dierna sit up suddenly, shading her eyes with her hand. Allectus had reined in, a tension in him like a good hunting dog. Teleri followed his gaze. One of the officers, elegant in a red tunic and a belt with plaques of gilded bronze, was coming toward them, followed by a sturdy, square-built man in a sleeveless sailor's tunic, faded by sun and salt till its original color could not be told.

Allectus slid down from his horse's back to greet them. But it was the second man whom he saluted. Teleri's eyes widened. Was this man, his fair hair stiffened by perspiration and the skin of his high brow reddened by the sun, the hero about whom they had been hearing such tales? He came forward with the rolling gait of a man who has spent much time at sea, and as he drew closer, she noted how his gaze swept from the water to the woods to the newcomers and back again even as he smiled. It reminded her, oddly, of the way Dierna surveyed the assembled priestesses before they began a ceremony.

Dierna herself was watching Carausius with a strange look, almost of approval, in her eyes. As the Roman came up to clasp arms with Allectus, his gaze swept once more over the horse litters, and as he looked at the High Priestess, Teleri saw his eyes widen in turn. Then the moment was lost in a babble of introductions. When she thought about it afterward, it seemed to the girl that the look had been one of recognition. But that must be only a fancy, for Dierna had said herself that she had never met Carausius before.

Beyond the low arm of land that protected the harbor the sun was setting. Carausius stood before the foundations of his fortress with his officers, watching the priestesses prepare for their ritual. The legionaries had been drawn up in formation before what would one day be the gate, with the native workers spreading out to either side behind them.

A moon before, when they began the digging, a priest had come down from the temple of Jupiter Fides at Venta Belgarum and sacrificed an ox, while a haruspex read the auspices. They had been encouraging—but in truth he could not recall a time, once the plans were all made and the funds committed, when a haruspex had not managed to find a favorable meaning in the entrails of the beast he had slain.

"For a thousand years and twice a thousand shall these foundations remain to praise the name of Rome in this land. . . ."

An excellent prophecy, thought Carausius. And yet the priest, a brisk, rotund fellow whose cook was the best in Venta, had not been very inspiring. Looking at the blue-robed priestesses, Carausius understood why he had felt the Roman ceremony was not enough, and why, when he had heard that the Lady of Avalon was in the area, he had requested her to come. The fortress of Adurni was Roman, but the land it was intended to protect was Britannia.

He had stood, sweating in his toga beneath the sun of noontide, throughout the Roman ritual. Tonight he wore a linen tunic dyed crimson, with native needlework around the borders, and a light woolen mantle held by a golden brooch pin. The gear was similar enough to the native dress of his own people in the fens of Germania to bring back memories of a past he had renounced when he swore to serve Rome. His father's people had made their offerings to Nehallenia. What goddess, he wondered, did they pray to here?

Brightness flared in the west. The Admiral turned in time to see the edge of the sun showing for a moment like a rim of molten metal above the curve of the hill. As it disappeared, a lesser radiance caught his eye. One of the women had kindled the torches. She lifted them, and for a moment he saw her standing like a goddess with her hands full of light. Then he blinked, and realized it was the youngest of the priestesses, the daughter, they said, of some local king. He had thought her aloof and cold, but now, with the firelight gleaming on her dark hair and her pale skin aglow, she was beautiful.

The High Priestess, her features a mystery behind her veil, fell in behind her, followed by the other two, one carrying a branch of rowan and the other a wand of apple wood hung with chiming silver bells.

"It is now the hour between day and night, when we may walk between the worlds," came the voice of the Lady Dierna from behind her veil. "The walls you will build here will be made from stone, strong to repel the weapons of men. But we, as we walk, will make another kind of barrier, a shield of the spirit that shall defeat the spirits of your enemies. Bear witness, you who serve Britannia and Rome!"

"I am your witness," said Carausius.

"And I," came the lighter voice of Allectus, behind him.

"And I," Cerialis said solemnly.

Dierna accepted their commitment with a little inclination of the head. Just so, thought Carausius, an empress might acknowledge a service. He supposed that the High Priestess of Avalon must be the equal of an empress, in her own sphere. Was she indeed the woman of his vision? And if so, did she recognize him as well? Her manner to him had been strange; he could not tell if she liked him, or accepted him only by virtue of his position.

But already the priestesses were beginning their circumambulation, turning to the right. Ever more faintly he heard the shimmer of the silver bells.

"How long must we stand here?" asked Cerialis after a time. The priestesses had reached the near left-hand corner and paused to make offerings to the spirits of the land. "I do not know why she wanted our witness. There is nothing to see."

"Nothing?" whispered Allectus in a shaking voice. "Cannot you feel it? They are singing up a wall of power. Can you not see the shimmer in the air where they pass?"

Cerialis coughed, casting an embarrassed glance at the Admiral as if to say, *He is only a boy, and full of fancies.* But Carausius had seen the Lady of Avalon walking upon the waves. He saw nothing now, but it seemed to him that some other sense was corroborating Allectus' words.

They waited while the priestesses continued their sunwise progress around to the far end of the rectangle and then came toward them once more. The long twilight of the north drew on, and the colors of the sunset deepened from gold to rose, and from rose to an imperial purple, as if an emperor's mantle had been drawn across the sky. The procession saluted the near right-hand corner, then moved toward the space where the main gate would one day be.

"Come, you who would hold this place against our enemies!" the Lady cried. For a moment Carausius did not understand. Then he realized she was pointing at him, and started forward. He came to a halt before her. Her face was hidden, but he could feel the intensity of her gaze.

"What will you give, man of the sea, to keep the folk of this land in safety?" Her voice was soft, but it held a weight of meaning that disturbed him.

"I have given my oath to defend the Empire," he began, but she shook her head.

"This is not a matter for the will, but for the heart," she said softly. "Will you shed your heart's blood, if need be, to preserve this land?"

This land . . . , he thought. In the years since he had been assigned to the Channel fleet, he supposed, Britannia had won his affection, as a soldier will become fond of any post at which he is stationed for long. But that was not what she was asking of him.

"I was born in a land across the sea, and blessed at my birth in the name of its gods . . ." he said softly.

"But you have crossed that sea, and been given your life again by the power of the Goddess I serve," Dierna replied. "Do you remember?"

He stared at her features, seen dimly through the veil as once he had seen them through the storm. "It *was* you!"

She nodded gravely. "And now I claim the price for saving you. Your blood will bind you to this soil. Hold out your arm."

In her voice was utter certainty, and he, who with one word could send the entire Britannic fleet to sea, obeyed.

Torchlight glinted from the small sickle in her hand. Before he could question, she drew the sharp point across the softer skin inside his arm. He bit his lip at the sting and watched as the dark blood welled from the cut and began to drip onto the ground.

"You feed this earth as she has fed you," whispered the Lady. "Blood to blood, soul to soul. As you are bound to guard, she is bound to provide, linked by service and destiny. . . ." She looked up at him suddenly, and her voice shook as she went on. "Do you not remember? Your body was bred by the Menapian tribe, who dwell across the sea, but your soul is much older. *You have done this before!*"

Carausius shivered and looked down at the dark spots where his blood had fed the earth. Surely he had seen that before. . . . He took a deep breath, abruptly noticing how the scent of the woods, released by the cooling air, mingled with the scent of the sea. A flicker of vision showed him a high hill crowned with standing stones. Enemies were all around him, Roman soldiers. Blood from his wounds spattered the earth as he swung a shining sword. . . .

Then one of the torches crackled and his consciousness was wrenched back to the present. But he understood now that what he felt for Britannia was something more than dutiful affection. He would defend her now not only out of ambition, but for love.

Dierna motioned to the youngest priestess, the one they called Teleri, who handed her torches to the others. She wiped his arm with a cloth that had been thrust through her belt, her face grave and intent, then bound the wound with a strip of white linen.

The High Priestess drew a sigil above the place where his blood had soaked into the ground. "To those who come in peace, this way shall be ever open," she chanted, "and ever defended against those who come in war!" She turned to face the east, lifting her arms, and as if in answer, the moon rose over the harbor like a silver shield.

⊲ ⊲ ⊲

The next day, Cerialis invited the Roman officers to a feast on the shore. Dierna was standing beneath an oak tree, watching his servants set up tables and benches, when the Roman guests arrived. Carausius had dressed to do their host honor in a white military tunic banded with red, his belt and sandals of red-dyed leather ornamented with gilded relief plaques and tags. Today he was instantly identifiable as a Roman commander. But last night, when they blessed the foundations of his fortress, he had looked like a king. . . .

What, she wondered, had that ceremony meant to him? He had not expected her summons, but he had answered it. Indeed, she had not intended to bind him. But when they came to the gateway, the image of the man on the ship and the man who stood watching from the hill had become one, and she had known that it was not stone and mortar that would protect her land, but the blood of those who were sworn to defend it. And now the land knew him, and the gods, but did he himself understand?

Something more was needed, something to make him *want* to do the duty to which he had been bound. Her night had been haunted by dreams of sacred kings and royal weddings. An image surfaced suddenly of torches against a night sky, and an idea came—*Teleri may not like it*, she thought then, *but it will serve*. She did not think to wonder how she herself would feel, seeing the girl as Carausius' bride.

One of Cerialis' slaves offered her a basket of berries, to take the edge from her appetite until the feast was served. Nodding, she took one, then touched the boy's sleeve.

"If there is a time yet to wait, I will walk upon the shore. Go to the Roman Commander and ask if he will escort me."

As Dierna watched the lad make his way toward the Romans, she reflected that she had not planned this either. But surely this impulse was not her own. Since her vision just before Midsummer, the gods had been leading her; if she opened her spirit to hear them, she must believe that she would be doing their will, not her own.

There was nothing wrong with the Admiral's manners. He maintained a correct distance between them as they walked slowly toward the water's edge, not quite touching, but close enough to steady her if she should stumble on the smooth stones. But his eyes were as wary as if he were steering toward some enemy.

"You are wondering what you have gotten into. And you do not trust me," she said quietly. "It is often so after such a moment. When the excitement fades, doubt creeps in. The morning after my initiation, I wanted to run away from Avalon. Do not fear, nothing was done that affects your honor."

He raised one eyebrow, and for a moment the hard crags and planes of his face softened. She noted the change with an odd flicker of emotion. *I would like to see him laugh*, she thought.

"It depends on what, exactly, I have sworn to—"

"To defend Britannia, even to death—" she began, but he shook his head.

"That was already my duty. This was something more. Did you work magic to compel me?"

They paced another few steps while Dierna considered. That he should be aware of the power the rite had raised was a good sign, but it meant she must be careful about what she said to him.

"I am no hedge-witch, but a priestess of the Great Goddess, and it would go against my own oaths to bind your will.... And yet I believe that you have been bound. By the gods themselves," she went on, "before we ever met in the flesh."

"When I saw you through the storm?" Carausius answered. Once more his face changed, not to laughter but to something deeper, almost dread. And once more Dierna felt that odd pang, sharper now, like a blade in her heart. In the ritual she had seen his face overlaid by that of another man, younger, with Roman features and hair. She knew that in that lifetime he had been a sacred king. *But who had she herself been, in that other life so long ago?*

"How could a living woman walk upon the waves?"

"My body lay in trance—it was my spirit-shape that you saw, enabled to journey by disciplines that are the Mysteries of Avalon."

"Druid lore?" he asked suspiciously.

"Wisdom that the Druids preserved, taught to them by those who came before, from the Drowned Lands across the sea. What remains of that knowledge is preserved by my sacred sisterhood. There is still power in Avalon," she added, "power that could be of great help to you in defending this land. With our help you could know immediately when the raiders strike, and sail to meet them when they turn for home."

"And how will that help come?" His lips twisted ruefully. "My duties will take me up and down this coast and back and forth across the sea. You cannot spend all your time in spirit form, advising me!"

"It is true that in my own world I have duties that are as demanding as your own. But if one of my people were with you, she could help in some things and, when greater effort was needed, speak in the spirit with me. What I propose is an alliance, and to seal it I will give you one of my priestesses."

Carausius shook his head. "The Army would not allow me to keep a woman in any official—"

"She will be your wife," Dierna interrupted. "You are not married, I have been told."

He blinked, and she saw his sun-reddened skin darken with quick color. "I am a serving officer . . ." he said, a little helplessly. "Whom did you have in mind for me?"

Inwardly Dierna sighed with relief. "You are no longer accustomed to being commanded," she said, smiling at him, "and think me very autocratic, I know. But it is your welfare I am thinking of as well as the service of this land. Teleri is the maiden I would give you, the daughter of Eiddin Mynoc. Her birth is high enough so that it will be considered a worthy alliance, and she is beautiful."

"The one who bore the torches in last night's ritual?" he asked. "She is fair indeed, but I have scarcely spoken two words to her."

Dierna shook her head. "I will not compel her into this alliance unwilling. When I have her consent I will speak to her father, and the world will think this has been arranged between you and him in the usual way."

Teleri might regret leaving Avalon, thought the priestess, but she must surely appreciate the opportunity to become the consort of a man of such proven power. Dierna surveyed the Admiral's broad shoulders and strong, clever hands with an involuntary quickening of the pulse, and for a moment wished she could have come to him at the Beltane fires.

But Teleri was younger, and more beautiful. She herself would do her duty in Avalon, and Carausius would be happy with Teleri in his arms.

The sky was beginning to cloud over. Teleri wiped her brow with her veil and took a deep breath of the muggy air. The motion of the horse litter that was carrying them along the rough track back to Venta Belgarum made her a little queasy, and the weather was not helping. It would only get worse, she knew, until the tension was released in rain.

At least on the way back she was riding with Dierna. She glanced at the older woman, who sat in balanced stillness, eyes closed as if she were meditating. When they left Portus Adurni, she had rejoiced, for they were on their way to Avalon. But the longer Dierna remained silent, the more tense Teleri grew.

Halfway to Clausentum, they detoured around a gang of soldiers who were leveling the roadbed and laying stones. From there on, the road was graveled and they traveled more smoothly. As if the change in motion had awakened her, the High Priestess stirred at last.

Teleri started to speak, but Dierna's words came first.

"You have been with us for over two years in Avalon. Soon you will be eligible to take your vows. Have you been happy there?"

Teleri stared at her. "Happy?" she managed finally. "Avalon is my heart's home. I was never happy anywhere, I think, until I came to you!" To be sure, she had sometimes chafed at the discipline, but it was far better than being caged in her father's hall.

Dierna nodded, but there was a bleak look in her eyes.

"I have studied as hard as I could," Teleri said then. "Are the priestesses not pleased with me?"

The other woman's grim look softened. "They are. You have done very well." There was a pause, then: "When we blessed the fortress, what did you see?"

For a moment Teleri gaped. Then she forced her mind back to the torchlit field and the stars.

"I think we raised power. My skin tingled. . . ." She looked at the older woman uncertainly.

"And the Roman Commander, Carausius—what did you think of him?"

"He seems strong . . . competent . . . and I suppose kindly," she said slowly. "I was surprised when you took his blood for the blessing."

"So was he." For a moment Dierna smiled. "Before Midsummer, when I went apart to seek visions, I saw him." Teleri felt her eyes widening as the priestess told her the tale. "He is the Eagle who will save us, the Chosen Defender," Dierna said finally. "I have offered him alliance with Avalon."

Teleri frowned. Carausius had not seemed to her to be the stuff of heroes, and to her he seemed old. But Dierna was continuing.

"The Goddess has given us this opportunity, and this man, who though not of our blood, is an ancient soul. But he is barely awakened. He needs a companion to remind him, and to be his contact with Avalon. . . ."

Teleri felt her former queasiness focus suddenly in her gut. Dierna reached over and took her hand. "It has happened before that a maiden trained in Avalon has been given to a king or a war-leader to bind him to the Mysteries. When I was a girl, Eilan, a princess of the Demetae who was called in the Roman tongue Helena, was given to Constantius Chlorus. But he was transferred out of Britannia. Now the need for such an alliance has come again."

Teleri swallowed, and whispered, "Why are you saying this to *me?*"

"Because you are the fairest and most gifted of our maidens yet unsworn, and you are of high birth, which the Romans will honor. It is you who must go with Carausius as his bride."

Teleri jerked away, the very thought of lying with a man bringing back memories of the Saxon's hard hands holding her down. Then nausea overwhelmed her and she grabbed for the side of the litter, pushing the curtains aside. She heard Dierna calling to the slaves to halt the horses. Gradually her emptied belly calmed and the world came into focus once more.

"Get down," came the calm voice of the priestess. "There is a stream here where you can wash and drink. You will feel better then."

Teleri allowed the slaves to help her descend from the horse litter, flushing with embarrassment as she felt the curious gaze of the other priestesses, and from Allectus, who was leading their escort, concern.

"There, now you will be well," said Dierna presently.

Teleri wiped her mouth and sat up. The water had revived her, and it was true that she felt better on solid ground. Indeed, she saw the gathering clouds, and the crimson of poppies growing in the grass, and the glitter of the stream with unusual clarity. A breath of wind stirred the damp hair on her brow.

"What you said," she whispered. "I cannot do it. I chose Avalon because I wanted to serve the Goddess. And you yourself know better than any why I cannot give myself to a man." Dierna could not know what she asked, to make her go into such bondage. A wife was a slave, and she did not even know this man!

Dierna sighed. "When they chose me as high priestess, I tried to run away. I was pregnant with my first child, and I knew that if this fate came upon me I would never be her mother—not really—for my first care would always have to be the good of Avalon. All one night I lay out in the marshes, weeping, while the mists swirled around me. And after a time it came to me that there were others who could care for my children, but there was indeed at that time no other who could take up the burdens of the Lady of Avalon. I mourned for the simple happiness I would not be allowed to enjoy, but still more I feared the guilt, greater than what I felt at not being able to give all my love to my child, that would weight me if I denied this duty. I think death might be kinder than what I felt then.

"But just before the sun rose, when I had no more tears, a warmth surrounded me, like a mother's arms. In that moment I knew that my child would have all the love she needed, because the Goddess would watch over her, and that I need not fear to fail those who depended on me, because She would work through me as well.

"That is why I can ask you to do this, Teleri, knowing how hard it will be. When we swear the vows of Avalon we promise to serve the Lady according to Her will, not our own. Do you not think I would rather have had you by my side always, growing in beauty like the young apple tree?" Dierna reached out once more, and this time Teleri did not shrink away. "The omens have been too clear to deny. Britannia needs this man, but he is too enmeshed in this life to remember the wisdom of his soul. You must be the Goddess to him, my dear, and awaken him!"

Dierna's voice caught. Teleri looked at her and understood that the older woman did indeed care for her.

"The Lady is cruel, to use us so!" she exclaimed. But in her heart she was crying out, *Don't you love me enough to keep me by you? Don't you see how much I want to stay?*

"She does what She must, for the good of all . . ." whispered the priestess, "and to serve Her we must do the same."

Teleri reached out then, and touched the older woman's bright hair, and Dierna gathered her into her arms.

After a time, Teleri felt moisture on her cheeks, and did not know if it was the Lady Herself, weeping in the skies, or her own tears.

Chapter Twelve

The grain had been gathered into shocks and the hay into mows. The peace of harvest lay across the land. The fields beyond the Vale of Avalon were checkered with gold. It was a good omen, Dierna told herself as the mists closed behind them. Marriages were usually performed in the spring or early summer, but surely it would be better for Carausius to take his bride when the beginning of winter put an end to the raiding season, and he would have time to know her before he must go away to fight once more. And if she herself felt weary, it was because for the past two moons she had been so furiously busy preparing Teleri for her wedding.

No doubt that was why Teleri herself looked so pale. As they climbed into the covered cart Eiddin Mynoc had sent to carry them to Durnovaria, Dierna gave the younger woman a reassuring pat. The girl had worked as hard as any, completing her training, and learning to look into the water and see visions there.

It was easiest, of course, in the sacred pool, but a silver basin would do as well, if the Seeress breathed enough of the sacred smoke and the water was blessed with the proper spell. The virtue was not in the water, but in the one who looked into it. She herself had learned the craft well enough so that at need she could have seen visions in a mud puddle, with only a few deep breaths and no herbs to help her at all. Sometimes it even happened that the Sight came upon her unbidden, and those visions, impelled by need, were the most important of all.

But Teleri still believed that holiness lay in the forms of things, and so amid the gear which was going with her was a casket which held an ancient silver basin, chased with labyrinthine spirals that drew the eye, and several jugs of water from the sacred pool.

Dierna watched Teleri as she stared through the gap in the leather curtains, gazing as if her gaze could pierce the mists that swathed the Tor. But all one could see was the Christian church and the scattering of huts that sheltered the monks who lived there. Farther up the hill, above the sacred well, were the houses of the holy sisterhood. Above them showed the rounded top of the Tor, bare since the time of the first High Priestess, when the monks had cast down the sacred stones. Sometimes it was hard, seeing it from the outside, to believe that those who had the power to pass through the mists would find instead the Great Hall of Avalon and the House of Maidens, the Processional Way, and the standing stones.

In her mind's eye they were more real than the scene she could see. Many things had changed after the Lady Caillean had worked the magic to separate Avalon from the world. It was in Sianna's time that they had begun to build in stone. By the time Sianna's daughter ruled, the walls of the Great Hall were rising, as long as those of a Roman basilica, though it was roofed with thatch instead of tiles. It was Sianna's granddaughter who had dedicated the first pillars of the Processional. Dierna's own grandmother built the new House of Maidens.

And what will I build? Dierna wondered then. She shook her head, for the answer to that lay in this journey. Her foremothers had built in stone, but she, the first for many years to turn her attention to the outside world, was building an invisible edifice in the hearts of men. Or one man. But he, if her foundation was laid well, would make a wall of ships and men to keep out the Saxons that was more effective than any barrier of stone.

Dierna settled back against the padded backrest and let the curtains fall as the cart began to move. Teleri had already closed her eyes, but her hands were clasped too tightly for sleep. The priestess frowned, noticing for the first time how thin the girl's wrists had become. After her first outburst, Teleri had made no objection to the marriage. Indeed, she had done everything they asked of her as obediently as any daughter of Avalon. Dierna had assumed Teleri had become reconciled, but she wondered now if she had used the press of preparation to avoid questioning too closely.

"Teleri." She spoke quietly, and saw the girl's eyelids twitch. "This craft of seeing in the pool works both ways. You will look in the water each night for visions of what is passing in Britannia— images that I send to you, or that in time you may begin to pick up on your own. But the pool can also be used to send messages. When you are in trance, if you have prepared yourself properly and your will is strong, you may also send a message to me. If something happens—if you are in need—call, and I will come to you."

Teleri answered without opening her eyes. "For more than two years I have been on Avalon. I had expected to be going to my consecration, not my wedding, by now. It was a fair dream. But now I am being cast out to return to the world. You have told me I am being given to a good man. My fate is no worse than' that of any other maiden of noble lineage. It will be better to make the break a clean one. . . ."

Dierna sighed. "As you say, you have spent two years among the priestesses. Avalon has set its mark upon you, Teleri, even if you do not wear the crescent between your brows. Your life will never be as it was, for you are no longer the same. Even if all is well, it would ease me to know how it is with you." She waited, but there was no answer. "You are angry with me, and perhaps you have reason. But never forget that the Goddess is there to comfort you even if you will not turn to me."

At this, Teleri straightened and looked at her. "You are the Lady of Avalon . . ." she said slowly. "You are the Goddess to me." Then she turned away once more.

Lady, what have I done? thought Dierna, staring at the girl's profile, as pure and unyielding as some Roman bas-relief. But it *was* done, or nearly, and the need that had compelled this betrayal—if that was what it was—had not changed. She closed her own eyes. *Lady, You know all hearts. This child cannot understand that what You have asked of us is just as hard for me as it is for her. Send her the comfort she will not take from me, Lady, and the love. . . .*

217

⊲

*Lady
of
Avalon*

⊲ ⊲ ⊲

Carausius hitched the loose end of his toga forward and tried to remember what Pollio had been saying. The man was a major landowner in the Durotrige territories, with trading interests in Rome, a man of influence and connections. But, then, almost everyone whom Prince Eiddin Mynoc had invited to his daughter's wedding was highborn or powerful, or both. Clad in togas or embroidered linen gowns, they could have been an aristocratic gathering anywhere in the Empire. Only the blue-robed priestess standing by the door reminded one that Britannia had her own gods and her own Mysteries.

"An excellent alliance," repeated Pollio. "Of course, we were encouraged to hear that Maximian had given you the command, but this connection with one of our most prominent families suggests a more personal interest in Britannia."

Suddenly it became easy to pay attention. The priestess had offered this marriage as a way to improve communication. Was there a political dimension to marrying the daughter of a British prince that he had not intended? Cleopatra had given all Egypt to Antony, but all he wanted from Teleri was a link to Avalon. He must find some way to make it clear to Prince Eiddin Mynoc and the others that he intended nothing more.

Pollio took a fried cake from the tray offered by one of the slaves and continued. "I have been to Rome. After three centuries they still think we are at the ends of the earth. When times grow hard and pressure is put on their defenses, they will think of us last, when all other needs are met. Have we not seen this, when they pulled troops from our frontier to fight for warring emperors?"

"I am sworn to the Emperor—" Carausius began, but Pollio had not yet finished.

"There are many ways to serve. And perhaps you will not be so swift to pursue your ambitions in Rome if there is someone waiting for you here, eh? Certainly your bride is beautiful enough to keep any man's attention at home." Pollio's grin made the Admiral bristle. "I remember her when she was a gawky child; she has certainly improved in the last year or so!"

Carausius looked across the room, where Teleri was standing with her father beneath a garland of wheat ears and dried flowers. He found it hard to imagine her as an awkward adolescent. Perfumed and jeweled and veiled in crimson silk imported from the eastern lands of the Empire, she was even more lovely than she had been at the fortress. But though she was robed like a king's daughter, her ornaments only accented her beauty, which owed more to the poise with which she wore them.

As if aware of his attention, she turned, and for a moment he glimpsed the pure lines of her face through the roseate haze of her veil, like the statue of a goddess at a festival. He looked quickly away. He was a man of normal appetites, and as he rose in rank women had come easily. But he had never, even when he went to courtesans in Rome, bedded a woman of a royal line, or one who was so beautiful. To worship her would be easy, he thought. He was not so sure how he would do as a husband.

"Nervous?" Aelius, who had left the *Hercules* being refitted in Clausentum and come to support him, squeezed his shoulder. "Don't blame you! But they say all bridegrooms feel that way! Don't worry— one woman's much like another when the torches are put out. Remember how you'd take a boat through the delta of the Rhenus and you'll be all right. Go slow and keep taking soundings!" He burst into laughter as Carausius glared.

He was relieved when a touch on his arm gave him the excuse to turn away. He met the dark, ardent gaze of the slight young man who stood before him, but for a moment could not remember his name.

"Sir, I have spent much . . . time in thought since last summer," said the boy. "It is a great thing you are doing for Britannia." There was a hint of a stammer, as if speech could not quite keep up with the emotions that drove it.

Allectus, that was it. The boy had come down to the ground-

breaking for the fortress of Portus Adurni with his father, and
escorted the priestesses home. Carausius nodded as he went on.

"My health was poor when I was younger, so I have not served in
the Army. But to achieve your purposes will take money. More, I
think, than the Emperor will give you. I know money, sir. If you will
take me onto your staff, I will serve you with all my heart!"

Carausius frowned, looking at the young man with a commander's eye. Allectus would never make much of a warrior, but he
seemed healthy, and if all the stories were true, he was not boasting.
Certainly he spoke truly; the Admiral had begun to realize that the
protection the citizens of Britannia expected of him might extend
beyond the brief given him by Maximian. But protection was all he
would give them, he told himself as the stories of various Army officers who had declared themselves Emperor came to mind.

"What does your father say?"

Light leaped in Allectus' eyes. "He is willing. I think it would
make him proud."

"Very well. You may join my staff—unofficially—and work with
us this winter. If you prove your worth, we will see about making it
permanent when the campaigning begins in the spring."

"Sir!" Allectus sketched a quasi-military salute with an enthusiasm that made him seem suddenly much younger. There was an
awkward moment as Allectus struggled with his emotions.

Carausius took pity on him. "And my first order is to go find out
for me when the rites are going to begin!"

Allectus straightened and strode away with what was obviously
intended to be a military swagger. Carausius wondered if he had been
right to take him on. The young Briton was a curious mixture of
callow youth and maturity, unsure and clumsy in society, but from all
accounts a clever and aggressive businessman. But the Army could
find a use for men of many talents. If Allectus proved able to meet
the physical demands of service and tolerate military discipline, he
might be very useful indeed.

For a moment the Admiral stood frowning, his thoughts on his
command. They had planned the wedding for the end of the sailing

season, but the weather had held fair longer than expected. It was convenient for those who had traveled to the wedding, but some bold Saxon might seize the opportunity for one last raid before the storms began. And if the Saxons did come, he would be here instead of waiting at one of the Channel fortresses, and by the time he found out about a raid, the sea wolves would be long gone. . . .

It was some sense more subtle than hearing that recalled him to the present. When he looked up, Dierna was standing before him.

He took a deep breath and gestured at the crowd in the room. "You have wrought well, and all of us do your bidding. Are you pleased?"

"Are *you?*" She met his gaze levelly.

"I count no battle won until the day is over."

Dierna raised one eyebrow. "Are you afraid?"

"Since I met you I have heard strange tales of Avalon. They say that Rome conquered the Druids but not their priestesses; that you are sorceresses, like those who dwelt on the Isle of Sena in Armorica, the heirs to ancient powers." He had faced down men who wanted to kill him, but it took all of his will to hold this woman's gaze.

"We are only mortal women," the priestess said gently, "though our training is arduous, and perhaps it is true that we guard certain Mysteries that the Romans have lost."

"I am a citizen, but not a Roman." He tugged the loose end of the toga back into place once more. "When I was a boy, wisewomen of the Menapii still dwelt in the fens of Germania, where the Rhenus flows into the northern sea. They had their own kind of wisdom, but in you I sense something more disciplined that reminds me of some priests I met in Egypt when I was there."

"Perhaps . . ." She looked at him with interest. "It is said that those who fled the Drowned Lands found harbor in many ports, and that the Mysteries of Egypt are akin to our own. Do you *remember?*"

Carausius blinked, unsettled by something particular in her tone. She had asked him something similar at Portus Adurni.

"Remember?" he asked, and she shook her head and smiled.

"It does not matter. And in any case, today you should be thinking about your bride. . . ."

Both of them turned to gaze at Teleri. "She is very beautiful. But I hardly expected to be marrying her in such a conventional Roman ceremony."

"Her father wished to make certain the union would be recognized," answered Dierna. "Some years ago one of our women was given to a Roman officer, Constantius, according to our own rites, and we have heard that she is now considered his concubine."

"And what are the rites of Avalon?" His voice was as quiet as hers.

"Man and woman come together as priest and priestess of the Lord and the Lady. He bears the power of the Horned One who brings life to field and herd, and she receives him as the Great Goddess, the Mother, and the Bride."

There was something in the timbre of her voice that stirred him. For the space of a breath he felt as if he were about to recall something long forgotten but vitally important. Then he heard the bleating of the sacrificial sheep outside, and the moment was gone.

"I would not have refused such a ritual," he said softly. "But now it is time to attend to the rites of Rome. Give us your blessing, Lady of Avalon, and we will do the best we may."

The haruspex stood in the doorway, motioning them to come. Carausius straightened, feeling along his forearms the familiar prickle of excitement that came when the waiting was over and battle began. This was not so different, he told himself as he moved forward and the wedding guests fell into place behind him. This was a celebration, but now he was sailing strange seas.

Outside the bedchamber, the party was still going on. The Prince, happy that instead of losing his daughter to Avalon he had married her off to a man of note, had purchased a large quantity of Gallic wine, and the wedding guests were taking full advantage of his bounty. Carausius looked at his bride and wished he had been able to do the same. But a good commander did not drink on duty.

And this was a duty. The woman who awaited him in the big bed was beautiful. He supposed she must be good-tempered as well, and, since she had been trained in Avalon, wise. But she was a stranger.

It had not occurred to him that this might be a problem. Certainly he had bedded courtesans and camp women without any need for introductions. But he realized now that from his marriage he wanted more. Teleri lay with the sheet pulled up to her chin, watchful as a threatened doe. Carausius smiled in an attempt to reassure her and pulled off his tunic. She was his wife by Roman law, but the custom of the British, like that of his own people, was that the wedding was not complete until the marriage feast was ended and the bride deflowered.

"Would you like me to blow out the lamp?" he asked.

Mutely, she nodded. Carausius felt a moment's regret—what was the point of marrying a beautiful woman if you could not look at her body? Still, too much beauty might unman him, whereas one woman felt much like another in the dark. He pulled back the covers and heard the bed groan as he lay down beside her, but Teleri was still silent. With a sigh he reached out to touch her hair. Her skin was very smooth. Without need for thought, his fingers slid from her cheek to her neck, and from there to the firm round of her breast. She took a quick breath and then stilled, trembling beneath his hand.

Should he woo her with love talk? Her silence unnerved him, and he could think of no words. But if his mind was unready, his body, reacting to the firm flesh his fingers were exploring, was responding eagerly. Carausius tried to slow down, to wait until she was ready as well, but Teleri lay still, passively accepting, as he parted her thighs. And then he could hold back no longer. With a groan he sank down upon her body, gripping her shoulders. She whimpered suddenly and began to struggle beneath him, but he was already claiming his prize.

It was over quickly. Afterward Teleri curled on her side with her back to him. Carausius lay for a long time, listening to her breathing, trying to hear if she wept. But she made no sound. Gradually he began to relax. He told himself it had not been too bad a beginning, and would get better as they became more accustomed. Love might be too much to hope for, but as he and Teleri lived together, surely respect and affection would grow, and that was as much as most couples ever knew.

Carausius was not accustomed to sharing a bed, and sleep was long in coming. He lay still, going over troop dispositions and supplies in his head and wishing he could light a lamp and work on them. But he could not tell if his wife was sleeping, and if she was, he feared to wake her. After a time he passed into an uneasy dream in which he stood on a heaving deck, battling against faceless foes.

When he heard the knocking, he thought at first that it was the sound of a ram, battering the side of his ship. There were voices; slowly he took in their words.

"Lady, it is the third hour. Nothing can be done until dawn—in Juno's name, it is the Admiral's wedding night! You cannot disturb him now!"

"If he is angry I will take the blame," answered a woman's voice. "Will you bear the responsibility for denying him news he needs?"

"News?" asked the guard. "No messenger has come. . . ."

"I need no human messenger." The woman's voice changed, and Carausius, already out of bed and pulling on his robe, felt a chill that owed nothing to the night air. "Do you doubt my word?"

The poor guard, caught between his orders and the priestess's power, was saved from having to answer as Carausius opened the door.

"What's wrong?"

Something that had been tensed in Dierna's face relaxed, and she smiled. She had wrapped a mantle over her night robe, and her hair, unbound, fell around her shoulders like flame. Then her expression grew grim once more.

"The Saxons have come again."

"How can you know—" he began, but she only laughed.

"You have kept your part of our bargain. Did you think I would not keep mine? I knew how you feared to leave the coast unguarded, and this night I looked into the Seeing bowl. I told you—this is what I have spent the autumn teaching Teleri to do."

He took a deep breath, coming to full wakefulness as he took in the implications of her words. "And what did you see?"

"A town in flames—I think it is Clausentum—and two keels drawn up on the shore. They will take their time in looting, thinking no help can come. If you are swift, you can catch the dawn tide and be waiting for them beyond the Isle of Vectis when they head home once more."

Carausius nodded. The guard was standing openmouthed, but he snapped to attention as the Admiral began to rap out orders. Carausius suppressed a smile; then all other considerations disappeared in the tide of anticipation that swept through him at the prospect of battle. *This* was something he knew how to do.

☙ ☙ ☙

They spent that winter in Dubris, the Roman fort on the southeastern coast, in the tribal lands of Cantium. Teleri had expected to hate it, for it was not Avalon. But if the villa above the chalk cliffs where Carausius had settled her was a cage, at least it was comfortable, and the big, fair-haired Cantiaci tribesmen, though different from her own more lively west-country folk, were kindly, and made her welcome. Her husband was often away, supervising the construction of the new fortress at Portus Adurni, or the additional improvements being made at Dubris.

Some of the spoils recaptured from the pirates Carausius had defeated the day after the wedding had been returned to their owners. He had sent to Rome for permission to sell items whose owners could not be determined and divert the proceeds to the protection of the Saxon Shore.

Even when Carausius was home he spent most of his time with his officers, poring over maps and arguing strategies. At first Teleri was relieved to see so little of him. She had feared that a man's touch would bring back memories of the reiver's attempt to rape her, but the disciplines of Avalon had stood her in good stead.

When Carausius lay with her, she had only to detach her mind from her body and she felt nothing—neither pain nor fear. She had not realized that her husband would notice, but after a time she began to suspect that he was deliberately avoiding her.

At Midwinter, the Romans celebrated Saturnalia. The Admiral granted his men their holiday and returned to the villa for some much needed rest. On the eve of the solstice they feasted. It was a time to make merry and the men drank deeply. Even Teleri allowed herself more of the sweet Gallic wine than she was used to. At Avalon, they would be celebrating this night with holy rituals, to midwife the newborn sun back into the world. She had seen them only once, and still she found herself weeping when she remembered their beauty.

And so she drank, and was surprised, when at last they rose from the table, to find her legs wobbling beneath her.

"I can't walk!" she exclaimed indignantly. The men began to laugh, and abruptly she found it funny too. But the laughter was too much for her precarious balance. Carausius caught her as she swayed and lifted her in his arms, his face perplexed as if he were wondering how she had gotten there.

"I'm your wife"—she nodded solemnly—"'s all right for you to carry me...."

The world spun dizzily as he bore her along the passageway, and she clung tightly, not releasing him even when he laid her on the bed.

"Shall I send your maid to undress you?" he asked, trying to detach her fingers.

"You undress me," Teleri mumbled, "husband...." She looked into his face and smiled. It was not lust, but loneliness that she was feeling, she knew. But if he was with her she would not think about Avalon.

"You've had a bit too much wine, you know," he said, but the muscles of his arms were no longer rock-hard beneath her fingers.

She giggled suddenly. "So have you!"

"That's true," he replied in the tone of a one who has made an unexpected discovery.

She tugged at his tunic and Carausius thumped down onto the bed beside her, and then, rather clumsily, kissed her. There was a comfort, she thought as he pulled at her clothing, in being close to another person. This time, she had intended to welcome him, but as matters progressed she found herself growing more detached from what was happening. When at last he lay atop her, she took refuge in random images, and found among them, unexpectedly, the face of Allectus.

In the morning, Teleri awoke with an aching head and a confusion of memories. She was alone in the bed, but Carausius' mantle lay where it had fallen on the floor. Lying with him had not been a dream. At least, she thought as she allowed her maid to dress her, she no longer feared him. But when they met for breakfast, he seemed uncertain how to respond to her, and a little ashamed. Or perhaps it was only that his head was aching as well.

But if it made their relationship no worse, neither had that night's encounter brought them any closer together.

As the dark days drew on, Carausius brought his senior officers to stay at the villa more frequently. Teleri found herself often in the company of Allectus, providing a sympathetic ear when the demands of military life pushed him to the edge of his endurance.

"The way in which we are funded is so inefficient!" he exclaimed as they walked along the cliffs. "The taxes are raised in Britannia, sent all the way to Rome; then, if the Emperor sees fit, a portion trickles back again. No trader could prosper that way! Would it not make more sense to calculate how much will be allotted for the defense of Britannia and keep back that amount from the taxes that are sent on?"

Teleri nodded. Certainly it made sense when he explained it. Accustomed to the civilian government, which was largely financed by contributions from the magnates who served as local magistrates, she had never thought about the problems of defending the entire province before.

"Could we not call for donations from the people here whom Carausius' forts are protecting?"

"We will have to, unless Maximian sends more." Allectus turned, hands on his hips, to stare out to sea. It seemed to Teleri that military life had improved him. The intense gaze was unchanged, but hours spent in training had bronzed his skin. He stood straighter too, and had more muscle on his thin frame.

"I have lent out some of the money at a percentage, to be repaid at the beginning of the sailing season, and that will bring us some gain. But it takes money to breed money. Asking for contributions from the magistrates is a good idea"—he gave her that smile that so transformed his features—"but it will take more than sound reasoning to screw gold out of our people. They can be generous when the results will be something they can use to impress their neighbors. To see benefits in fortifications to defend another tribe's lands strains their imaginations. You must come with me, Teleri, and charm them into generosity! Surely they will not be able to resist your smile...."

She blushed involuntarily, thinking that, despite his complaints, the Army had been good for him, socially as well as physically. He would never have had the wit to pay her such a compliment a year ago.

The weather grew warmer, though storms still lashed the land. Carausius shifted his quarters to the fortress itself, and took Teleri with him. The alliance with Prince Eiddin Mynoc and the aura of Avalon were themselves of considerable use, but they were not the major reason he had married Teleri. It was time now to learn if the other, secret purpose in having her with him could be achieved. Teleri took to retiring early—no hardship now, when Carausius needed to spend his evenings with his men. They did not know that she rose in the dark hours before dawn and sat staring into the water in the silver bowl, clearing her mind and waiting for word from Avalon.

At first she found it hard to concentrate, but presently she began to think of this time apart as the best part of her day. In those quiet hours when the great fortress slept around her she could almost imagine herself back in the House of Maidens. Teleri occupied her mind by reflecting on the things she had learned there, and was surprised to find how much she remembered, and how much her understanding of what she had been taught seemed to have grown.

On a night near the end of the month of Mars, she found herself thinking of Dierna with regret, rather than with the anger that had so often tinged her thoughts before. And as if that shift in attitude had been like the movement of a stone that releases the water pent behind a dam, she saw the features of the High Priestess forming in the water into which she gazed.

From the widening of the other woman's eyes, Teleri could tell that Dierna saw her too, and she felt an unexpected pang as she realized that the other woman was gazing at her with relief and with love. Dierna's lips moved. Teleri heard nothing, but she sensed a question and smiled reassuringly, then gestured as if she were asking how they fared on Avalon in return. She saw Dierna close her eyes, frowning. Then her image blurred. For a moment Teleri glimpsed Avalon, lying peaceful under the stars. She saw the House of Maidens and the dwelling of the priestesses, the weaving sheds and dye house and kitchens, the shed where they dried and processed herbs. There was the apple orchard, the oak grove, and the glimmer of the holy well, and, watching over all, the pointed silhouette of the Tor.

Teleri closed her own eyes then, striving to picture the fortress of Dubris and the harbor where the tethered warships rose and fell on the tide. Her thought moved to Carausius, broad-shouldered and intent, with more silver strands in his hair than there had been a year ago. Unbidden, the image of Allectus appeared at his shoulder, eyes alight with excitement. But in the next moment her will, unused to this labor, faltered, and she blinked and saw in the bowl only the dull sheen of the water, and in the window, the pale light of dawn.

⊲ ⊲ ⊲

Carausius straightened from looking at the map of the coastline, wincing as the muscles of his back protested. How long, he wondered, had he been bending over it? The map was made of leather so that it could be rolled up and carried, or pegged to a board. Wooden counters representing ships and supplies were set by the pictures of fortresses or towns, easy to count and easy to shift. If only it were so easy to move ships and men. But the vagaries of the weather and the human heart could upset the most logical plans.

The fortress lay in the stillness of the hours between midnight and dawn, when everyone was asleep but the guards on the walls. And himself and Allectus. The younger man moved three more wooden "bags of grain" from the painted image of Dubris to Rutupiae and glanced at his commander.

"I think we'll have enough." He made a tally mark on his slate. "We won't get fat, but everyone will be fed." He tried to suppress a yawn.

"And everyone must sleep," said Carausius, surveying him with a smile. "Even you and I. Go to bed, Allectus, and sleep well."

"I'm not tired, truly. The other forts—"

"Can wait until tomorrow. You've done more than enough for now."

"You're pleased with my work, then?" Allectus asked. Carausius frowned, wondering why he needed to ask.

"Last fall, you took me on unofficially," Allectus went on. "The officers on your staff know me, but I would have more authority when I go elsewhere if I were in uniform. That is," he added with sudden diffidence, "if I've earned my place here. . . ."

"Allectus!" Carausius gripped his shoulder, and the younger man straightened, his dark eyes shining as if he were holding back tears. For a moment the Admiral was reminded of Teleri—both had the fine bones and dark coloring of the tribes that lived in the west country. They might well be related, somewhere along the line.

"My boy, can you doubt it? I can scarcely imagine how I managed before you were here. But if you want a uniform, then that is what you shall have."

Allectus smiled blindingly and, bending, kissed the Admiral's hand. Carausius let go of his shoulder, a little surprised by his intensity, but touched as well. "Go on now, and sleep," he said gently. "You do not need to exhaust yourself in my service to prove your loyalty."

When Allectus had gone, Carausius stood looking after him, still smiling. *If Teleri bore me a son he might look like that,* he thought suddenly. He had taken her for other reasons, but she was his wife. Why should he not hope for a son, born of this land, to follow him?

He strode down the corridor toward his quarters more eagerly than usual. Teleri had made it clear that she did not welcome his embraces, but most women wanted to bear children. And perhaps, if she did so, she would come to feel a kindness for the father of her child.

But when he came to his chamber, the bed was empty.

For a moment Carausius stood staring, astonished by the depth of pain at the thought he had been betrayed. Then reason reasserted itself. Even if Teleri had been the kind of woman to engage in a love affair, she was too intelligent to have done so by night, when every sleeper was accounted for and guards paced the grounds. Softly, he crossed the floor and pushed open the door to the inner room.

Upon a low table a lamp was burning. Light gleamed from the rim of the silver bowl before it, and glowed in Teleri's white robes. The flame rippled as he entered, but she did not stir. Scarcely daring to breathe, he knelt beside her.

Her eyes were fixed on the dark surface of the water, and her lips moved.

"Dierna . . ." she whispered, then stilled, as if listening.

"Lady," Carausius said at last in a voice scarcely louder than her own, "let your vision seek the coasts of Britannia. What do you see?" He himself was not sure to which of them he was speaking, and when Teleri stirred again he could not tell who replied.

"Dark waters . . . I see a river, low banks, treetops dark against the stars." Her breath caught and she swayed. "A strong current . . . Ripples gleam. . . . Oars lift shining from the water. . . ."

"Are they warships? How many?" Carausius snapped. She twitched, but in a moment she was answering.

"Six . . . going upstream . . ."

"Where?" This time he kept his voice low, but he could not control its intensity. "Which river? Which town?"

"I see a bridge . . . and red stone walls," the answer came slowly. "Dierna says . . . it is Durobrivae! Go! You must go quickly!" The last words, though Teleri's mouth had spoken them, sounded so much like Dierna's voice that Carausius blinked. Then the woman swayed and he caught her in his arms.

Pulse pounding, he lifted Teleri and carried her to the bed. Though he twitched with the need to be gone, he took the time to tuck the covers around her. She did not wake, but her breathing was already deepening to the regular rhythms of sleep. Her closed features had the remote serenity of a Vestal's, or a child's, and in that moment he could not imagine how he had ever looked at her with desire.

"My Lady, I thank you." Carausius bent and kissed her on the brow. Then he strode from the room, already forgetting her as he called out the first of the orders that would take him to sea once more.

◁ ◁ ◁

From the military point of view, the season that followed was largely successful. Dierna's sight was not always true, and Teleri was not always able to understand her sendings. And there were also times when Carausius was already at sea and could not be warned. But as the High Priestess had promised, the alliance with Avalon gave the Admiral an edge that enabled him, if not to destroy the enemy, at least to maintain a kind of parity. If the Romans could not always come to the rescue before the raiders had finished looting a settlement, they were often in time to avenge it. And the traders who sailed from the ports of Britannia grew heavy with the unclaimed spoils that Carausius sent to Rome.

At the end of the summer, when the haystacks stood heaped high in the meadows and the barley was nodding before the reaper's scythe, Carausius called a council of British leaders from all the territories of the Saxon Shore to discuss the future defense of Britannia. With Teleri's help, he had done far more than Maximian expected of him. But it was not enough. For the land to be truly safe, he must somehow persuade those who lived inland to help him. They met in the great basilica at Venta Belgarum, the only place in the region that was large enough to contain them all.

◁ ◁ ◁

Carausius stood up, automatically twitching the folds of his toga so that they would fall in the graceful sweep familiar from Roman statuary. In the past two years he had been required to wear the toga often enough so that he no longer chafed at the inconvenience. But as he draped the loose end over one arm and lifted his hand to call the assembly to order, it occurred to him that the stately movements required if one wanted to keep the garment in place no doubt went far to explain the Roman ideal of *dignitas*.

"My friends, I have no gift of oratory such as they teach in Rome. I am a soldier. If I were not charged with the duties of the Dux Tractus Armoricani et Nervicani, the coasts to either side of the Channel, I would not be here, and so, if I speak with a soldier's bluntness, you must forgive me." Carausius paused, looking at the men who sat, swathed in their own togas, on the benches before him. By their dress, he might have been addressing the Senate of Rome, but here and there he saw a man with the fair skin and ruddy hair of pure Celtic blood, or the fine-boned intensity of a race that was older still.

"I have called you here," he went on, "to speak of the defense of the lands which gave you birth, and which have become a home to me."

"That is the Army's job," responded a man from one of the back benches. "And you have been doing it well. What does this have to do with me?"

"Not as well as he might." Another turned to glare at him, and then back to scowl at Carausius. "Not two months since the scum hit Vigniacis and destroyed my workshops. Where were you then?"

Carausius frowned, and Allectus, at his elbow, whispered, "His name is Trebellius and he owns a bronze foundry. They supply many of our ship fittings."

"I was chasing a reiver who had sunk a boat carrying one of your cargoes, I believe," answered the Admiral smoothly. "Indeed, your goods have served us well, and I pray to the gods that you will be back in production swiftly. Surely you cannot think I would choose to risk an industry whose output I so desperately need." There was a murmur of appreciation.

"The fleet is doing its best for us, Trebellius. Let's not complain," said Pollio, who had helped organize the meeting.

"We *are* doing our best," echoed Carausius, "but sometimes, as our friend here has pointed out, it is not enough. We have only so many vessels, and they cannot be everywhere. If we could improve the fortresses we have and build more, and if we had the ships to serve them, you would not have to weep over looted houses and burned walls."

"That's all very well," a man from Clausentum replied, "but what do you expect us to do?"

Carausius sought inspiration from the frescoed wall, where a Jupiter who bore a strong resemblance to Diocletian was offering a wreath to a Hercules with the face of Maximian.

"—Your duty as civic fathers and leaders of your towns. You are accustomed to stand the cost of public works and civic buildings. I ask only that you apply some of those resources to defending them. Help me build more fortresses and feed my men!"

"That has stung them where they live," murmured Allectus as the hall erupted in disputation.

"It is one thing to build our own cities." Pollio stood up at last as spokesman. "We have been bred up to do that, and our resources are, if barely, adequate to the task. But defense is the Emperor's responsibility. Why else do we tax our people so heavily and send the money to Rome? If we pay for our own defense, will he squander the money we send him on Syria, or throw it away in another campaign against the Goths?"

"Leave the taxes that are levied in Britannia here, to support our government, and we will gladly pay for our defenses," said Prince Eiddin Mynoc, "but it is not justice to take all and give nothing in return."

The walls shook as most of the others began to shout their approval. Carausius tried to tell them that he could only make reports and recommendations and had no way to make the Emperor listen, but he could not be heard.

"The Emperor must help us," came the cry. "If you petition Diocletian for support we will stand behind you. But support us he must. Any man who wants to be called Emperor of Britannia must earn the name!"

◁ ◁ ◁

"What will you do?" Allectus asked. Carausius winced, recognizing the anxiety in his eyes.

Cerialis had set the dining couches in his garden. The late-summer twilight laid a golden haze like a veil across the trees, through which they could hear the river lapping softly against the reeds. To break this dream of peace with talk of war seemed sacrilege.

"We will send to Diocletian." Carausius spoke in a low voice, as if afraid to be overheard, though only Allectus and Aelius were near. "Of course we must do that, but I know how severely his resources are stressed already, and I have no great hopes for relief from Rome."

He drained his goblet, hoping the wine would deaden his headache, and held it out to be refilled by the slave who hovered nearby. "I do not understand how you British can be so shortsighted! It does no good to ask the Emperor for funds. He has to watch over the whole Empire, and from where he sits, there may be other places in greater need than Britannia."

"There lies the difficulty," answered Cerialis soberly. "It is hard enough to get my countrymen to look beyond the walls of their own cities, much less beyond our shores. As they see it, they have paid for protection, and should not have to pay again. . . ."

Carausius closed his eyes; his head was pounding, as if someone were trying to split it in two. On one side, the responses drilled into him by twenty years in uniform railed against these provincials who did not understand that all the parts of the Empire depended on the strength of the whole. But the other, the self that had been born when the priestess spilled his blood on the soil, yammered that nothing, not even his oath to the Emperor, was as important as the safety of Britannia.

"I have done what I can to raise money, but by the means I have available there is little more to be gained." Allectus' voice seemed to come from a great distance.

"By the means available . . ." the Admiral repeated, an idea surfacing from his inner turmoil. If neither the Emperor nor the British princes would give in, then he had to find a third way. He raised himself on one elbow, looking at them somberly.

"The gods know I have tried to play by the rules! But if my duty requires me to bend them, then that is what I will have to do. When we take a ship, even the Emperor's law allows me a portion of the plunder. From now on Britannia will receive a proportion of the spoils as well. I trust you, Allectus, to word our reports in a way that will . . . obscure what is going on."

Chapter Thirteen

High and clear, the whistle of the watcher came floating over the marshes. At the foot of the Tor it was heard, and a trilling cry carried the message upward.

"One comes. Call the mists and send out the barge that will bring him to Avalon!"

Dierna draped her long veil over her head and shoulders. Her heart had begun to beat with unaccustomed excitement; she paused a moment, surprised it should be so, then took a deep breath and stepped out from the shadows of her house into the brightness of the summer's day. She cast a critical eye over the priestesses who awaited her.

Crida, seeing the look, tossed her head. "Are you afraid we will not do you credit? Why are you so careful? It is only a Roman."

"Not entirely," answered the High Priestess. "He is a tribesman from a people not so different from our own, forced, like so many of our young men, into a Roman mold. And he is a man marked by the gods. . . ."

Silenced, Crida covered her own face with her veil. Dierna nodded and led the way down the winding path. As they neared the shore, Ceridachos came out to meet her, dressed in all the Arch-Druid's regalia, attended by Lewal, who had met their visitor before.

She wondered how the Tor would appear to the Admiral's eyes. Over the years the first whitewashed wattle buildings had been replaced by stone, but they nestled against the side of the hill. Only the great Processional Way, with its paired pillars, had a majesty as mighty as the works of Rome, if different in kind. And the standing stones that crowned the Tor had been ancient when Rome was only a scattering of huts upon the seven hills.

The great barge of Avalon lay drawn up on the shore below the apple trees. It had been built in her mother's time, large enough to carry horses as well as men, and it was paddled—not poled, like the smaller craft in which the marsh dwellers slipped through the reeds. Dierna stepped in and took her place in the prow, and at her word the boatmen pushed off and the barge slid silently across the mere. Before them, a bright haze glimmered on the water, veiling the far hills with gold. When they reached the middle of the lake, Dierna got to her feet, balancing with the ease of long practice, though indeed today the water was as smooth as a dancing floor.

She took a deep breath and lifted her hands, her fingers twitching as if she were spinning an invisible thread. The boatmen raised their paddles and the barge floated, waiting, on the threshold between the worlds. The spell that called the mists was woven in the mind, but it manifested in the outer world, linking one to the other by such movements as these. Her breath gathered power; she could feel the muscles of her throat begin to vibrate, though there was still no sound. Dierna closed her eyes, calling upon the Goddess within and gathering all her forces into one mighty act of will.

She felt the lurch of shifting levels and resisted the temptation to look, knowing that the instant between times was the most dangerous of all. In the years since the Lady Caillean had raised the barrier of mist to protect them, many priestesses had been taught this spell. But in every century there had been one or two who were sent out for their testing and disappeared, lost between the worlds, when they tried to part the mists to return.

Then a sudden damp cold swirled around her. Dierna opened her eyes, and saw grey water, and a blur of trees, and as the mists parted, the crimson cloak of the man who waited for her on the shore. Teleri was not with him. When they communicated through the Seeing bowl, the other woman had seemed to forgive her. Up to this moment, Dierna had hoped that she would come.

For a moment, her thought winged southwestward. *Teleri, I still love you. Don't you understand? It was necessity, not I, that banished you from Avalon!*

⊲ ⊲ ⊲

And Teleri, walking in her garden in the villa at Dubris, swayed, for a moment as dizzy as if she had been looking into the Seeing bowl. She stumbled to a stone seat and sat down upon it, and behind her closed eyelids she saw the Lake of Avalon. The image made her almost ill with longing.

Carausius is arriving there now, she told herself. *He will sit by Dierna's side, and perhaps she will allow him to climb the Holy Tor.*

Had Teleri been wrong to decline the High Priestess's invitation? As much as she had ever wanted to go to Avalon in the first place, she wished she could return. She had refused to go back, not because she no longer cared, but because she cared too much.

I wish them joy of one another! Her fingers clenched in the folds of her gown. *As for me, if I ever return to Avalon, alive or dead, I will never leave it again. . . .*

⊲ ⊲ ⊲

"Behold the Vale of Avalon," said Dierna as the barge passed through the mists once more and slid over the water toward the Tor. Carausius blinked and straightened, like a man emerging from a dream. The men of the escort, protesting, had been left behind to wait with the horses. But the priestess, accustomed to reading men's features, had seen relief in their eyes and known that they too had heard tales of the holy isle. Even princes of the British royal houses were rarely allowed to tread this sacred soil. When there was need, the priestesses went out to them to bless the land.

It was not because Carausius was a man of rank and power in the Roman world that Dierna had extended this invitation, but because she had had a dream. It boded well for her purposes, she felt, that even at this season, when the demands on him were at their greatest, the Admiral had answered her call. But it was true that since Carausius had decided to use the profits from captured raiders to support his operations at the end of the preceding summer, things had gone well. The fleet had had an extremely successful season and had taken many rich prizes, whose profits were speeding the strengthening of the ships and the protection of the shore. Perhaps the enemy was too exhausted to trouble them.

Blue-robed priestesses stood beneath the apple trees with a line of Druids behind them. As the barge drew nearer, they began to sing.

"What are they saying?" asked Carausius, for the words were an ancient dialect of the British tongue.

"They hail the Defender, the Son of a Hundred Kings. . . ."

He looked taken aback. "That is too much honor, if it is intended for me. My father poled a barge not unlike this one through the channels of the delta where the Rhenus flows into the northern sea."

"The spirit has a royalty that transcends blood. But we will speak more of that another time," she answered him.

The barge grounded and Carausius stepped out upon the shore. Crida came forward to offer him the cup of welcome, made of plain earthenware but filled with the clear, iron-tasting water of the holy well. Dierna was glad to see that, if her face showed any resentment, it was hidden by the veil.

Then she gave her guest into Lewal's keeping, to be fed and shown around the buildings grouped at the foot of the Tor, while she led the priestesses back to their tasks. It was not until after the evening meal that they met once more.

"The Druid priesthood work their rituals on the Tor by daylight," said Dierna as she led Carausius toward the Processional Way. "But by night it belongs to the priestesses."

"The Romans say that Hecate rules the hours of darkness and the witches are her daughters, who use its shadow to hide deeds they dare not do by day," he answered her.

"Do you think we are sorceresses?" The stone pillars that guarded the path were before them. She paused, looking back at him, and saw a tension in the tilt of his head and the line of his shoulders that had not been there before. "Well, there may be times, when the good of the land demands it, when that is true. But I promise I mean you no ill, nor shall I bind your will with any magic."

He followed her between the pillars and stopped suddenly, blinking. "Perhaps you will not need to.... There is magic enough here already to maze any man."

Dierna held his troubled gaze. "So you *do* feel it! You are a brave man, Carausius. If you keep your nerve, the Tor will do you no harm. This much I will say—if my visions are truthful, you have walked this way before...."

He gave her a startled look, but climbed the rest of the way in silence. The moon, lacking only a day of her fullness, had risen above the hills and was climbing the eastern sky. They passed from darkness to light and back again as they circled the hill. By the time they reached the summit, the moon was sailing halfway up the heavens; the shadows of the ringstones stretched sharp and black across the circle, but the altar in the center was fully illuminated, and the silver vessel of water upon it shone as if lit from within.

"Lady, why have you brought me here?" His words were rough, but his voice trembled, and she knew that he was trying to control the very awareness he denied.

"Be still, Carausius," she said softly, moving to the other side of the altar stone. "When you stand on your deck, do you not listen to the wind, and reach out to sense the mood of the sea? Be silent, and allow the stones to speak to you. You have seen Teleri look into the silver bowl, so you know it will do no harm. Now it is your turn."

"Teleri was trained by you as a priestess," he exclaimed. "I am a soldier, not a priest. I know nothing of spiritual things—any honor I have gained has been by using my wits and the strength of my arm."

"You know more than you can remember!" retorted Dierna. "It is not like you to admit failure before you have tried. Gaze into the bowl, my lord"—her voice softened—"and tell me what you see...."

They stood facing each other while the moon rose higher, and if the time seemed long to him, to Dierna, accustomed to such vigils, it was a respite from the cares of the world. As the silence deepened, it came to her more and more strongly that in another time and place she had faced this man across an altar before.

Presently she saw him sway. He staggered forward, gripping the stone as he bent over the silver bowl. His head sank as if the water were drawing it. Dierna set her own hands over his, steadying him and balancing the power that pulsed through him with her own. She looked down at the bowl with the unfocused gaze of vision, and as the images began to form, knew that what she and Carausius were seeing was the same.

Moonlight shone on water; she looked on an island lapped by silver seas. Dierna had never seen it with her waking eyes, but she recognized the alternating rings of land and water, the rich fields near the sea and the ships in the inner harbor, and in the center an isle within an island, stepped and terraced and crowned with temples that gleamed pale in the moonlight. It was as great as the entire Vale of Avalon, but its contours, drawn larger, were those of the Holy Tor. It was the old land, mother of mysteries. Dierna knew that she was seeing the island from which the teachers of the Druids had fled, which now lay drowned beneath the sea.

Vision expanded; now she gazed upon the island from a terrace with a marble balustrade. A man stood beside her. Tattooed dragons twined the strong forearms that gripped the rail, and the royal diadem of the sun, its disk paled now with moonlight, gleamed on his brow. His hair was dark and his features were aquiline, but she knew the spirit that looked out of his eyes.

He turned to her and those eyes widened. "Heart of Flame!"

Uncalled and unexpected, Dierna felt her own need rise up in answer. He reached out to her, and suddenly the vision was swallowed by a flood of water that poured over them in a great wave.

Heart pounding, Dierna fought with a lifetime's discipline to regain her composure. When she could see again, Carausius was on his hands and knees and the silver basin, overset, had spilled its waters in a shining stream across the stone. She hurried to his side.

"Breathe deeply," she whispered, holding on to his shoulders until his shudders ceased. "Tell me—what did you see?"

"An island . . . in the moonlight . . ." He sat back on his haunches, rubbing his forearms, and looked up at her. "You were there, I think. . . ." He shook his head. "And then there were other scenes. I was here!" He looked wildly around him. "There was fighting, and someone was trying to destroy the stones!" Frowning, he stared up at her. "It's gone. I cannot remember anymore. . . ."

Dierna sighed, wanting to take him in her arms as she had held that other one, so long ago. But it was not for her to tell him of the link between them, if he did not know. Indeed, she herself was not certain of the vision's meaning, only of the emotion that had come with it. She had loved this man in another life—perhaps in more than one—and, thinking back over the time since their first meeting, she understood that she loved him still. She was a priestess, trained to control both heart and will, and even for the men who had fathered her children she had never felt more than respect and the passion of the ritual. How could she have been so blind?

"You were a sea king," she said quietly, "long ago, in a land now passed away. Britannia's bulwark has always been the sea. And here, some small part of that tradition survives. As for the stones . . ." She swallowed. "Long ago a man called Gawen died here defending them. He too was a sacred king. I do not know if you were he, or whether it is only that you, a warrior, have seen a vision of that fight. But I do believe that you have been reborn in order that you may serve once more as Britannia's protector."

"I am sworn to serve the Emperor . . ." Carausius said in a shaken voice. "Why has this been shown me? I am not a king."

Dierna shrugged. "The title does not matter. Only the dedication, and you have made that already when you gave your blood to consecrate your fortress. Your soul is royal, sea lord, and bound to the Mysteries. And I think that a day is coming when you may have to choose whether or not to claim your destiny."

He got to his feet, and she felt his spirit walled against her. There was strength in the man for certain, untrained though it might be. She had done as the Goddess bade her. Whatever his choice, she must accept it. In silence, she led him back down the hill.

In the morning, word came to them from across the marshes of an urgent message for Carausius. Dierna had the messenger brought to the island, blindfolded, and waited as the Admiral slid the scroll from its leather case.

"It is the reivers?" she asked as she saw his face change.

He shook his head, his expression halfway between exasperation and anger. "Not the Saxons—this is from the thieves in Rome!" He looked back at the scroll, translating roughly as he read.

"I am charged with colluding with the enemies of Rome and defrauding the Emperor. . . . They say I have deliberately waited to attack the pirates until after they are on their way home so that I can seize their booty! The fools—do they think I can be everywhere, or read the barbarians' minds?" He turned the parchment, and grunted with mirthless laughter. "Evidently they do, for here they accuse me of making secret treaties with the raiders, directing them where to strike and dividing the spoils." He shook his head. "There will be nothing secret about it, if ever I take action against Rome!"

"But you have spent the money on Britannia!"

"True, but will they believe me? I am summoned to Rome to be judged by the Emperor. Even if I am acquitted, no doubt they will post me to the other end of the Empire and never let me return to Britannia again."

"Don't go!" she exclaimed.

Carausius shook his head. "I swore an oath to the Emperor—"

"You swore an oath to this land, and other vows before that, to defend the Mysteries. Is there another man in all Diocletian's armies that could do the same?"

"If I refuse, I will be a rebel. It will mean civil war." He looked up at her and his face was grim.

"Who can stop you? Maximian is embroiled with the Franks on the Rhenus, and Diocletian with the Goths on the Danuvius. They have no forces to spare for the discipline of a wayward admiral who, whatever they may think of his methods, is protecting the Empire. But if it comes to war, it will not be the first time." She held his stony gaze. "Diocletian himself was a son of slaves whose glory was foretold by a Druid priestess in Gallia. I speak with no less authority than she."

His eyes widened. "I do not seek to be Emperor!"

Dierna bared her teeth in a smile. "Go back to your fleet, Carausius, and see if they will support you. I will pray to the gods to guard you. If it comes to fighting, you may find that you have no choice but to accept the fruits of victory!"

✣ ✣ ✣

Teleri was instructing her maidservant which gowns should be packed for the journey from the fort of Dubris to the villa when a legionary appeared at the doorway of her quarters.

"Lady, there's a messenger. Will you come?"

"Has something happened to the Admiral?" Her heart pounded suddenly, and for a moment she did not know whether it was with hope or with fear. The year before, Carausius had defied the emperors and built up his fleet, and the Saxon raids had begun to decline. This season he meant to do more.

Carausius had set sail three days before to carry the war to the Saxons. If he could burn their villages, perhaps they would not be so eager to raid Britannia again. But in the heat of battle even a commander could be struck down. She felt disloyal. Her husband had been kind to her, and he was the defender of her people. She was appalled to realize how much she resented the duty that kept her at his side.

"I don't think so," said the legionary. "I think the message is *for* Carausius, not from him. But the fellow has hardly a word of Latin, and his British is some dialect that none of us can understand."

"Very well." With a last word of instruction to her maid, Teleri followed the soldier to the gatehouse.

The messenger, a weathered fellow in the faded tunic of a fisherman who gazed at the stone walls as if he thought they would fall on him, was waiting. When she greeted him in the accent of Durnovaria he brightened.

"He's from Armorica," she murmured as he burst into speech.

"Their folk trade often with our own, and their manner of speaking is much the same." Teleri leaned forward, frowning, as he went on. The man was still speaking when Allectus came into the room.

"Is Maximian coming against us?" asked Allectus in Latin when the story was done.

"That is what he says," Teleri replied. "But why should the emperors act now? I thought that Diocletian had accepted Carausius' denial of the accusations against him, and forgiven him for not obeying the command to return."

"That was last year," Allectus said grimly, "when the emperors were fighting on the Rhenus. But we had word this spring that Maximian has made peace with the Franks in Belgica. Did you really think that Rome would tolerate our defiance forever? I suppose we should not be surprised that the junior Emperor has used the respite to build ships in Armorica." His lips twisted. "After all, we have been building up our own fleet here. I only wish we had had more time to prepare!"

"But Carausius does not want to fight Maximian! He is oathsworn to the emperors!" Teleri exclaimed.

"The oath he offered with his blood at Portus Adurni binds more deeply. You were there—you heard him pledge himself to defend this land."

The longer Allectus spent in the Army, thought Teleri, seeing how straight he stood now, the more he improved. Carausius might be a great warrior, but it was the younger man whose financial skills had given him the resources needed to pursue this war. The diffidence that had made Allectus seem younger than his years had been replaced by pride.

"You want him to rebel . . ." she said slowly. "To proclaim himself Emperor of Britannia!"

"Yes. I do. The Christians say a man cannot serve two masters, and the time has come when Carausius must choose." Allectus strode to the open gateway and stood staring out to sea. "As trade improves it is not only the merchants who benefit. Perhaps you cannot see it, but I know where the money comes from, and where it goes. Now everyone is prospering. In the temples they pray for Carausius, did you know, as if he were already Emperor. . . . Let him be, then, the lord we need. Maximian will force him to choose!"

With a shake of his head Allectus dug out the wax tablets from the pouch at his side and turned back to the fisherman.

"Ask the man how many ships he saw, and how many men they were carrying. Ask him when they set sail," he said briskly. "If I cannot stand by my commander's side with a sword in my hand, I will give him what may be of more worth—the information he needs to plan his battle, and a fleet alerted and prepared to follow him! Quickly—the ship that carries this message must catch the tide!"

Romans fighting Romans! Even the thought of it made Teleri shiver. *Goddess, protect Carausius!* she prayed, shamed by the fervor she saw in Allectus' eyes, *and forgive my doubts! Tonight I will look into the silver bowl again. Perhaps Dierna will have news for me as well.*

The fisherman looked from one to the other, trying to understand. Teleri took a quick breath, and began to question him.

◁ ◁ ◁

Carausius stood on the afterdeck of the *Orion,* swaying a little as the trireme rocked in the swell, sails furled. The lowest rank of oarsmen were sufficient to keep her in position, while the others rested. The other ships of his command held position in three columns, except for one swift liburnian which he had sent ahead to look for the enemy. The land was a blur of green off his port bow, low hills and sandspits rising into rocky bluffs to the west. The shore looked peaceful, but an occasional ridging of water that ran across the line of the waves revealed the hidden currents there.

Orion had been completed over the winter, the largest ship in his command, in size a throwback to the big triremes of ancient days, and her wood gleamed white in the sunshine. At the prow the carven hunter took aim at an invisible foe. The image was Roman, but it was Dierna who had suggested this name for the flagship. There was a power, she had said, in the constellation of that name that would bring him victory. But the shrine at the stern sheltered a goddess, her statue helmed and armed with shield and spear. The Roman officers addressed her as Minerva, but this choice had also been guided by the High Priestess, and she had told Carausius to pray to the goddess as Briga, who was honored in Avalon on the Maiden's Isle.

"Lady, with heavy heart I call you," Carausius murmured. "I do not want to fight Maximian. Give me an omen, that I may see my way, and if we fight, then, for the sake of the brave men who have followed me, look upon us with gracious aspect, and give us the victory."

He cast another handful of barley upon the altar, and poured out a libation of wine. Menecrates, the man he had chosen as *Orion's* captain, took a pinch of frankincense and cast it on the coals. The tang of the sea air mingled pleasantly with the sweetness of the incense burning in the shrine.

But even as he prayed, a part of the Admiral's mind was calculating, planning, preparing for the fray. Allectus' message had brought Carausius speeding back from the delta of the Rhenus, and when he reached Dubris, the Rutupiae and Adurni squadrons had been waiting to join him. There was new word from Teleri as well— Maximian's fleet had put to sea and was beating up-Channel. Teleri herself had seen them in vision, three squadrons of ten ships each, crammed with men. Carausius' total command was larger, but his forces must be spread out to defend the province, whereas Maximian could bring his whole strength to bear on whichever fortress he chose.

Teleri wrote that the High Priestess had promised to call the winds to slow Maximian's advance, but she could only delay their meeting for a little while. It would be enough, thought Carausius, for that same wind was bearing them down-Channel so swiftly that they were passing Portus Adurni now.

Their numbers were unequal, but Maximian must make do with slaves and drafted fishermen, seasoned by a few officers drawn off from the Mediterranean and the Rhenus patrols. The Emperor would be hoping to trap his foe against the shore and force a boarding battle, where he could make use of the legionaries he carried on board.

The ships of the British fleet, on the other hand, could make up in maneuverability for what they lacked in manpower. Carausius told himself to beware overconfidence. The Saxons he was accustomed to fighting were good sailors, but as warriors they sought individual glory rather than a shared victory. Carausius' men had never fought ships under Roman discipline. Still, the enemy did not know the Channel, and that in itself might be advantage enough today.

Realizing that the men were watching him, he completed his prayer and fastened the doors of the shrine. Menecrates took the censer and tossed the coals over the side. Carausius looked around him and grinned. He had a good ship, from the bronze ram that cut the waves just below her waterline to the heavy linen sails. And he had good men—ship's officers whose naval training had been completed by two years' experience against the pirates, two dozen legionaries of long service, and one hundred and sixty-two free oarsmen committed to the defense of Britannia. And the gods had sent him a fair spring day, with a few wisps of cloud and a light following wind to set an edge of froth on waves as deeply blue as lapis, a day on which to meet death gladly or to rejoice in victory.

He missed Allectus, whose keen wit and sardonic humor had lightened many a dismal hour. But though the younger man had truly earned his place on the Admiral's staff, he had no stomach for the sea.

Gulls flew yammering around the mast, then swooped landward, feathered pirates greedier than any Saxon. *Be patient,* thought the Admiral, *soon enough you will be fed.*

From the prow the lookout shouted, and Carausius stiffened, shading his eyes with one hand as he peered over the sea.

"The liburnian!" the man cried again. "She's approaching under full oars—"

"What signal?" rapped the Admiral, taking the steps down to the catwalk between the banks of oars two at a time and running forward.

"Enemy in sight!"

Now Carausius could see the bobbing mast and the froth of white as the oarsmen dug into the waves. Steadily the little ship grew larger, until she drew up with a swirl of oars like a duckling returning to its mother's side. His stomach tightened. The moment of decision was upon him now.

"What strength?" called the Admiral, gripping the rail.

"Three squadrons—coming up-Channel in cruising formation under easy sail."

Carausius felt the momentum of events begin to seize him. "They'll be preparing for a landing at Portus Adurni, thinking to lie offshore till nightfall and take us by surprise. We'll surprise them instead, lads." He turned to his crew. "Hoist the shield!"

As the gilded shield swung upward, it caught the sun like a fallen star. The brightness was a risk, but even if some keen-eyed enemy caught the flash he would be puzzled to interpret it, if he could see no sails. Behind Carausius, the awning that had sheltered the rowers was being rolled up in a rattle of canvas. Men checked to make sure their swords were handy, and the middle and upper ranks stood to their oars.

The lapping of waves against the side seemed loud in the sudden silence. A shadow passed across the foredeck; Carausius looked up and saw the stark shape of a sea eagle. The sun was almost overhead, the bird a black silhouette against the sky. It slid past, banked with a flash of white-and-black feathers, and circled the ship, once, twice, and again. Then with a cry it sped away westward, as if to lead the British to their enemy.

"An omen!" Menecrates' exclamation came faintly through the sudden roaring in Carausius' ears. The gods had answered him; all his regrets fled away.

"The Lord of Heaven himself gives them into our hand. Forward! The Eagle has shown us our road!"

The deck shivered beneath his feet as one hundred and eight oars lifted and then bit into the sea. *Orion* lurched forward, rolled a little, and finally began to move more smoothly as the rowers found their rhythm and gathering momentum gave her headway through the waves. Behind her, the line of larger triremes followed, masts aligned so that it was hard to see how many there were. To either side, the lighter ships kept pace, holding, he was glad to see, their own columns in as steady a formation as good seamanship could achieve.

Carausius blinked and shaded his eyes with his hand. On the horizon the flicker of white showed again, and he grinned. "Come, my pretties, come on—you cannot see our numbers—tell yourselves we will be easy meat and come on!"

The enemy appeared to have heard him. As the rest of Maximian's fleet came into view, he saw the severe shapes of the sails crumpling as they were hastily taken in, and white wakes exploding into froth as the ships shifted to oars. The wedge formation in which they had been sailing tightened, but they did not slacken speed. Carausius motioned to his trumpeter.

Menecrates snapped an order. *Orion*'s helmsman leaned on the rudder, and the deck tilted as the great ship began a smooth turn to starboard. The line of masts behind him shivered as one by one the other ships in the column followed and repeated his turn. *Orion*'s rowers continued their steady stroke, but the ships behind her were putting on speed, and the smaller, swifter craft in the outer two columns were flashing through the water and veering away to either side.

"Orion," he whispered, "there go your hounds! May the gods give them good hunting!" The Roman Commander would seek to grapple and board in the traditional manner, whereby superior numbers might carry the day. The goal of the British fleet must be to destroy or disable as many of the enemy ships as possible before they came to grips with their foe.

They were closing fast. Carausius' body servant brought him shield and helmet. The javelins had been brought up as well, and *Orion*'s marines were piling them at the after- and foredecks, while the slingers readied their stones. Now he could see the gleam of enemy armor on the deck of the oncoming trireme. He cast a last glance around him. As Admiral he could plan strategies, but it was up to the individual captains to judge, in a situation that changed from moment to moment, how to carry out the orders they had received. Now that the die was cast, thought Carausius with a curious relief, he himself was no more important than any other marine.

Orion lurched as an order from Menecrates altered her course toward the smaller ship he had selected as her first prey. The enemy, seeing her danger, started to veer, and the chance to ram her bows was lost, but the British trireme's momentum made collision inevitable. Portside oars swung high out of the water as the two vessels came together, and *Orion*'s newly sharpened ram sheared through her enemy's waving oars and gouged a groove along her side. She was not destroyed but, for the moment at least, out of action. A javelin struck the deck and clattered past; then *Orion*'s oarsmen set to their work once more and pulled her out of range, driving onward into the mass of the foe.

Shouts and trumpets to either side told Carausius that the squadrons on his wings were beginning to envelop the enemy's wedge from the rear; even light ships could do great damage by ramming from astern.

The next enemy, her attention engaging *Hercules,* noticed too late the new threat bearing down on her. Carausius leaped down to the catwalk and grabbed one of the struts, bracing himself as *Orion* smashed into her foe. Timbers shrieked and a few javelins came whistling over the side, but Menecrates' men were backing oars, pulling *Orion* free before her victim could settle in the water and hold her fast. A marine fell with a javelin in his shoulder, but his companions held on to their weapons, knowing that the sea would avenge him soon.

A burst of yelling and the clash of arms told him that someone from another ship had managed to grapple and battle was joined. But *Orion* surged onward. Masts swayed on the water like treetops in a storm. Beyond them he could see the rocky bluffs that edged the shoreline, closer now.

A flight of slingstones buzzed past his head, and the lookout was knocked down. In a moment one of the marines hauled him upright again, swearing, with blood streaming from a graze on his temple. The ship from which the missiles had come was turning toward them, but not fast enough. A shout from Menecrates sent *Orion* charging toward her unprotected side.

They struck, shattered oars flying through the air like kindling. A hunk of wood punched through a rower's neck like an arrow, and he collapsed. *Orion*'s bow dipped as her enemy's weight bore down. Grapples came whipping through the air, but the marines managed to bat them away. For a few moments Carausius feared the two ships would be stuck together, but once more *Orion* managed to pull free. The shore was growing steadily closer. Carausius glanced up at the sun and realized that the afternoon tide must be setting landward. He grabbed the trumpeter by the arm and shouted in his ear.

In another moment the signal to disengage blared above the clamor of dying ships and men. *Orion* backed oars, drawing away, and the Romans began to cheer. But they did not know this coast and its tides.

As the British ships began to pull back, the Romans tried to follow them, but the enemy triremes, heavier and less well manned, moved slowly. The Romans shouted imprecations while their more agile opponents regrouped, waiting as the tide strengthened and drew their foes inexorably toward the hostile British shore. Roman captains realized their danger and began to turn their attention from battling men to fighting the sea. A few, already too close to escape, turned their prows shoreward, looking for a cove in which to ground. The others, oars thrashing the choppy waters, angled slowly away from the coastline, seeking the open sea.

Carausius waited, his brain busy with calculations of time and distance, as *Orion* paced her enemies, ready to cut off their escape if they should progress too far. Beyond the bluff the coast curved back into a shallow bay. As the Admiral glimpsed it, he spoke once more to the trumpeter.

The horn blared across the waves as *Orion* hallooed her hounds to the attack once more. Carausius pointed toward the largest of the remaining foes, and the deck dipped as the ship began to turn. Ever more swiftly flashed the oars, in the all-out stroke that can only be sustained for as long as it takes to close the last few ship-lengths that separate two foes.

Carausius could make out faces now. He saw a centurion whom he had served with on the Rhenus when both were little more than boys, and brought up his sword in salute. The enemy ship, seeing her danger, tried to turn; the Admiral glimpsed the carven sea-nymph that ornamented her prow. But she was rowing against the tide, whereas *Orion* had the force of the sea behind her. They struck with a rending crash that lifted both ships, spilling men overboard.

Carausius was flung to his knees, staring as armed men rained down around him. The impact had carried them halfway through the other vessel; no need for grappling irons to hold them fast this time, and no way that any strength of oars could pull them free. The rowers were already abandoning their benches and snatching up weapons. Then a sword flared toward him; the Admiral scrambled to his feet, bringing up his shield to guard, and all thought beyond the need to defend himself was swept away.

The men he was fighting were veterans of a thousand such mêlées. They recovered quickly from the shock of the collision and began to regroup, cutting their way across the foredeck of *Orion* with deadly efficiency. Carausius took the shock of their blows on his shield and thrust with all his might. A glancing hit to his helm sent him reeling, but in the next moment a marine and an oarsmen locked in a death grapple fell against his opponent and knocked him overboard.

With a gasped prayer of thanks Carausius got back to his feet. Bodies thrashed in the water or lay tangled among the oars. Where there was room to stand, fighters hacked with sword or thrust with *pilum*. The fight had spread to the other ship, but he could not tell who was winning. He took a quick breath as he saw the bluff looming above them.

Its shadow fell across the locked ships, and a few men looked up, but most were too intent on their own struggles to see. And in another moment it was too late. The Roman vessel's port side hit the rocks, slid upward on the swell, and settled back with a crackling of timbers. And *Orion*'s prow, dislodged by the impact, groaned and began to slide free.

The Roman ship was dead, but her crew could still carry the day by taking the fight to *Orion*. Carausius gritted his teeth and summoned the last of his strength as more legionaries leaped to his deck from the enemy's settling rail.

He had thought the battle hot before, but now it was ten times fiercer, more desperate than any fight against Saxon pirates. Carausius' sword arm began to tire; his shield arm ached from the shock of blows. He was bleeding from a dozen scratches; soon loss of blood would slow him down. They had floated free of the Roman vessel and were now themselves at the mercy of the tide; there was no man free to take the helm.

Dead men lay all around him, but a centurion and another man scrambled over the bodies and came in swinging. Carausius set his feet and prepared to defend himself. Perhaps he should have contented himself with planning the battle and stayed ashore; no doubt that was what Maximian had done. Young men never believed they could be killed, he remembered as a swordstroke slammed into his helmet, snapping the strap and knocking it away; or older men either, he thought as he forced his weary arm up to block the next blow.

He slipped in someone's blood and went down on one knee. Glancing over his shoulder, he realized that the fight had brought him back to the Lady's shrine. He sucked in breath and let it out more slowly, his desperation giving way to a great calm. *Lady, my life is yours,* his spirit cried.

A shadow rose above him, Carausius tried to raise his shield, knowing it would not be in time. Then he felt a quiver in the boards; the deck jerked, and the blow that would have split his head went awry. He glimpsed the man's neck unguarded and swung; blood spurted in a crimson stream as the Roman fell.

Carausius struggled to get upright, supporting himself on his sword. No living man stood near him. He levered himself to his feet and realized that the shore was no longer moving. The soil of Britannia herself had reached out to save him; *Orion* was aground.

On her deck, the fighting had ended. The survivors straightened, and beneath the blood, Carausius recognized them as his own men. Other ships still floated just offshore, and most of them were British as well.

I am alive! He stared around him, gripped by a great wonder. *We have the victory....* And on the face of the statue in the shrine he thought he saw a smile.

⊲ ⊲ ⊲

That night, the larger British vessels anchored in the shallow waters of the cove with their prizes in tow, while the smaller ships were run up on the sandy shore. The men made camp in the meadow above and shared their provisions, and as word spread through the countryside, wagons came lumbering down to the sea bearing food and drink for the celebration.

They had enthroned their commander on a pile of driftwood covered with cloaks taken from their enemies. Carausius told himself he ought to be giving orders, making new plans, but he was light-headed with blood loss and the wine that someone had found on the enemy flagship. And he was too happy. The evening was beautiful, and the men, his men, were the bravest and best that any commander had ever led. He beamed upon them all like the setting sun, and they returned his warmth with praises that grew ever louder as the wine went round.

"They won't sneer at us now for provincial clods!" cried an oarsman.

"British ships are the best, and so are her crews!"

"Shouldn't have to take the orders of some idiot in Rome," muttered one of the marines.

"These waters belong to Britannia, an' we'll defend 'em!"

"Carausius will defend them!" The shoreline echoed with his name.

"Carausius for Emperor!" cried Menacrates, brandishing his blade.

"Imperator, Imperator..." Man by man, all the fleet took up the cry.

Carausius felt himself overwhelmed by their emotion. The Eagle of Jupiter had led him into battle, and the Lady of Britannia had saved him. He could doubt no longer, and when the men of the fleet raised him on their shields to acclaim him Emperor, he lifted his arms, accepting their love, and their land.

Chapter Fourteen

There were times, when the air thickened over the hills and mist rolled down across the moors below the Wall, that Teleri could almost imagine herself back in Avalon. And she was always surprised that the thought should give her such pain. This was not the Summer Country, she told herself as her pony carried her along the road, but the marches of the Brigante lands; and she was no longer a priestess of Avalon, but Empress of Britannia.

The rider ahead of her reined in and looked back inquiringly, as if he had heard her sigh. Teleri managed a smile. In the two years since Carausius had been acclaimed Imperator, Allectus had become a good friend to her. He did not have the stamina for long marches, and he was no sailor, but behind a desk he was a wonder, and an emperor, even more than a commander, needed such men around him in order to survive.

It amazed her, sometimes, that Carausius had maintained his position for so long. When he accepted the Army's acclamation and proclaimed himself Imperator, she had expected Rome to descend with fire and sword before the end of the year. But it would appear that a lord of Britannia could rebel with more impunity than a general from any other province—at least he could if he ruled the seas, and had the favor of Avalon. Still, it seemed to her that even Carausius had been surprised when Maximian, having lost the sea battle, had responded to his proclamation with a stiffly formal letter welcoming him as a brother emperor.

No doubt the Romans had their reasons: Maximian's peace with the Franks had not lasted; he was still trying to keep their clans from overrunning Gallia, as well as pacifying the Alamanni on the Rhenus, and Diocletian was fighting Sarmatians and Goths on the Danuvius. There were rumors of trouble in Syria as well. Rome had no men to spare for fighting elsewhere. So long as Britannia did not threaten the rest of the Empire, the emperors must think they could afford to leave her to her own devices—and defenses. And Carausius himself was learning that there was more to ruling Britannia than defending the Saxon Shore.

Teleri cast an anxious glance toward the grey line of masonry that undulated across the hills. On the other side of that line the Picts ran free, and for all that they were as Celtic as the Brigantes on this side of the Wall, the wild tribes of Alba had laid a terror upon the hearts of their Romanized cousins that was as great as the fear the southern British felt of the Saxons, and had lasted far longer.

Teleri pulled the hood of her heavy cloak forward as the fog thickened, contracting the world to a patch of road surrounded by a grey blur. Moisture darkened the sand that surfaced the road, and beaded on the heather. If this kept up they would have to light the torches, even though it was only midafternoon. Their guide stopped, holding up his hand, and she halted her own pony, listening. Sounds were difficult to distinguish in such weather, but something was coming. . . .

Her escort spread out around her, spears ready. They could fight, but it would be madness to flee when even on the road they could scarcely see their way. Straining, she made out a rhythmic tramp and jingle, too regular, surely, for the undisciplined clatter of Pictish horsemen. Closer and louder it came. Allectus reined his horse back to block the road before her. Teleri heard the scrape of steel as he drew his sword. She wondered how well he could use it. She knew he had been practicing with one of the centurions, but he had not begun his training until two years ago. Still, his determination to stand between her and danger pleased her.

For a moment nothing moved. Then shapes seemed to precipitate from the gloom, and a detachment of legionaries strode out of the mist, and came to a precise halt before her.

"Gaius Martinus, optio, from the garrison at Vindolanda, detached for escort duty to the Empress." He saluted smartly.

"But the Lady Teleri has an escort—" Allectus began.

"We're here to reinforce you on your way into Corstopitum," the optio said dourly. "Last night the Picts broke through at Vercovicium. The Emperor has gone after them, but he sent us to make sure you got safely to shelter." The man looked as if he resented having pulled guard duty when his comrades were out having all the fun.

Carausius had wanted her to stay safely in Eburacum, and now Teleri understood why. She had always thought of the Wall as a barrier as unbreakable as the mists that surrounded Avalon, but that ribbon of stone looked fragile against the expanse of the moors. It was only a work of men, and what one group of men built could be breached by another.

By the time they reached Corstopitum, darkness was falling and the mist had turned to a fine, soaking rain. The town was well sited on the northern bank of the river, where the military road crossed the old trackway into Alba. In earlier years its population had been increased by the numbers of craftsmen brought in to produce military supplies and those who managed the imperial granaries. But to Teleri, riding up the High Street toward the hostel, with moisture seeping down her neck and aching thighs, the place seemed sad. Many of the buildings had been abandoned, and others were badly in need of repair.

But over the years every emperor who came to inspect the Wall had stayed at Corstopitum, and the official hostel was both spacious and comfortable. If it had no mosaics, the planked floors were covered by thick rugs striped in the manner of the local tribes, and there was a crude charm in the hunting scenes some soldier-artist had painted on the wall. Dry clothes and a glowing brazier gradually drove away the chill, and by the time Teleri rejoined Allectus in the big dining chamber, she had recovered enough to listen to his worries with some sympathy.

"The Emperor is a strong man, and our gods protect him," she responded when for the third time he had wondered if Carausius had found shelter. "A man who is accustomed to balance on a heaving deck in a howling storm will not be troubled by a little rain."

Allectus shuddered and then grinned at her, the lines of worry that usually made him seem older than his years disappearing.

"He can take care of himself," she repeated. "I am very glad you are here with me!"

"It has worked out well, our partnership." He sobered, but his face still held the boyish look that had made her heart go out to him. "He has the strength and power to make men follow him. I am the thinker, who calculates and remembers and anticipates what the man of action has not time to see. And you, my lady, are the Sacred Queen. Yours is the love that makes it all worthwhile!"

Love? Teleri raised one eyebrow, but kept silent, reluctant to trouble his faith. She had loved Dierna, and Avalon, and they had been taken from her. Carausius came to her bed more often now that he was Emperor and needed an heir, but she had no child. Perhaps a baby would have drawn them closer together; as it was, she had learned to view her husband with respect, and even some affection, but duty was their primary bond.

Did she love Britannia? What did that mean? She was fond of the Durotrige lands where she had been born, but she had seen nothing on these northern moors to make her love them. Perhaps, if she had been allowed to study the Mysteries as long as Dierna, she would have learned how to love an abstraction as well.

But it was Dierna's ability to care for abstractions that had sent Teleri into exile. Teleri had no more wish to be Empress of Britannia than she did to rule Rome itself. To her, they were equally unreal. She no longer even dreamed of freedom. She wondered suddenly if she was capable of caring deeply for anything anymore.

◁ ◁ ◁

The next word they had of Carausius came barely an hour before the Emperor himself arrived, lying in a horse litter with a great gash in his thigh where a Pictish horseman had got in under his guard.

"I can fight well enough on shipboard, even when the deck is leaping beneath my feet with the swell," he told them, wincing as the Army surgeon put a new dressing on his wound, "but to fight from the back of a horse is something else again! But we stopped them, and scarce half a dozen got away to tell their chieftains that the British Emperor will protect his lands as well as ever they were when they belonged to Rome."

"But you cannot be everywhere, my lord, even if you could stick a horse as well as a Sarmatian. The strength of the Wall is in men, but they must have something to defend. The last Emperor to refortify was Severus, and that was two generations ago. This whole region needs rebuilding, and we don't have the funds to bring in new wood and stone."

"True," said Carausius, "but the population here is less as well, and many buildings have been abandoned. The stones from the structures we demolish will serve to strengthen the rest. They will be smaller, but stronger—" He bit his lip as the surgeon bound a dressing over the wound. "Just like Britannia . . ." he finished rather quickly, beads of perspiration standing out on his brow.

Allectus shook his head impatiently. "Is it bad?" he asked as the surgeon began to put away his instruments. "Will the wound do any lasting harm?"

The surgeon, an Egyptian who still went wrapped in shawls and mufflers after decades away from his native sun, shrugged and smiled.

"He is a strong man. I have treated many worse wounds from which men recovered to fight another day."

"I will take charge of your sickroom," said Teleri. "When an empress orders, even an emperor must obey."

The surgeon nodded. "If he lies still and lets his body heal he will do well, but there will be a scar."

"Another scar, you mean . . ." said Carausius ruefully.

"It is what you deserve for risking yourself in an engagement that any cavalry commander with five years' service could have led as well!" commented Allectus severely.

"If we had one to spare," answered the Emperor. "That is the problem. Now that the taxes no longer go to Rome, Britannia is more prosperous, but that only makes her more tempting to the wolves, whether they come by land or by sea. The men of the southern tribes have been forbidden to bear arms for so many generations that they are no use as a militia, and most will not leave their homes to serve in the Army. The same thing happened, I am told, in the early days of the Empire in Rome."

"And how did they solve the problem?" asked Teleri.

"They recruited soldiers from newly conquered barbarian lands whose sons had not forgotten they were fighting men."

"Well, I hardly think Diocletian will allow you to raid his recruiting grounds," said Allectus.

"True . . . but I will have to find men somewhere. . . ." Carausius fell silent, and did not protest when the surgeon ordered the others out so that he could rest.

He would be a bad patient when the first pain faded away, thought Teleri. He looked oddly helpless, lying there, and she felt an unfamiliar pang of compassion for his pain.

Throughout the winter, while his wound was healing, Carausius brooded on the problem of how to balance his resources of money and manpower. His government had prospered wonderfully under Allectus' hand, but money was no help laid up in his treasury. He must use it to buy men. The wild tribes of the north were the old enemy, unacceptable to the people of Roman Britannia even if they would have hired out to an emperor. He knew he must look elsewhere.

More and more often Carausius found himself dreaming of the sandy heaths and reed-bordered marshes of his own country across the Channel, and the rich soil of the fields that had been wrested from the sea. The men who made those fields were solid and steady, but good fighters, and there was never enough land for the younger sons. Surely, he told himself, if he sent a message, some would answer his call.

And as for the Saxons: Their coast, east of the land of the Jutes and facing the northern sea, was as hard a place to make a living as the Menapian lands. When they went out raiding it was not for glory only, but because the booty they took would buy food for the hungry mouths at home. If he came to them as a countryman, he might bind them by a treaty, and if he purchased the safety of his own lands with tribute, he would not be the first emperor to use the taxes he collected to buy off his enemies.

When he returned to Londinium he would do it. This was the only solution he could see.

On the ides of the month of Maia, three sails appeared off the southeastern coast of Britannia. In the past years, even the lowliest shepherd lad had learned to recognize the patchwork-leather sails of a Saxon keel. Alarms clanged in the villages, then fell silent as the longships sailed by.

The lookouts at Rutupiae, remembering their orders, watched in grim silence as the boats entered the estuary of the Stour and made their way upriver under oars. As the day was ending, they came to Durovernum Cantiacorum, the tribal city of the Cantiaci, with its newly built walls glowing pink in the light of the setting sun.

Carausius watched from the porch of the basilica as the German chieftains marched up the High Street with their warriors, closely escorted by legionaries bearing torches, uneasily aware that they might have to defend these ancient enemies from the hatred of the inhabitants of the town. If the Saxons noticed the tension they gave no sign of it, or perhaps the occasional grins as they looked around them indicated they considered the danger a challenge to be enjoyed.

But Carausius had issued his invitation in terms they could understand, and if he forgot how to speak to them, the young Menapian warriors whom he had brought over from Germania Inferior to be his bodyguard were there to assist him. To reinforce the message, he had had clothing made for himself in the German fashion: long trousers, gathered at the ankle, of fine wool dyed a rich gold, and a linen tunic of blue much ornamented with bands of Greek brocade, with armrings and a torque of gold. From its belt, glittering with golden medallions, hung a well-worn Roman cavalry sword, to remind them he was a warrior. And over all he had draped a mantle of the imperial purple clasped with a brooch of heavy gold, to remind them that he was an emperor.

Here, said the clothing, was a chieftain of rank and power, no sly Roman who would sell his honor for gold, but a king and ring-giver with whom a free fighter might honorably make alliance. But as he watched his guests march toward him, it was not of the outfit's symbolism that Carausius was thinking, but of how much more comfortable it was than Roman gear.

In the basilica they had set up a long table for feasting. Carausius sat at its head with the German chieftains on either side. Their men sat on benches farther down the table, where the slaves kept them well supplied with Gallic wine. The British were accustomed to think of all the pirates as Saxons, but in fact they were from several tribes. The tall man on the Emperor's right was Hlodovic, a saltwater Frank of the breed who were even now causing such trouble for Maximian. Next to him, a thickset man with a grey beard was one of the last Heruli remaining in the north, who had joined his warriors to those in the following of the Anglian leader, Wulfhere. Last came a dour Frisian called Radbod.

"Your wine is good," said Wulfhere, draining his cup and holding it out to be refilled.

"I drink to you," answered Carausius, lifting his own. He had taken the precaution of having the depth of his own cup decreased by filling it partway with wax beforehand. He had learned to drink deep in the Navy, but the capacity of German warriors was legendary, and to win their respect it was essential to keep pace with them.

"We will drink your wine gladly, but we have amphorae that are just as good at home," put in Hlodovic.

"Paid for in blood," said Carausius. "Better to receive such wine as a gift, and spill your blood on nobler quarrels."

"Is it so?" Hlodovic laughed. "Does not your wine come from Gallia? Are not your stocks grown lower since you became unfriends with Maximian?"

"For the past few seasons your cousins have kept him busy in Belgica." Carausius laughed. "He has neither the ships nor the men to impede trade with Britannia."

"Wine is good," agreed Radbod, "but gold is better."

"I have gold... for my friends. And silver from the Mendip mines." Carausius signaled, and the slaves began to bring in baskets of bread and platters with eggs and cheese, and oysters, followed by joints of veal and venison.

"And what gifts do you expect your 'friends' to give you in exchange?" asked Hlodovic, slicing another chunk from the shank before him. They sat at table in the barbarian fashion, but the chieftains, who valued such things as much as any Roman, ate from silver plates and drank from glass goblets.

"Let your young men seek glory on other shores. The rewards will be even greater if you yourselves go against those who would attack us by sea."

"But you, lord, are a noble fighter. Why should you deprive yourself of such a challenge?" asked Wulfhere, laughing and draining his cup again.

"It is true I would rather fight upon the sea. But now that I am High King here, I must spend much time in the north, making war against the Painted Peoples there."

"And you would set the wolves to guard the sheep while you are gone?" Wulfhere shook his head in amusement.

"If the wolves are honorable beasts, I would place more trust in them than in dogs," Carausius replied. The first meats served had been devoured, and now the warriors were working on the whole roast boar glazed with honey and surrounded by apples.

Wulfhere stopped eating to look at him. "You are no Roman, for all they call you Imperator...."

Carausius smiled. "I was born in the Menapian fens. But I belong to Britannia now."

"We wolves are hungry, and we have many cubs to feed," put in Radbod. "How much would you give?"

As the meats were replaced by dishes of stewed fruit and sweet-ened breads and pastries, the discussion became more specific. One after another, the amphorae of Gallic wine were emptied. Carausius matched his guests cup for cup, and hoped he would remember all that had been said when morning came.

"So now we have a bargain," Hlodovic said at last. "And I have only one more thing to ask of you."

"And what is that?" asked Carausius, feeling the wine sing in his veins, or perhaps it was victory.

"I want you to tell us all the tale of how you defeated the fleet of the Emperor Maximian. . . ."

Carausius stood up slowly, holding on to the table until the world stopped whirling, then, taking each step with conscious care, began the long journey toward the door. He had done it! In the name of Jupiter Fides he had sworn to pay the tribute, and the barbarian chieftains had pledged troth to him, swearing by Saxnot and Ing, and by Woden of the Spear. Now they lay at the table with heads pil-lowed on their arms, while their men snored on the beds that had been spread for them on the floor of the hall. But he—Carausius—was the conqueror, in drinking as in negotiation, for he was the only one still able to walk under his own power from the hall.

He wanted his own bed. No—it was Teleri's bed he wanted. He would come to her straight from his battlefield and offer her his vic-tory. At the door, Aedfrid, the youngest of his Menapians, was waiting. He leaned on the boy's shoulder, laughing as he found him-self stumbling on the words. But he had made his meaning clear enough for the man to guide him along the corridors and across the road to the nearby house, belonging to the leading magistrate of the city, where the imperial party had been lodged.

"Do you need any help, lord?" asked Aedfrid as they neared the bedchamber. "Shall I call your body slave, or—"

"No..." Carausius waved genially. "'m a sailor, y'know? In th' Navy they'd laugh at a man... couldn't hold his wine. I'll get m' clothes off—" He missed a step, and reached out for support to the wall. "Maybe m' wife will help me...." He laughed again.

Shaking his head, the warrior opened the door to the Empress's chamber, holding up the torch so that the light streamed past Carausius across the floor.

"Teleri!" he called. "I have done it! I have won!" He lurched toward the bed, and the flickering torch sent his shadow in distorted waves before him. "The sea wolves have sworn alliance!" He had been using the German tongue all evening, and did not realize that he was speaking it now.

The bedclothes heaved; in the torchlight he glimpsed her white face and widening eyes. Then she screamed.

Carausius took a step backward and felt himself falling. The last thing he remembered, as all the wine he had drunk at the feast finally caught up with him, was the terror in Teleri's eyes.

⊲ ⊲ ⊲

In the morning the Emperor woke with a pounding head and a mouth like the kitchen midden. He grimaced, hoping the German chieftains felt worse. Was he getting old, that one night's drinking could make him feel so ill? Then he opened his eyes, and saw that he was in Teleri's bed. Alone.

He groaned aloud, and the door opened. Deft and tactful, his body servant got him out of his wine-stained German clothing, washed him, and put him into a clean tunic.

Carausius found Teleri in the smaller dining chamber, where they often breakfasted. She looked up as he entered, and he stopped short, for what he saw in her face, as he had seen it the night before, was stark fear.

"I apologize," he said stiffly, "for disturbing you." Teleri stared at her platter and did not answer. "I wanted to tell you about my victory. We have a treaty. The German chieftains will send warriors."

"Saxons ..." she hissed, fists clenching in the skirts of her gown.

"Frisians and Franks and Heruli," he corrected, wondering what was wrong with her. She had known they were coming here.

"They are all Saxon wolves to me! I thought it would not matter—that enough time had gone by—" Teleri shook her head, and he saw that she was weeping.

"Teleri!" he exclaimed, moving toward her.

"Don't touch me!" she cried, rising so quickly the bench crashed over behind her. "You're one of them! I thought you were a Roman, but when I look at you it is *his* face I see now!"

"Who, Teleri?" asked Carausius. His voice shook with the effort he was making not to shout.

"The Saxon . . ." she answered, so quietly he had to strain to hear, "the man who tried to rape me when I was eighteen years old."

⊲ ⊲ ⊲

Summer drew on, and with it a year for the southern part of the province more peaceful than any its people could recall. The Saxons, with their oaths still fresh on their lips and their purses full of British gold, turned their attention to other shores. But the Irish had no such inhibitions. They began to raid into the lands of the Silures and Demetae, and the Emperor and his household rode westward to defend them.

Teleri had asked to remain with her father, but the Emperor, knowing the value the western tribes placed on their queens, judged it wise to show his confidence in his ability to defend them by bringing his wife along. Teleri thought that perhaps he had hopes that if she came he might woo her to his bed once more. She had tried to discipline her feelings, but since the feast at Cantiacorum she had not been able to bear his touch. Even when he was not wearing his Menapian clothing or surrounded by his barbarian bodyguard, when she looked at him she still saw an enemy.

As Empress, she had her own servants and household. She rode in a horse litter with her people around her, and if she did not share her husband's bed it was easy to say that she had been tired by travel and needed to sleep alone. When they reached Venta Silurum they would be expected to live together, and explanations would be more difficult. And so, as they neared the mouth of the Sabrina, she begged permission to turn south to Aquae Sulis and take the waters there. Carausius, perhaps hoping that time would heal the rift between them, agreed.

The night before the two parties were to separate, they rested at Corinium, the old capital of the Dobunni, where the Fosse Way intersected the main road to the west. The town was small but wealthy, famous for the artistry of the makers of mosaics who based their industry there. The *mansio* was positively opulent, thought Teleri as she settled onto one of the couches. Surely Rome itself could produce nothing more luxurious. It was all the more disconcerting, therefore, when the door opened and Dierna walked into the room.

As always, the High Priestess dominated her surroundings, which seemed abruptly overdone, even tawdry, behind the classic simplicity of her blue gown. Then Teleri remembered that she herself was now an empress who must outrank any priestess ever born, and sat up, demanding to know what Dierna was doing there.

"My duty—I have come to speak with your husband, and with you." The priestess settled herself on one of the benches. Teleri gave her a narrow look, and saw that the older woman's hands were clasped tightly, belying her air of calm.

"Does he know you are here?" Teleri sat back again, adjusting the folds of her crimson palla to fall more becomingly.

There was no need for answer: the door was opening again and Carausius himself came through, with Allectus at his heels. Behind them she glimpsed the tall figures of his barbarian bodyguard and tensed involuntarily. Then the door shut the sight away.

The Emperor stopped short, staring. He saluted Dierna. "Lady, you honor us."

"It is true," she answered, "I have honored you, but you do not honor us by those barbarian garments you wear."

Teleri took a quick breath. This was getting to the point indeed! Carausius glanced down at his German breeches and flushed, but when he looked up again, there was no yielding in his gaze.

"I was born a barbarian," he said quietly. "These are the garments of my youth, and comfortable. And they are the clothes of my allies."

Dierna's eyes flashed. "Do you, then, reject the gods of Britannia, who have raised you so high? It is no shame for a pig to rootle in the mud, but a man knows better. You have stood upon the Holy Tor and heard the singing of the summer stars. You bore the dragons on your arms before Atlantis sank beneath the waves. Will you deny the wisdom won through so many lives and sink back into the mire where infant races strive? You belong to them no longer, but to Britannia!"

"Indeed. But what is Britannia? The tree that shelters the peoples lifts its arms to heaven," Carausius answered slowly, "but it must be rooted in the earth or it will die. Britannia is more than Avalon. In my travels around this island I have seen men from every corner of the Empire whose sons cherish this land as their own. I will protect all of them—all those who have been given into my hand. You must not blame me if I take what comfort I may where I can...." His gaze sought Teleri and then fell away.

"Your support comes from the princes of Britannia," exclaimed Allectus, "from the men of the old Celtic blood who made you Emperor! Will you give their gifts to slaves?"

Carausius straightened, the high color flaming into his face once more. "Do you attack me as well? I thought that I could count on *your* loyalty!"

"Then perhaps you had better reconsider your own," Allectus said bitterly. "If you are determined to revert to your roots, you must not complain if I remember that my fathers were kings among the Belgae!"

For a long moment Carausius stared at him. His gaze passed to Dierna, and then to Teleri, and she had to look away. At last he sighed.

"You will do as you must. But you are wrong. I remember very well who made me Emperor—it was the soldiers and the men of the fleet who first acclaimed me, not the British princes, who no longer bear arms. Britannia was Celtic once, but that is so no longer. In Moridunum there are men—of many races—who are spilling their blood to defend you. My place is beside them. I will leave you to debate philosophies."

◁ ◁ ◁

The Empress of Britannia was journeying to Aquae Sulis to bathe in the waters and make offerings to the Goddess there. But Teleri, the woman, sought in those pungent waters healing for her troubled soul. She wondered if she would find it. Dierna had decided to come with her, and even an empress found it impossible to deny the Lady of Avalon. But as her horse litter swayed over the stone bridge across the Avon, Teleri looked up at the wooded hills that rose above the town and felt the beginnings of peace.

The temple precinct had been built in the Hellenic style by the Emperor Hadrian. In its day, thought Teleri as she approached the shrine, it must have been magnificent. But the years had smoothed the stones and faded the frescoes. It seemed to her that this place had become an extension of the Goddess, friendly and comfortable as a gown worn until it takes on its owner's form.

In the courtyard she paused before the altar opposite the spring and cast a few pinches of incense on the coals. She could feel Dierna beside her, her power hidden behind the veil that covered her like light behind a shade. The priestesses of Sulis had greeted the Lady of Avalon as a colleague, but in this cult she had no authority, and that knowledge gave Teleri a certain satisfaction.

They moved across the courtyard and up the steps of the temple, whose Gorgon guardian glared down from the pediment, surrounded by nymphs. Inside, lamps shone softly on the life-size image of Minerva Sulis, her gilded features gleaming beneath the bronze helm. Despite her martial trappings, her expression was calmly reflective.

Lady, thought Teleri as she gazed up at her, *can you teach me wisdom? Can you give me peace?* Unbidden, memories came to her of priestesses chanting on the Holy Tor, bathed in the silver radiance of the moon. She had felt the presence of the Goddess then, filling her with light. Here she sensed only an echo of power, and could not tell if the difference lay in the nature of the temple, or in her own soul.

On the second day of her visit, she bathed in the waters. All other visitors had been denied the precinct to give privacy to the Empress and her ladies. Through the colonnade that surrounded the Great Bath she could see the courtyard and the altar where she had worshipped the day before. Light refracted from the water and glimmered on the timbered ceiling; a haze of moisture from the heated pool in the next chamber veiled its shadows in mystery. The water was tepid, and one soon became accustomed to the sulfur smell. Teleri lay back, letting it support her, and tried to relax. But she could not forget the unhappiness she had seen in her husband's eyes when she left him, and the pain, equal in intensity if different in cause, in those of Allectus. It seared her soul to see them at odds.

Presently the priestess of Sulis instructed them to move to the hot pool, fed, like the others, from the sacred spring, but heated by a hypocaust. Teleri gasped at the heat, but Dierna was stepping down into the pool as eagerly as if it had been the lake of Avalon; she bit her lip and forced herself to follow. For a time, then, she could think of nothing but her body's reactions. She felt her heart begin to pound, and sweat started from her brow.

Just when she thought she would faint, their guide assisted her to climb out and escorted her to the frigidarium, whose chill waters seemed scarcely cold at all. Then, with every nerve tingling and the blood humming in her veins, she was allowed to return to the Great Bath. The extremes in temperature had both stimulated and exhausted her. This time she found it easy to sink into a mindless reverie.

"This is the womb of the Goddess," said Dierna softly. "The Romans call her Minerva, and those who came before them, Sulis. To me, she comes as Briga, Lady of this land. When I float in these waters, I am returned to my source and renewed. I thank you for allowing me to accompany you."

Teleri turned to her, brows lifting. But she told herself that such a courteous comment deserved an answer. "You are very welcome. I cannot claim such lofty meditations, but there is peace here."

"There is peace in Avalon as well. I am sorry now that I sent you away from it. My purpose was worthy, but it was a hard fate for one unwilling. I should have found another way." Dierna lay half floating in the green water, her long hair spiraling around her face in bronze curls, her full breasts, nipples darkened by childbearing, breaking the surface.

Teleri's amazement became complete. She had sacrificed three years of her life, and now her mentor was suggesting it had not been necessary after all? "You gave me to understand that the fate of Britannia depended on my cooperation. What other way could there be?"

"It was wrong to bind you by a marriage such as is made between any Roman citizens." Dierna stood up, water streaming from her hair. "I did not understand then that Carausius was destined to be a king, and must be mated to a sacred queen in the old way."

"Well, it is done now, and past mending—" Teleri began, but the priestess shook her head.

"Not so. To bind the Emperor to the ancient Mysteries is even more important now, when he is tempted to follow other ways. You must bring him to Avalon, Teleri, and perform the Great Rite with him there."

Teleri stood up so swiftly that the water rolled away from her in a great wave. "I will not come!" she hissed. "By the Goddess of this sacred spring I swear! You cast me out from Avalon, and I will not come running just because you changed your mind. Work what magic you please on Carausius, but the earth will shake and the heavens will fall before I come crawling back to you!"

She splashed toward the stepped edge of the pool, where slaves waited with towels. She could feel Dierna's gaze upon her, but she did not look back again.

When Teleri woke the next morning, they told her that the Lady of Avalon had gone. For a moment she felt a pang of loss. Then she remembered what had passed between them, and was glad. Before the noon meal, trumpets announced another arrival. It was Allectus, and she was too glad to see him to ask why he was not with the Emperor. The tree-clad hills around Aquae Sulis had become a prison to her. Suddenly she was homesick for the rolling hills above Durnovaria and the sight of the sea.

"Take me to my father's house, Allectus!" she cried. "Take me home!" The hot blood rose and fell in his face, and he kissed her hand.

Chapter Fifteen

That winter a general in Egypt followed Carausius' example and proclaimed himself Emperor. In response, the masters of Rome raised two of their younger generals to the authority and title of Caesar—Galerius to assist Diocletian in the east, and Constantius Chlorus in the west. The decision appeared to be a good one, for not only were the Egyptians reminded where their duty lay but, with Constantius' support, Maximian was able to contain the Franks and the Alamanni on the Rhenus. And with peace restored to the rest of the Empire, the emperors of Rome were at last free to deal with lesser annoyances, such as Britannia.

When the seas calmed with the coming of a new year, a liburnian flying Constantius' pennant rounded the Isle of Tanatus and beat up the estuary of the Tamesis to Londinium. The scrolls she carried bore a simple message. Diocletian and Maximian Augustus called upon Carausius to renounce his usurpation of the province of Britannia and return to his allegiance. He was summoned to Rome for trial. If he refused, he must prepare to face their wrath, with all the power of the Empire behind it.

The Emperor of Britannia sat in his office in the Governor's Palace in Londinium, gazing down at Diocletian's message with unseeing eyes. He no longer needed to read it—he had memorized the words. Within the palace all was silence, but from outside there came a murmur like lapping waters, which periodically swelled to a storm.

"The people are waiting," said Allectus, who was sitting nearer to the window. "They have a right to be heard. You must tell them what you intend to do."

"I hear them," answered Carausius. "Listen—their noise is like the roar of the sea. But I understand the ocean. The men of Londinium are far more fickle, and more dangerous. If I resist this demand, will they stand behind me? They cheered when I assumed the purple. I have brought them prosperity. But I fear they will greet my conqueror with equal enthusiasm if I fall."

"Perhaps," Allectus said evenly, "but you will not win them by indecision. They want to believe that you know what you are doing; that their homes and livelihood will be safe. Tell them that you will defend Londinium and they will be satisfied."

"I want more than that. I want it to be true." Carausius pushed back his chair and began to pace across the mosaic floor. "And I do not think that purpose will be served by camping across the Dubris road with my army and waiting for Constantius to come."

"What else can you do? Londinium is the heart of Britannia, from which its lifeblood flows, or why else did you establish a mint here? It must be protected."

Carausius turned to face him. "The entire land must be protected, and seapower is the key to defending her. Even strengthening the forts of the Saxon Shore is not the answer. I must take the battle to my enemy. He must not be allowed to land so much as a single legionary on these shores."

"You will go to Gallia?" asked Allectus. "Our people will think you are abandoning them."

"The sea base of Gesoriacum is in Gallia. If Constantius takes it, our forward defense is lost—and with it the shipyards, and the supply lines that link us to the Empire."

"And if you lose?"

"I beat them before. . . ." Carausius stood still, fists clenching.

"Your fleet was fresh from fighting the Saxons then, at the peak of its efficiency," observed Allectus. "Now half your marines are in the north reinforcing the garrisons on the Wall. Will you call on your barbarian allies?"

"If I must—"

"You must not!" Now Allectus was on his feet as well. "You have given up too much to them already. If you win by their aid they will want more. I am as dedicated as you are to maintaining Britannia in freedom, but I would rather be ruled by Rome than by Saxon wolves!"

"You are being ruled by a Menapian now!" Carausius could hear his own voice rising and fought for control. "Britannia's governors have come from Gallia and Dalmatia and Hispania; the Legions that defend you bear foreign names."

"Perhaps they were born barbarians, but they have been civilized. They recognize that this is a Celtic land. The Saxons care only to fill their bellies. Their breed will never take root in British soil."

Carausius sighed, remembering how the priestess had shed his blood to feed the land. "I will go south, where the people still remember how I saved their homes, and raise men to sail with me to Gesoriacum. You understand these merchants of Londinium, Allectus. Stay here and rule in my place while I am gone."

A swift, unexpected flush came and went in the younger man's sallow cheeks. Carausius wondered why. Surely, after all this time, Allectus must know how the Emperor trusted him. But there was no more time to worry about anyone's feelings. He opened the door and called for his clerk, already marshaling the instructions that must be given before he could depart.

On the Tor, the beginning of summer was customarily set aside for dyeing the skeins of flax and wool that had been spun during the long winter. It was the tradition also for the Lady of Avalon to assist in the labor. The reason given was that she might thereby set an example for the maidens, but it had always seemed to Dierna that the custom had been retained because by the time one became high priestess the task of preparing the dye and dipping the yarn was a welcome diversion from her other responsibilities. Not that the work was simple—to mix the dyestuffs correctly and time the immersion to produce just the right shade of blue required experience and a good eye. Ildeg was their dyemistress, and Dierna was content to work under her direction.

Several skeins of wool already swung, dripping, from the branches of the willow tree behind her, its bark still faintly stained from having served the same purpose the year before. Farther along the bank of the stream other cauldrons were steaming. Ildeg walked from one to another, making sure that all was done correctly. Little Lina, who was assisting Dierna, brought two skeins and laid them on the mat, then added another piece of wood to the fire. It was important to keep the liquid simmering without allowing it to boil.

Dierna hooked up one of the skeins and lowered it carefully into the pot. The dye was woad, in this light as deep a blue as the waves of the open sea. She had only once been out of sight of the land, when Carausius took her out into the Channel on his flagship. He had laughed at her ignorance and said she needed to understand the waters that protected her beloved isle. She looked into the cauldron and saw the sea once more, her dipper creating the currents that flowed through it, and the white froth on the waves.

Carausius might be at sea even now, she thought, fighting his battle. Word had come that he was on his way to Gesoriacum with every ship he could command. But he had not taken Teleri, and even if the priestess had seen something in vision that would be helpful, without another trained priestess to receive the message, or the ritual of preparation and the sacred herbs to increase her own power, she had no way to communicate what she saw. She had not expected to care so much whether she knew what was happening.

"Pull the wool out now, my dear, or it will be too dark." Ildeg's voice startled Dierna back to awareness of the present. She lifted the skein and carried it, steaming, to the willow tree, and Lina went off to get more.

Dierna took a deep breath before dipping the next one, for the acrid fumes from the dyepot could be dizzying, then carefully lowered it into the deep-blue sea.... A leaf fell and drifted in lazy circles on the surface. The priestess started to lift it, then dropped the dipper with a soft cry. It was not a leaf, but a ship, with a dozen more around it, appearing and disappearing through the swirling steam. She gripped the rim of the pot, unaware of the heat that seared her palms, and bent closer, desperate to see.

Her vision was as that of a seabird, circling the ships that battled below. She recognized *Orion* and some of the others. Even if she had not known them by sight, she would have known them by the speed and agility with which they moved. The remaining ships—bigger, heavier, and more clumsily handled—must be the Roman enemy. Behind them she could make out a long sandspit; the engagement was taking place inside a great harbor, where the British superiority in ship handling gave little advantage. How had Carausius allowed himself to be trapped this way? His fight against Maximian's Armorican fleet had been a test of seamanship, but as one Roman after another managed to grapple and board her victim, it became clear that this battle would be won by brute force, not skill.

Flee! her heart cried. *You cannot win here, you must break free!* Dierna strained downward; for a moment she saw Carausius clearly, a bloody sword in his hand. He looked up. Had he seen her? Had he heard? Then a tide of red rolled across her vision. The sea was turning to blood! She must have screamed, for in the next moment she heard voices calling her name as if from a great distance, and felt soft hands pulling her away.

"It's red . . ." she whispered. "There is blood in the water—"

"No, Lady," answered Lina, "the dye in the water is blue! Oh, my Lady, look at your hands!"

Dierna gasped at the first pulse of pain. Then the others were gathering around her, and in the tumult of dressing her wounds, no one thought to ask her what she had seen.

The next morning she summoned Adwen to pack for her, and Lewal and one of the younger Druids to escort her, and the men of the marshes to pole them through the mists to the outer world. There was that in her manner that defied questioning, but in any case she dared not speak of her vision, if indeed it had been a true Seeing and not a fancy born of her fears. If Carausius had been defeated, either he himself or word of his death would come first to Portus Adurni, and it was there that she must go. If he lived, he would need her help. She had to know.

The journey took them a week of hard traveling. By the time they reached Venta Belgarum, Dierna's hands were healing and one anxiety had been replaced by another. Bad news spread like the wind, and all of the west country knew that a great battle had taken place at Gesoriacum. Throughout one night Dierna tossed sleepless, too anxious even to seek him on the spirit-roads, not knowing if Carausius had survived.

In the morning more news followed: the flagship had made it home with the Emperor on board, but the ships that followed him were pitifully few. The fleet that had struck fear into the hearts of the Saxons was lost, along with most of the men who had manned it, and Constantius Chlorus was gathering a force to invade Britannia. Everywhere men were murmuring. Men who had profited under the rebel regime feared to lose all they had gained. Others shrugged, unconcerned at the prospective change of masters, or speculated on the rewards in store for those who helped the invaders.

But whatever the Romans did about the others, if Constantius conquered there would be no mercy for Carausius. Dierna's pony tossed its head and broke into a trot as she urged it forward.

◁ ◁ ◁

The air at Portus Adurni seemed heavy, despite the fresh wind off the sea. Dierna thought that she would have known there was trouble even if she had not heard the rumors. The atmosphere in the fortress was not yet that of defeat, but she could almost taste the apprehension. It was significant that the officer in charge made no objection when she asked to see the Emperor. She was a civilian, with no business on a military post in what would soon become a war zone. But it was clear that the forces Carausius retained were desperate enough to welcome even whatever nebulous help a native witchwoman might bring.

He was leaning on a table on which a map of Britannia had been spread, moving chips of wood back and forth as he calculated movements and dispositions. There was an ugly gash on his cheek and a bandage around one calf. For a moment Dierna stood in the doorway, so weak with relief at the sight of him that she could not move. Then, though she had made no sound, he looked up.

"Teleri?" he whispered. Dierna took a step forward, turning so that the light fell full upon her. Carausius blinked, the hope that had for a moment animated his face giving way to something else, perhaps fear.

Why should I be surprised? she told herself, willing her pounding heart to slow. *I wanted him to love her. I should not have come. . . .* But he was already moving toward her.

"Lady," he said harshly, "have you come to prophesy good fortune or despair?" His gaze had steadied, but it was the calm of a man who wills himself to face his doom. Was that what she was to him? She bit her lip, realizing that was all she had allowed herself to be.

"Neither. I came to help you if I can."

He frowned, thinking. "You have come swiftly if you were on Avalon. Or did Teleri send—" As she shook her head she saw the sorrow, swiftly veiled, in his eyes.

"Is she not here with you?"

"She is in Durnovaria, with her father." There was a short silence.

Now it was Dierna's turn to frown. It had been clear, at Aquae Sulis, that Teleri was unhappy. But the situation must be worse than she thought. *She blames me for it,* she realized then. *That is why she would not talk to me.* But there was nothing she could do about Teleri right now. Suppressing her unease, she came to his side and looked down at the map.

"Where do you think Constantius will land, and what forces can you bring to meet him?"

"His first concern must be to take Londinium," said Carausius. She could see that to discuss the problem gave him a measure of comfort. It was action, of a sort, and this was not a man to accept his fate meekly, as the Christian priests enjoined their followers.

"He might strike for it directly," he continued, "but a landing would be difficult if the city is defended. Constantius might try instead to land on Tanatus and march across Cantium; however, he knows the southeast supports me strongly. If I were in his place, I would try a two-pronged attack and land the second force elsewhere, perhaps between here and Clausentum. Allectus' subsidiary mint is here, and it would be wise to seize it as soon as possible."

As he spoke he moved the colored counters around the map, and for a moment Dierna saw, as if she were gazing into the sacred well, soldiers marching across the land. She shook her head to rid it of the fancy, and focused on the map once more.

"And you are mustering your defenses?"

"Allectus holds Londinium," he replied. "I have stripped the garrisons on the Wall to the bone, and those forces are marching south to reinforce her garrison. I will put more men here, and in Venta as well. We must base our defenses on the cities. Except for the naval fortresses, we have no forces in the south. Since the time of Claudius, the fighting has all been on the coasts and the northern border, and there has been no need. You could help me, if you would, by going to Durnovaria and asking Prince Eiddin Mynoc if he will raise a war band from among his young men."

"But Teleri—"

"Teleri has left me," he said flatly, confirming her fears. "I ask no condolences. You know better than any that our marriage was only the symbol of an alliance. She never wanted me, and I never really had the time to try and win her. I wish I could have made her happy, but I would not hold her against her will. Yet I still need the alliance, and I cannot ask her to plead for me."

His face had that complete absence of emotion that masks deep pain. Dierna bit her lip, knowing better than to insult him with sympathy. She had arranged the marriage, as she thought, for the good of all, but the result had been to hurt the girl she loved as a sister and the man whom she—respected? Could respect account for the way she felt now? She told herself that her own feelings did not matter. There was too much to do.

"I will go, of course," she said slowly, wondering if Teleri would be willing to talk to her now. "But I would feel better," she added, "if you put someone else in command of Londinium." She was not quite sure what was bothering her—was it something Allectus had said at Corinium?

"A more experienced officer?" asked Carausius. "Allectus knows enough to be guided in military matters by the commander of the garrison. It is the civilian population which must support our cause, and Allectus is on excellent terms with every merchant in Londinium. He will be able to persuade them if anyone can. I trust him all the more just because he is not regular Army. An officer of long service, faced with Caesar's legionaries, might remember that his first oath was to Diocletian. But I am certain that Allectus will never willingly give Britannia back to Roman rule."

"You are right," Dierna said, thinking of royal bloodlines, "but is he as loyal to you as he is to this land?"

Carausius straightened, looking at her, and she stilled, aware of a sudden tension between them.

"Why," he asked tiredly, "should that matter to you?"

Dierna stood silent, unable to answer him.

"You didn't want an emperor for Britannia, you wanted a sacred king," he went on. "You called me to this isle by your magic and gave me a royal bride; you persuaded me to forsake my oath of allegiance and my own land. But Allectus belongs here. *He* will never disgust you by wearing the garments of a barbarian. . . ."

He too was remembering how they had argued in Corinium. The sadness in his smile wrenched her heart, but in the next moment she recognized in his eyes not only pain but pride.

"I may be barbarian born, my Lady, but I am not stupid. Do you think I did not understand that I was only your tool for the defense of Britannia? But a tool can break, and when it does, the craftsman takes up another. Can you face me and say that you will cease trying to free this land from Rome if I should fall?"

Dierna felt her own eyes sting unexpectedly with tears, but she could not look away. His patience demanded an answer.

"No ..." she whispered at last, "but that is because it is the Goddess who wields the tools, and I also am in Her hand. ..."

"Then why do you weep?" He took a step toward her. "Dierna! If we are equally bound, then will you just this once cease trying to manipulate everyone according to your own notions of duty and give truth to me?"

The truth ..., she thought desperately. *Do I even know it? Or is duty all I can allow myself to see?* "I weep," she said at last, "because I love you."

For a moment Carausius was completely still. She saw the tension go out of him, and his head bowed.

"Love ..." He whispered it as if he had never before heard the word.

And why should he love me? she wondered then.

"It makes no difference," Dierna said quickly. "You asked and I answered."

"You are the High Priestess of Avalon, as holy as one of the Vestals in Rome." He looked up at her, and she flinched from the intensity of emotion suddenly revealed. She had no right to expect love from him, but she did not think she could bear his hatred. "To say that what you feel means nothing demeans you, and me." Carausius continued to stare at her, as if her features were a book written in some strange language that he was trying to read.

"I did not speak as High Priestess, but as a woman ..." she whispered. Her eyes again filled with tears.

"And it has been a long time since she was allowed to feel?" he asked with a ghost of humor. "The Emperor of Britannia might say the same."

To her blurred vision, his features seemed to alter. She had seen them before, when he and she sought visions in the silver bowl upon the Tor. With a sudden conviction she thought, *I have loved this man before.*

Carausius straightened. Slowly the aura of power that always made him seem the biggest man in any room returned. It was not the power of the Emperor he had become that she recognized, but the aura of the King. He had been right, she thought, in identifying what she wanted for Britannia. But the Sacred King she sought was not Allectus but himself. He strode to the door and said something to the guard outside. Then he closed it firmly and turned back to her.

"Dierna . . ." He spoke her name once more.

Her heart began to pound, but it seemed the power of voluntary motion had abandoned her. Carausius gripped her shoulders and bent to kiss her as a thirsty man bends to a pool of water. She sighed, her eyes closing, and as he felt her yield he pulled her hard against him. Dierna trembled, suddenly achingly aware of everything he was feeling, because his need was her own. And in that moment she did not care whether he was king or emperor, or only a man.

After a time her released her, fumbling for the fastenings of her gown. Dierna could not protest: her hands were as eager on his body as his upon her own. The small part of her mind not yet over-whelmed by passion observed in amusement that she was as clumsy as a virgin. Indeed, she had never known a man except in the ceremonial joinings of the Druid rituals, never taken a lover simply for desire. She wondered vaguely how they would consummate their union, for there was no bed in the room.

Carausius kissed her once more and she clung to him; her bones were melting, she flowed to meet him as the river seeks the sea. Then he lifted her and laid her down upon the map of Britannia that cov-ered the table. Dierna laughed softly, in a single flash seeing the sym-bolism, and understanding that the Goddess had blessed even this hasty coupling, for, without design or ceremony, High Priestess and Emperor were celebrating the Great Rite after all.

◁ ◁ ◁

The walls that Eiddin Mynoc had built around his city were high and strong. Teleri could walk all day if she wished, and never have to look at the sea. Since she had come down from Aquae Sulis, she had spent a great deal of time walking, to the despair of the maidservants her father had assigned to attend her. And since Dierna's visit, she found it impossible to be still.

Sometimes Teleri wondered what the High Priestess had

wished to say to her. She had refused to see her, afraid Dierna would try to persuade her to go back to her husband, or to Avalon. But the other woman had spent a great deal of time talking to the Prince, so perhaps she had not really been interested in Teleri after all. In any case, the priestess was gone now, and Teleri's brothers and their friends were happily practicing cavalry maneuvers on their blooded horses, and learning how to adapt the skills of the hunt to the battlefield. Soon they would leave as well, and then there would be nothing to remind her of Carausius and his war.

A gull swooped across her path, yammering, and she jumped, her fingers making the sign to avert evil.

"Oh, my lady, you must not give way to such superstitions," said her maid Julia, who had recently become a Christian. "Birds are not evil, only men."

"Unless it was no natural bird, but an illusion of the Evil One," said Beth, her other attendant, laughing as Julia crossed herself.

Teleri turned away, their bickering as meaningless as the squawking of the bird. "We will go to the market to look at plates and bowls."

"But, lady, we were there only two days ago—" began Julia.

"A new shipment of Castor-ware is expected," answered Teleri, and set off at such a pace that the girl had no breath to spare for another objection.

By the time they returned to her father's town house, the maids carefully carrying two dark-brown pots embellished with bas-relief hunting scenes, the sun was sinking in the west. The purchase of the pots had distracted Teleri for a little while, but already they had ceased to interest her, and when the girls asked her what to do with them, she shrugged and said they might take them to the housekeeper or the rubbish heap, for all she cared.

Teleri went to her rooms and cast herself upon the couch, then rose once more. She was tired, but she feared to sleep, because so often she had troubled dreams. She had just sat down again when one of the house slaves came bowing to her door.

"Lady, your father says that you should come. The lord Allectus is here!"

Teleri stood so suddenly she felt faint, and grasped the curved end of the couch for support. Had Allectus come as the Emperor's advocate, or was there another reason? Suddenly self-conscious, she pulled off the stola she had worn to the market, smudged with the dust of the day, and cast it aside.

"Tell them to bring me water for washing, and tell Julia to lay out the rose silk tunica and the matching veil!"

By the time Teleri joined her father and his guest in the dining chamber, she was composed in appearance, if not inwardly. When she had been seated, the conversation returned to the coming invasion.

"And does your intelligence indicate that the Romans will come soon?" asked the Prince.

"I do not think that Constantius has enough transports for the men he will need to bring, and he will need to build more warships as well. He defeated Carausius in Gesoriacum, but our lads gave them a good savaging."

Allectus sipped at his wine, his gaze slipping sideways to Teleri. He had colored when she came in, but his greeting had been formal. He looked fit, she thought then, his skin browned from much riding in the sun. And he looked older—all the boyish softness had been worn away.

"And the lads we have here," said the Prince, "will they, as you put it, give the Romans 'a good savaging' as well?"

"If we are united," said Allectus. "But as I travel about, I hear murmurs. Our people—the men of the old Celtic blood—are awakening. To escape from the Roman yoke is much, but some say we should go further, and choose a king who is not himself a foreigner."

Teleri's gaze moved to her father, who continued to peel the apple he was holding.

"And how would a high king be chosen?" asked the Prince. "If our people had been able to unite, Caesar—the first one—would never have gotten a foothold on these shores. Our tragedy is that we have always been more eager to fight each other than any foreign foe."

"But if they could agree? If there were some sign to mark the man our gods have chosen?" asked Allectus softly.

"There are many omens, and many interpretations. When the time comes, a chieftain must judge by what he sees. . . ."

Teleri stared, wondering if she dreamed or they did. What about Carausius? But already the talk had become more general, turning to the training of men and the supplies that fed them, and routes for moving one or another where they must go.

The night was warm, and when dinner was done, Allectus asked Teleri if she would walk with him in the atrium. For a time, they paced in silence. Then Allectus stopped suddenly.

"Teleri—why did you leave Carausius? Was he cruel? Did he hurt you?"

She shook her head wearily. She had been expecting something like this. "Hurt me? No—he never cared enough for that. Carausius did nothing, but when I looked at him I saw a Saxon."

"You never loved him?"

She turned to face him. "Never. But you did, Allectus, or at least he was your hero! What do you want me to say?"

"I thought he would save Britannia!" Allectus exclaimed. "But it was only a change of masters. And I was always in his shadow. And you belonged to him. . . ."

"Did you mean what you said to my father, or were you only testing him?" Teleri asked then.

He let out his breath in a long sigh. "Teleri, I could lead this land. A government runs on money, and I control it. I come of the Belgic princes, and the Silures on my mother's side. That is not enough, I know. But if you could love me—they would follow me if you consented to be my Queen."

She fingered the fabric of her gown. "And do you love me, or do you only want to marry me, as *he* did, because it will help you to gain power?" She looked up and realized that Allectus was trembling.

"Teleri," he whispered. "Don't you know what I feel for you? You have haunted my dreams. But when we met, you were a priestess of Avalon, and then, suddenly, the wife of Carausius. I would give you my heart on a platter if it would please you, but I would rather offer you Britannia. Give me your love and you shall be, not Empress, but High Queen."

"And what of my husband?"

His gaze, which had been so luminous and open a moment before, grew hard. "I will reason with him until he agrees. . . ."

Even if the Emperor relinquished her, Teleri could not imagine Carausius voluntarily giving up his power. But Allectus was kneeling before her, and she found it hard to care. He took her hand and kissed it, then turned it gently and pressed his lips to her palm.

Such a gentle touch, she thought. Allectus would not stop her if she rose and walked away. But as Teleri looked down at his bent head, she felt a surge of protective pity, and for the first time realized that she too had power. Carausius had needed her as a link to the British, and to Avalon. This man needed her love.

Gently, she stroked his hair, and when he looked up, she accepted him into her arms.

◁ ◁ ◁

The messenger Prince Eiddin Mynoc sent to the Emperor had said the Prince's men would be leaving Durnovaria on the ides of Junius. He had recommended that an officer be sent to take charge of them at Sorviodunum, where the main road from the southwest met the routes coming down from Aquae Sulis and Glevum.

A few days before Midsummer, Carausius, exasperated by a week of conferences with the local senators at Venta, decided to ride over himself to meet them. He still wore his German breeches for riding, but his advisers had persuaded him to put his Menapian bodyguard in Roman gear. They looked now, he thought as he glanced at the file riding behind him, like any other recruits sent to serve at the other end of the Empire.

When they came to Sorviodunum, the Durotriges had not yet arrived, but the weather was fair and bright; it was not a day for a man to sit inside when he might be out in the clean air. What he wanted, thought Carausius as he led his men out along the

Durnovaria road, was to be on the deck of a ship. It would have been a fine day for sailing. But he would sway instead to the motion of the horse beneath him, and pretend that the undulations in the land before him were the rolling waves of the sea.

It was nearing noon when one of the Menapians called out and, looking up, Carausius saw a cloud of dust on the road. The past few years had taught him to judge cavalry, and he estimated that perhaps two score horsemen were coming, pushing their mounts harder than an experienced commander would have recommended, out of exuberance, probably, rather than emergency. He squeezed his own mount's sides, and the Menapians speeded into a trot behind him as they hurried to meet the Durotriges.

With a smile he recognized Teleri's eldest brother, more heavily built than she, though with the same dark hair. But, then, he had already figured out whose these riders must be. They looked good, he thought as he scanned the others—their gear, all aflutter and jingling with ornaments and tassels, was more suited for parade than the field—but they seemed energetic and determined. And of course they rode well.

Only one man sat his horse without the easy grace of the others. Carausius shaded his eyes with one hand, blinking as he recognized Allectus. It had taken him a moment, for he had never seen the younger man in anything but Roman dress, whereas now he rode in a saffron tunic and crimson mantle, like the Belgic Prince he was.

It would appear that he himself was not the only one to feel the tug of his native roots, now that they were fighting Rome, thought Carausius. He grinned as the Durotriges pulled up in a swirl of dust before him, and waved.

"Allectus, my boy, what are you doing here? I thought you were in Londinium."

"This is my country and my people," answered Allectus. "It is here I should be."

Carausius felt a faint prickle of uncertainty, but he continued to smile. "Well, you have certainly brought the Durotriges here in prime fettle." He looked back at the riders and his unease deepened, for they were not smiling.

Teleri's brother moved his mount a little forward. "Did you think that you Romans—or you Germans, I should say—were the only ones who can fight? Celtic warriors made the walls of Rome tremble when your people were still crawling out of the mire."

Theudibert, one of Carausius' Menapians, growled, but he motioned to him to be still.

"If I did not believe in your courage," he said calmly, "I would not have asked your father to send you. Britannia needs all her sons to fight for her now—those whose forebears battled Caesar, and the children of the Legions, brought from Sarmatia and Hispania and every corner of the Empire to take root in this land. We are all Britons now."

"Not you," said one of the Durotriges. "You were born across the sea."

"I have given my blood for Britannia," said Carausius. "The Lady of Avalon herself accepted my offering." Even now the thought of Dierna lifted his heart. At Portus Adurni he had given more than blood; he had poured out his seed, his very life, in her embrace that night, and been renewed.

"The Lady of the Britons rejects it," said Allectus. The warriors reined aside to let him through. "The daughter of Eiddin Mynoc is your wife no longer. The alliance is ended, and our allegiance withdrawn."

Carausius stiffened with anger. Had the boy gone mad?

"The tribes breed brave men," he said in a last attempt at conciliation, "but for three hundred years they have not borne arms except for hunting. Without the help of the British Legions, you will be easy meat for Constantius when he comes."

"The Legions"—Allectus snorted contemptuously—"will follow whoever pays them. Is that not the history of your Empire? And the mints belong to me. Whether for love or for money, all of Britannia will fight the invader. But they must be led by a man of the old blood."

A vein pulsed in Carausius' temple. "By you . . ."

Allectus nodded. "It might have been different if you had had a son by Teleri, but she rejected your seed. She has bestowed the sovereignty on me."

Carausius stared at him unseeing. He knew that he had never won Teleri's love, but he had not realized that she hated him. That hurt, for he still thought of her with affection, even though Dierna had shown him what it meant to love. The part of his mind that was still capable of reason told him that Allectus was saying these things to wound him. And if Dierna had not given herself to him so fully, Allectus might have succeeded. But with the memory of her love like living water within him, no taunt Allectus might make could shake his manhood. It was she, not Teleri, who was the giver of sovereignty.

But the Durotriges clearly believed Allectus, and he could not betray Dierna by telling them of her gift to him.

"These men are not bound," he said slowly, "but you, Allectus, swore an oath to me. How can they trust you if you betray me?"

Allectus shrugged. "I swore by the gods of Rome—the same gods by whom you swore to serve Diocletian. One broken oath deserves another—'an eye for an eye,' as the Christians say."

Carausius brought his horse up closer, forcing the other man to meet his eyes. "It was more than an oath, Allectus, between us," he said softly. "I thought I had your love."

The younger man gave a little shake of the head. "I love Teleri more."

Teleri, thought Carausius, *not Britannia.*

"You may have her with my blessing," he said grimly, "and may she be more comfort to you than ever she was to me. But as for Britannia, I believe that the Legions have more sense than to obey an untried boy, even one whose hands flow with gold. And it may be that the other tribes will not be so eager to obey the Belgae, who conquered them before the Romans came. You are welcome to try, Allectus, but I do not think the people of this land will follow you, and I will not abandon those who swore faith to me. . . ."

Contemptuously, he reined his horse away. He had gone perhaps two horses' lengths forward when one of the Menapians shouted a warning. Carausius began to turn, and so it was that the lance that Teleri's brother had thrown took him not in the back but through the side.

For a moment all he felt was the impact. Then the weight of the lance pulled it free. As it clattered to the road, Carausius felt a gush of warmth below his ribs, and then, finally, the first fiery stab of pain. He heard shouts, and the clash of swords. A horse screamed. He blinked, trying to focus, and saw one of his bodyguard go down.

I am not dead yet, he told himself, *and men are dying for me!* A deep breath brought him a moment's clarity, and he drew his sword. He kicked his mount toward Allectus, but there were too many men between them. A blade flashed toward him; he knocked it away, thrust, felt the jar as it bit, and saw his enemy fall. That had been luck, he thought, but his battle rage was rising, and with every moment he felt stronger. His Menapians, seeing him fighting, took courage and attacked with equal fury.

Time blurred. Suddenly there was no foe before him. He heard hoofbeats, and saw that the Durotriges were regrouping around Allectus and wheeling away. Arms waved as if they were arguing.

"My lord," cried one of his men. "You are bleeding!"

Carausius managed to sheathe his sword and pressed his hand to his side. "It is not serious," he gasped. "Tear me a strip from your mantle to stanch it. They outnumber us, but we've made them bleed. If we draw off now, they may think twice about following."

"Back to Sorviodunum?" asked Aedfrid.

The Emperor shook his head. Allectus' treachery had shaken all his assumptions, and until he was healed he dared trust no one's loyalty. Carausius twisted to look down at his side. Blood welled from the wound, making it hard to see, but he sensed it was bad. Though he had spoken stoutly, this might be beyond the skill of any surgeon closer than Londinium. He straightened in the saddle, gazing westward, where the hills rolled away into blue haze.

"Bind up my side," he said to Theudibert.

"Lord, this is very deep. We must get help for you."

"That way," said Carausius, pointing. "The only healing for this hurt is in the Summer Country. We'll go back as if we were returning to the town, and turn off as soon as we are out of sight. They will lose time looking for us on the road. Swiftly now, and do not falter because of me. If I cannot sit a horse, tie me to the saddle; if I cannot speak, keep asking for the road to Avalon."

Chapter Sixteen

Dierna gasped as agony stabbed her side. The thread snapped between her fingers and the spindle rolled across the grass.

"Lady! What is it?" cried Lina, the maiden assigned this month to serve her. "Did a bee sting you, or did you prick your hand?" Her words were lost in a babble of concern as the other women came running.

The priestess clapped her hand to her side and took a deep breath, fighting to control the pain. It was not her heart; the burning ache pulsed lower, beneath her rib cage, as if something had broken there. And the agony was not entirely internal. The skin itself was tender as she probed it carefully; and yet, when they unpinned her tunic, she could see no wound.

No spell or ill-wishing could break through Dierna's wardings against her will. And there was only one person living to whom she had opened herself so fully that she would feel *his* agony. She realized that in their lovemaking she had given Carausius more than her body—she had given part of her soul away. She sent her spirit winging outward along the path by which the pain had come, and sensed his longing for her.

"She is elf-shot," said old Cigfolla soberly. "Lift her carefully, my daughters. We must take her to her bed."

Dierna got control of her voice again. "It is not . . . *my* . . . pain. I must rest, but you . . . Adwen . . . go to the holy well. Someone . . . is coming. . . . Try if the Sight will show him to you!"

That whole afternoon Dierna lay in the cool darkness of her

dwelling, using all the disciplines she had learned to maintain a state of trance that would put her beyond the pain. Gradually the physical agony became bearable, but the sense of need grew. Carausius was seeking her, but would he reach her in time?

⊲ ⊲ ⊲

The plan had been a good one, thought Carausius, reining in and drawing breath in deep gasps, but he had overestimated his own endurance. Despite the binding, every step jarred his side to new agony. When it came to a choice between stopping or losing consciousness, he judged it would take less time to pause. But he was having to do so more and more often, and at their previous halt, the rearguard had come galloping up to tell them that the Durotriges were on their trail.

"Let us stop here, lord, and make a stand," said Theudibert. Carausius shook his head. The foliage was too thick for maneuvering, but not high enough for cover. "Then let some of us continue on down the valley, where the ground is soft and will show our tracks well," said the warrior, "while you slip away across the heath. With luck they will follow us."

The Emperor nodded. This way at least some of his men would be saved. It was the only way, he knew, that he would be able to get any of them to leave him. Allectus might be false, but these lads had sworn the oath of a *comitatus,* and would never willingly outlive their chieftain.

"May Nehalennia bless and guard you." He called their own goddess to guard them as they thundered away.

"Come," said Theudibert, "let us go on now, while their noise still covers our own."

Theudibert had his rein, for it was all Carausius could do now to stay in the saddle; he bit back a cry as the motion sent pain through him in dizzying waves.

This scene was repeated several times during the two days that followed. The Menapians were hardy and used to rough traveling, but the Durotriges knew the land. Though subterfuges might work for a time, eventually their enemies always found them. Carausius could only hope that when he reached Avalon he would be protected by the Britons' respect for the holy isle.

On the afternoon of the third day, approaching from the east, they reached the marshes of the Summer Country. By this time, Carausius was too weak to sit a horse alone, and rode roped to Theudibert. The marshes were a terrain that the Menapians understood, but no good for horses. Two men were sent off with their mounts. Retaining only the beast Carausius rode, the six who remained began to work their way around the edge of the lake, seeking the village of the marsh folk who could take him to Avalon.

It had not occurred to them that the British, familiar with the country, would know by now where they must be heading and ride ahead along the ridge of the Poldens to forestall them. Carausius, who might have foreseen it, was by this time almost past thinking. He did not rouse until the shock of a sudden stop and an oath from Theudibert brought him upright, staring.

Dusk was falling. Across still water he saw the huts of the marsh dwellers on their poles. Before them, a spur of solid ground curved down from the ridge, and there, silhouetted against the light, a line of horsemen was waiting.

"I will hide you in the marshes," said Theudibert, undoing the rope that had tied them together and knotting the loose end around his lord's waist.

"No . . ." rasped Carausius. "I would rather die fighting. But send Aedfrid to that village. He must beg them to summon the Lady of Avalon."

A few moments before, he could not have moved, but now, with his foe before him, Carausius found himself able to get off the horse and draw his sword.

"This is good," said Theudibert as the riders started toward them. "I too am tired of running away." He smiled, and after a moment Carausius grimaced back at him.

In the end, it always came back to this terrible simplicity. He had felt it before at the beginning of a battle, when all the plans and preparations had become irrelevant and he stood face-to-face with his foe. But other times he had at least begun the fight unwounded. This time the most he could hope for was to get in one or two good blows before they struck him down.

The clatter of hoofbeats thundered in his ears. One horse misstepped and went down, but the others loomed over him with frightening speed. Carausius swayed aside and stabbed as a rider went past him. Theudibert's spear flashed and the Briton fell. Another rider was upon them; the Emperor stepped backward into muddy water, staggering to keep his balance, but the horse stopped suddenly, mistrusting the ground. The rider coming toward him also slipped, and grabbed the mane to keep his balance; Carausius' sword took him in the side.

The moments that followed passed in a series of disjointed images. He stood back-to-back with Theudibert, half leaning against the other man. Carausius felt an impact, and then another, and knew he had been hit, but he was beyond pain. He blinked, peering around him, and wondered if it was darkness or blood loss that was making it so hard to see. More riders came at them; behind him, Theudibert made a sound of surprise, and Carausius lurched as his support disappeared. A last access of fury brought Carausius around, swinging. His blow took Theudibert's slayer in the neck as the Briton bent to pull out his spear.

Carausius swayed, struggling to being up his blade. But there was no one left to fight. A dozen bodies lay around him, moaning, or deathly still. Upon the ridge he heard the sounds of battle, though he could not see them. Then they too faded. *My brave Menapian boys have bought me this last respite*, he thought. *I must not waste it.*

To his right, the willows grew in a tangle down to the waterside. If he hid among their branches, no one would find him. He was lightheaded with blood loss, but somewhere he found the strength to make his way to the shelter of the trees.

⊲ ⊲ ⊲

For three days and three nights Dierna had maintained her vigil, as her spirit yearned toward that of the man she loved. By the end of the second day, the contact was becoming intermittent, as if he were moving in and out of consciousness. On the third day, agony reawakened, and with it an anxiety that she could hardly bear. It was not until a little past midnight that she fell into a fitful sleep, full of nightmares through which she fled, pursued by faceless demons, struggling in a bloody sea.

Dierna woke again as the pale light of the longest day was outlining her doorway, and realized that what had roused her was a tap on the door.

"Enter . . ." she whispered. She sat up, feeling for the first time in three days free of pain. Was Carausius dead? She did not think so, for there was still a weight upon her spirit.

Lina stood silhouetted against the dawn sky. "Lady, one of the marsh folk has come to us. He says there was a fight at the lake edge. One of the warriors made it to their village, babbling that they must find his lord and take him to the Lady of Avalon. . . ."

Dierna got to her feet, surprised to find herself to unsteady, and gathered up her mantle. Lina was already carrying the basket in which she kept her healer's supplies. The priestess leaned on the girl's shoulder as they made their way down the path, but by the time they reached the barge, the fresh air had begun to revive her.

They passed through the mists and came to the village of the marsh men, its houses set on poles among the reeds. The little dark folk were up and about already, and among them one tall, fair-haired lad who walked up and down along the shore, peering about him distractedly.

"Domina," he saluted her in rough camp Latin. "The Durotriges attacked us—Allectus led them. In the fight Lord Carausius was wounded. He told us to bring him. And by the holy gods, we did what he asked."

"Where is he?" Dierna cut in.

The boy shook his head in distress. "He sent me to the village for help. But the people saw the fighting and were afraid. I understand"—he gazed around him at the little dark folk of the marshes— "they look like children to me, though I know they are men. I went back to the battlefield and found only the dead. But my lord's body was not among them. The small ones would not stir during the hours of darkness for fear of demons. Since first light we have been looking, but Carausius has not been found!"

◁ ◁ ◁

The Emperor of Britannia lay half on land and half in the lake, watching his blood cloud the water with crimson in the light of the new day. He had never known that dawn could be so beautiful. The night had been filled with horrors. He had struggled for hours, it seemed, crawling over tree roots and floundering in mud that tried to suck him into its slimy embrace. For part of it he thought he had been fevered, but he was cold now—too cold—he could neither feel nor move his lower limbs at all. This was not how he had expected to meet his end.

The white shape of a swan moved out of the mists that clung to the water and swam past him, graceful as if this were a dream. Lying here, where he could not see the hills, he might have been in the marshes of his own country, where the father of rivers branched into many channels as it sought the sea. In his homeland, he remembered, they had given men to the gods by a triple death. His lips twisted wryly as he realized that he had already suffered two-thirds of it— being speared in a dozen places, and half drowned.

It is a gift, he thought. *I have been restored to myself, instead of dying in delirium. The least I can do is finish the job. . . .* With a wisdom from beyond this lifetime he remembered—the Goddess never dies, but the God gives his life for the land. He knew now that he had done this before, by an act of will transformed from the victim of senseless violence to an offering, made in faith that the Goddess would find a use for it somehow.

The rope that had bound him to Theudibert was still tied around him. With clumsy fingers he loosened the knot and tugged it up around his neck, then wound the other end around the root of a tree. For as long as he could, he would stay upright, for the morning was very beautiful, but he did not think it would be for long.

Somewhere beyond those mists lay the Empress of his heart.

Would she know, he wondered, how he had loved her? *This gift is for you,* he thought, *and for the Goddess you serve. I was born across the sea, but my death belongs to Britannia.* Perhaps it did not matter. Dierna had once told him that, behind the faces they wore, all gods were one. His only regret was that he had not seen the sea once more.

The sun rose higher, dancing brightly on the water. Those sequined dimples were very like the sunsparks on the ocean, he thought vaguely . . . and then they *were* the waves, and the singing in his ears was the wind in a ship's rigging, and his vertigo the swoop of the craft that was bearing him over the sea. It came to him then that if the gods were one so were the waters, all of them the womb of the Goddess, the most ancient of seas.

Before him, an island rose from the ocean, girded with cliffs of red stone and green fields. In its center was a pointed hill from whose summit the gilding of a temple roof challenged the sun.

He knew that place, and in that recognition knew himself also, with the insignia of a priest upon his brow and on his forearms the dragons of a king. He stepped forward, arms lifting in salutation, uncaring that the body he had left behind slumped lifeless in its bonds.

From across the water he could hear the voice of the woman who from life to life had always been his beloved and his Queen, calling him.

Dierna walked on the lakeshore, calling her lover's name. Surely now, when Carausius was so near, the link between them would draw her. She knew the others were coming along behind her, but she kept her eyes shut, following a scent of the spirit between the worlds. Success, when it came, was an awareness on both levels that the other part of her soul was near.

Dierna opened her eyes and saw the shape of a man, tangled in tree roots and half underwater, so smeared with mud and bits of reed he seemed already part of the earth on which he lay. Aedfrid ran past her, stopping short as he saw the rope around Carausius' neck and making a sign of reverence before he reached out and with trembling hands untangled it and drew his lord's body fully up onto the shore.

The marsh men were chattering in horror, but Aedfrid looked at her in appeal. "It was not a shameful death. Do you understand?"

Throat closing, she nodded. *Could you not wait a little longer?* her heart cried. *Could you not stay to say goodbye to me?*

"I will take him and give him a hero's burial—" said the warrior, but Dierna shook her head.

"Carausius was chosen by our Goddess to be King. In this life or another, he is bound to this land. And through him," she added as new knowledge came to her, "through him, your people also are bound to Britannia, and will belong to her one day. Wrap him in my mantle and lay him in the barge, and we will make a tomb for him in Avalon."

⊲ ⊲ ⊲

Throughout that day, the longest of the year, the Lady of Avalon sat in the sacred grove above the well, watching beside the body of her Emperor. As the wind shifted, she could hear snatches of singing from the Druids on the Tor. Ildeg was taking the part of the High Priestess. Dierna had been trained to suppress her emotions when there was work to be done, but she had learned also that there came a time when even training could not overcome the cry of the heart. An adept bore the responsibility of knowing when that time had come and stepping aside, lest the magic go awry.

And surely if I were in the circle today I would destroy it, thought Dierna, looking at Carausius' still features. *I am still in my fertile years, but I feel all the Death Crone now....*

They had washed Carausius in the water of the holy well and bound up his dreadful wounds. Even now a grave was being prepared for him beside that of Gawen, son of Eilan, who according to some tales had been partly Roman too. She would bury him like a king of Britannia, but that was a cold bed for the man with whom she had lain down in joy.

If I dared, I would cast myself into the grave with him, and celebrate the Great

Rite as they did in ancient days, when the Queen followed her lord into the Other-world. . . . But she was not his wife, and that grief weighed on her even more than her loss, and she cursed the pride that had blinded her to the voice of her own heart. For all this was her doing, she saw now— the decisions that had forced Carausius and Teleri into a loveless union and led to Allectus' treachery had been her own. If she had never meddled, Carausius would still have been sailing his beloved sea, and Teleri would have been happy as a priestess of Avalon. Dierna rocked, hugging her breasts, and wept for them all.

It was much later, when the sounds of revelry had faded and the long dusk of Midsummer was veiling the land, that the grief that had gripped her itself grew weary and Dierna sat up, blinking and looking about her. She felt emptied, as if her tears had washed all other feeling away. But one thought remained. Though she might weep, there were other women who would lie tonight in their husbands' arms, their children sleeping peacefully nearby, because Carausius had defended Britannia.

A drumbeat, slow as the beating of her own heart, throbbed in the air. Dierna rose to her feet as the procession of white-robed Druids wound down from the Tor. She stepped aside to let them lift the bier, and took her place behind it as they began to move once more. Down to the edge of the lake they passed, where the black-draped barge was waiting to bear the sea lord on his final voyage.

The grave had been dug on the Watch Hill, the farthest island that remained within the mists, the Gateway to Avalon. To those who could not pass them, it bore nothing of interest but a poor village of marsh folk huddled at its foot, just as there was nothing but a few Christian hermitages at the foot of the Tor. But long ago, another Defender of Avalon had been buried there, that his spirit might continue to protect the Vale. The Druids had hailed Carausius by those titles when he came here before. It was fitting that his body should lie beside that of the man for whom that song had been made.

By the time they reached the Watch Hill, darkness had fallen. Torches circled the gravesite; their light cast an illusory warmth across the features of the man who lay beside it, and glowed on the pale robes of the Druids and the priestesses in their blue. But Dierna was swathed in black, and though the firelight sparked and glittered like falling stars from the bits of gold sewn into her black veil, no light could penetrate its shadow, for tonight she was the Lady of Darkness.

"The sun has left us..." the priestess said softly when the singing ceased. "This day it reigned supreme, but now the night has fallen. From this moment onward, the power of light will lessen, until the cold of midwinter overwhelms the world." As she spoke, even the light of the torches seemed to weaken. The teachings of the Mysteries placed great importance on the cyclical movements of Nature; now she understood them in the depths of her soul.

"The spirit of this man has left us...." Her voice scarcely shook as she went on. "Like the sun he reigned in splendor, and like the sun has been cast down. Where does the sun go when it leaves us? We are told that it walks in the southern lands. Just so, this spirit journeys now to the Summerland. We mourn his loss. But we know that in the heart of midwinter's darkness the light shall be reborn. And so we give this body back to the earth from which it was made, in hopes that his radiant spirit will once again take flesh and walk among us in the hour of Britannia's need."

As they laid the body in the grave and began to fill it in, Dierna could hear someone weeping, but her own eyes were dry. Her words had not given her hope—she was beyond that. But Carausius had not given up the battle when his fate turned against him, and she knew now that she would not do so either.

"Carausius has his victory. But it is in the world of the spirit. In this world, his murderer still lives and boasts of his deed. It is Allectus who has done this—Allectus, whom he loved—Allectus, who must pay for his treachery! At this moment, when the tides of power begin to turn toward disintegration and decline, I will set my curse upon him."

Dierna took a deep breath and raised her arms to heaven. "Powers of Night, I call you by no mean magic but by the ancient laws of Necessity, to fall upon the murderer. May no day seem bright to him, no fire warm to him, no love true to him, until he has atoned for his crime!"

She turned, gesturing toward the lake that lapped below.

"Powers of the Sea, womb from which we are all born, mighty ocean on whose currents we are all carried, may all courses he may choose go awry! Rise up to engulf the murderer, O Sea, and drown him in your dark tides!"

She knelt beside the grave and buried her fingers in the loose soil.

"Powers of Earth, to whom we now release his body, may the man who killed him find no peace upon your surface! May he doubt every step he takes, and every man on whom he depends, and every woman he loves, until the chasm yawns beneath him and he falls."

Dierna got to her feet again, smiling grimly at the shocked faces around her. "I am the Lady, and I set upon Allectus, son of Cerialis, the curse of Avalon. Thus I have spoken, and thus it shall be!"

◁ ◁ ◁

The year-wheel rolled toward harvest, but though the weather held fair, a summer storm of rumor racked the land. The Emperor had disappeared. Some said he was dead, murdered by Allectus. But others denied it, for where was the body? He was in hiding from his foes, they believed. Still others whispered that he had fled over the sea to make submission to Rome. Certain it was that Allectus had proclaimed himself High King, and was sending his riders up and down Britannia to summon chieftains and commanders to a great oath-taking in Londinium.

The people of Londinium were cheering. Teleri flinched at the sound, and drew the leather curtains of the carriage closed. It was stuffy inside, but she could not bear the noise, or perhaps it was the pressure of so many eyes, so many minds, all focused on her. It had not been like this when she was here before, with Carausius. But by the time she joined him here, he had already been accepted as Emperor. The difference, she supposed, was that this time she was part of the ceremony. She ought to have been proud and excited.

Why, she wondered, did she feel like a captive being paraded in the triumph of some Roman conqueror?

It was better once they reached the basilica, though here also there were too many people. Tables had been set up for feasting. The princes and magistrates who sat there eyed her with less curiosity and more calculation. Teleri tried to hold her head high, but she clung to her father's arm.

"What are you afraid of?" asked the Prince. "You are an empress already. If I had guessed, when you were a gawky girl, that I was raising the Lady of Britannia, I would have bought you a Greek tutor."

She gave him a quick look and saw the glint in his eye, and tried to smile.

A blaze of color at the end of the long aisle resolved itself into figures. She saw Allectus, arrayed in a purple mantle over a crimson tunic, dwarfed by the bigger men beside him. His eyes brightened as he saw her.

"Prince Eiddin Mynoc—be welcome," he said formally. "You have brought your daughter. I ask now if you will give her to me as a wife."

"Lord, it is for that we have come. . . ."

Teleri looked from one man to the other. Was no one going to ask *her*? But perhaps, she told herself, her consent had been given that night in Durnovaria, and the rest—the killing of Carausius and all that had ensued—was only its sequel.

She stepped forward, and Allectus took her hand.

The feast that followed seemed endless. Teleri picked at the food, listening halfheartedly to the conversation. There was some discussion of the gift which Allectus had given to the soldiers upon his proclamation. It was traditional for an emperor at his accession, especially when he was a usurper, but Allectus' contribution had been generous even by those standards. The merchants, on the other hand, seemed to be hoping for more favors. Only the chieftains of the old Celtic blood paid her any attention, and she realized that her father had been right, and it was partly because of her that they had come.

By the time bride and groom were put to bed, Allectus had drunk a great deal. Teleri, bracing herself as he staggered against her, realized that she had never seen him in less than full command of himself. Her first husband's embrace had been something to endure. As she helped Allectus out of his clothes, she began to wonder if her second man would be able to do a husband's duty at all.

Teleri got Allectus into the great bed and lay down beside him. Now that they were alone, there were things she must ask him—not least of them how Carausius had died. She had not been surprised to feel guilt when she learned of his murder; from the moment when she accepted Allectus' love, she had understood, at some level, what he meant to do. She had not expected the pain.

But when she turned to him, he was already snoring. In the dark hours of the night Allectus woke, crying out that Constantius was coming with a great army of men with bloody spears. Sobbing, he clung to her, and Teleri soothed him as if he were a child. He had been happier when he still served Carausius. And she, if not happy, had at least retained her honor. On which of the three of them could she blame this tragedy? Perhaps it was Dierna she should blame, she thought bitterly.

After a time Allectus began to kiss her, his embrace becoming more frantic until he took her with a desperate urgency. Eventually he slept once more, but Teleri lay for a long time wakeful in the darkness. She, who had dreamed of freedom, had chosen this cage. But it was done now, and must be endured.

As Teleri at last fell into a fitful slumber, she found herself praying to the Goddess as she had not since she was a girl, dreaming of escape from her father's hall.

⊲ ⊲ ⊲

In Avalon, Dierna endured as well. Her curse had gone out against Allectus; its fulfillment must be left to greater powers. But for a time, it seemed that those powers did not care. The anniversary of Carausius' death went by, and the world rolled on unheeding. The priestess waited, but for what she could not say.

Another year passed. If Britannia was not happy with Allectus' rule, no one dared speak too loudly against him. But he continued his payments to the barbarians, and the Saxon Shore stayed peaceful. As for Constantius, though his fleet had overcome that of Carausius, it had taken a beating, and as the latter himself had predicted, it would take time and money to build enough transports and the galleys to guard them to invade the island.

⊲ ⊲ ⊲

The moon rode high in the heavens. Though it was beginning to wane, it still was bright enough to dim the summer stars. The thatching on the House of Maidens glistened, and the pillars of the Processional Way glowed. Dierna took a deep breath of the cool night air. Around her all was silent. The restlessness that had kept her from sleep must be a thing of the spirit. Something was changing, and its reverberations resounded on the inner planes.

Another year had come and gone since Britannia rejected the lord that Avalon had chosen, and in that time the High Priestess had not left her isle, but from time to time rumors reached them. Constantius had launched his invasion at last. Some said he had landed near Londinium, and the High King's forces were fighting him there. Other reports spoke of a force that had landed at Clausentum and was marching on Calleva. If Carausius had lived, she would have been using all the magic of Avalon to aid him. But never again would she interfere in the affairs of the outside world.

Dierna was about to return to her bed when she glimpsed someone running up the hill. It was Lina, who as a part of her training had been assigned to keep vigil beside the holy well. Frowning, the High Priestess hurried toward her.

"Hush, I am here." She got an arm around the girl and guided her to one of the benches. "Take a deep breath, and another. You are safe now...." She held Lina until the girl's sobs became shuddering gasps and her trembling stilled. "Tell me, daughter, what has frightened you?"

"The well!" Lina drew a shaky breath. "The moonlight was

shining on the water, mirror-bright. I looked into it, and suddenly mist swirled around me and I saw men fighting with swords. It was horrible! So much blood! I was glad I could not hear their screams."

"Was it the Romans? Did you see Allectus?"

"I think so—Roman soldiers were attacking a British camp. Tents were blazing. By the light of the moon and fire it was easy to see. The Romans were fully armed, but our people had been sleeping. Some of them had time to grab their shields, but most had no armor at all. The fiercest battle was around a thin, dark-haired man with a golden headband. He fought bravely, but not very well."

Allectus! thought Dierna. *At last my curse strikes home.*

"One by one the men of his guard were killed. The Romans called on the King to surrender, but he would not, and so they speared him, again and again, until he finally went down."

"He is dead, then," Dierna said aloud, "and Carausius avenged. Be at rest, my dear one, and you, who betrayed him. In another lifetime, perhaps, we will meet again."

That autumn, while Emperor Constantius basked in the adulation of the capital he had reconquered for Rome, rains lashed the land. In the Vale of Avalon, clouds swathed the Tor and lay low across the waters, as if the mists that protected it were blotting out the world. But despite the leaden skies, Dierna felt as if a great weight had been lifted from her, and her priestesses, taking heart from her mood, began to speak of building new walls around the sheep pen and replacing the tattered thatching of the meeting hall.

On a morning shortly after the equinox, the maiden in charge of the sheep came in weeping because one of the ewes had gotten through the temporary fencing and disappeared. And because, after a week of solid rain, the clouds had thinned to a misty drizzle that might even soon admit a few rays of sun, and after so many months of lassitude she found herself actually wanting exercise, Dierna volunteered to search for it.

It was not easy going. The waters had risen with all the rain, and some places that were usually dry had become marsh as well. Dierna chose her path carefully, wondering what the silly creature had been thinking of to leave the hill. But the soft ground made for easy tracking, and she followed the trail around the hill above the holy well and down through the orchards. Still it went on, back along the edge of the lake toward the low hill of Briga, whose shrine was circled by apple trees.

Dierna paused, frowning, for the hill, ordinarily on an isle by courtesy, had become in truth an island. Mist lay low across the water, as yet too thick for her to see the sky, though it glittered in the light of the sun. And yet it seemed to her that she could see something grey beneath the trees. She knew where the path must be, though she could not see it. Picking up a pole that had drifted onto the shore with which to probe the ground, she began to wade out into the water.

Mist swirled around her, at the first step a veil, but by the third a curtain that hid both the place from which she had come and her goal. An ancient panic stopped her, muddy water lapping her ankles. *This is my own land!* she told herself. *I have known these paths since I could walk—I should be able to find my way blindfolded or in a dream!* She took a deep breath, calling on disciplines she had practiced to induce calm for almost as many years as she had lived on Avalon.

And as the roaring in her ears faded, she heard a call.

"D'rna—help me!"

It was faint with distance or exhaustion, hard to tell which, for the mist deadened sound. But Dierna splashed forward.

"Someone, please . . . can anyone hear at all?"

Dierna gasped, her sight darkened by memory. "Becca!" Her voice cracked. "Keep calling! Becca, I'm coming for you!" She stumbled ahead, feeling out the way with her staff.

"Oh, Goddess, please—I've tried so hard to find my way. . . ." The words faded to disjointed mumblings. But they were enough. Dierna turned and found herself in deeper water, reached out with senses beyond sight as she had when she searched for Carausius, and at last glimpsed the shape of a tree and, clinging to its roots, a woman's form.

She saw draggled dark hair, limp as waterweed, and a thin, mud-smeared hand. The body she hauled onto the higher ground was as light as a child's. But it was not a child. Dierna cradled the woman against her breast and gazed into Teleri's eyes.

"I thought . . ." Her mind reeled in confusion. "I thought you were my sister. . . ."

The wonder in Teleri's face faded, and she closed her eyes. "I was lost in the mist," she whispered. "Ever since you sent me away I think I have been lost. I was trying to come back to Avalon."

Dierna stared down at her, wordless. When she heard of Teleri's marriage to Allectus she had wanted to curse her too, but she had lacked the energy. It would appear that, even without her cursing, Teleri had been punished by the same powers that brought Carausius' murderer down. But Teleri was still alive. Mist drifted around them like a clammy veil. In all the world, she could see nothing living but Teleri, and herself, and the apple tree.

"You came through the mists . . ." Dierna said slowly. "That can only be done by a priestess, or by passing through Faerie."

Thought came slowly, as if from deep waters. Could she forgive this woman, for whose love Allectus had turned against his master? Could she forgive herself, for being so certain she knew the will of the Goddess that she had tangled them all in this doom? Dierna sighed, releasing a burden she had not known she bore.

"I am not the one you were looking for. . . . Forgive me . . ." Teleri whispered then.

"Are you not? *I promise that I will treat every woman in this temple as my sister, my mother, and my daughter, as my own kin. . . .*" The voice of the priestess gathered strength as she repeated the oath of Avalon.

"Dierna . . ." Teleri gazed up at her, those dark eyes, still so lovely in her ravaged face, filling with tears. Dierna tried to smile, but now she was weeping herself, and could only hold the other woman close, rocking her like a child.

She did not know how much time had passed before calm returned. A cloud of white still surrounded them, and it was cold.

"We seem to be trapped here, until the fog goes away," she said with a cheerfulness that belied her words. "But we will not starve, for there are still apples on this tree." Gently she settled Teleri against the trunk and stood up to pluck one. As she did so, she saw a stirring in the air beyond the island, and then, as if it had precipitated out of the mist, the shape of a woman poling a small flat craft of the kind the marsh folk used.

She stilled, squinting as she tried to see. The woman seemed familiar, and yet, as the priestess reviewed the people of the marsh villages, she could not remember her face or name. Despite the chill, the stranger was barefoot and clad only in a deerskin wrap, with a garland of bright berries on her brow.

"Hello." She found her voice at last. "Can your craft carry two lost ones back to the Tor?"

"Lady of Avalon that is, and Lady of Avalon that will be, that is why I am here . . ." came the answer.

Dierna blinked, and then, understanding at last who had come for them, she bowed.

Swiftly, lest the Queen of Faerie disappear as she had arrived, Dierna lifted Teleri into the boat and clambered after her. In another moment the punt was sliding into the cloud. The mist was very thick here, and bright, the way it sometimes appeared when one passed through it to reach the outside world.

But the radiance that encompassed them as they emerged was the clear light of Avalon.

Dierna speaks:

Last night, when the moon first came full after the equinox of spring, Teleri ascended the seat of prophecy. It has been long since this way of Seeing was prac-ticed, not since the time of the Lady Caillean, before the priestesses lived on Avalon, but the long memories of the Druids had preserved the ritual. The Sight comes to me rarely now, and our need was great, and worth the risk of the experiment.

Constantine, the son of Constantius, now rules the world, and the Chris-tians, who for a time seemed about to be destroyed by their own quarrels, have been united by the persecutions of Diocletian, and now reign as the favorites of his successor. The gods of Rome were content to share in the devotion of the people of Britannia without supplanting them. But the god of the Christians is a jealous master.

In Avalon, Teleri ascended the high seat, her dark hair falling like a veil around her, and the sacred herbs granted her a vision of what shall be.

She saw Constantine ruling in splendor, to be succeeded by unworthy sons. Another, coming after, strove to bring back the old gods and died young in a dis-tant land. In his time, the barbarians once more raided Britannia, and after them, the men of Eriu. But despite all, our island flourished as never before, except for the temples of the old gods, despoiled by the Christians, who called our Goddess a demon, whose roofless ruins reproached the sky.

In time, another British general, inspired by Carausius, proclaimed himself Imperator and sailed with his Legions to Gallia. But he was defeated, and the men he had taken away remained in Armorica. Now wave after wave of barbarians began to pour into the Empire from Germania, marching at last through the gates of Rome. Britannia, abandoned by the Legions, proclaimed herself independent at last.

More than a century had passed, and the Painted Peoples were sweeping down from the north, devastating the land. Teleri spoke then of a new lord, whom men hailed as Vortigern, the High King. In blood he was of the old line, like Allectus, but, like Carausius, to protect his people he brought in Saxon warriors from over the sea.

I tried to halt the flow of vision, to ask what part, in this strange future, might be played by Avalon.

She cried out in wordless answer, possessed by images too chaotic for comprehension. I acted quickly then to bring her back to herself, for indeed she had journeyed far.

Teleri sleeps now. It is my peace that is broken, for, as I rest, the images she saw live in my memory, and I fear, in a land which rejects the Goddess and all Her works and wisdom, for the priestesses who shall come after us on this holy isle.

PART III

Daughter of Avalon

A.D. 440–452

A rare hard freeze held all of Britannia gripped in cold. Though it lacked ten days yet to Samhain, the last storm had leached all color from the land and left a rime of ice in every rut, and there was a chill edge to the wind. Even on the straight Roman roads the going was treacherous. The Isle of Mona, separated from the mainland of Britannia by a narrow channel, lay wrapped in icy peace. The folk of the island had seen no stranger for days.

Viviane was all the more surprised, therefore, when she looked out the door of the cowshed to see a traveler turning up the path leading to the farm. The big, rawboned mule the stranger rode was mud-splashed to the belly; the stranger's own body so swathed in cloaks and shawls she could make out nothing but his feet. She blinked, for a moment certain she knew him. But of course that was impossible. She bent to lift the heavy pail of milk, then started back to the house, her small feet crunching through the ice that had formed in the puddles on the path.

"Da, there's a man coming, an outlander—"

Her speech had the musical lilt of the north, though she had been born in a place they called the Summer Country. Her foster-brother had whispered once that she was from a place that sounded even more unlikely, an island called Avalon that was not really part of this world at all. Her father had hushed him, and in truth, when she was awake she did not believe it, for how could a place in the middle of the land be an island? But sometimes in dreams she almost remembered, and would wake with an odd sense of loss. Her real mother was its Lady, and that was all she did know.

"What sort of an outlander?" Her father, Neithen, came around the corner of the house from the woodshed with an armful of kindling.

"He looks like a rag heap, all bundled to keep off the cold, but, then, so do you and I." She grinned up at him.

"Get in with you, lass"—Neithen made a shooing motion with the wood—"before the milk freezes."

Viviane laughed and stumped through the door, but Neithen remained outside, watching as the mule picked its way up the path. Viviane, setting down the pail and shrugging off her cloak, heard voices and paused to listen. Bethoc, her foster-mother, stopped stirring the pot and listened too.

"Taliesin! So it is you," they heard Neithen say. "What ill wind has blown you this way?"

"A wind from Avalon, that will not wait for the weather to smile," came the answer in a voice of peculiarly resonant beauty, even when it was hoarse with cold.

"Somehow, I do not think you have come all this way only to give Viviane Samhain greetings from her mother!" they heard Neithen reply. "Come in, man, before you *do* perish of cold. I'll not have it said that the best bard in Britannia froze on my doorstep. No—go on, I'll stable your beast with my cows."

The door opened, and a tall figure, slender beneath the wrappings, came through. Viviane backed away, staring, as he began to unwind them, scattering little chips of ice to melt upon the well-scrubbed stones of the hearth. Underneath all the layers he wore the white woolen robe of a Druid. The thing that had distorted his shape was a sealskin harpcase, which he eased off his shoulder and set carefully on the floor.

He straightened gratefully. He had beautiful hands, she saw, and hair so pale she could not tell if it was gold or silver, receding from a high brow. He would look much the same, she thought, until he grew old; indeed, he seemed old to her. Then he saw Viviane watching and his own eyes widened.

"But you are only a child!"

"I am past fourteen, and old enough to be married!" she retorted, drawing herself up, and was astonished by the sudden sweetness of his smile.

"Of course you are—I had forgotten you are just like your mother, who is in truth no higher than my shoulder, only one always remembers her as being tall."

He bowed to her foster-mother, whose glower softened to a kind of bleak acceptance. "A blessing on this house and the woman of it," he said softly.

"And on the traveler who honors our hearth," Bethoc replied, "although I do not think it is a blessing that you bring."

"Nor do I," said Neithen, coming through the door.

As he hung up his cloak, Bethoc poured cider into a wooden cup and offered it to their visitor, adding, "But I will bid you welcome. Supper will be ready soon." She turned back to the cauldron that hung over the fire, and Viviane began to get out the carved wooden bowls.

"So," said Neithen, "what is your news?" Viviane paused to listen, a bowl still in her hand.

Taliesin sighed. "The Lady's daughter Anara died a moon ago."

My sister, thought Viviane, wondering if she ought to feel sorrow, since she could not remember the girl at all.

"Was that the one who was married to the son of Vortigern?" asked Bethoc in an undertone.

Her husband shook his head. "That was Idris, but she is dead too, in childbed, I have heard." He turned back to Taliesin. "I am sorry to hear it...." He waited, clearly wondering why the bard should have made this journey to tell them so.

"The Lady Ana has sent me to bring Viviane to Avalon ..." Taliesin said.

"My home is here!" exclaimed Viviane, looking from her father to the bard.

Taliesin's face grew somber. "I know. But the Lady Ana has need of you."

"Father! Tell him you will not let me go!" she cried.

Startled, Taliesin looked at the other man. "You have not told her?"

"What has he not told me?" Viviane's voice rose. "What does he mean?"

Neithen flushed, and he did not meet her eyes. "That I am not your father, and have no right to keep you here, a truth I had hoped you would never need to know."

She turned on him. "Whose daughter am I, then? You say you are not my father. Will you next say the Lady is not my mother?"

"Oh, she is your mother, right enough," said Neithen glumly. "She gave this house to me and Bethoc when she gave me you to foster, with the promise that the land should be ours always, and you our daughter, unless by some chance both your sisters should die without leaving a female child. If the elder, whom she kept by her to train as a priestess, is dead, then you are her only heir."

Viviane felt her face turn pale. "And it makes no difference if I say I do not wish to go?"

"The need of Avalon outweighs all our wishes," Taliesin said gently. "I am sorry, Viviane."

She drew herself up proudly, fighting tears. "Then I will not blame you. When must we leave?"

"I would say now, but my poor mule must be allowed a little rest or he will founder. We must leave with tomorrow's dawn."

"So soon!" She shook her head. "Why could she not give me more warning?"

"It is death, my dear, that has given no warning. You are old already to begin your training, and soon the weather will make travel impossible. If I do not bring you now, you could not come to Avalon before spring."

As Viviane climbed into the loft to begin her packing, the tears began to fall. She felt orphaned. It was clear that her mother's summons had been motivated by need, not love. Avalon was a fair dream, but she did not want to leave the man and woman who had been her family, or the rocky island she had learned to call home.

⊲ ⊲ ⊲

Taliesin sat by the fire, a cup of heated cider in his hand. He had slept warm and well, for the first time in days. There was peace in this house. Ana had chosen well when she gave her daughter to Neithen to raise. It was a pity she could not have left her here. Memory brought to mind the face of the Lady as he had last seen it, the broad brow marred by new lines, mouth drawn tight above the pointed chin. A little, ugly woman, some might call her, but from the day Taliesin first came to the Druids twenty years before, she had been the Goddess to him.

Ana had been trained by her own mother, and she by her aunt, as he had been told. The inheritance was not always mother to daughter, but over the centuries many children of Avalon had married into the princely houses of Britannia, and sent their own daughters back to the holy isle to become priestesses in their turn. Indirectly, Ana's child could trace her descent all the way back to Sianna, who was said to be a daughter of the Queen of Faerie.

A movement caught his eye and he looked up. A pair of legs, swathed in breeches and leg wrappings, was emerging from the loft. He stared as the odd figure, topped by a loose tunic, made its way down the ladder and, on reaching the bottom, turned to face him, frowning defiantly. Taliesin lifted one eyebrow, and the frown became a crinkle of amusement that transformed Viviane's face.

"Are those your foster-brother's things?"

"I have been taught to ride like a man; why should I not dress like one when I do so? You are glowering—would not my mother approve?"

His lips twitched with quickly suppressed mirth. "It will not please her." *Holy Briga*, he thought, *she is just like Ana. How interesting the next few years are going to be.*

"Good!" Viviane sat down beside him, elbows planted on her knees. "I don't want to. If she objects I shall tell her I object to being taken from my home!"

Taliesin sighed. "I cannot blame you." *It was ill-done of her to send you away so young and then call you back with no warning at all, as if you were a puppet to be jerked this way and that for show,* he thought then, *but Ana has always been too fond of her own will. And I too have felt her hand on my strings. . . .*

He saw Viviane's face stiffen in shock and realized she had heard him. Without thinking, he made a subtle gesture with his left hand; her surprise faded and she reached for a cup. He must be more careful. This little one might well have all her mother's talent, though it was still untrained. And he had never been able to hide anything from the Lady of Avalon.

⊲ ⊲ ⊲

The sun was declining a little from the height of noon when they set out, Taliesin on his mule and Viviane on one of the tough little hill ponies of the north. The water between the isle and the mainland had frozen solid, and they were able to ride across. They passed through the village that had grown up near the legionary fortress at Segontium and started along the road the Romans had built across the top of the Deceangli country, heading for Deva.

Viviane had never ridden farther than across the Isle of Mona, and she quickly grew weary. Nevertheless, she managed to keep up with him, without betraying fatigue or weakness; though the Druid, trained to ignore the claims of his body, scarcely considered that a young girl might find such long hours in the saddle hard. But Viviane, small and fine-boned though she might be, had the tough constitution of the dark people of the marshes from whom she had gotten her looks. She had not seen her mother since she was five years old, but she was determined to show her no weakness. She could not help wondering who her real father might be, and whether he too lived in Avalon. Perhaps he would love her.

And so she rode with the tears freezing on her cheeks and lay down at night too tired, almost, for sleep, aching in every limb. And gradually, as they moved south through the valley of the Wye, she grew accustomed to the exercise, though she still did not like riding, or the pony she rode. The beast appeared to be possessed by some demon of independence—he insisted on going his own way, and it was not hers.

Between Deva and Glevum, Rome had made little mark upon the land. At night they sought shelter with herdsmen, or little families who scratched a living from the hills. They reverenced the Druid as a visiting god, but Viviane they welcomed as one of their own. As the two approached more southern lands, though the cold was still fierce, the roads were better, and now and again they would see a tile-roofed villa surrounded by broad fields.

Just north of Corinium, Taliesin turned up the road leading to one such, a comfortable old place with buildings set around a courtyard.

"The time was," the Druid said as they rode in, "when a priest of my calling would have been an honored guest at any British house, and treated by the Romans with respect as a priest of a kindred faith. But in these days, the Christians have poisoned so many people's minds—calling all other believers worshippers of demons, even when they follow kindly gods—that I travel in the guise of a wandering bard, and only to those who hold by the old ways am I revealed."

"And what sort of household is this?" asked Viviane as the dogs began barking and people stuck their heads out of doors to see who had arrived.

"These people are Christians, but not fanatics. Junius Priscus is a good man, who cares for the health of his people as well as his animals but lets them worry about their own souls. And he dearly loves to hear harp-playing. We will get a good welcome here."

A strongly built man with a fringe of red hair was coming out to greet them, surrounded by dogs. Viviane's pony chose this moment to try and bolt, and by the time she had it under control Priscus was welcoming them.

They dined in the old Roman way, the men reclining while the women sat on benches near the hearth. Their host's daughter, Priscilla, a wide-eyed child of eight who was already nearly as tall as Viviane, found the visitor fascinating and sat on a stool at her feet, offering her more to eat whenever she finished what she had. This was often, for of recent days their hosts had been poor folk, and Viviane had feared the food they were sharing would be needed as the cold season went on. It seemed to her now that it had been a century since she had eaten her fill, or been truly warm. She ate without paying much attention to the conversations around her, but presently her hunger began to ease, and she realized the talk had turned to the High King.

"But can you really say that Vortigern has done so badly?" asked Taliesin, setting down his wine cup. "Do you not remember how, when Bishop Germanus visited from Rome, we were so desperate that the bishop was called to lead troops against the Picts, for he had served in the Legions before he went into the Church? That was in the same year that this child was born." He smiled at Viviane, then turned back to his host.

"The Saxons that Vortigern has settled in the north have kept the Painted People at bay; by moving the Votadini to Demetia, and the Cornovii down to Dumnonia, he has put strong tribes where they can protect us against the Irish; and that Anglic chieftain, Hengest, and his men are guarding the Saxon Shore. It is only when we are at peace that we can afford to quarrel among ourselves, but it seems hard that Vortigern should be punished for his success by civil war."

"There are too many Saxons," said Priscus. "Vortigern has given Hengest the whole of Cantium to support his people without a by-your-leave from its king. While the Council supported Vortigern, I accepted him, but Ambrosius Aurelianus is our rightful emperor, as his father was before him. I fought for him at Guollopum. If one or the other had won decisively, we would know where we were—as it is, poor Britannia is likely to fare like the child whom King Solomon offered to divide between two mothers, slaughtered to appease their pride."

Taliesin shook his head. "Ah well, I seem to remember that the King's threat brought the quarreling women to their senses, and perhaps our leaders will do the same."

His host sighed. "My friend, that will take more than a threat. That will take a miracle." For a moment longer he frowned; then he roused himself, smiling at his wife and the two girls. "But this is gloomy talk for such a chilly evening. Now that I have fed you, Taliesin, will you cheer us with a song?"

They stayed for two nights at the villa, and Viviane was sorry to go. But the Druids taught their priests to read the weather, and Taliesin said that if they did not leave now they would not reach Avalon before the snows. Little Priscilla clung to her when they parted, promising never to forget her, and Viviane, sensing the child's good heart, wondered if she would find any companion she liked so well on Avalon.

They pushed hard that day and the next, catching a few hours' sleep in a herdsman's hut by the road. Viviane spoke little during the long ride, except for an occasional muttered curse aimed at the pony. Another night they spent at an inn at Aquae Sulis. Viviane retained an impression of splendid buildings beginning now to fall into decay, and an occasional whiff of sulfur-scented steam. There was no time for sightseeing, however, and the next morning they set off along the Lindinis road.

⊲ ⊲ ⊲

"Will we reach Avalon tonight?" Viviane called from behind him. Taliesin turned; the road was climbing into the Mendip Hills, and their beasts had slowed.

He frowned. "On a good horse I would be certain of doing so, but these beasts will go at their own pace or not at all. We will try."

By midafternoon he felt a wet touch on his hand and, looking up, saw the sky had turned to solid cloud, which was flaking away into the first snow. Oddly, with the snowfall it seemed warmer, but the bard knew that was illusory. The girl had not complained, but when, soon after they crossed the road that served the lead mines, darkness began to fall, he turned down a path toward a cluster of buildings surrounded by trees.

"They make tiles here in the summer," said Taliesin, "but at this season the works will be empty. As long as we bring more wood in to replace what we use, they will not mind if we sleep here; I have done it before."

The place had the damp chill of disuse, which resisted the warmth of the fire. Viviane sat close to the flame, shivering, while the bard began to boil water for gruel.

"Thank you," she said when it was ready. "It is true that I never asked to go on this journey, but I thank you for your care of me. My father—my foster-father, that is—could not have done more."

Taliesin gave her a quick look, and then began to scoop gruel into his own bowl. Her olive skin had gone sallow with cold, but sparks of flame burned in her dark eyes.

"Are you my father?" Viviane asked then.

For a moment, shock held him still. But his mind was racing, for in truth during this long ride he himself had wondered. He had been newly made priest at the festival at which she had been begotten, come for the first time as a man to the Beltane fires. And Ana, though she was five years older than he and had already borne two daughters, had worn the beauty of the Goddess like a crown.

He remembered kissing her, and the taste of the mead she had drunk was honey on her lips. But, then, they had all been drunk that night, meeting and parting in the ecstasy of the dance. And from time to time a couple would touch, and cling, and stumble off into the shadows to join in the oldest dance of all. He remembered a woman crying out in his arms as he poured out his seed and his soul. But that first time, the ecstasy had overwhelmed him, and he could not remember her face or name.

The girl was still waiting, and she deserved an answer.

"You must not ask me that." He managed a smile. "No pious man can claim to have fathered a child to the Lady. Even the beastly Saxons know better. You are born of the royal line of Avalon, and that is all that I, or any man, can tell you."

"You are sworn to Truth," she said, frowning. "Cannot you give truth to me?"

"Any man would be proud to claim you, Viviane. You have borne the pains of this journey well. When you have come to the Beltane fires yourself, perhaps you will understand why I cannot answer. The truth is this, my child—it is possible, but I do not know."

Viviane lifted her head, and for a long moment held his gaze so that he, for all his training, could not look away.

"If one father has been torn from me," she said finally, "I

must find another, and I know no man I would rather call my father than you."

Taliesin stared at her, huddled like a little brown bird beside the fire, and for the first time since he had been made bard could find no words. But his thoughts were tumultuous. *Ana may come to regret she sent me on this journey. This daughter is no Anara, to go meekly, whether to fetch water or to seek her death, at my Lady's call. But I will not regret it—what a priestess this girl will make for Avalon!*

Viviane was still waiting.

"Perhaps we had best say nothing of this to your mother," he said finally, "but I promise you this—I will be as good a father to you as I may."

◁ ◁ ◁

They came to the lake just as dusk was falling. Viviane surveyed the scene without enthusiasm. Yesterday's snow crusted the mud and edged the reeds, and more was falling. The puddles were frozen solid, and ice extended into the pewter-colored water in sheets that glistened faintly in the failing light. Farther along the shore she saw a few huts, raised on poles above the mud of the marsh. On the other side of the water she could make out a hill, its top swathed in clouds. As she looked, from that direction she heard the faint clangor of a bell.

"Is that where we are going?"

Taliesin's face brightened momentarily in a grin. "I hope not—though, if we were not of the People of Avalon, Inis Witrin is the only holy island we would ever see."

He plucked down a cowhorn, its surface carved in spirals, that was hanging from a branch of a willow tree, and blew. The sound rang hard and throaty in the still air. Viviane wondered what was supposed to happen. The bard was gazing toward the huts, and it was she who saw the first quiver when what she had taken for a pile of brush began to move.

It was an old woman, bundled in woolen wrappings topped with a tattered cape of some grey fur. To judge from her size and the dark eye that was all Viviane could see of her face, she must be one of the marsh folk. Viviane wondered why Taliesin was staring at the woman oddly, at once amused and wary, like a man who finds an adder in his path.

"Gracious lord and young lady, the boat cannot come in such cold. Will it please you to rest in my house until a better time?"

"No, it does *not* please," said Taliesin decidedly. "I took oath to bring this child to Avalon as swiftly as could be, and we are weary and exhausted. Would you have me forsworn?"

The woman laughed softly, and Viviane's skin prickled, though it might have been from the cold. "The lake is frozen. Maybe you can walk across." She looked at Viviane. "If you are priestess-born, you must be foresighted, and will know where it is safe to go. Do you have the courage to try?"

The girl stared back silently. She had *seen* things, in fragments and flashes, as long as she could remember, and knew that, untrained, such Sight was not to be trusted. But she was aware enough to sense meanings in this conversation she did not understand.

"Ice is treacherous—it seems solid, and then it cracks and you go down," said the bard. "It would be a pity, after bringing the child all this way, to see her drown. . . ."

The words hung in the chill air, and Viviane thought she saw the old woman flinch, but that must have been an illusion, for in the next moment she was turning, clapping her hands, and trilling a call in a language the girl did not know.

Immediately, small dark men bundled in furs swarmed down the ladders, so swiftly that they must have been watching all the while. From the shelter of the reeds they dragged a barge, long and low enough to accommodate even their mounts, with some dark stuff draped around the prow. Ice cracked and shattered as they pulled it forward, and Viviane was glad she had not been tempted to show off. Would the old woman have allowed her to try? she wondered. Surely she had known the ice was thin.

There were more furs heaped inside the barge. Viviane snuggled into them gratefully, for as the boatmen pushed off with their poles and the craft began to slide away from the shore she could feel the chill fingers of the wind. She was surprised to see the old woman, whom she had thought one of the villagers, sitting in the prow— upright, as if she did not feel the cold. She looked different, almost familiar somehow.

They came to the center of the lake. The marsh men had switched to paddles now, and as the wind strengthened, the barge rocked on the swell. Viviane had just realized that through the falling snow she could now see the shadowed shore of the island, with its round church built of grim grey stone, quite clearly, when the boatmen lifted their paddles from the water.

"Lady, now you call the mists?" one of them asked in the British tongue.

For one horrified moment, Viviane thought he was talking to *her;* then, to her astonishment, the old woman got to her feet. She did not look so little now, nor so old. The girl's face must have shown her feelings, for she glimpsed on the Lady's face a mocking smile as she turned to face the island. Viviane had not seen her mother since she was five, and could not recall her features, but she knew her now. She glanced at Taliesin accusingly—he might have warned her!

But her father, if he *was* her father, was gazing at the Lady, who moment by moment gained in height and beauty as she lifted her arms. For a breath she stood, body arched in invocation; then a string of strange syllables left her lips in one clear call, and her arms curved down.

Viviane felt in her bones the tremor that moved them from one reality to the other. Even before the mists began to shimmer she knew what had happened, but her eyes still opened wide in wonder as they parted, and she saw the Isle of Avalon glimmering in the last light of a sun that had not been shining in the world she knew. There was no snow on the ringstones that crowned the Tor, but white sparkled on the shore and lay like blossom on the apple boughs, for Avalon was, even now, not completely apart from the human world. To her dazzled eyes, it was a vision of light, and in all the years she lived after, Viviane never beheld anything so beautiful.

The boatmen, laughing, dug in with their paddles and brought the barge swiftly to the landing. They had been seen—white-cloaked Druids and girls and women in shades of natural wool or priestess-blue were running down the hill. The Lady of Avalon, shedding the wrappings that had disguised her, stepped first onto the shore, and turned to reach for Viviane's hand.

"My daughter—be welcome to Avalon."

Viviane, about to take her hand, stopped short, all the frustration of her journey suddenly bursting free in words.

"If I am so welcome, I wonder it has taken you so long to send for me, and if I am your daughter, why did you tear me, without a word of warning, from the only home I have known?"

"I never give reasons for what I do." The Lady's voice abruptly chilled.

Suddenly Viviane remembered that tone from when she was very small; she would be ready for a caress and instead the cold would come, more shocking than a blow.

Then, more gently, the Lady added, "My daughter, a time will come when you may do the same. But for now, for your own sake, you must undergo the same discipline as any peasant-born novice on this isle. Do you understand?"

Viviane stood speechless as the Lady—she could not think of her as "mother"—gestured to one of the girls.

"Rowan, take her to the House of Maidens and give her the dress of a novice priestess. She shall be pledged before the evening meal in the hall."

The girl was slender, with fair hair showing beneath the shawl she had wrapped around her head and shoulders. When they were out of sight of the Lady, she said, "Don't be frightened—"

"I am not frightened. I am angry!" hissed Viviane.

"Then why are you shaking so hard you can hardly hold on to my hand?" The fair girl laughed. "Truly, there is nothing to fear. The Lady does not bite. She does not even bark much if you are careful to do what she says. A time will come, believe me, when you will be glad you are here."

Viviane shook her head, thinking, *If my mother showed her anger, I might believe she loved me. . . .*

"And she always lets us ask questions. She is impatient sometimes, but you should never show that you are afraid of her—it
makes her very cross. And you should never let her see you cry."

I have started well, then, with my defiance, thought Viviane. When she
thought about her mother on the way here, this was not how she
imagined their reunion would be.

"Had you ever seen her before?"

"She is my mother," said Viviane, momentarily enjoying the girl's
consternation. "But I am sure you know her better than I do—I have
not seen her since I was very small."

"I wonder that she did not tell us!" exclaimed Rowan. "But perhaps she thought we would treat you differently. Or perhaps it is
because we are all, in a sense, her children. There are four of us
novices now," the girl chattered on, "you and me and Fianna and
Nella. We will sleep together in the House of Maidens."

They had reached the building. Rowan helped her strip off her
travel-stained clothing and wash. By this time Viviane had no regrets
for the clothing of the world. She would have happily donned a
sack, as long as it was clean and dry. But the gown into which Rowan bundled her was of thickly woven oatmeal-colored wool, and
the cloak of grey wool, pinned around her shoulders, both soft
and warm.

When they came to the hall, they found that the Lady had
changed as well. All traces of the old woman were gone. She stood up
now in a robe and mantle of dark blue, and a garland of autumn
berries rested on her brow. This time, as Viviane looked into those
dark eyes, she recognized, not the mother she remembered, but the
face she saw when she herself looked into a forest pool.

"Maiden, why have you come to Avalon?"

"Because you sent for me," said the girl. She saw her mother's eyes
darken with anger, but remembered what Rowan had said and faced
her boldly. The ripple of nervous laughter that had started among
the girls who stood behind her faded at the Lady's glance.

"Do you seek admission among the priestesses of Avalon of your
own free will?" the Lady said tightly, holding her gaze.

This is important, thought Viviane. *She could order Taliesin all the way to*

Mona to fetch me, but he cannot compel me to stay here, nor can she, for all her power. She needs me, and she knows it. For a moment, she was tempted to refuse.

In the end she decided to stay neither from love for her mother nor out of fear, nor even from the thought of the cold world outside, but because, during that journey across the lake and earlier, traveling with Taliesin, senses that had been dormant while she lived on the farm had begun to awaken. When her mother brought them through the mists, Viviane had tasted the magic that was her heritage, and she wanted more.

"For whatever reason I came, I wish to stay here—of my own free will," she said clearly.

"Then I accept you in the name of the Goddess. Henceforth you are consecrated to Avalon." And for the first time since she had arrived, her mother took Viviane into her arms.

The rest of that evening was a blur to her—the admonitions to hold all the women of the community as her kin, and the names by which they were introduced to her; her own promise to remain pure. The food was simple but well prepared, and, exhausted as she was, the warmth of the fire had sent her half to sleep before the meal was done. Laughing, the other girls bore her along with them to the House of Maidens, showed her a bed, and gave her a linen shift that smelled of lavender to wear.

But she did not fall asleep immediately. The bed was strange to her, as was the breathing of the other maidens, and the way the building creaked in the wind. Like a waking dream, all that had happened since Taliesin came riding up to her foster-parents' farm passed through her memory.

In the next bed she could hear Rowan turning. Softly she called her name.

"What is it? Are you cold?"

"No." *Not in body,* thought Viviane. "I wanted to ask you—for you have been here for some time—what happened to Anara? How did my sister die?"

There was a long silence, and then, finally, a sigh.

"We only heard whispers," said Rowan. "I don't know for sure.

But . . . she finished her training, and they sent her out beyond the mists to make her own way back. More than that, perhaps even the Lady does not know. And you must not say I told you—since then Anara's name has not been spoken. I only heard that when she did not return they went out searching, and found her floating in the marshes, drowned. . . ."

Chapter Eighteen

The Lady of Avalon walked through the orchard above the holy well. On the branches the hard green apples were beginning to show the first blush of color. Like the maidens who sat at the feet of Taliesin, she thought, they were small and unripe, but they would grow. She could hear the girls' voices now, and his deeper tones answering. Drawing about her the glamour that would allow her to pass unseen, she moved closer.

"Four Treasures there are that have been guarded at Avalon since the Romans came to this land," said the bard. "Do you know what they are, and why they are held holy?"

The four novices were sitting together on the grass, their cropped heads tilted as they listened, fair and red and dark and brown. Their hair had been cut for convenience, as was customary in the summer. Viviane had protested, for her hair had been her chief beauty, glossy and thick as a horse's mane. But if the girl cried, she had done so only when she was alone.

The fair girl, Rowan, was lifting her hand. "One of them is the Sword of the Mysteries, is it not? The blade borne by Gawen, who was one of the ancient kings?"

"Gawen bore it, but it is far older, forged from the fire of heaven...." The bard's voice took on the cadence of poetry as he recounted the legend.

Viviane sat with a rapt face, listening. Ana had thought of telling her that the hair-cutting had not been meant as a punishment. But the Lady of Avalon did not explain her actions, and she would do the child no favor if she coddled her. Her breath caught as a vision of Anara's pale face beneath the water, her hair tangled in the reeds, superimposed itself upon Viviane's. Once more she told herself that Anara had died because she was a weakling. For her own sake, Viviane must do and suffer whatever was necessary to make her strong.

"And what are the other Treasures?" Taliesin was asking now.

"There is a Spear, I think," said Fianna, sun gleaming on her autumn-colored hair.

"And a Platter," added Nella, as tall as Viviane, though she was younger, with a tangled mop of brown curls.

"And the Cup," Viviane added in a whisper, "which they say is the same as the Cauldron of Ceridwen, and the Grail that Arianrhod kept in her temple of crystal, all set about with pearls."

"It is all of those things, for it contains them, as it both *is* and contains the holy water of the well. And yet, if you were to look upon them unprepared, they might seem no different from any other such gear—and that is to teach us that there can be great holiness even in the things of everyday. But if you touched them"—he shook his head—"that would be another matter, for it is death to touch the Mysteries unprepared. And that is why we keep them hidden away."

"Where?" asked Viviane, her gaze sharpening. With what, wondered her mother—curiosity, or reverence, or desire for power?

"That also is one of the Mysteries," Taliesin answered, "that only those initiates know who are called to be their guardians."

Viviane sat back, her eyes narrowing, as he went on.

"For you, it is enough to know what the Treasures are, and what they mean. We are taught that the Symbol is nothing and the Reality is all—and the reality that these symbols contain is that of the four elements from which all things are made—Earth, and Water, and Air, and Fire."

"But haven't you told us symbols are important?" said Viviane. "We talk about the elements but we can't really understand them. Symbols are what our minds use to make magic—"

Taliesin looked at the girl with a smile of peculiar sweetness, and

Ana felt an unexpected pang. *She is too eager,* she told herself. *She must be tested!*

She saw Viviane shiver, and then turn, and, despite the glamour, the girl saw her mother standing there. Ana returned her gaze coldly; and after a moment Viviane flushed and looked away.

The Lady turned then herself and passed swiftly back through the trees. *I am in my thirty-sixth year,* she thought, *and still fertile. I can make more daughters. But until I do, that girl is my only child, and the hope of Avalon.*

◁ ◁ ◁

Viviane sat on her heels, rubbing the small of her back. Behind her the scrubbed stones of the path steamed gently; before her the dry stones lay waiting. Her knees hurt too, and her hands were red and chapped from constant immersion. As they dried, the stones she had finished looked just like the ones ahead of her, which was not surprising, since this was the third time they had been washed.

The first time was understandable, since the cows had strayed from their pasture and fouled the path. And there had been justice in assigning Viviane to do the cleaning, since she had been herding the cows at the time.

But the second and third scrubbings were unnecessary. She was not afraid of hard work—she had been accustomed to work on her foster-father's farm—but what was the spiritual significance of repeating a job she had done carefully and well? Or of herding cattle, for that matter, which she could have done at home?

They would have her believe that Avalon was now her home, she thought sullenly as she dipped the brush into the pail and made a careless swipe across the next stone. But a home was where you were loved and welcome. . . . The Lady had made it perfectly clear that she had brought her daughter to Avalon not out of love but from necessity. And Viviane reacted by doing what was asked of her sullenly and without joy.

It might have been different, she told herself as she went on to another stone, if she had been learning magic. But that was for the senior students. The novices got only children's tales and the privilege of acting as serving maids for the community. And she couldn't even run away! Occasionally one of the older maidens would attend upon the Lady when she traveled, but the younger girls never left Avalon. If Viviane tried, she would only lose herself in the mists, to wander until she drowned in the marshes as her sister had done.

Perhaps, if she begged him, Taliesin would take her away. She believed that he loved her. But he was the Lady's creature—would he risk her wrath for a daughter who might not even be his own? In the year and three quarters since she had been here, Viviane had seen her mother truly angry only once, when Ana learned that the High King had put aside his wife, a woman trained in Avalon, and taken the daughter of the Saxon Hengest as his bride. With the true target out of reach in Londinium, there had been no outlet for the Lady's fury at the insult to Avalon, and the atmosphere of the isle had throbbed with such tension Viviane had been astonished to look up and see the sky still blue. Clearly what her teachers said about the necessity for an adept to control his or her emotions was true.

I will just have to outwait her, Viviane told herself as she inched forward. *I have time. And when I reach the age for initiation and they send me through the mists, I will simply walk away from here. . . .*

The sun was setting, turning the clouds to banners of gold, and the air had the hush that comes when the world is poised between night and day. Viviane realized that she would have to hurry to be done before dinnertime. And the water was almost gone. She pushed herself to her feet and started down the path, the pail clanking by her side, to get more.

An ancient stone chamber surrounded the well shaft, which was only uncovered for certain ceremonies. A channel led the water to the Mirror Pool, into which the priestesses looked when they wished to see the future, and from there the overflow was diverted around through the trees to a trough from which it might be drawn for drinking or for other purposes, such as scrubbing the stones.

When Viviane passed the Mirror Pool, she found her steps lagging. As Taliesin had taught her, it was the Reality, not the symbol, that mattered, and the reality was that the water in the trough was exactly the same as the water in the Pool. She looked around her. Time was passing, and there was no one to see.... Viviane took a quick step sideways and bent to dip her bucket in.

The Pool was full of fire.

The bucket slipped from her grasp and clattered over the stones, but Viviane sank to her knees, staring. She clung to the rim of the Pool, whimpering at the images she saw there, unable to look away.

A city was burning. Red flames licked at the houses, shooting up in tongues of gold when they seized some new source of fuel, and a great pillar of black smoke stained the sky. Figures were moving, black against the brightness, carrying goods out of the burning houses. For a moment she thought the people were trying to save their possessions; then she saw the flare of a sword. A man fell, blood spouting from his neck, and his murderer laughed and tossed the casket he had been carrying onto a blanket where more such fragments of people's lives were already piled.

Bodies lay in the streets; in an upper window she saw a face, its mouth opening in a silent scream. But the fair-haired barbarians were everywhere, laughing as they slew. Vision recoiled, expanded to take in a wider scene; on the roads that led out of the city people were fleeing, some of them with animals to draw the carts that held their possessions, others pulling the carts themselves, or dragging bundles, or, worse still, staggering onward with nothing, even their eyes emptied of sense by the horrors they had seen.

She had seen the name "Venta" on an overturned stone, but the broad lands that surrounded the city were flat and marshy; this was not the Venta of the Silures. What she was seeing must lie far to the east—the capital of the old Iceni lands. Her mind clung to such calculations, seeking to distance itself from what she had seen.

But the vision would not release her. She saw the great city of Camulodunum with its gate in flames, and many another Roman town shattered and burning. Saxon rams battered down walls and smashed gateways. Ravens hopped aside as bands of plunderers swaggered down deserted streets, then returned to feast on the unburied bodies once more. A mangy dog, grinning triumphantly, trotted across the forum with a severed human hand in its jaws.

In the countryside the destruction was less complete, but terror swept the land clean with its dark wing. She saw the folk of isolated villas bury their silver and make their way westward, trampling the ripening grain. The whole world, it seemed, was fleeing the Saxon wolves.

Fire and blood ran together in crimson swirls as her eyes filled; she sobbed, but she could not look away. And gradually she became aware that someone was speaking, had been speaking for a long time.

"Breathe deeply.... That is well.... What you see is distant, it cannot harm you.... Breathe in and out, and calm yourself, and tell me what you see...."

Viviane released her breath in a shuddering sigh, took the next more easily, and blinked away the tears. The vision still held her, but now it was as if she were seeing pictures in a dream. Her consciousness floated somewhere outside her body; she was aware, without much caring, that someone was asking her questions and her own voice was answering.

◁ ◁ ◁

"I suppose the girl is truthful? There is no possibility that she was hysterical or making this up to get attention?" asked old Nectan, Arch-Druid and chief of the Druids of Avalon.

Ana smiled sardonically. "Do not comfort yourself with the thought that I am protecting my daughter. The priestesses will tell you I have shown her no favor, and I would kill her with my own hands if I thought she had profaned the Mysteries. But what purpose in inventing such a tale unless she had an audience? Viviane was alone until her friend wondered why she had not come in to dinner and went to look for her. By the time I was called, she was deep in trance, and I think you will admit that I must know the difference between true vision and playacting."

"Deep in trance," echoed Taliesin, "but she does not yet have the training!"

"True. And it took all of mine to bring her back again!"

"And after that, you continued to question her?" asked the bard.

"When the Goddess sends a vision so sudden and overwhelming, it must be accepted. We dared not refuse the warning," said the Lady, repressing her own unease. "In any case, the damage was done. All we could do was to learn as much as possible, and tend the girl after—"

"Will she be all right?" asked Taliesin. His face had lost all color, and Ana frowned. She had not realized he was so fond of the girl.

"Viviane is resting. I do not think you need to worry—she comes of a tough breed," Ana said dryly. "She will be sore when she awakens, but if she remembers anything it will seem distant as a dream."

Nectan coughed. "Very well. If this was a true vision, then what must we do?"

"The first thing I have done already, which is to send a messenger to Vortigern. It is now high summer, and the girl saw fields ready for harvest. If the warning comes now, he will have a little time."

"If he will use it," Julia, one of the senior priestesses, said dubiously. "But that Saxon witch leads him about by his—" At Ana's expression she fell silent.

"Even if Vortigern mustered his whole houseguard and rode against Hengest he could do little," Taliesin put in quickly. "The barbarian numbers are now too great. What are the words you have told us Viviane cried out at the end?"

"The Eagles have flown forever. Now the White Dragon arises and devours the land . . ." whispered Ana, shivering.

"It is the disaster we feared," said Talenos, a younger Druid, heavily, "the doom we hoped would never come to be!"

"And what, besides wailing and beating our breasts like the Christians, do you suggest we do?" Ana asked acidly. It was as bad as he had said and more, she thought, remembering the horror in Viviane's words—and her belly had been too tense for her to eat since she had heard them. But she must not let them see that she was sick with fear.

"What can we do?" asked Elen, oldest of the priestesses. "Avalon was set apart to be a refuge; since the time of Carausius we have kept it secret. We must wait until the fire burns itself out around us. At least we will be safe here. . . ." The others looked at her in scorn and, confused, she fell silent.

"We must pray to the Goddess to help us," said Julia.

"It is not enough." Taliesin shook his head. "If the King is unable, or unwilling, to sacrifice himself for the people, then it is for the Merlin of Britannia to do so."

"But we don't have—" started Nectan, his ruddy cheeks paling, and Ana, despite the first twinge of alarm as she guessed where Taliesin was heading, felt a bitter amusement at the old priest's obvious fear that they would expect *him* to take on the role.

"—a Merlin," finished Taliesin. "Nor have we had a priest to hold that title since the Romans first invaded Britannia, when he died so that Caractacus could fight on."

"The Merlin is one of the masters, a radiant soul who has refused to ascend beyond this sphere so that he can continue to watch over us," said Nectan, settling back onto his bench. "To incarnate again would diminish him. We may pray for his guidance, but we must not ask him to walk among us once more."

"Even if that is the only thing that might save us?" asked Taliesin. "If he is so enlightened, then he will know whether it is right to refuse. But it is certain he will not come unless we ask!"

Julia leaned forward. "It did not work in the time of Caractacus. The King for whom the Merlin died was captured, and the Romans slew the Druids on the holy isle."

Nectan nodded. "And though that was a disaster, the Romans who conquered are the very people whose destruction we are lamenting now! Is it not possible that one day we will live as peacefully with these Saxons as we have lived with Rome?"

The others all looked at him, and he in turn became silent.

The Romans, thought Ana, had possessed a civilization as well as an army. The Saxons were little better than the wild wolves of the hills.

"Even if he were born tomorrow," she said aloud, "it might be too late by the time he became a man."

"There is another way that I have heard of," said Taliesin in a low voice, "when a living man opens his soul to let the Other in—"

"No!" Fear made her voice a lash to strike him. "In the name of the Goddess I forbid it! I don't want the Merlin—I want you yourself, here!" She held his gaze with her own, summoning all her power, and after an agonizing interval that seemed to go on forever, saw the hero-light in his grey eyes dim.

"The Lady of Avalon has spoken, and I obey," he murmured. "But I will tell you this." He looked up at her. "In the end, there will be a sacrifice."

◁ ◁ ◁

Viviane lay in her bed in the House of Maidens, watching dust motes dance in a last ray of sun that slanted past the curtain across the door. She felt bruised inside and out. The older priestesses had told her this was because she had been unprepared for her vision. Her body, tensing in resistance, had set one muscle against another until it was a wonder she had no broken bones. Her mind had been drawn into that other reality. If her mother had not opened her own mind and reached out to find her, she could have been lost.

To Viviane, that was the greatest wonder, that her mother had been willing to run such a risk, and that her own spirit had accepted the other woman's touch without fear. Perhaps the Lady had only wanted to hear the vision, said the other part of Viviane's mind that was always doubting. Nonetheless, there was something in Ana's mind that her daughter's had apparently recognized. Viviane suspected they were more alike than either would have liked to admit. Perhaps, she thought smiling, this was why it was so hard for them to get along.

But the Lady of Avalon was a trained priestess. Viviane might have all her mother's talent and more, but unless she learned to use it she would be a danger to herself and everyone around her.

This experience had sobered her more effectively than any punishment her mother might impose. And she had to admit that she deserved it. True, the winter after she arrived had been one of the hardest in memory; the ice that had been an illusion at Samhain had frozen the lake by midwinter, and the marsh folk had brought food to them on sledges pulled across the ice and snow. For a time, they had all been too concerned with survival to think much about training. But since then, Viviane had been mostly going through the motions, almost daring her mother to make her learn.

The door curtain moved, and she smelled something that made her mouth water. Rowan made her way past the beds and set the covered tray she was carrying on a bench with a smile.

"You have slept a whole night and all the day again. You must be hungry!"

"I am," answered Viviane, wincing as she pulled herself up on one elbow. Rowan pulled back the cloth, revealing a bowl of stew, and Viviane spooned it up eagerly. There were bits of meat in it, which surprised her, for the priestesses in training were mostly kept on a light diet to purify their bodies and increase their sensitivity. No doubt her seniors felt that more sensitivity was the last thing she needed just now.

But, hungry as she was, she found that her stomach refused to accept any more than half the bowl. She lay back with a sigh.

"Will you sleep now?" asked Rowan. "I must say, you look as if you had been beaten all over with sticks."

"I feel like it too, and I want to rest, but I am afraid I will have nightmares."

Rowan's gaze became avid, and she leaned closer. "In the hall they would only say you had seen some disaster. What was it? What did you see?"

Viviane stared up at her, shuddering, even the simple question conjuring back the images of horror. They heard voices outside the door, and the other girl straightened. Viviane sighed in relief as the curtain was pushed aside and the Lady of Avalon came in.

"I see that you have been cared for," Ana said coolly as Rowan made a quick reverence and scurried away.

"Thank you . . . for bringing me back," said Viviane. There was an uncomfortable silence, but it seemed to her there was a little more color in her mother's cheeks than there had been before.

"I am not . . . a maternal woman," Ana said with some difficulty, "which is probably just as well, since I must put the obligations of the priestess ahead of those of the mother. As your priestess, I would have done the same. But I am pleased to see you recovering."

Viviane blinked. It was not much—certainly not the kind of speech she had dreamed of when as a child she had wondered about her mother. But Ana had given her more kindness just now than in the almost two years she had been here. Dared she ask for just a little more?

"I am better, but I am afraid to sleep again. . . . If Taliesin could play his harp, it would give me better dreams."

For a moment her mother looked angry. Then some new thought seemed to cross her mind, and she nodded.

When, later that evening, the bard came to sit by her side, he too looked anxious and strained. Viviane asked what was wrong, but he would only smile and say that she had had enough troubles for one day and he would not burden her with his own. And there was no sorrow in the music he drew from the harp's shining strings; when sleep claimed her, it was deep and without dreams.

🜨 🜨 🜨

The year that followed proved Viviane a true prophet. It gave her a certain standing among the priestesses, but she would far rather have endured their scorn, for the news that began to reach them with the harvest, though insulated by distance, was as bad as it could be. Hengest the Saxon, complaining that Vortigern had not delivered the promised payments, had fallen upon the cities of Britannia with fire and sword. In a few short months all the south and east were devastated, and refugees streamed into the west country.

Numerous though they were, the Saxons had not the force to occupy the entire island. Cantium was in the grip of Hengest; the Trinovante territories north of the Tamesis were the hunting grounds of the East Seax; and the Iceni lands were firmly held by their Anglian allies. Elsewhere, the raiders struck and retreated again. But the Britons who fled did not return to their homes, for how could they make a living when there were no markets in which to sell their produce and their wares? The conquered lands were like a sore on the body of Britannia, and the nearby places grew numb even before the fever reached them.

Farther to the west, life continued more or less unaffected, except for the fear. In Avalon, separated from the world, the priestesses found it hard to enjoy their safety. From time to time, some refugee wandering in the marshes would be found by the little folk. Those who were Christian were sheltered by the monks on their isle, but several of the others came to Avalon.

The High King, despite his Saxon wife, did not sit idle. Little by little, they began to hear how Vortigern had held Londinium, and how his sons were attempting to rally the people and take back their lands, calling for men and support from the undamaged lands of Britannia.

In the spring of the following year, when Viviane was seventeen, one of the marsh folk came through the mists with a different message. The son of the High King had come to seek the aid of Avalon.

In the House of Maidens, the girls had huddled together with all their blankets, for it was early spring, and still cold.

"But did you *see* him?" whispered little Mandua, who had come to them the summer before. "Is he handsome?"

The girl was young but precocious, and Viviane did not think she would last here long enough to be made a priestess of Avalon. But, then, she herself was still a novice, and though she was not the tallest, she was the oldest of them all. Only her friend Rowan remained of the girls who had been here when she arrived.

"All princes are handsome, just as all princesses are beautiful," said Rowan, laughing. "It is part of the job."

"Was not this one once married to your sister?" asked Claudia, who had been a refugee of good family from Cantium, though she never spoke of it now.

Viviane shook her head. "My sister Idris was the wife of Categirn,

Vortigern's older son. This is the younger one, Vortimer." She had caught a glimpse of him as he came in, thin, as dark of hair as she was herself, but taller. Still, she had thought he looked absurdly young to be carrying a sword, until she saw his eyes.

The wooden winter-door at the end of the hall was pulled open, and they all turned. "Viviane," came the voice of one of the elder priestesses, "your mother wants you. Come, and wear your ceremonial robe."

Viviane stood up, wondering what on earth this could mean. Five pairs of rounded eyes watched as she settled her cloak around her shoulders, but no one dared to say a word. Would she still be a maiden, she wondered, when she returned? She had heard tales of magics that required such an offering. The idea made her shiver, but at least if it happened they would have to make her a priestess.

The Lady was waiting with the others in the Great Hall, already robed in the crimson garments of the Mother, while old Elen, swathed in black, was clearly the priestess who had been chosen to take the part of the Crone. Nectan wore black as well, and Taliesin was resplendent in scarlet. But no one there matched her white. *It is the Prince we are waiting for,* she thought then, beginning to understand.

Her mother turned, though Viviane had heard nothing, and told her to put on her veil. Prince Vortimer came in, shivering in a white woolen tunic borrowed from one of the young Druids. His gaze fixed on the Lady of Avalon, and he bowed.

Are you frightened? You should be. Viviane smiled behind her veil as, without a word, the Lady led them from the hall. But as they started up the path to the Tor, she realized that she was frightened too.

Tonight the moon was still a maiden, her shining bow already arching westward as the world turned toward midnight. *Like me,* thought Viviane as she gazed upward. She shivered, for the torches they had set to either side of the altar gave out no heat, and only a fitful light. She took a deep breath as she had been taught, willing her body to ignore the chill air.

"Vortimer, son of Vortigern"—the Lady spoke softly, but her voice filled the circle—"why have you come here?"

The other two priests moved forward, escorting the Prince so that he faced the Lady across the altar stone. From her place at her mother's shoulder Viviane saw his eyes widen, and knew he was seeing not the little dark woman who was her mother, but the tall and stately High Priestess of Avalon.

Vortimer swallowed, but managed to speak steadily when he replied.

"I have come for Britannia. The wolves tear at her body, and the priests of the Christians can do nothing but tell us that we are suffering for our sins. But there is no sin in the little children burned in their houses, or the babe whose head is smashed against the stones. I have seen these things, my Lady, and I burn to avenge them. I call on the old gods, the ancient protectors of my people, for aid!"

"You speak well, but their gifts are not given without a price," said the High Priestess. "We serve the Great Goddess, who is nameless, and yet called by many names, and though formless, yet has many faces. If you come to dedicate your life to Her service, then perhaps She will hear your call."

"My mother was trained on this holy isle, and brought me up to love the old ways. I am willing to give whatever is required for the favor of Avalon."

"Even your life?" Elen stepped forward, and Vortimer swallowed, but he nodded. The old woman's laughter was dry as bone. "Your blood may one day be demanded, but not today...."

Now it was Viviane's turn. "It is not your blood that I ask of you," she said softly, "but your soul."

He turned, staring as if his burning eyes could pierce her veil.

"It belongs to you...." He blinked suddenly. "It has always belonged to you. I remember ... I have made this offering before."

"Body and spirit must both be given," Ana said sternly. "If you are truly willing, then offer yourself upon the altar stone."

Vortimer pulled off his white garment and lay back, naked and shivering, upon the cold stone. *He thinks we are going to kill him,* thought Viviane, *despite my words.* He looked younger lying there, and she realized that he could not be more than a year or two older than she.

Elen and Nectan moved to the north and the south, while she took her place in the east and Taliesin moved westward. Humming softly, the High Priestess came to the edge of the circle and, turning sunwise, began to dance in and out among the stones. Once, twice, and thrice, she wove the circle, and as she passed, Viviane felt her own awareness shifting, and saw with altered sight a flicker of radiance pass through the standing stones that seemed to hang in the air. When she had finished, she returned to the center.

Viviane straightened to her full height, setting her feet firmly as she reached out to heaven, and the circle filled with the scent of apple blossom as she called on the powers that guarded the Eastern Gate by their ancient and secret names.

Old Elen's voice grew resonant as the warmth of the south filled the circle; then Taliesin called the west in a voice of music, and Viviane was lifted by a tide of power. Only when Nectan's invocation summoned the guardians of the north did she feel herself rooted once more. But the circle to which she returned was no longer entirely in the world. Even Vortimer had ceased to shiver; indeed, it was quite warm within the circle now.

Ana had unstoppered the glass phial that hung at her girdle, and the scent of the oil hung heavy on the air. Elen poured oil on her fingers and bent to Vortimer's feet to draw the sigil of power.

"To the holy earth I bind you," she whispered. "Living or dying, you belong to this land."

The High Priestess took the oil, and gently anointed his phallus, and he blushed as it stiffened beneath her hand. "I claim the seed of life you carry, that you may serve the Lady with all your power."

She offered the phial to Viviane, who moved to his head and began to draw the third sigil on his brow. She blinked, memories that were not of this lifetime showing her a fair-haired man with eyes as blue as the sea, and then another boy, with the dragons of kingship newly emblazoned on his arms.

"All your dreams and aspirations, the sacred spirit within you, I consecrate to Her now . . ." she said softly, and was astonished to find her own voice so sweet in her ears. She wondered if, in those other lives, she had loved him. Lifting her veil, she bent and kissed his lips, and for a moment saw a goddess reflected in his eyes.

She moved to join her mother and old Elen at Vortimer's feet. As they linked arms, she felt the dizzying shift and a moment's panic as her former self fell away, and began to tremble. She had seen this, but had never experienced it before.

Then her own consciousness was replaced by that Other, focused in the three figures that stood in the circle but were not contained by them, whose being embraced the world. She was aware of the other faces of Her triple nature, and yet she was One; though she spoke through three pairs of lips, it was in one voice that Her words came to the man who lay below.

"You who seek the Goddess and believe you know what you have asked for—know now that I shall never be what you have expected, but always something other, and something more. . . ."

Vortimer had gotten himself upright, and was kneeling on the stone. How small he looked, and how frail.

"You listen for My voice, but it is in silence that you will hear Me; You desire My love, but when you receive it, then shall you know fear; You beg Me for victory, but it is in defeat that you will understand My power.

"Knowing these things, will you still make the offering? Will you give yourself to Me?"

"I come from You—" His voice wavered, but he went on, "I can only give You back Your own. . . . It is not for myself I ask this, but for the people of Britannia." As Vortimer answered, the radiance within the circle grew.

"I am the Great Mother of all things living," came Her answer, *"I have many children. Do you think that by any act of men this land can be lost, or that you can be separated from Me?"*

Vortimer bowed his head.

"You are great of heart, my child, and so, for a time, you shall have your desire. I accept your service, as I have accepted it before. Sacred King you have been, and Emperor. Yet again you shall preserve Britannia. What one man may do, your arm shall accomplish, but it is not yet time for the Saxons to be conquered. It is another

name that the ages will remember. Your labors in this life will but prepare the way. . . . Will that content you?"

"It must. Lady, I accept Your will . . ." he said in a low voice.

"Rest, then, for as you have served Me, I will keep faith with you, and when Britannia has need, you shall return. . . ."

His face grew radiant as the Goddess reached out to enfold him, and when Her embrace was ended, laid him curled on the altar stone, sleeping like a little child.

Chapter Nineteen

At the end of the summer, the sun blazed in a cloudless sky and turned the grass to gold. The Druids dug out a pool at the edge of the lake, where the priestesses went to bathe. When the weather was so warm, there was no need for clothing, and the women spread cloths on the grass and dried off in the sunlight, or sat chattering on benches in the shade of the spreading oak tree.

Viviane's hair had grown out a little from its yearly shearing, but a good shake was enough to get rid of the moisture. By now she had become accustomed to having it short, and on such a day as this, the lack of weight was very welcome. She spread out her tunic on the grass and lay down, letting the sun toast the rest of her body to the brown that arms and legs had already acquired. Her mother was sitting on a tree stump, her body in shadow but her head tipped back to catch the sun as Julia combed out her hair.

The Lady's hair was usually worn coiled on her head and held with pins, but it fell past her hips when unbound. As the comb lifted each dark strand, auburn highlights ran down it in waves of flame. Through slitted eyes Viviane watched the other woman stretch with pleasure like a cat. She had been used to thinking of her mother as little and ugly, all frowns and angles, except, of course, when she wore the beauty of the Goddess in ritual. But Ana was not ugly now.

Sitting there, she was a goddess in miniature, her body carved from old ivory, with a smooth belly etched with the silver scars of childbearing and breasts high and firm. She even looked happy. Curious, Viviane let her eyes unfocus as she had been taught, and saw

Ana's aura ablaze with rosy light. It was brightest over the belly. No wonder if even to normal sight she seemed to glow.

Her skin chilling with a sudden, outraged suspicion, Viviane sat up. Trailing her tunic behind her, she made her way to her mother's side.

"Your hair is beautiful," she said evenly. Ana's eyes opened, but she was still smiling. Definitely, something had changed. "But, then, you have had a long time to grow it. You were made priestess when you were fifteen, were you not? And had your first child the next year," she added thoughtfully. "I am turned nineteen. Do not you think it is time for my initiation, mother, so that I may begin to grow my hair out too?"

"No." Ana had not changed position, but there was a new tension in her body.

"Why not? I am already the oldest novice in the House of Maidens. Am I destined to become the oldest virgin in the history of Avalon?"

Ana did sit up then, though anger had not yet quite overcome her benevolent mood. "I am the Lady of Avalon, and it is for me to say when you are ready!"

"In what lesson am I unlearned? In what task have I failed?" cried Viviane.

"Obedience!" The dark eyes flashed, and Viviane felt, like the blast of a hot wind, her mother's power.

"Is it so?" Viviane reached for the only weapon left to her. "Or are you simply waiting for me to become expendable, when you have been delivered of the child you now bear?"

She saw her mother's face flush, and knew it was true. It had happened, she supposed, at Midsummer. She wondered who the father was, or if he even knew.

"You ought to be ashamed, at an age when I should be making you a grandmother, to be pregnant yourself once more!"

She had meant to sound defiant, but even she could hear the petulance, and now it was her own face that was aflame. As Ana began to laugh, Viviane turned, pulling on her tunic, and her mother's laughter followed her like a curse as she ran away.

After an active summer, Viviane was hard and fit. She did not care where she went, but her feet chose a safe path around the edge of the lake, away from the Tor. The summer had dried much of the marshland, and soon she found herself farther from Avalon than she had been since the day she arrived. But she kept on running.

It was not exhaustion that stopped her, but mist, which rose up suddenly to blot out the light. Viviane slowed, her heart pounding. She told herself it was only a land-fog, drawn up from the boggy ground by the heat of the day. But such fogs were normally released when night began to cool the air, and when she last saw the sun it had only been midafternoon. The light she saw now was all silver, and had no direction that she could see.

Viviane came to a halt and looked around her. It was said that Avalon had been withdrawn to a place partway between the world of humankind and Faerie. Those who knew the spell passed through the mists to reach the human shore. But from time to time something would go wrong, and a man or a woman would be lost in the other realm.

My mother would have been wiser, she thought as the sweat dried clammy on her skin, *to let me try the mists from the direction of the mortal world.*

The veil was thinning; she took another step, then stopped short, for the hillside it revealed was lush and green and starred with unfamiliar flowers. It was beautiful, but it was no land she knew.

On the other side of the rise, someone was singing. Viviane frowned, for the voice, though pleasant enough, was having some trouble maintaining the tune. Carefully she parted the bracken, and looked over the rim of the hill.

An old man sat singing among the flowers. He was tonsured across the forehead like a Druid, but he wore a nondescript tunic of dark wool, and at his breast hung a wooden cross. In her astonishment she must have made some sound, for he saw her, and smiled.

"A blessing on you, fair one," he said softly, as if he feared she would vanish away.

"What are you doing here?" she asked, coming down the hill.

"I might ask the same of you," he said as he took in her scratched legs and the perspiration on her brow. "For, though indeed you have the look of the folk of Faerie, I see that you are a mortal maid."

"You can *see* them?" she exclaimed.

"That gift has been given me, and though my brothers in the faith warn me that these creatures are demons or delusions, I cannot believe evil of anything so fair."

"Then you are a very unusual monk, from all I have heard," said Viviane, sitting down beside him.

"I fear it is so, for I cannot help feeling that our own Pelagius had it right when he preached that a man might by living virtuously and in peace with all gain heaven. I was made priest by Bishop Agricola, and took the name of Fortunatus. He considered the doctrine of Augustine, that all are born sinners and can hope for salvation only at the whim of God, to be heresy. But they think otherwise in Rome, and so we in Britannia are persecuted. The brothers at Inis Witrin took me in and set me to keep the chapel on the Isle of Birds."

He smiled; then his gaze sharpened and he pointed past her. "Ssh—there she is, the pretty, do you see?"

Slowly, Viviane turned her head, just as the iridescent shimmer which was emerging from the elder tree resolved itself into a slender form crowned with white blooms and clad in glossy blue-black draperies.

"Good mother, I greet you," murmured the girl with bowed head, her hands moving in the ritual salutation.

"Here's a maiden of the old blood, sisters—let us welcome her!" As the sprite spoke, suddenly the air was aswarm with bright beings, clad in a hundred hues. For a few moments they swirled around her; her skin tingled to the caress of insubstantial hands. Then, with a chime of laughter, they whirled away.

"Ah—now I understand. You are from the *other* island, from Avalon." Father Fortunatus nodded.

She nodded. "I am called Viviane."

"They say it is a very blessed isle," he said simply. "How came you to wander away?"

She stared at him suspiciously, and he looked back at her with a transparent innocence that was disarming. He would never use anything she said against her, she sensed, or against her mother—it was because he cared about her that he had asked.

"I was angry. My mother is pregnant—at *her* age—but still she tries to keep me a child!" Viviane shook her head; it was hard to remember now why that had made her so furious.

Father Fortunatus opened his eyes. "I have no right to advise you, for indeed I know little of womankind, but surely a new life is cause for rejoicing, and all the more if its coming is a kind of miracle. She will need your help to tend it, surely. Will not the sweet weight of a child in your arms bring you joy?"

Now it was Viviane's turn to wonder, for, in her resentment, she had not really thought about the child. Poor little mite, how much time would the Lady have to mother it? The baby would need her, even if Ana did not. Father Fortunatus was a funny old thing, but talking with him had eased her.

She looked up, wondering if she could find her way out of here, and realized that the directionless silvery light was darkening to a purple gloaming shot with glimmers of fairy light.

"You are right—it is time to go back to the world," said the priest.

"How do you find the way?"

"Do you see that stone? It is so old it stands also on the Isle of Birds, and when I step upon it I can come a little ways into Faerie. There are many such places of power, I think, where the veils are thin between the worlds. I come after I have said Mass on a Sunday, to praise God in His creation, for if He is Maker of All, surely He created this place too, and I know of none more fair. You are welcome to come back with me, maiden. There are holy women on Briga's isle who would shelter you. . . ."

It is the chance I was longing for, thought Viviane, *to escape and make my own way in the world.* But she shook her head.

"I must go back to my own home. Perhaps I will find another such place where the veils grow thin."

"Very well, but remember the stone. You will always be welcome if you have need of me." The old man got to his feet and extended his hands in blessing, and Viviane, as if he had been one of the elder Druids, bent to receive it.

Goddess, guide me, she thought as he disappeared into the dusk. *I spoke bravely, but I have no idea where to go.*

She stood up and closed her eyes, picturing in her mind the Isle of Avalon at rest in the purple twilight with the last rosy glow from the western sky gleaming in the waters below. And as she stilled her thoughts, the first notes of music began to fall into her silence like a silver rain. Their beauty was almost unearthly. But now and again the music would falter, and in those moments of human imperfection she knew it was not elven music she was hearing, but the song of a harper great almost beyond the measure of humankind.

If the sky of Faerie was never completely bright, it never reached utter darkness either. The purple dusk allowed her to see her way, and slowly Viviane moved toward the music. Now it was louder, calling so plaintively she wanted to weep. It was not only the harmonies that wrenched the soul, but the longing that throbbed through them. The harper sang sorrow, he sang longing, across the hills and waters he called the wanderer home. . . .

> *"The winter snow is white and fair—*
> *Lost, 'tis lost, and I sit mourning—*
> *It melts and leaves earth moist and bare.*
> *Oh, it may come again,*
> *but never twice the same."*

And Viviane, following that music, found herself finally walking across a meadow where the evening mist was just beginning to drift from the damp ground. In the distance, the familiar silhouette of the Tor stood stark against the sky. But her gaze was fixed on something nearer, on the figure of Taliesin, who sat, playing his harp, upon a worn grey stone.

"The flower that blooms proclaims the spring—
*   Lost, 'tis lost, and I sit mourning—*
For it must fall, the fruits to bring.
*   Oh, it may come again,*
*   but never twice the same."*

Sometimes when he played, the visions Taliesin conjured with his music became so vivid he was sure he could have touched them if he had lifted his fingers from the strings. At first, the girl who was coming toward him, her slim form wreathed in the mists of Faerie, seemed one of its people, her head high and her step so light he could not tell if she touched the ground. But if she were a vision, it was of Avalon, for that gliding step was the gait of a priestess.

"The summer fields with grain blaze gold—"

Dazed, he watched her, and his fingers continued to move upon the strings. He knew her, but she was a stranger, for his heart had called out to the child he loved, and this was a woman, and beautiful.

"Cut down for bread ere winter's cold."

Then she called his name, and that broke the spell. He had only time to set down the harp before she was sobbing in his arms.

"Viviane, my dear—" He patted her back, aware that it was not a child's body in his arms. "I have been anxious for you."

She pulled away, looking up at him. "You have been terrified—I could hear it in your song. And my mother, was she terrified too? I wondered if they would be dragging the marsh for me by now."

Taliesin thought back. The Lady had said little, but he had recognized the sick fear in her eyes.

"She was frightened. Why did you run away?"

"I was angry," said Viviane. "Do not be afraid. I will not do it again . . . even when the child is born. Did you know?" she added suddenly.

She deserved the truth, he thought, and nodded.

"It happened at the Midsummer fires." He saw comprehension dawn in her eyes, and wondered why he should feel ashamed.

"So this time," she said in a thin voice, "you did remember. And now I am needed neither by you nor by her."

"Viviane, it is not so!" Taliesin wanted to protest that he would always be a father to her, especially now, when her mother was carrying his child, but at this moment, when she looked so much as Ana must have appeared when she was young, he recognized that his feelings were not entirely fatherly, and he did not know what to say.

"She will not initiate me as a priestess! What *can* I do?"

Taliesin was a Druid, and, confused though the man in him might be, the priest in him responded to that cry.

"There is one thing you can do just because you are a maiden," he said, "something of which we have great need. The Four Treasures are in the keeping of the Druids. Sword and Spear can be handled by our priests, and the Platter by a woman, but the Cup should be tended by a maiden. Will you accept that trust?"

"Will my mother allow it?"

He saw the anguish in her face transform to awe.

"I think it is the will of the Goddess that you do this, Viviane, and that is something that even the Lady of Avalon will not gainsay."

She smiled, but in Taliesin's heart there was still sorrow, and in his mind a new verse that seemed to be part of his song—

> *"The child who used to laugh and run—*
>   *Lost, she's lost, and I sit mourning—*
> *Walks now a woman in the sun.*
>   *Oh, she may come again,*
>   *but never twice the same."*

In the west country, men hurried to harvest their fields as the year ripened toward harvest, for the Saxons were reaping a harvest of their own with bloody swords. Rumors flew like chattering crows through the countryside. One war band, under Hengest, had burned Calleva;

another, led by his brother Horsa, had failed to take Venta Belgarum but gone on to savage Sorviodunum. Surely, if they had the will to press onward, they would go north, to the rich pickings of Aquae Sulis and the Mendips. But there was another track, less traveled, that led straight westward to Lindinis.

If the Saxons did not have the numbers to settle these lands, they had enough warriors to cripple them so that they would be easy prey to some later attack. The barbarians, it was said, had no care for cities or workshops. Once they had drunk up all the plundered wine, they would go back to swilling beer. What they wanted was land—fertile land, *high* land, which would not be swallowed, as their homeland had been, by the salty waves of the sea.

The people of the Summer Country nodded and told each other that they should be safe enough in their marshes, but in so dry a year as this, the grasses of the higher meadows had been cut for hay, and places that were at most times hidden by water now were covered by a carpet of radiant green.

But Viviane paid little attention. Whatever else the barbarians might devour, it was certain they could never come to Avalon. She was not even disturbed when her mother's pregnancy became more apparent, for Taliesin had proved as good as his word, and at last she had a purpose of her own. With the other novices she had studied the lore of the Four Treasures, but now she was learning that this was barely a beginning, even though it was far more than most people ever knew. What she needed now was not more knowledge—to handle the holy things required the wisdom not of the head but of the heart. To become the Guardian of the Grail, she herself had to be transformed.

It was, in its way, as strenuous a training as her novitiate, but far more focused. Each day she bathed in the waters of the sacred well. That water had always been the drink of the priestesses, but now she ate more lightly, and her diet was fruit and vegetables only with a little grain, not even milk or cheese. She grew thinner and sometimes lightheaded; she moved through the world as if she walked underwater, but in that glimmering light all things became transparent to her, and ever more clearly she began to see between the worlds.

As Viviane's training progressed, she understood why finding a maiden for this duty was a problem. A girl would not have the strength of mind or body, but in the usual way of things, a young woman her age would already have been made priestess, and exercised her right to go to the Beltane fires. It did not displease her that the younger girls, who had wondered what fault had delayed her initiation, now looked on her with a kind of awe.

As she watched her mother's body become misshapen with pregnancy, Viviane walked serene and graceful, exulting in her own virginity. She was aware that the Grail, like the Goddess, had many manifestations, but it seemed clear to her that the most important was the one in which the Druids guarded it, as a radiant vessel of unsullied purity.

On the eve of the equinox of autumn, when the year balances on the threshold between sun and shadow, the Druids came for Viviane. They dressed her in a robe whose white was even more spotless than their own, and in silent procession she was led to an underground chamber. A sword lay there on a stone altar, its sheath cracked and flaking away with age. Against the wall leaned a spear. Beside it, set into the wall, were two niches. In the lower a broad platter rested on a white cloth. In the upper—Viviane's breath stopped as for the first time she looked upon the Grail.

How it would have appeared to an uninitiated eye she could not say—perhaps an earthenware cup, or a silver chalice, or a bowl of glass glittering with a mosaic of amber flowers. What Viviane saw was a vessel so clear it seemed made not from crystal but from water itself, which had willed to form the shape of a bowl. Surely, she thought, her mortal fingers would pass through it. But they had told her that she must take it up, and so she walked forward.

Closer, she could feel, first pressure, and then a current against which she pushed as if she were walking through a stream. Or perhaps, she thought hazily, it was a vibration, for now, if it was not her own ears ringing, she could hear a sweet humming. It seemed soft, but quickly it overwhelmed all other sound. Closer still, she wondered if it would dissolve her bones.

At that, Viviane felt a tremor of fear. She looked back—the Druids were watching her expectantly, willing her to continue. She told herself that the terrors that were suddenly attacking her were irrational, but still they came.

What if this were a plot between Taliesin and her mother to get rid of her? Truth or fancy, she knew well that it would be death to touch the Grail while she was afraid. She told herself that she did not have to do this. She could turn and walk away, and live with the shame. But if death were to be preferred to living as she had been, then she had nothing to lose by embracing it.

She looked once more at the Grail, and this time saw a cauldron that held the sea of space, pregnant with stars. A voice came from that darkness, so soft that she could scarcely hear, and yet she felt it in her bones.

"I am the dissolution of all that has passed; from Me springs all that is to come. Embrace Me, and My dark waters will sweep you away, for I am the Cauldron of Sacrifice. But I am also the vessel of Birth, and from My depths you may be reborn. Daughter, will you come to Me, and bear My power into the world?"

Viviane felt the tears rolling down her cheeks, for in that voice she heard not Ana but the true Mother for whom she had always longed. She stepped to the point of balance that lies between the Darkness and the Light, and took up the Grail.

A coruscating radiance that was both and neither pulsed through the chamber. One of the Druids cried out and dashed from the room; another fainted dead away. But the other faces were open and amazed, and as the Maiden, knowing herself now as something more than Viviane, lifted the Grail, they grew luminous with joy.

She passed through the midst of them and ascended the stair, bearing the sacred vessel between her hands. With measured tread she took the path that led to the holy well, and there, where the water rose ceaselessly from its secret sources, knelt and let it fill the bowl. From the niche in the well house came an answering glow, where the vial of holy blood that Father Josephus had left in the care of the priestesses lay hidden. Clear and pure flowed the water from the sacred spring, but it left a bloody stain upon the stones. As Viviane brought it brimming up again, the Grail began to pulse with a rosy glow.

That lovely light shone like dawn at midnight as she continued down the path that led to the lake. There she lifted the Grail once more and poured its contents into the greater water in a glistening stream. To her altered sight, the water of the well carried with it a glow that spread in shimmering motes, until the entire lake bore an opalescent sheen. Everything that water touched, she knew, would receive a part of the blessing, not only in Avalon, but in all the worlds.

  ◁ ◁ ◁

For Viviane, the ceremony of the Grail left a great peace behind it. But in the outer world the Saxons still roamed.

One evening a few weeks later, when the days had begun to darken earlier with the approach of Samhain, one of the girls came running up from the lake with word that a boat was approaching. It was paddled by Heron, one of the marsh men who knew the spell to pass through the mists to Avalon, but its passenger, by his dress, was one of the monks of Inis Witrin. Before the High Priestess could say a word, everyone within earshot was hastening down the path to see.

The boat slid up onto the mud, and, leaving the monk, who was blindfolded, seated in the stern, the waterman splashed through the shallows to shore.

"Father Fortunatus!" exclaimed Viviane, hurrying forward. Ana gave her an astonished look, but there was no time for questions.

"Heron, why have you brought this stranger here without my leave?"

The voice of the High Priestess lashed the marsh man to his knees. He bent, forehead touching the mud, while the monk sat turning his head as if he could see with his ears. His hands were not bound, but Viviane noted that he made no effort to remove the cloth.

"Lady, I bring him to speak for me! The wolf people—" He shook his head and fell silent, shivering.

"It is the Saxons he speaks of," Fortunatus said then. "They have sacked Lindinis and now come hither. Heron's village, which lies on the southern shore of the lake, is already in flames. His people have taken refuge in our abbey, but if the Saxons come there, as they seem likely to do, we cannot oppose them.

"Do not blame this man, for it was my idea to come to you. We of the abbey are willing to be martyred for our faith, but it seemed hard that innocent men and women and little children should die. We have labored to convert them, but they still have more faith in the old gods than the new. There is no power I know that can protect them, unless it be the power of Avalon."

"You are a strange monk if you believe so!" exclaimed the High Priestess.

"He is one who can see the fairy folk, and has their favor," said Viviane.

His head tipped in her direction, and he smiled. "Is that you, my fairy maiden? I am glad to know that you came safely home."

"I hear your plea, but this is not a decision to be made in a moment," said Ana. "You must wait while I confer with my council. Better still, let Heron take you back to your own place. If we decide to come to your aid, we will not need you to show us the way!"

◁ ◁ ◁

The debate in the meeting hall went on until full dark.

"Since the time of Carausius, Avalon has stayed secret," argued Elen. "Before that, I have heard, the High Priestesses sometimes interfered in the affairs of the world, and it went badly. I do not think that we should change a policy that has served so well."

One of the Druids nodded vigorously. "That is so, and it seems to me that this attack, dreadful as it is, only proves the value of our isolation."

"The Saxons themselves are heathens," said Nectan. "Perhaps they are doing us a favor to cleanse the land of these Christians, who would call our Goddess a demon and kill us all as worshippers of their Devil."

"But it is not only the Christians they are killing!" pointed out

Julia. "If they slaughter all the marsh folk, who will man the boats that take us back and forth when we must travel in Britannia?"

"It would be shameful to desert them, who have served us so long and well," put in one of the younger Druids.

"And the Christians of the abbey are different," offered Mandua shyly. "Did not Mother Caillean herself befriend their founder?"

"If not now, when will we use your power?" asked the young Druid. "Why learn to work magic at all if we do not use it when there is need?"

"We must wait for the Deliverer whom the gods have promised," said Elen. "He will take up the Sword and drive these evil ones from the land!"

"May he be born soon!" breathed Mandua.

They were still arguing when Viviane, no longer able to control her exasperation, left the hall. Father Fortunatus had given her no more than his good wishes, but she could not get him out of her memory. Surely not all the Christians could be fanatics if such men as he were among them. And she knew there was still a connection between Avalon and Inis Witrin. Despite the protections of which the priestesses had been boasting, she could not help wondering how Avalon might be affected if Inis Witrin were destroyed.

As often happened these days, Viviane found that her steps had brought her to the sanctuary where the Treasures were guarded. She had the right to come and go as she pleased, and the Druid on watch stepped aside for her.

Why is he guarding them? she wondered, contemplating the ghostly shimmer of power that came through the cloths with which they were veiled. True, she had used the Grail to bless the land, but Avalon was already holy. The land that needed blessing was in the outside world. No one had wielded the Sword since Gawen; she did not even know the last time anyone had used the Platter or the Spear. Who were they saving them *for?*

As if it had sensed her thought, from the direction of the Grail came a brighter glow. *It wants this,* thought Viviane in wonder. *It wants to work in the world!*

She thought back over the past few days. Although the ritual restrictions of the weeks before the equinox had been relaxed, she had become accustomed to keeping to that diet, and with all the excitement, today she had eaten nothing since noon. Taking a deep breath, she moved toward the Grail.

"What are you doing?" Taliesin was standing in the doorway, fear stark in his eyes. "There has been no preparation, no ceremony—"

"What has to be done. You are all too divided to take action, but I see only the need, and I feel that the Grail desires to answer. Will you deny that I have the right?"

"You have the right. You are the Guardian." The answer was wrenched from him. "But if you have misunderstood its wishes, the Grail will blast you—"

"It is my own life I am risking, and I have the right to do that too . . ." she said gently, and saw his face change as the fallible human was replaced by something greater, as she had seen happen to him in ritual and at certain other times before.

"How will you pass to the other isle?"

"If I am meant to go there, then surely the Grail has the power to show me the way."

He bowed his head. "It is so. Go to the well and walk three times around it, holding in your mind the place you would go, and when you have finished the third circuit, you will be there. I may not forbid you, but I will follow, if you will, to watch over you. . . ."

Viviane nodded, and then the glory washed away all human perception as she brought forth the Grail.

Taliesin understood that the Powers of Avalon had preserved their secrets, for the Maiden who carried the Grail away from its treasury was no longer Viviane. But he himself retained enough awareness to feel both fear and awe in full measure as they passed between the worlds. And then the sweet darkness of Avalon was replaced by the scent of smoke, and the night song of the crickets by the screams of dying men.

The men of the White Dragon were attacking Inis Witrin. Some of the outlying buildings were already in flames. The dark people of the marshes attempted to defend it, but they fell like children before the strength of the Saxons. A running fight had spread away from the hermitages clustered around the old church through the monks' orchard and the sheds they had built below the well.

The Maiden stood before it, looking down at the scene. The Grail, still veiled, was cradled against her breast, and her whole body seemed to shimmer. In the depths of the well house, like a reflection, Taliesin saw a ruddy glow. Presently someone saw her, and shouted. The marsh folk hung back, but the Saxons, hearing the word "treasure," started to run toward her, giving tongue like wolves on a trail.

The Saxons had attacked with fire. It was right, thought Taliesin, that the power of Water should combat them. Though their howling unnerved him, as they charged he stood fast behind the Maiden, who faced them with untroubled serenity. And then, when he could see firelight glinting on the first man's bared teeth, she pulled the cloth away from the Grail.

"Oh, men of blood, behold the blood of your Mother!" she called in a clear voice, and began to pour out the water she had dipped up from the well on Avalon. "Men of greed, receive the treasure you desired, and come to Me!"

To Taliesin, it was a river of Light that poured toward them, so bright that he could scarcely see. But the Saxons began to blunder about as if they had been blinded, shrieking about darkness. And then the water engulfed them, and they drowned.

In the days that followed, there were as many accounts of that moment as there had been eyes to see. Some of the monks swore that the holy Joseph himself had appeared, the flask containing the blood of the Christos which he had brought with him to Britannia blazing in his hand. Those Saxons who survived swore that they had seen the great queen of the Underworld herself just before the river that encircles the world rose up to sweep them away. The marsh men, smiling their secret smiles, spoke among themselves of the goddess of the well who had once more come to help them in their time of need.

It was Taliesin, perhaps, who came closest to truth when he reported to the High Priestess what had occurred, because he was wise enough to know that human words can only distort the reality when something transcendent passes through the world.

Viviane herself could tell them nothing. For her there was only a memory of glory, and from Father Fortunatus, sent by the hand of one of the marsh folk, a wreath of fairy flowers.

Chapter Twenty

The winter passed quietly. The first cold had sent the reivers back to their lairs in the east, and their victims bound up their wounds and set about rebuilding their homes. News came that the sons of Vortigern had driven Hengest back to the Isle of Tanatus and besieged him there. Patiently, the world waited for spring; and in Avalon, all waited for the birth of the Lady's child.

After the raid, Viviane had asked once more for initiation, but she had not been surprised when her mother refused. As Ana had said, she ought to have been disciplined for taking matters into her own hands. The only thing that excused her was the fact that she had succeeded. The council would never have authorized such a thing, but failure would have brought its own punishment. What the Grail itself had approved, the High Priestess could not condemn. Still, she did not have to reward her daughter's presumption.

But this time, Viviane did not complain. She and her mother both knew that whenever she pleased she could simply walk away. After the baby was born there would be a decision, for, whether the child was a boy, or a girl who might supplant her, its birth would change everything. And so Viviane, like Ana, waited with increasing impatience for spring.

The feast of Briga passed, and the blossoms began to fall from the apple trees. As the spring moved toward its equinox, the meadows, lushly green after the winter's flooding, began to adorn themselves with dandelions, little purple orchids, and the first white stars of cow parsley. In the wetlands one might find a few white blossoms of the water crowfoot and the scattered gold of marsh marigold; on the banks, the yellow flag began to show her colors, and the first forget-me-nots lay like bits of fallen sky. The weather grew changeable, one day stormy with a hint of winter chill and on the next smiling a promise of summer. Safe in her mother's womb, Ana's child continued to grow.

❧ ❧ ❧

Ana levered herself up from the bench with the aid of her staff and resumed her climb. Until now, it would not have occurred to her to consider something the younger priestesses did a dozen times a day a "climb," but in her current state, the bench that had been placed halfway between the shore of the lake and the meeting hall for the benefit of the older members of their community was very welcome. The staff was not for support, but for balance, to keep her from falling if her foot turned on a stone she could not see.

She gazed over the swell of her belly with mixed exasperation and pride. She must look like a horse pushing the cart. A pregnancy that on a taller woman would have looked stately, on her was grotesque. Taliesin might be thin, but he was a tall man, and she suspected that this child was going to take after him. She reminded herself that she had borne her first two daughters without much trouble, and they had been big and fair. Viviane's birth had been easy, for she was small.

But, then, she thought wryly, *I was not nearly forty years old.* At sixteen she had scampered up and down the Tor without pausing for breath up to the day of her delivery. This time, though the euphoria of pregnancy had brought her through the first two-thirds in good spirits, these last three months had made it quite clear that her body no longer had the resilience of youth. *This should be my last child. . . .*

Some sense more subtle than hearing made her pause. Looking up, she saw her daughter watching her. As always, the sight of Viviane evoked both pain and pride. The girl's sharp features showed no emotion, but Ana sensed the same mingling of envy and scorn Viviane had felt since she first learned about the child. As her mother's belly had grown, however, the envy had been diminishing.

Now she is beginning to understand. If only she realized that the rest of it—the work of a priestess, especially the role of the Lady of Avalon—brings just as much pain as joy! I have to make her see that somehow!

With her thoughts on her daughter, Ana paid less attention to the path, and when her foot slipped on a patch of mud even the staff was not enough to save her. She tried to twist her body sideways as she went down, and felt the wrench of overstressed muscles in her arm as it took the first impact. But nothing could prevent her distended belly from taking the rest of her weight. The breath went out of her in a grunt as she landed, and for a moment the shock took all her senses away.

When she could see again, Viviane was kneeling beside her.

"Are you all right?"

Ana bit her lip as one of the small tremors that she had been experiencing at intervals for the past week tensed the muscles of her abdomen. This time, however, it left a deeper, meatier ache in her womb. She let out her breath in a long sigh.

"I will be," she whispered. "Help me to get up again."

With the aid of Viviane's strong arm, she got her legs under her and rose to her feet. As she did so, she felt a trickle of warmth between her legs and, looking down, saw the first drops of waters from her womb soaking into the ground.

"What is it?" cried Viviane. "Are you bleeding? Oh—" Connecting what she was seeing with the training in midwifery that all the novices received, she looked at her mother, a little paler than she had been, and swallowed.

Ana grimaced at the girl's confusion. "Just so. It has begun."

⊲ ⊲ ⊲

Viviane watched in fascination as her mother's belly distorted with another contraction. Ana stopped walking and gripped the edge of the table, sucking in her breath. She could bear no clothing, and they had built up the fires in her dwelling to keep her warm. Viviane found herself sweating in her thin robe, but Julia, who was their most experienced midwife, and old Elen seemed comfortable as they talked by the fire.

In the hours since Ana's labor had begun, it had occurred to Viviane more than once that this was an exceedingly unlikely way for human beings to come into the world. It was almost easier to believe in the Roman tales of births from the eggs of swans and other unusual beginnings. She had watched animals give birth when she was a child on Neithen's farm, but that was a long time ago, and although she recalled the babies sliding forth, wet and squirming, the process itself had never been so visible as it was now, when she could see the muscles ridge beneath her mother's bare skin.

Ana sighed and straightened, arching her back.

"Would you like me to rub it?" asked Julia. Ana nodded and braced herself against the table as the midwife began her massage.

"How can you keep walking?" asked Viviane. "I should think you would be tired. Wouldn't it be easier if you lay down?" She gestured toward the bed, where a clean cloth covered a pile of fresh straw.

"Yes," answered her mother, "I am tired, and no"—she gritted her teeth, motioning to Julia to stop until the next contraction went by—"it is not easier, at least not for me. When I stand, the baby's own weight helps bring her down."

"You are so sure it is a girl!" exclaimed Viviane. "What if you are carrying a boy? Perhaps it is the Defender of Britannia who is struggling to come into the world."

"At this point," the laboring woman gasped, "I would give thanks for a hermaphrodite."

Julia made a warding sign, and Viviane blinked. This contraction was stronger, and when it ended, there was perspiration on Ana's brow.

"But perhaps you are right. I think . . . that I will rest for a little while." She let go of the table, and Viviane assisted her to lie down. It was clear that in this position the contractions were more painful, but at the moment being off her feet made it worthwhile.

"There is a point in every labor . . . when one would like to forget the whole idea. . . ." Ana closed her eyes, breathing carefully, as the next contraction rolled through. "Girls call for their mothers. . . . Even priestesses. I have heard it often. I did it myself, the first time."

Viviane moved closer, and when the next pain came, Ana gripped her hand. She could tell by the strength of that squeeze what it cost the other woman not to cry aloud.

"Have you reached that point?"

Ana nodded. Viviane looked down at her, biting her own lip as her mother's fingers dug into her hand once more. *She went through this to bring me into the world. . . .* It was a sobering thought. For the past five years she had fought her mother without compunction, hoping, at most, to be able to hold her own. But now Ana lay in the hand of the Goddess, helpless to withstand Her power. Allowing Viviane to see her in this moment of vulnerability was the last thing the girl would have expected her to do.

The contraction passed, and Ana lay panting. Moments went by without another. Perhaps they were like the showers that come and go as the clouds pass by in a storm.

Viviane cleared her throat. "Why did you want me here?"

"It is part of your training to see a child born. . . ."

"*Your* child? I could have gotten this experience assisting one of the marsh women—"

Ana shook her head. "They drop their babes like kittens. I did myself, the first three times. They say that later children come more quickly, but I think my womb has forgotten how." She sighed. "I wanted you to see . . . that there are some things that even the Lady of Avalon cannot command."

"You won't even make me a priestess. Why should that matter to me?" Hurt sharpened Viviane's tone.

"Do you think I have not wanted to see you initiated? Yes, I suppose I can see why you would. The reason—" She broke off, shaking her head. "The claims of the mother and the priestess are often difficult to reconcile. This child might be a boy, or a girl of no talent at all. As high priestess, it is my duty to raise up a successor. I cannot risk you until I know—" A new pain took away her breath.

And as a mother? Viviane did not quite dare to say the words.

"Help me up," said Ana hoarsely. "It will take longer if I stay lying down."

She pulled herself up on Viviane's arm, and held on to the girl's shoulder. Viviane was the right size to support her, as none of the others could. Ana had always seemed so imposing, her daughter had never before realized how very much alike they really were.

"Talk to me . . ." said Ana as they made their way back and forth across the room, stopping when a contraction came. "Tell me about . . . Mona . . . and the farm."

Viviane glanced at her in surprise. Ana had never seemed to care about her daughter's childhood before. She wondered sometimes if she even remembered Neithen's name. But the woman who hung on her arm, gasping, was not the mother she had hated, and pity opened her heart, and her memories. She spoke of the green, wind swept island whose trees huddled on the shore that faced the mainland and whose far end braved the grey sea. She told her of the scattered stones that had once been a Druid temple, and of the rites that the families descended from the survivors of Paulinus' massacre still practiced there. And she spoke of Neithen's farm and the calf she had saved.

"I suppose she is an old cow now, with many calves of her own."

"It sounds like a healthy and happy life. . . . I hoped it would prove so, when I let Neithen take you away." As the pain passed, she straightened, and they began to walk again, but more slowly.

"Will you foster out this child?" asked Viviane.

"I should . . . even if she is clearly priestess-born," Ana said in a rush. "But in these days I wonder if there is anywhere she could grow up in safety."

"Why should she not stay? Everyone kept telling me I was old to begin my training here."

"I think . . ." said Ana, "I had better lie down." A little blood was trickling down her leg. Julia came over and examined her, remarking that the womb was four fingers open, which they seemed to think was making good progress, though it all still seemed rather unlikely to Viviane.

"It is best . . . if a child has some experience of the world outside. Anara was raised here. I think in some ways it made her weaker." Her gaze went inward and the muscles of her jaw tightened as she clenched her teeth against a new pain.

"What happened to her?" whispered Viviane, leaning close. "Why did my sister die?"

For a moment she thought her mother was not going to answer. Then she saw sliding from beneath the closed eyelids a tear.

"She was so beautiful, my Anara...not like us," whispered Ana. "Her hair was as bright as a wheatfield in the sun. And she tried so hard to please...."

Not like us, indeed! thought Viviane with grim humor, but she kept silent.

"She said she was ready for her testing, and I wanted to believe her.... I wanted it to be so. And so I let her go. I pray, Viviane"—she gripped her arm—"that you never hold the dead body of your own daughter in your arms!"

"Is that why you have put off my initiation?" Viviane asked in amazement. "Because you were afraid?"

"For the others I can judge, but not for you...." She whimpered softly as the next pang came, then eased back again. "I thought I knew when Anara was ready.... I thought I knew!"

"Lady, you must relax!" Julia bent over her, glaring at Viviane. "Let the girl go now, and I will stay with you awhile."

"No..." whispered Ana. "Viviane must stay too."

Julia frowned, but said no more as she began lightly massaging Ana's taut belly. In the silence that followed, Viviane heard a ripple of music, and it came to her that she had in fact been hearing it for quite a long time. No man was allowed in the birthing chamber, but Taliesin must be sitting just outside it.

I wish he could be here! Viviane thought angrily. *I wish every man could see what a woman goes through to give him a child.*

Now the contractions were beginning to come quickly. It seemed that Ana had scarcely time to gasp for breath before her body contorted again. Elen had one of her hands, and Viviane took the other, while Julia probed once more between her thighs.

"Will it be long?" whispered the girl as the laboring woman moaned.

Julia shrugged. "Not as such things go. This is the time when the body finishes opening the womb and gets ready to push out the child. Be easy, my Lady," she said to Ana, massaging her belly with fluttering fingers once more.

"Oh, Goddess . . ." whispered Ana, "Goddess, *please!*"

This, thought Viviane, was intolerable. She leaned forward, murmuring she knew not what words of encouragement and praise. Her mother's eyes, dilated with pain, fixed on hers, and then suddenly they seemed to change. For a moment she looked young; her long, sweat-dampened hair shortened to a mass of tangled curls.

"Isarma!" she whispered. "Help me, and the child!"

And like an echo came words: *"May the fruit of our lives be bound and sealed to thee, O Mother, O Woman Eternal, who holdest the inmost life of each of Thy daughters between the hands upon her heart. . . ."* And as she gazed at the white face before her, she knew that the other woman heard them too. And in that moment they were not mother and daughter but women together, sister souls bound to each other and to the Great Mother from life to life since before the wise ones came over the sea.

And with that memory came other knowledge, learned in another life, in a temple whose birthing lore was deeper than anything the women of Avalon had ever known. With her free hand she drew the sigil of the Goddess upon the laboring womb.

Ana lay back with a long sigh, and Viviane, dropping back into her self with dizzying suddenness, had a moment of stark fear. Then her mother's eyes opened again, blazing with new purpose.

"Get . . . me . . . upright!" she hissed. "It's time!"

Julia began to snap out directions. They helped Ana swing her legs over the edge of the bed so that she was squatting while Elen and Viviane knelt in the straw to support her. Julia hastily spread another clean cloth below and waited as Ana grunted and bore down. Again and again she pushed; to hold her was like trying to grasp some great force of nature. But Julia was urging her on, saying that she could see the baby's head now—another push, a good one, would bring it through.

Viviane, feeling the tremors that pulsed through her mother's frame, found herself calling upon the Goddess as well in a prayer as fervent as any she had ever made. She sucked in breath, and felt heat explode within as if she had breathed in fire. Light flared through every limb, a force far too great to be contained in any human frame; but for that moment she *was* the Great Mother, giving birth to the world.

When she exhaled, the power rushed out of her with the force of lightning and through the body of the woman she held, who convulsed, bearing down with all her might. Julia cried out that the head was coming, and Ana pushed again with a yell they must have heard all the way to Inis Witrin, and something wet and red and wriggling slid forth into the midwife's waiting hands.

A girl ... In the sudden, echoing silence, they all gazed at the new life that had just entered the world. Then the baby turned her head and the stillness was broken by a faint, mewling cry.

"Ah, there's a fine lass," murmured Julia, wiping the tiny face with a soft cloth and holding her up to let the blood drain from the cord. "Elen, support the Lady while Viviane helps me here."

Viviane had been told what she would need to do, but her hands trembled as she tied off the cord with two thongs and then, when the section between grew slack, took the knife and sliced it through.

"Good. Now you may hold her while I deliver the afterbirth. The cloth to wrap her is on the table there."

Viviane scarcely dared to breathe as the midwife set the infant in her arms. Beneath the streaking of birth blood the baby's skin was rosy, and the wisps of drying hair promised to be fair. No fairy child this, but one of the golden people of the race of kings.

Elen was asking what the baby should be named.

"Igraine ..." Ana murmured. "Her name is Igraine. ..."

As if in answer, the baby opened her eyes, and Viviane's heart was lost. But as she looked into that vague blue gaze, the Sight came upon her suddenly. She saw a fair young woman she knew to be this child grown, with a baby of her own. But this was a lusty boy, and in the next moment she was seeing him grown up as well, riding into battle with the hero-light in his eyes and the Sword of Avalon at his side.

"Her name is Igraine"——her own voice seemed to come from

very far away—"and the Defender of Britannia shall come from her
womb...."

🜃 🜃 🜃

Taliesin sat by the hearth in the great meeting hall, playing his
harp. He had played often this springtide. The priests and the priestesses smiled when they heard him and said that their bard was giving
a voice to their rejoicing to match that of the migrating waterfowl
that the warming weather had brought to the marshes around Avalon.
Taliesin would smile and nod and continue making music, and hope
they would not notice that the smile did not reach his eyes.

He should have been happy. Although he could not claim her, he
was the father of a fine daughter, and Ana was recovering well.

But she was recovering slowly. Although she had not screamed
during the delivery, as some women do, he had been sitting close
enough to her door to hear the sounds she did make as the labor went
on and on. He had played then as much to keep himself from hearing
as to cheer those within. How did they do it, these men who fathered
a child every year? How did a man bear the knowledge that a much-
loved woman was risking death to bring forth from her womb the
babe that he had planted there?

Perhaps they did not love their wives as he loved the Lady of
Avalon. Or perhaps it was only that they were not cursed with the
Druid-trained senses that had allowed Taliesin to share her agony.
The harper's fingertips had been bloody from the intensity of his
playing as he tried to make from music a barrier against that pain.

And now he had a new grief. His memories of Viviane's birth
were dim—he had been busy with his usual tasks, and the birth had
gone easier, and he had not known the child was his own. But, whoever had begotten her, Viviane was his daughter now. And Ana had
given permission for her initiation at last. He understood now why
the High Priestess had delayed so long. He too would live in fear
until the girl made her own way safely back through the mists once
more.

And so he played, the great harp lamenting all those things that pass away, which, though they may return, are not the same. And in the music, his pain and his fear were transmuted into harmony.

                                                     ◃ ◃ ◃

Viviane walked upon the shores of the lake and gazed across the water at the pointed shape of the Tor, gathering her courage for the test that would make her a priestess of Avalon. If anything had been needed to convince her that she was no longer in the world in which she had spent the last five years, it would be this, for instead of the familiar crown of ringstones, she saw on the summit a half-built tower. It was dedicated to a god called Mikael, she had been told, though they called him *angelos*. He was a Lord of Light, whom the Christians had called upon to combat the dragon-power of the earth goddess who had once dwelt in the hill.

And still does, she thought, frowning, *in Avalon.* But, whatever the builders' intentions, that phallic tower seemed less a threat to earth than a challenge to heaven, a beacon to mark the flow of power. These Christians had inherited so much from the older faiths, and understood so little of its true significance. She supposed she should be glad if, even in this distorted form, some of the Mysteries were preserved in the world.

And this was the only Mystery she would ever see, if she could not make her way back to Avalon. The test and the initiation were the same, for it was in the act of transforming the reality of Inis Witrin, which lay in the human world, to that of Avalon, that a priestess came into her power.

Viviane turned to gaze at the land behind her, where the flood-plain of the Brue stretched away in a tangle of marsh and meadow toward the estuary of the Sabrina. If she breathed deeply, she fancied she could catch a hint of the salt tang of the distant sea.

She continued to turn, seeing the white trace of the road winding back and forth in three great curves to the grey ridges of the Mendip Hills and, on the other side, the friendlier heights of the Poldens. Somewhere beyond them lay Lindinis and the Roman road. It occurred to her that if she chose she could set out in any direction and find a new life there. That much she could have done before. But now she could also choose to return. She had nothing but the shift on her back and the little sickle knife at her belt, but her mother had at last set her free.

Viviane sat down upon a weathered log and watched a kingfisher dart and soar like the spirit of the sky. Sunlight sparkled on the water, and glowed in the worn wood of the little flatboat they had left for her, a punt such as the marsh folk used. The air still retained the warmth of noon, but a light breeze was stirring in the west, bearing with it the cool breath of the sea. She smiled, letting the sun relax muscles that had gone tight with tension. Even to have a choice in whether to go out into the world or return to Avalon was a victory; but she already knew what her decision would be.

For too many nights she had dreamed of this testing, envisioned each moment, plotted out what she should do. It would be a shame to waste all that planning. But that was not what had compelled her decision. She no longer cared whether she or little Igraine became High Priestess someday, but she did need to prove to her mother that in her the old blood ran true. The euphoric aftermath of the birthing had faded enough for Viviane to know that she and Ana would continue to quarrel—they were too much alike. But they understood each other better now.

Although Viviane's purpose had not changed, since her sister's birth the motives behind it had altered. To maintain this new understanding, she had to prove herself a priestess. And she *wanted* to go back, to bicker with her mother, and watch Igraine grow, and listen to Taliesin sing.

Which was all very well, she thought, getting up again and walking along the shore. But she still had to *do* it.

Magic, she had been taught, *is a matter of focusing the disciplined will. But sometimes the will must be abandoned. The secret lies in knowing when to exercise control, and when to let go.* The sky was clear now, but as the sea-wind strengthened, the mist would come, rolling in from the Sabrina in a moist wave, as inexorable as the tide.

It was not the mists she must transform, but herself.

"Lady of Life, help me, for without You, I cannot cross to Avalon. Show me the way. . . . Make me understand," she whispered, and then, realizing it was not an exchange but a simple statement of fact, "I am your offering. . . ."

Viviane settled herself more comfortably on the log, resting her open hands upon her knees. The first step was to find her center. She breathed in, held the breath, and let it slowly out again, and with it, all the thronging thoughts that would distract her from her purpose here. In and out, she repeated the pattern, counting, as consciousness drew inward and she rested in timeless peace.

When her mind was empty of all thoughts but one, Viviane drew in a deep breath and sent her awareness downward, deep into the soil. Here on the marshes it was like reaching into water, not the solid foundation into which one locked on the Tor, but an elusive, fluid matrix upon which one must float. But though these depths might be unstable, they were a well of power. Viviane sucked it in through the roots her spirit had extended and drew it upward in a tingling rush that fountained from the top of her head to seek the skies.

In that first exaltation she thought her soul would leave her body; but responses which had become instinctive pulled the energy back downward, sending it all the way back along her spine and into the earth again. Once more it welled upward, and this time Viviane stood up, arms lifting as the power pulsed through her. Gradually, the current became a vibration, a column of energy from earth to heaven, and she herself the conduit between.

Her arms drew down, stretching outward, and with them her spirit expanded to encompass everything within the horizontal plane. She sensed everything about her, lake and marsh and meadow, all the way to the hills and the sea, as shadows of light within her vision. The mist was a moving veil across her perceptions, cool to the skin but tingling with power. Eyes still closed, she slowly turned to face it, and focused all her need into a silent call.

And the mist rolled in as a great grey wave, blotting out meadow and marsh and the lake itself, until Viviane seemed the only living thing left in the world. When she opened her eyes it made little difference. The ground was a darker shadow at her feet, the water a hint of movement ahead. She felt her way forward until the long shape of the punt appeared—faint, as if the mist had leached away its substance, as well as its color.

But it felt solid enough, even to her altered senses, and when she stepped into it and pushed off she felt the familiar lurch as it floated free. In moments, the shadowed masses of the shore had disappeared. Now she had not even the solid earth for an anchor, and no destination was visible to her mortal eyes. Her choices were two—she could sit here until dawn, when the land-wind blew the mists away, or she could find the way through the mists to Avalon.

From the depths of her memory she began to summon up the spell. It was, she had been taught, slightly different for each one who used it—sometimes each time it was used it seemed to change. The words themselves were not what mattered, but the realities to which they were the key. And it was not enough simply to say the spell—the words were only a trigger, a mnemonic to catalyze a transformation in the spirit.

Viviane thought of a mountain she had seen which became the figure of a sleeping goddess when looked at in a certain light. She thought of the Grail, itself only a simple cup until you viewed it with the eyes of the spirit. What was mist when it was not mist? What, in truth, was the barrier between the worlds?

There is no barrier. . . . The thought precipitated into her awareness.

"What is the mist?"

There is no mist. . . . *There is only illusion.*

Viviane thought about it. If the mist was an illusion, then what about the land it hid? Was Avalon a mirage, or was it the Christian isle that was not real? Perhaps neither existed outside her mind, but in that case, what was the self that imagined them? Thought pursued illusion down an endless spiral of unreason, at each turn losing coherence as more of the boundaries by which humans defined existence disappeared.

There is no Self. . . .

The thought which had been Viviane trembled at the touch of

disintegration. A flicker of insight told her that this was the darkness in which Anara had drowned. Was that the answer, that nothing existed at all?

Nothing . . . and Everything . . .

"Who are You?" Viviane's spirit cried.

Your Self . . .

Her self was nothing, a flickering point on the verge of extinction; and then—in the same moment, or before, or after, for there was no Time here—it became the One, a radiance that filled all realities. For an eternal moment, she participated in that ecstasy.

Then, like a leaf not quite light enough to float on the wind, she fell downward, inward, reintegrating all the parts that had been lost. But the Viviane who returned to her body was not entirely the same one who had been reft away. And as she redefined herself, her voice returned to her and she sang out the rippling syllables of the crossing spell, and with it redefined the world.

She knew, even before the mists began to part, what she had done. It was like the moment when she had emerged once from a tangled wood, certain that she was going in the wrong direction, and then, between one step and the next, felt the shift in her head and known her way.

Later, when Viviane wondered how she had come to succeed where Anara had failed, she thought that perhaps it was because her five-year battle with her mother had forced her to build a self that could withstand even the touch of the Void. But lest she fancy herself too holy, she understood also that there were some who were lost during their testing because they were already so close to the One that their separate souls joined it without distinction, as a drop of water becomes one with the sea.

The ecstasy of that union was still near enough that Viviane blinked away tears as it faded. She recalled with sudden anguish how she had wept when her mother sent her away with Neithen. Until now, she had not allowed herself to remember that day.

"Lady . . . do not leave me alone!" she whispered, and like an echo came that inner awareness, *"I never left you; I never will leave you. While life lasts, and beyond, I am here. . . ."*

But if the inner light was dimming, the mist had become a shimmer of brightness as it thinned, and in the next moment Viviane stood dazzled by the full light of the sun.

She blinked at the brightness of light on water and the pale stone of the buildings and the vivid green grass of the Tor, and she knew there was no sight more beautiful in all the worlds. Someone shouted; she shaded her eyes with her hand and recognized Taliesin's bright hair. Her eyes searched the slope, seeking her mother, and she tensed against the old pain. Taliesin had been watching for her, probably since the moment she went away. Did her mother not care, even now, whether Viviane succeeded or failed?

And then her spirit lifted: abruptly she knew that her mother was hiding because she would not admit to herself or anyone else just how much she did care whether her oldest living daughter came safely home.

Chapter Twenty-one

"Up! Fivy, pick me *up!*" Igraine held up her chubby arms and Viviane swept her up to her shoulder, laughing. They had played this game all the way around the garden, the child wanting first to get down and explore and then to be picked up so she could see.

"Ouf—I think it's time for Fivy to put you down, love, while I still have a back!" At four, Igraine was almost half Viviane's height already, and there was no doubt she was Taliesin's daughter: though the little girl's hair was a redder gold, the deep blue of their eyes was the same.

Igraine gurgled with enjoyment, and trotted off down the path in pursuit of a butterfly.

Sweet Goddess, thought Viviane as she watched the sun gleaming on those curls, *what a beauty the child is going to be!*

"No, sweetheart," she cried suddenly as Igraine veered toward the bramble hedge, "those flowers don't like to be picked!" But it was too late. Igraine had already made a swipe at the blossoms, and little dots of red were welling from the scratch on her hand. Her face grew crimson and she drew breath for a yell as Viviane scooped her into her arms.

"There, there, sweetness, did the nasty flower bite you? You have to be careful, do you see? There, now, I'll kiss it and it will be well!" The wails began to diminish as Viviane rocked her in her arms.

Unfortunately, the child's lungs were as well developed as the rest of her, and everyone within earshot, which was almost everyone on Avalon, seemed to be running to the rescue.

"It's just a scratch—" Viviane began, but first among those approaching was her mother, and suddenly she felt like the youngest novice, despite the blue crescent on her brow.

"I thought I could trust *you* to keep her safe!"

"She *is* safe!" exclaimed Viviane. "Let her learn caution from those things that will do her no real harm. You cannot keep her forever cushioned in goosedown!"

Ana reached out and, reluctantly, Viviane let the little girl go.

"You may raise your children in your own way when you have them, but do not tell me how to raise mine!" she spat over her shoulder as she carried Igraine away.

If you are so wise a mother, why is it that the first two daughters you *raised are both dead, and only the one you sent away survived?* Crimson with embarrassment, for they had attracted quite an audience, Viviane bit back the reply. She was not angry enough to say the one thing she knew her mother would not be able to forgive, just because it might be true.

She dusted off her skirts and fixed Aelia and Silvia, two of the newest novices, with a stern glare. "Is that sheepskin you were scraping completely bare? Come, then," she continued, reading the answer in their lowered eyes, "the hide will grow no sweeter with keeping, and we must get it clean and salted down."

Viviane marched down the hill toward the tanning shed, which was located well downwind of all the other buildings, with the two girls in tow. At times like this she wondered why she had wanted to be a priestess. Certainly her work had not changed. The only difference was that now she had more responsibility.

As they neared the lake, she saw one of the marsh men's punts being poled through the water at speed.

"It's Heron," exclaimed Aelia. "What can he want? He seems to be in a dreadful hurry!"

Viviane stopped short, remembering the Saxon attack. But it could not be that—Vortimer had beaten Hengest back to Tanatus for a second time two years before. The two girls were already running down the shore. More slowly, she followed them.

"Lady!" Even in his desperate haste, Heron gave her the full salutation. Since she had brought the Grail to save them, the marsh folk had honored her equally with the Lady of Avalon, and she had not been able to make them cease.

"What is it, Heron? Has there been an accident? Have the Saxons come?"

"No danger for us!" He straightened. "They take the good priest—Father Lucky Man—men came to take him away!"

"Someone is taking Father Fortunatus?" Viviane frowned. "But why?"

"They say he has bad ideas that their god does not like." He shook his head, obviously unable to comprehend the problem.

Viviane shared his confusion, although she did remember Fortunatus' saying that some of the Christians considered his ideas to be what they called a heresy.

"You come, Lady! They listen to you!"

Viviane doubted it. His faith was touching, but scaring off a band of Saxons seemed an easy matter compared with dealing with a squabble between Christian factions. Somehow she doubted that Fortunatus' superiors would be favorably impressed by a testimonial from Avalon.

"Heron, I will try to help. Go back, and I will speak to the Lady of Avalon. That is all that I can promise you...."

Viviane had expected her mother to dismiss Heron's tale with polite regret, but to her astonishment she appeared to consider it a cause for concern.

"We are separate from Inis Witrin, but there is still a connection," Ana said, frowning. "I am told they dream of us sometimes, and our workings are disturbed when there is trouble there. If Christian fanatics fill the isle with fear and fury, surely we will feel the effects in Avalon."

"But what can we do?"

"It has been in my mind for some time that Avalon should know more about the leaders in the outside world and their policies. In former days, the Lady of Avalon traveled often to counsel princes. That has seemed unwise since the Saxons came. But the land is more secure now than it has been in years."

"Will you go, Lady?" asked Julia in amazement.

Ana shook her head. "I had thought to send Viviane. And along the way she can inquire concerning this Fortunatus. The experience will be useful."

Viviane stared. "But I know nothing of politics or princes—"

"I would not send you alone. Taliesin shall go with you. To the Romans you will say you are his daughter—that is something they will understand."

Viviane gave her mother a quick glance. Was this an answer to the question neither she nor Taliesin had ever dared to ask? Or was the Lady telling her how she ought to feel? Whatever Ana's reason, thought the girl as she went off to prepare for the journey, she had chosen the only companion with whom Viviane would have been willing to leave Avalon.

⊲ ⊲ ⊲

Fortunatus' trail led them to Venta Belgarum, its stout walls scarred by barbarian attacks but still unfallen. They were told that the chief magistrate, a man called Elafius, was playing host to the visiting bishop, the same Germanus who had made himself so useful against the Picts ten years before. On this visit, however, he seemed to have confined his attacks to his fellow Christians. Two British bishops had been deposed and a number of priests confined until they should see the error of their ways.

"No doubt Fortunatus is among them," said Taliesin as they rode through the fortified gateway. "Pull your shawl up to cover your hair, my dear. You are a modest virgin of good family, remember?"

Viviane gave him a mutinous glare, but she complied. She had already lost the argument about traveling in men's clothing, but she had sworn that if she ever came to be Lady of Avalon she would wear what she pleased.

"Tell me about Germanus," she said. "It is unlikely he will speak to me, but it is as well to know your enemy."

"He is a follower of Martinus, the bishop of Caesarodunum in Gallia, whom they revere now as a saint. St. Martinus was a man of property who gave away all his possessions, even dividing his cloak to share it with a poor man who had none. Germanus preaches against inequality of wealth, which makes him popular with the people."

"That does not seem so bad," observed Viviane, reining her pony up beside his mule. After Lindinis and Durnovaria, she was becoming accustomed to towns, but Venta was by far the biggest city she had seen. Her pony twitched nervously at the crowds, and so did she.

"No, but the mob is easier to sway by fear than by reason. So he tells them that they will burn in hell unless they have faith and their god decides to forgive them, and of course it is only the priests of the Roman Church who have the power to say if he has done so. He preaches that the Vandal occupation of Rome, and our own troubles with the Saxons, are a divine punishment for the sins of the rich. In uncertain times like these, such a philosophy has a great appeal."

Viviane nodded. "Yes ... we all want someone to blame. And I take it that Pelagius, and those who follow him, don't agree?"

They were passing now along the wide street that led to the forum. The gatekeeper had said that the heretics were being tried in the basilica.

"Pelagius himself has been dead for many years. His followers are mostly men of the old Roman culture, well educated and accustomed to thinking for themselves. They find it more logical that a god would reward benevolence and right action than blind faith."

"In other words, they feel that what a man does is more important than what he believes, whereas for the Roman priests it is the other way around ..." Viviane observed dryly, and Taliesin gave her an appreciative grin.

Her pony shied as two men ran past them. Taliesin reached down to take her rein, then peered ahead, his greater height and taller mount enabling him to see farther.

"Some kind of disturbance—perhaps we should stay—"

"No," said Viviane, "I want to see." More slowly, they continued forward until they reached the square.

A crowd was gathering in front of the basilica. She could hear a murmur like the first mutter of thunder that precedes a storm. Many wore the rough dress of workmen, but the garments of some of the others had once been much finer, though now they were stained and worn. Refugees, most likely, eager to find a scapegoat on whom to blame their sorrows. Taliesin leaned down to ask what was going on.

"Heretics!" The man spat on the cobbles. "But Bishop Germanus will sort them, that he will, and save this sinful land!"

"We seem to have come to the right place," said Taliesin evenly, but his face was grim.

At the wrong time . . . , thought Viviane, too appalled to speak at all.

The door of the basilica opened, and two men in the dress of guards came out and took up positions to either side. The muttering of the people deepened. There was a gleam of gold and a priest emerged, wearing an embroidered cape over a white tunic. It must be the bishop himself, she thought, for he had an oddly shaped hat and he was carrying an ornately gilded version of a shepherd's staff.

"People of Venta!" he cried, and the babble fell to a murmurous silence. "Sorely have you suffered from the sword of the heathen. The men of blood have ravened like wolves across this land. You cry out to God—on your knees you have asked why you should be punished."

The bishop's staff swept over their heads and they bowed, wailing. Germanus considered them for a moment, then, more calmly, continued.

"You do well to ask, O my children, but you would do better to call upon the Lord of Heaven for mercy, for He does as He will, and it is only by His mercy that we shall escape damnation."

"Pray for us, Germanus!" shouted a woman.

"I will do better—I will purify this land. Every one of you was born in sin, and only faith will save you. As for Britannia, it is the sins of your great ones who have brought this plague upon you. But the mighty are brought low. The heathen have been the scythe in the hand of God. They who ate at rich tables now beg for their bread, and those who wore garments of silk walk in rags." He stepped forward, sweeping the air with his crooked staff.

"It is so! It is true! God have mercy upon us all!" People were beating their breasts, prostrating themselves on the hard stones.

"They boasted that their own deeds could save them, and said that their wealth proved God's favor. Where is God's favor now? The foul heresies of Pelagius have led you astray, but by the grace of our Heavenly Father we will purge them!"

He looked as if he had taken a purge himself, thought Viviane, his eyes bulging with passion, and spittle flying from his jaws. How could anyone believe such things? she wondered. But the people were crying out in an ecstasy of agreement. Her pony pressed up against Taliesin's mule, as if even the little mare felt a need for protection.

The shouting increased as more guards came through the door, shoving three men before them. Viviane stiffened, unwilling to believe that one of these shuffling prisoners could be Fortunatus. But as if he felt the thought, the first one straightened, surveying the crowd with a wistful smile. His face was bruised and his hair awry, but she recognized the monk who had been her friend. Then the guards began to push them down the stairs.

"Heretics!" cried the people. "Devils! You have brought the pagans down upon us!"

If only they had, thought Viviane. With an army of pagans she could have swept this rabble away.

"Stone them!" called someone, and in another moment the whole forum had taken up the cry. Men bent to pry up paving stones. Viviane could see them throwing; she glimpsed Fortunatus, his head bloodied; then the crowd closed around him.

For a long moment the bishop stood watching, on his face a kind of appalled satisfaction. Then, as if he had regretfully remembered that Christians were supposed to be lovers of peace, he spoke to one of the guards, and the soldiers waded into the mêlée, swinging the blunt ends of their spears.

Once it was on the receiving end of the violence, the mob began to disintegrate, and presently dispersed in struggling knots herded by the guards. The churchmen had disappeared back into the basilica when the fighting began. As soon as Viviane could see clear across the forum, she dug her heels into her pony's sides.

"Viviane, what are you doing?" Taliesin's mule came clattering after. But she had already reached the crumpled forms of those downed in the fighting. Some were beginning to sit up, moaning, but three lay motionless, surrounded by scattered stones.

Viviane slid off the animal's back and bent over Fortunatus. New blood covered the wounds he had already. One eye was swollen shut. Frantic, she felt for a pulse, and as she touched him, the other eye opened. Gently she turned his head so he could see her.

"Lovely lady..." He blinked in confusion. "But this is not Faerie."

"Fortunatus, how do you feel?" For a moment longer he stared, then began to smile.

"It is you ... my maiden of the hillside. But your hair has grown long. ... what are you doing here?"

"I came to help you. If only I had gotten here sooner! But we'll get you away now and tend your wounds and all will be well!"

Fortunatus started to shake his head, winced, and lay still. "I could have escaped the bishop's men," he whispered. "I thought about simply stepping into Faerie. But I owed him obedience."

"I won't let you go back so they can try to kill you again!" exclaimed Viviane.

There was a great sweetness in his smile. "No ... now I have only a little way to go."

From time to time one of the patients the marsh folk brought to Avalon had died, and now, beneath the blood, she could recognize a similar pallor, and the blue, pinched marks at nose and temples. A younger man might have survived his injuries, but Fortunatus' heart was failing him now.

"Will you pray for me?"

It was Viviane's turn to stare. "But I am a pagan—a priestess!" She pointed to the crescent on her brow.

"I fear I am a greater heretic than even Germanus knows," whispered Fortunatus, "for I cannot think that God is confined to these boxes men try to put Him in. If He is a father, then cannot He also be a mother, and if so, is not the Goddess you serve another way in which He can be seen?"

Viviane's first reaction was outrage; then she remembered the moment of Union when she returned through the mists to Avalon. The Power she had felt then had been neither female nor male.

"Perhaps it is so . . . ." she murmured. "I will pray to the One who is beyond all differences to bring you gently to the Light." She saw pain ripple across his features; then his breathing eased.

"I have often thought . . . dying might be like moving into Faerie. A step inward and sideways . . . out of this world."

Tears pricked Viviane's eyelids, but she nodded, and took his hand. His lips moved as if he were trying to smile. Then the smile began to fade.

Viviane sat beside him, feeling his life seep away like water from a cracked bowl. It seemed a long time, but when she looked up from the emptied body, Taliesin was reining in beside her. She shook her head, trying not to weep.

"He's dead, but I won't let them have his body. Help me get him away."

The bard turned in the saddle, making a sign with his fingers and murmuring a spell of confusion. Understanding his purpose, Viviane began to reinforce the spell. *"You do not see us. . . . You do not hear us. . . . No one was here at all. . . ."* Let the Christians think Fortunatus had been carried off by demons if they pleased, so long as they did not see.

Taliesin heaved the old priest across his own saddle and lifted Viviane back into her own, then spread his cloak across the body, took both reins, and led them back across the square.

The illusion protected them until they left the city. Viviane would have liked to bury the old man on his own holy isle, beside the stone from which he stepped to Faerie, but Taliesin knew of a Christian chapel, now abandoned but still sacred ground. And there they laid him, with such rites as the Druids used, and Viviane, remembering that moment in the mist when she had been united with the Light and known all Truth to be One, thought that Fortunatus would not mind.

⊲⊲ ⊲⊲ ⊲⊲

If the first part of their journey had ended in failure, the remainder was more successful, though Viviane found it hard to care. They journeyed to Londinium, where the High King struggled to maintain a semblance of rule with his strong sons beside him. Viviane recognized Vortimer, the one who had come to Avalon, though he looked older now. At first he thought she was her mother; she did not tell him that she had been the veiled priestess who represented the Maiden in his ritual. He was quietly proud of his successes against the barbarians, and she had no doubt of his loyalty to Avalon.

His father, Vortigern, was another matter: an old fox, married now to a redheaded Saxon vixen. He had ruled long and survived much, and would welcome any alliance, she judged, that would help him hold on to power. She spoke to him of Bishop Germanus, and how his fanaticism was dividing the land, though she had little hope that the High King would, or could, act against him. But to her message from the Lady of Avalon he did listen; for the sake of Britannia he would meet with his old rival Ambrosius to discuss cooperation, if an encounter could be arranged on neutral ground.

After that their way led to the western strongholds, where the Saxons had not yet come. In Glevum, Ambrosius Aurelianus, whose father had called himself Emperor and contested with Vortigern for the sovereignty, was gathering men. He heard the Lady's message with interest, for although he himself was a Christian of the rational sort, he respected the Druids as philosophers, and had met Taliesin before.

He was a tall man in his forties, dark-haired with the eagle look of the Romans, but most of his warriors were young. One of them, a lanky, fair-haired fellow called Uther, was no more than her own age. Taliesin teased her with having acquired an admirer, but she ignored both of them. Compared with Prince Vortimer, Uther was only a boy.

Ambrosius heard her complaint against Germanus with some sympathy, for the men of culture whom the Gallic bishop was so fond of attacking were the class from which he himself had come. But Venta Belgarum was in a part of the island which no longer gave allegiance either to himself or to Vortigern, and in any case, a secular lord had little control over churchmen. His response had been much more courteous than that of the High King, but Viviane sensed that his actions would not be any more useful.

As she and Taliesin started back down the road toward Avalon, she meditated darkly on cursing Fortunatus' murderers, and was only stopped by the suspicion that the old priest himself had probably forgiven them.

In persuading Vortigern and Ambrosius to consider an alliance, Viviane had sown the seeds of British unity, but it was not until the following year that the first shoots appeared. Word had come that the Saxons were once more building up their strength in the east of Cantium, and Vortimer, determined that this time he would crush them, appealed to Avalon. And so it was that, just before Beltane, the Lady of Avalon departed from the holy isle and journeyed eastward with her older daughter and her priestesses and her bard to meet with the princes of Britannia.

The place appointed for their council was Sorviodunum, a small town located on the banks of a river where the track from the north crossed the main road from Venta Belgarum. The crossing was a pleasant place, shaded by trees, looking northward across the broad expanse of the plain. When the party from Avalon arrived, the flat meadows around it had sprouted tents like some new kind of spring flower.

"We of the east have poured out our blood to defend Britannia," said Vortigern from his bench beneath the oak tree. He was not a large man, but still solid, his hair more grizzled than it had been when Viviane saw him before. "In the last campaign my son Categirn traded his life for that of Hengest's brother at the ford of Rithergabail. The bodies of our men have been the wall that kept the Saxons from yours." He gestured at the tiled roofs of Sorviodunum, basking peacefully in the sun.

"And all Britannia is grateful," said Ambrosius evenly from across the circle.

"Are you?" responded Vortimer. "Words are easy, but words will not stop the Saxon." He looked older too, no longer the ardent youth who had dedicated himself to the Goddess, but a proven warrior. The lean features were the same, however, and the fierce falcon's pride in his green eyes.

A hero, thought Viviane, watching him from her place at her mother's side. *He is the Defender now.* Everyone knew that the priestesses had arranged this meeting, but it was not politic to admit it publicly. The Avalon contingent had been placed in the shade of a thorn hedge, close enough for them to see and hear.

"Can anything stop them?" asked one of the older men. "However many we kill, Germania seems to breed more. . . ."

"Perhaps, but if we are strong, they will seek easier prey. Let them fall upon Gallia, as the Franks have done. They *can* be expelled! In one more campaign we can do it. It is keeping them out that concerns me now."

"And so it should," said Ambrosius. He looked watchful, as if seeking a deeper meaning in Vortimer's words. Vortigern gave a bark of laughter. Rumor was that he had come only at his son's urging, and had little hope that anything would be achieved.

"You know as well as I do what is required," said the High King. "I fought your father over this very question for many years. Whether he be called emperor or king, there must be one ruler whom all of Britannia will obey. Only thus did Rome hold off the barbarians for so many centuries."

"And you want us to follow *you*?" exclaimed one of Ambrosius' men. "To turn over the sheepfold to the man who invited in the wolves?"

Vortigern rounded on him, and for a moment Viviane understood how the old man had held power for so many years.

"I set wolves to fight wolves, as the Romans themselves have done, time and time again. But before I dealt with Hengest, I had worn out my voice in pleading with my people to take up the sword in their own defense—begging them, as I am pleading with you now!"

"We could not pay Hengest, and he turned upon us," said Vortimer more calmly. "Since then what little his hordes have left has been spent to fight him. What have you done, sitting in your peaceful hills? We must have men and we must have the resources to support them, not only for this campaign, but every year, to protect what we have regained."

"Our lands are battered, but with a few years of peace, they can heal." Vortigern took up the argument once more. "And then our united strength will be enough to break through the marshes and forests behind, which the Angles are sheltering, and take back the Iceni lands."

Ambrosius sat silent, but his gaze was on Vortimer. In the nature of things, he could expect to outlive the old man; it was the young one who would be his real rival, or his ally.

"You have won all men's respect for your valor, and your victories," he said slowly, "and surely all of Britannia must be grateful. Were it not for you, the wolf would now be at our throats as well. But men want some say in who spends their money and whom they follow. Your own people owe you their loyalty. The men of the west do not."

"But they will follow *you!*" exclaimed Vortimer. "All I ask is that you and yours fight at my side!"

"That may be all you ask, but your father, I think, wants me to acknowledge him as leader," Ambrosius replied. There was a heavy silence. "This much I will do," the western Prince said then. "I will open our storehouses and send you supplies. But I cannot, in conscience, ride under the banner of Vortigern."

The conference disintegrated into a babble of disputation. Viviane's eyes pricked with tears of disappointment, but as she blinked them away, she realized that Vortimer was looking at her with a kind of desperate hope. The wisdom of men had failed him. What was left but to seek the counsel of Avalon? She was not surprised when he turned his back on the others and strode toward them.

☙ ☙ ☙

All her life Viviane had heard of the Giants' Dance, though she had never been there. Riding north along the river, she watched eagerly for the first dark speck of stone to emerge from the plain. But it was Taliesin, tallest among them, who first saw it, pointing for Vortimer, and then for Viviane and Ana, to see. Viviane was grateful to the Prince for creating this opportunity. When he had asked the Lady of Avalon to foretell the future, she had replied that it could be done best by drawing on the power of an ancient site nearby. Viviane wondered if that was true, or whether Ana had simply not wished to work magic near so many unsympathetic eyes.

Certainly a ride of nearly three hours ought to be enough to discourage idle curiosity. Though the afternoon sun was warm, Viviane shivered. The plain seemed endless under an immensity of open sky; it made her feel oddly vulnerable, like an ant crawling across a paving stone. But slowly the dark specks grew larger. Now she could make out the separate stones.

She was familiar with the stone circle atop the Tor, but this one was larger, surrounded by a great ditch, its stones shaped with precision, and many of those that remained standing capped with lintels, so that the effect was more like a building than a sacred grove. Some of the stones had fallen, but that had done little to diminish their power. Though the grass grew green and thick around the circle, it was sparse and struggling within. She had heard that no snow fell inside that circle, nor would it stick to the stones.

On closer examination she could see portions of surrounding stones poking through the soil. Inside the ring was a smaller circle of pillars, and four taller trilithons in a semicircle around the altar stone. She wondered to what realities one might pass through those dark doorways. They dismounted and hobbled the horses—there were no trees to which to tether them on the plain. Curious, Viviane walked around the bank above the ditch.

"And what did you think of it?" asked Taliesin when she returned.

"It is odd, but I kept thinking of Avalon—or, rather, of Inis Witrin, where the monks dwell. Two places could hardly be more different, yet the circle of trilithons is almost the same size as the circle of huts that cluster around the church that is there."

"That is so," said Taliesin, speaking swiftly, almost anxiously. He had fasted since the night before to prepare for his own part in this magic. "According to our traditions, this place was built by the men of wisdom who came oversea from Atlantis in ancient times, and we believe also that the saint who founded the community in Inis Witrin was one of those adepts reborn. Certainly he was a master of the ancient wisdom, who knew the principles of proportion and number. And there is another reason you might feel the presence of Avalon." He pointed westward across the plain. "One of the lines of power runs straight cross-country to the holy well."

Viviane nodded and turned once more to survey the surrounding countryside. To the east a row of mounds marked the burial sites of ancient kings, but beyond that there was little sign of humanity, and only a few clusters of wind-sculptured trees broke the undulating expanse of grass. This was a lonely place, and though elsewhere the people of Britannia might be preparing to celebrate a joyous Beltane, there was something stark here that would be forever alien to the innocence of spring.

And none of us shall go from here unchanged. . . . She shivered again.

The sun was sinking, and the shadows of the stones rayed out in long bars of black across the grass. Instinctively Viviane moved away from them, but that brought her to the single pillar that stood sentry in the northeast, guarding the approach to the henge. Taliesin had passed over the ditch to a long stone that lay flat on the ground just within it. He knelt beside it, the red piglet they had brought with them bound and squirming in his hands, and as she watched, he drew his knife and stabbed precisely beneath the angle of its jaw. The pig jerked with a shrill squeal, then fell silent, gasping. The bard held it, his lips moving in prayer as the red blood spurted onto the pitted surface of the stone.

"We shall try the way of the Druids first." Ana spoke in a low voice to Vortimer. "He feeds his spirits, and the spirits of this land."

When the animal had bled out and its spirit fled, Taliesin pulled back a strip of skin and sliced off a little of the meat. He stood up, his gaze already distant, the morsel, reddened further by the light of the dying sun, in his hand.

"Come," said Ana in a low voice as Taliesin, walking like a man in a dream, moved toward the ring of stones. Viviane twitched as she crossed over the ditch and passed the place where the pig had been sacrificed, for the sensation, though less intense, had been like the way she felt when she parted the mists to cross over to Avalon.

The Druid stopped again just outside the henge. His jaws were working, and after a moment he took the bit of meat from his mouth and laid it at the base of one of the stones, murmuring a prayer.

"My lord, we have come to the place of power," Ana said to the Prince. "You must say once more why you have brought us here."

Vortimer swallowed, but he spoke steadily. "Lady, I seek to know who shall rule over Britannia, and who shall lead her warriors to victory."

"Druid, you have heard the question—can you now give answer?"

Taliesin's face was turned toward them, but his eyes were unseeing. With the same dreamlike deliberation, he passed beneath the stone lintel and into the henge. The sun was almost at the horizon, and the black shapes of the stones were edged with flame. As Viviane followed, she experienced another moment of disorientation. When she could focus again, it seemed to her that dancing flickers of light pulsed in the air. The Druid held up his hands to the dying light, turned them, and murmured another incantation into his palms.

He let out a long sigh, then curled up against the flat stone in the center, his face hidden by his two hands.

"What happens now?" whispered Vortimer.

"We wait," said the High Priestess. "This is the sleep of trance, from which the oracle shall come."

They waited while the sky faded to dusk, but though darkness was falling, everything within the circle remained dimly visible, as if by some light that came from within. The shining stars began their march across the sky. Still, time had little meaning. Viviane could not tell how long it was before Taliesin muttered and stirred.

"Sleeper, awaken; in the name of Her who gives birth to the stars I call you. Speak in the tongue of humankind and tell us what you have seen." Ana knelt before him as he pushed himself upright, supported by the stone.

"Three kings there shall be, struggling for power: the Fox, who rules now, and after him the Eagle and the Red Dragon, who shall seek to hold the land." Taliesin's voice came slow and heavy, as if he were still in a dream.

"Shall they destroy the Saxons?" asked Vortimer.

"The Falcon shall set the White Dragon to flight, but the Red Dragon alone shall make a son to come after him; it is he who shall be called the White Dragon's conqueror."

"What of the Falcon—" Vortimer began, but Taliesin interrupted him:

"In life the Falcon will never rule; in death he may ward Britannia forever. . . ." The Druid's head sagged on his chest and his voice became a whisper. "Seek to know no more. . . ."

"I don't understand." Vortimer sat back on his heels. "I am dedicated to the Goddess already. What does She want of me? This is too much to know, or not enough. Call the Goddess, and let me hear Her will."

Viviane looked at him in alarm, wanting to warn him to be careful what he said, for words spoken in this place, on this night, had power.

Taliesin struggled to his feet, shaking his head and blinking as if emerging from deep water.

"Call the Goddess!" Vortimer spoke now as a prince, accustomed to command, and the Druid was still close enough to trance that without question he obeyed.

Viviane's body jerked as the flickering energies in the circle responded to that call. But it was in her mother that they focused. Vortimer gasped as the small figure of the High Priestess seemed abruptly to expand to more than mortal size. Low laughter echoed from the stones. For a few moments She stood, stretching out Her arms and moving Her fingers as if to test them; then She stilled, looking from Viviane's appalled face to that of Taliesin, whose consternation showed that he now realized just what, unprepared and without consultation, he had done.

But Vortimer, hope flaming in his eyes, had cast himself at Her feet. "Lady, help us!" he cried.

"What will you give Me?" Her voice was lazy, amused.

"My life—"

"You have offered that already, and indeed, I will require it of you. But not yet. What I ask on this night"—She looked around Her and then laughed once more—"is a virgin sacrifice...."

The appalled silence that followed seemed very long. Taliesin, his hand gripping the hilt of his knife as if he were afraid it would escape his grasp, shook his head.

"Let the blood of the sow suffice You, Lady. The girl You may not have."

For a long moment the Goddess considered him. Watching her, Viviane seemed to see the shadow shapes of ravens flying, and understood that it was the Dark Mother of the cauldron who had come to them tonight.

"You have sworn—all of you—to serve Me," She said severely, "and yet you will not give the one thing I ask."

Viviane found herself speaking without intending it, her own voice tremulous in her ears. "If You had it, what would You gain?"

"*I* would gain nothing. I already have everything." The amusement had crept back into Her tone. "It is you who would learn ... that it is only through death that life can come, and sometimes defeat brings victory."

It is a test, thought Viviane, remembering the Voice in the mist. She unclasped her cloak and let it fall.

"Druid, as a sworn priestess of Avalon I command you, in the name of the powers we are sworn to serve. Bind me, lest the flesh flinch, and do as the Goddess commands." She walked to the stone.

As Taliesin, shaking, took the belt she handed him and bound her arms to her sides, Vortimer found his voice at last.

"No! You cannot do this!"

"Prince, would you obey if I begged you to hold back from the battle? This is my choice, and my offering." Viviane's voice was clear, but it seemed to come from very far away.

I have gone mad, she thought as Taliesin lifted her onto the slab. *The dark spirits of this place have seduced me.* At least she would die cleanly; she had seen him kill. The woman who was and was not her mother watched implacably from the foot of the stone. *Mother, if indeed this is your doing, I shall be revenged, for I shall be free, but when you return to yourself you will have to bear this memory.*

For a moment the stone was cold; then it began to feel warm and welcoming. Taliesin was a dark shape against the stars. He had drawn his knife; light glittered on the edge as his trembling communicated itself to the blade. *Father, do not fail me . . .* , she thought, and closed her eyes.

And in that darkness, she heard once more the Goddess laughing.

"Druid, put the blade away. It is another kind of blood I demand, and it is the Prince who must take the sacrifice. . . ."

For a moment Viviane could not imagine what She might mean. Then she heard the tinkle of a thrown knife striking stone. She opened her eyes and saw Taliesin crouched against one of the outer menhirs, weeping. Vortimer was standing as if he had been turned to stone.

"Take her . . ." the Goddess said more gently. "Did you think that even I would demand her life on Beltane Eve? Her embrace will make you a king." Softly She came to the Prince, and kissed him on the brow. Then She walked out of the circle, and after a few moments Taliesin followed Her.

Viviane sat up. "You may unbind me," she said when Vortimer still did not move. "I will not run from you."

He laughed shakily and knelt before her, fumbling with the knot.

Viviane looked down at his bent head with a sudden tenderness which she knew was the beginning of desire. When the cord fell away at last, he laid his head to rest in her lap, embracing her thighs. The pulsing warmth between them intensified; suddenly breathless, she ran her fingers through his dark hair.

"Come to me, my beloved, my king ..." she whispered at last, and he rose up and stretched himself beside her on the stone.

Vortimer's hands grew bold, until she felt herself dissolving. Then his weight pressed her into the rock of the altar, and consciousness diffused along all the lines of power that rayed from these stones. *This is death....* A flicker of thought fled away. *This is life—* His cry brought it back again.

That night they died many times, and were reborn in each other's arms.

Chapter Twenty-two

When Prince Vortimer returned to the east, Viviane went with him. Ana sat her pony beside Taliesin's mule, watching them ride away.

"After so many years, you still surprise me," said the bard. "You did not even argue when she said she wanted to go."

"I have lost the right," the High Priestess said hoarsely. "Viviane is better away, where she will be safe from me."

"It was the Goddess, not you . . ." Taliesin began, but his voice wavered.

"Are you so certain? I *remember.* . . ."

"*What* do you remember?" He turned to her, and she saw lines in his face that had not been there before.

"I heard myself speaking those words, and I felt *glee*, seeing you standing over her with that knife, seeing you all so afraid. All these years I have been certain I was doing the Lady's will, but what if I was deceived, and what spoke through me was only my own pride?"

"Do you think *I* was deceived?" Taliesin asked.

"How can I tell?" she exclaimed, shivering as if the sun had no power to warm her anymore.

"Well . . ." he said slowly, "I will give truth to you. That night my own judgment was clouded by fear. Of us all, I think that only Viviane could see clearly, and in the end, I honored her right to make the offering."

"Had you no thought for me?" Ana cried. "Do you think I could have lived with the knowledge that my word had condemned my own child?"

"Or I," he said very softly, "knowing she died by my hand?"

For a long moment they looked at each other, and Ana understood the question in his eyes. And once more, she refused to answer. Better that he should think the girl his daughter, even now.

Presently he sighed. "Whether it was your true self that willed to save her, or the Goddess who changed Her mind, let us give thanks that Viviane is safe and has a chance for happiness." He managed to smile at her.

Ana bit her lip, wondering how she had deserved that this man should love her. She was no longer young, and she had never been beautiful. And now her woman's courses had become so irregular, she did not even know if she was fertile any longer. "My daughter has become a woman, and I have become the Death Crone. Take me back to Avalon, Taliesin. Take me home...."

Durovernum was hot and crowded, as if half of Cantium had taken refuge within its stout walls. The Saxons had attacked it several times—but the city had never fallen. Today, pushing through the crowds on Vortimer's arm, Viviane thought that if any more people were packed in, it might explode.

People nudged each other and pointed to Vortimer as they passed. From their comments, it was clear that they found the sight of him reassuring. Viviane squeezed his arm, and he smiled down at her. When they were alone, she could let down her defenses and *know* what he felt for her. But in such a crowd she had to set up mental shields as stout as Durovernum's walls or the clamor would have driven her mad, and could only judge by the tone of his voice and the look in his eyes. No wonder people in the world outside had so many misunderstandings—she wondered if she would ever know the peace of Avalon again.

The house where they were going lay in the southern part of the city, near the theatre. It belonged to Ennius Claudianus, one of Vortimer's commanders, who was hosting a party. Viviane had found it strange that Vortimer and his captains should waste time on entertainment practically on the eve of a battle, but as he explained, it was important to display to the people their confidence that the life they had known would go on.

Darkness was falling, and slaves ran ahead of them with torches. Above, the clouds blazed as if they had been set afire. Viviane suspected that they owed their brilliant color to the smoke from burning thatch, for the Saxons were marching on Londinium, but the effect was certainly spectacular. Remembering the many abandoned farmsteads in the countryside through which they had ridden to come here, she was surprised the people had anything left to burn.

Why had she come? Did she truly love Vortimer, or had she simply been seduced by her body's response to him? Was it distrust of her mother that had driven her away? She did not know, but as they moved into the atrium and she looked at the elegantly dressed Roman women around her, Viviane felt like a child dressed up in her mother's clothes. In blood these people might be British, but they were clinging desperately to the dream of Empire. Flute-players twittered in the garden, and in the atrium, acrobats leaped and tumbled to the beat of a drum. The refreshments, she was told, were scanty compared with what would have been served in better days, but what they had was exquisitely prepared. For all her efforts to deaden her inner senses, Viviane wanted to weep.

"What is it?" Vortimer's hand on her shoulder brought her out of her reverie. "Are you unwell?"

Viviane looked up and shook her head, smiling. They had wondered if she would come from that first encounter in the stone circle pregnant, but in the two months since she and the Prince had been together her courses had been regular. Vortimer had no child; it was instinct, she supposed, for a man who faced death to want to leave something behind him. She had hoped for a child as well.

"Only tired. I am not used to such warm days."

"We can go soon," he said with a smile that made her pulse beat more quickly. He glanced around him with that watchful look that made her wonder.

All day, she thought, he had been waiting for something; when they were alone she would make him tell her what it was. That first time they made love, at the Giants' Dance, they had known each other utterly. Since then, when she lay with him in places that were not protected, her instinctive defenses had kept her from so complete a union. Vortimer had not complained; perhaps he, with his greater experience, did not consider it a problem; perhaps, she thought ruefully, this was what relations between men and women were usually like, and her own initiation the anomaly.

Suddenly impatient, she set her hands on his arms and willed the barriers away. She sensed first the warmth of his feeling for her, a blend of passion and affection and more than a little awe. Then all the awareness she had blocked came upon her in a rush, and she *saw.* . . .

Vortimer stood like a wraith before her. Her hands told her that his flesh was still solid, that this was an illusion, but to her Vision, he was fading away. With a gasp she made herself look away from him, but it did little good. Of the men in the room there was scarcely a one who had not become a ghost. She stared out toward the city, and images came to her of the streets deserted, buildings fallen, and gardens overgrown.

She could not bear it, she would not see it! With a last effort she closed her eyes and shut all sight away. When she could think again, they were outside and Vortimer was holding her.

"I told them you were feeling ill and I would take you home . . ."

Viviane nodded. That was as good an explanation as any. She must not allow him to suspect what she had seen.

That night, they lay in each other's arms with the shutters thrown open so that they could watch the three-quarter moon climb the sky.

"Viviane, Viviane . . ." Vortimer's fingers stroked down her thick hair. "The first time I saw you, you were a goddess, and again when you first gave yourself to me. When I asked you to come to Cantium, I was still dazzled, certain that you would be my talisman of victory. But now it is the mortal woman I care for." He lifted a strand of hair to her lips. "Marry me—I want you to be protected."

Viviane shivered. He was doomed, if not in the next battle, then another. "I am a priestess." She fell back on her old answer, even though she no longer knew if it were true. "I may not marry any man except as we were joined, in the Great Rite, before the gods."

"But in the eyes of the world—" he began, but she laid a finger across his lips.

"—I am your mistress. I know what they say. And I am grateful for your care of me. For all to accept me, the Church would have to bless our union, and I belong to the Lady. No, my love, while you live, I need no protection but Hers, and yours. . . ."

For a few moments he was silent. Then he sighed. "This morning word came that Hengest is moving on Londinium. I do not think he can take it, and if he does not, he will retreat back through Cantium and I will be waiting. The great fight for which I have been preparing is coming. I believe that we will be victorious, but a man puts his life at hazard every time he goes to war."

Viviane's breath caught. She had known that there must be another battle, but she had not expected it so soon! She forced her voice to remain even as she replied:

"If you should fall, is there anywhere, do you think, that your name would protect me? If you were . . . gone, I would return to Avalon."

"Avalon . . ." He let out his breath on a long sigh. "I remember it, but it seems to me a dream." His hand moved from her hair to trace the curve of cheek and brow, caressed the smooth skin of her throat, and rested above her heart. "It is like you—your bones are a bird's, I could break you with one hand, but inside you are strong. Ah, Viviane, do you love me at all?"

Wordless, she turned in his arms and kissed him, and only realized that she was weeping when he wiped away her tears. By then, it seemed, her lover was beyond speech as well, but their bodies communicated with an eloquence beyond words.

That night Viviane dreamed that she was back on Avalon, watching her mother weave. But the roof of the weaving shed had grown higher; the beams of the loom extended into its shadows, bearing the fabric of the tapestry. She peered upward, and glimpsed men marching, the lake and the Tor, her child-self riding with Taliesin through the rain; but as the weaver worked, the finished tapestry moved beyond her vision into the darkness of forgotten years. Lower down, the images were clearer. She saw the Giants' Dance and herself and Vortimer, and armies, always more armies, marching across the land in blood and fire.

"Mother!" she cried. "What are you doing?" And the woman turned and Viviane saw that it was herself at the weaving, as it was she who was watching, separate, but the same.

"The gods have strung the loom, but it is we who make the figures," said the Other. "Weave wisely, weave well. . . ."

Then she heard thunder, and the loom began to pull apart into fragments. Viviane tried to catch them, but they slipped through her fingers. Someone was shaking her. She opened her eyes and saw Vortimer, and heard the hammering at the door.

"The Saxons—the Saxons have been thrown back from Londinium and are retreating! My lord, you must come—"

Viviane shut her eyes as he went to open it. It was the news he had waited for, she knew, and she wished desperately it had not come. In memory she saw her dream-weaver and heard her warning. *Weave well. . . .*

What did that mean? Vortimer was going to war and she could not stop him. What could she do?

Vortimer was already pulling on his clothing. She flung her arms around him, her head against his breast; she could feel his heartbeat quicken as he let his tunic fall and held her. There was more noise at the door. Vortimer stirred, and her arms tightened around him. He sighed, and she felt his lips brush her hair. Then, very gently, he freed himself from her embrace.

"Vortimer . . ." She reached for him again and he took her hands. She realized she was weeping when he reached out to wipe away her tears.

"So"—his voice shook—"you do love me . . . as I love you. My beloved, farewell!" He stepped away from her, took up his tunic and belt, and started for the door.

Viviane stared after him, waiting until she heard the latch click behind him. Then she collapsed back onto the bed that still bore the imprint of their twined bodies, weeping as if to spend a lifetime's worth of tears.

Eventually, even her weeping came to an end.

As Viviane lay listening to the silence, it occurred to her finally that she was still a priestess. Why had she spent all that time learning magic if she could not use it to protect the man she loved?

Before the sun was high, Viviane was on her way. She encountered no difficulty. The road behind an advancing army was as safe a route as you might find, so long as you brought food of your own. And she had taken the precaution of dressing in a boy's tunic she got from one of the gardeners and hacking off her hair. After so many years, she had become accustomed to having it short, and if she needed to look respectable afterward, she could always cover it with a veil.

Even her mount was no temptation—an ugly and evil-tempered roan gelding that had been judged too slow to take to war. But once she persuaded it to move, its rough paces covered the ground. That night she slept within sight of Vortimer's campfires, and the next day, unrecognized and unsuspected, she attached herself to the camp cooks as a kitchen lad.

On the third day, the British vanguard encountered a band of Saxons and engaged them briefly. Hengest was falling back on his old stronghold on Tanatus. Vortimer's hope was to cut him off and destroy him before he could cross the channel to the isle. Now they turned east, moving with all their speed.

That night they made camp reluctantly, knowing the enemy might continue marching. But it is only men who will outrun strength and reason; the horses must be rested if the British were to preserve their advantage in cavalry. Viviane shivered in the dank sea air, for their road lay near the estuary of the Tamesis, and wished she were in Vortimer's arms. But it was better he should think her safe in Durovernum. She made her bed on a little rise from which she could look down on the softly glowing leather of the field tent where he lay. And there, in the darkness, she called upon the old gods of Britannia to ward his body and strengthen his arm.

The British rose at first light, and by the time the sun rose the warriors were on their way, leaving their supply train to follow as best they might. Now Viviane cursed her nag's slow paces; her link with Vortimer had become strong enough for her to know when they were making contact with the enemy.

They could hear the battle before they saw it. The ears of the horses flicked as the changing wind brought bursts of sound, like the roar of a distant sea. But the nearest water was the channel that separated Tanatus from the rest of Cantium, and it was too shallow to have waves. What they were hearing was the clamor of men in combat.

The two forces had met on the plain beside the channel. Beyond them rose the fortress of Rutupiae, its back to the sea. At this time of year the water meadows were dry, and a thin haze of dust rose in the air. Crows circled, cawing in an ecstasy of anticipation.

The carts came to a halt. Their drivers watched the battle in fascination, pointing when they thought they could make out some maneuver, their voices hushed and tense. Viviane reined her horse a little forward, straining to see. The first charge must have broken the Saxon shieldwall, and the battle had disintegrated into struggling knots of men. From time to time a group of horsemen would combine to attack a larger group of enemies, or scattered Saxons would join and try to re-form their line. It was impossible, in the confusion, even to guess which side might be getting the upper hand.

So intent was she on the struggle below that when men began to shout behind her she paid no attention, and it was only when a bearded figure grabbed for her horse's rein that she realized a band of Saxons had fled the main battle and saw a means of escape in the horses of the baggage train. It was the gelding that saved her, with a vicious snap of long-toothed jaws. The warrior, judging the horse more dangerous than its rider, reeled back. It was a fatal mistake, for Viviane, shocked into action, sank her dagger into his neck. His own weight pulled it through the flesh as the horse sprang free.

Another man ran toward them. Viviane clutched the mane as the nag lashed out with its heels. She dropped the reins as the horse bolted, but it hardly mattered, since she heartily agreed with its instinct to flee. By the time the roan came to a halt, sides heaving and sweat frothing on its neck, she had recovered enough to think again. The bloody dagger was still clutched in her hand. She shuddered and started to cast it away; then a thought came to her.

She had, in the blood, something of the enemy to work with, and the dagger itself was one that Vortimer had given her, which had been his as a boy. Gazing back over the distant struggle, she rested the reddened blade across her palms, and began to sing a spell.

Viviane sang sharpness to the swords of the Britons, that like this dagger they should let out the lives of their foes; she sang more blood spurting from the wounds of the Saxons as her assailant's blood had flowed. She sang to the spirits of the land, that the grasses should tangle the feet of the invaders, the air choke in their throats, the waters drown them, and put out the fire in the belly so that they would have no will to fight any more.

She knew not what she sang, for as she chanted she passed into trance, and her spirit soared like a raven above the battlefield. She saw Vortimer hewing his way toward a big man with a golden torque and grizzled braids who swung a great war-ax as if it were a toy. Screaming, she swooped over Vortimer's head and dove at his enemy.

The man was more sensitive than his fellows, or perhaps she had in truth projected her fetch into the battle, for he flinched, his next blow faltering, and she saw the battle-fury in his eyes giving way to doubt.

"*You are doomed, you are doomed, you must flee!*" she cried. Three times she circled his head, then sped toward the sea.

Vortimer fell upon him. They traded blows, but the big Saxon was defending now. The horseman wheeled, his sword flashing down. The ax swung up to meet it with a resounding clang, and deflected, arced down through the rings of the mailshirt across Vortimer's leg, and sank into the horse's side. The animal screamed and staggered; in another moment it was down, pinning Vortimer in the mud, but instead of following up his advantage the barbarian shouted something in his own tongue and began to run toward the water.

A half-dozen Saxon keels were drawn up onshore. The other warriors, seeing their leader retreating, followed him. In moments one warship had filled and pushed off; men who had not reached it in time splashed helplessly. The British came after them, baying like hounds, and the water grew red. The second ship, laden almost beyond her capacity, began to wallow away. The Saxon leader stood before the third, holding off his attackers single-handed while his war band surged past him. The boat began to move, and, shouting, they hauled him aboard.

Only three Saxon shiploads escaped from that doomed field, plus a few who managed to swim the channel to the other shore. But the British warriors reaped a bloody harvest of those who remained. Viviane floated above the fray, watching until men came to drag the horse off their leader's body, and she saw Vortimer hauled to his feet, exhaustion becoming exaltation as he realized they had the victory.

When Viviane came to herself again, she was lying in the grass. The roan nag was complacently cropping grass nearby. Wincing, for her muscles ached as if she had fought in body as well as spirit, she got upright, plunged the dagger into the earth to get the blood off, then wiped and sheathed it. Murmuring praises in her most soothing tone, for the horse was beginning to eye her suspiciously, she managed to grab the reins, and pulled herself onto its back once more.

One of the few things she had brought from Durovernum was a bag packed with healer's gear, knowing that after a battle there was sure to be use for it. When Vortimer's horse went down he must have been hurt. Frantic to get to him, she urged her horse down the hill.

By the time she caught up with him, the victors had withdrawn into the fortress of Rutupiae. Even then, he was so furiously busy giving orders that she could not get near him, and so began her work on others, wounded far more severely than he.

To Viviane, the very air of the place seemed weighted with

history. It was not by chance that Hengest had made Tanatus his stronghold. It was the gateway to Britannia. Rutupiae itself had risen from the marching fort thrown up to protect the first beachhead to be established when Caesar came to Britannia. For a time it had been the chief port of the province, and the great monument whose ruins formed a foundation for the signal tower had been erected to celebrate its importance. Now what trade remained came in through Clausentum or Dubris, but the walls and ditches of Rutupiae had been rebuilt a century earlier, when Rome strengthened the other forts of the Saxon Shore, and were still in good repair.

Night had fallen before Vortimer finally sat down and Viviane could approach him. He had taken off his armor, but done nothing about his wound. Somebody had found the fort's store of wine, and the British leaders were already beginning to toast their victory.

"Did you see 'em running? Weeping like women, they were, drowning as they tried to climb into their keels. . . ."

"Ah, but they killed a good many of our brave lads," said another. "We'll make a song for them, so we will, to praise this day!"

Viviane frowned. She had already gathered that Vortimer had lost a dozen of his commanders as well as many lesser men. Perhaps that was why his face, as he stared into the fire, was so grim. Still, Hengest himself had fled and left them the field. It was a notable victory. Quietly she moved to stand at his shoulder.

"My lord has cared for everyone else. It is time for his own wound to be tended."

"It was only a scratch—there are others far worse off than I."

She was not surprised he had not recognized her, for the light was uncertain, and she must look a sight in the garden slave's loose tunic and breeches, dirty and splattered with the blood of wounded men.

"And I have done what I could to help them. Now it is your turn. Let me see." She knelt before him, her cropped head bent, and laid her hand on his knee.

Perhaps his flesh recognized her touch, for he stiffened, frowning in uncertainty.

"You are so young—do you have the experience to know—" He stopped short as she grinned up at him.

"Do you doubt my experience—my lord?"

"Dear God! Viviane!" He winced as she began to examine the ugly gash along his thigh.

"Dear Goddess, surely!" She stood up, no longer laughing. "And in Her name I am telling you that, if you will not find a room where I can deal with this wound in private, I will strip off your breeches and tend it in front of them all."

"I can think of a number of other things I would rather do with you in a private room . . . but have it as you will," he answered in the same undertone. "I have a few things to say to you as well." He grimaced as he got to his feet, for the wound had stiffened, but he managed to keep from limping as he led the way into the quarters of the tribune, who was one of the commanders who had been killed.

Carefully, Viviane soaked the fabric of his breeches until the dried blood dissolved enough for her to remove them, and then began to cleanse the wound. Vortimer lay on his side as she worked, distracting himself from the pain of her ministrations with a blistering analysis of all the reasons why she had been a fool to follow him. If she had been one of his soldiers, she thought, she would have been annihilated. But she had developed excellent defenses living with her mother, whose scoldings had been accompanied by a psychic blast that truly could destroy, and mere words had little power to wound her. Especially when the emotion that fueled them was not anger but love.

"It's true that if I were your wife you could have ordered me to stay behind," she answered him finally. "Aren't you glad you didn't? Not many have the privilege of being nursed by a priestess of Avalon."

The wound itself was not so bad, but it had been further mangled when the horse fell on his leg, and there was a great deal of dirt and other matter to be removed. He continued to mutter as she worked on him.

"And you cut off your beautiful hair!" he finished as she set the cloth aside.

"I could hardly have passed myself off as a boy with it long," she answered him. "You're a Roman; don't you like me this way?"

"It's the Greeks you're thinking of. . . ." He blushed charmingly. "I hope I have demonstrated to you what I like. . . ."

She smiled back and handed him a piece of leather. "Bite on this—I'm going to pour wine into the wound." He jerked as the alcohol bit, perspiration starting on his brow. "Keep chewing the leather while I sew it. You'll have an interesting scar. . . ."

When she was finished he was pale and shaking, but beyond a few grunts he had made no sound. She took his head between her hands and kissed him, and not until his skin grew warmer did she let him go. Gently she washed the rest of his body and got him into a clean tunic. By the time Ennius Claudianus came looking for him, Vortimer was sleeping, and she had found a tunic of the dead tribune's which was long enough to serve her as a gown, and used the rest of the water to improve her own appearance sufficiently so that he recognized her and accepted her orders that the Prince should not be disturbed.

◁ ◁ ◁

The battle of Rutupiae had been costly, but there was no doubt that it was a victory. Even the grim business of counting the dead and burying the bodies could not entirely dispel their euphoria. Hengest was gone—not merely from the mainland, but from Britannia. His three keels had fled away across the sea—to Germania or the German Hel, the British neither knew nor cared. Whichever it was, he was likely to stay there, for, after so great a defeat, where would he find more men foolish enough to follow him?

"Then it's over? We have won?" Viviane shook her head in amazement. The Saxons had been a threat for so long.

Vortimer sighed and shifted position on the bench, for his leg still pained him. "We've beaten Hengest, and he was our most dangerous foe. But Germania breeds barbarians as a corpse breeds worms, and they are still hungry. More will come one day, and if not, we still have the Picts and the Irish. It's not over, my little one, but we've won a respite." He gestured toward the new graves. "Their blood has bought us time to rebuild. There is still wealth in the west and the south. Now, surely, they will help us!"

She looked at him curiously. "What do you mean to do?"

"I want to go to Ambrosius. In God's name, I've saved Britannia—he and my father will have to listen to me now. I could proclaim myself Emperor over both their heads, but I won't further divide this land. Still, it gives me room for negotiation. My father is old. If I promise Ambrosius my support when he is gone, perhaps he will give me the help I need now."

Viviane smiled back at him, exhilarated by his vision. It seemed to her now that all that had happened since their joining at the Giants' Dance had been fated, and at last she understood the impulse that had prompted her to go with him. She had heard that Carausius, the first to proclaim himself lord of Britannia, had been married to a woman of Avalon. For what could be more appropriate than that the Savior of Britannia should have a priestess as his consort, to protect and advise him?

⊲§ ⊲§ ⊲§

Vortimer offered her another mount for the journey, but Viviane had become fond of the roan gelding and would not be parted from it. And despite its rough gait, it seemed to her that she rode more comfortably on the roan than Vortimer did on his fine grey stallion. She had urged him to stay in Rutupiae until his wound had healed, but he was convinced that he must meet with Ambrosius now, while all Britannia was still ringing with the news of his victory.

Their stay in Londinium was marred by a major row between Vortimer and his father, who, having prepared himself to hail his son as heir apparent, was understandably upset when he learned of Vortimer's intention to, as he put it, throw away his victory. It occurred to Viviane that Vortigern and her mother could commiserate quite comfortably about their disobedient children, but she did not say so. Vortimer suffered all the more because he could see his father's point of view. He had spoken often of how Vortigern had labored to undo the mistake he had made by inviting the Saxons into Britannia. Though admitting the old man's faults, he honored his father, and it hurt to be at odds with him. When at last they took the Calleva road he was pale and silent.

But it was not until they reached the relative comfort of the *mansio* in Calleva that Viviane realized that not all of Vortimer's suffering was of the soul. When they stripped to bathe, she saw that the flesh around his wound had grown red and swollen. He swore it did not hurt him, and she swore he lied, and made him promise to let her treat it with hot compresses.

That night he seemed much easier, and when they went to bed, for the first time since the battle he drew her to him.

"We should not," she whispered as he kissed her throat. "It will hurt you—"

"I won't notice. . . ." His lips found her breast, and she gasped.

"I don't believe you," she said in a shaken voice, astonished to realize how accustomed she had become to their lovemaking, and how much she had missed it.

"Then we will have to be inventive. . . ." He raised himself on one elbow, and then eased onto his back, but one hand was still caressing her. "You are such a little thing—if you could ride that roan nag all this way, surely you can ride me!"

Viviane felt herself blushing even in the darkness, but his roving hand was waking a need she could not deny. After that, the intensity of their lovemaking escalated rapidly beyond the power of either of them to control. It was like that first time, when their joining had become a channel for forces beyond humanity, and for that night, the bedchamber in Calleva was also holy ground.

"Ah, Viviane . . ." he whispered when the glory departed and they began to remember they were only mortal once more. "How I love you. Don't leave me, my dear one. Don't let me go. . . ."

"I will not," she said fiercely, kissing him once more. And only much later did she wonder why she had not said she loved him as well.

⊲ ⊲ ⊲

In the morning they rode out toward Glevum, but by noon on their second day of travel, Vortimer grew fevered. He refused to stop, however, and he would not allow her to examine his wound. As the afternoon drew on, the men in their escort began to share her concern, and when she ordered them to turn toward Cunetio instead of taking the northerly fork in the road they did not argue.

That night the leg was very hot and hard. It was clear to Viviane that, despite her care, some dirt must have been caught in the wound: after soaking it, she cut through the stitches, and foul matter poured from the opening. The *mansio* at Cunetio was small and poorly maintained, but she did her best to make Vortimer comfortable. Still, he slept uneasily, and so did she, worrying about how long her supply of herbs would last and what she would do when they were gone.

She judged Vortimer's pain by the fact that he did not object to staying another day. His wound was still draining, and if it was not much better, at least it was not worse. On the following morning, she sat down beside his bed and took his hand.

"You cannot ride, and in this condition you cannot go to Glevum," she said soberly. "And this is not a good place to nurse you. But we are not so far from Avalon. Their stores of herbs are great, and their skill in using them surpasses mine. If you will let us build a horse litter to take you to Avalon, I am sure you will be healed."

For a long time, it seemed, he gazed into her eyes. "When we went into the Giants' Dance," he said, "I knew that one of us would be sacrificed. I am not afraid. It comes to me that I have died for Britannia before." And then, at her look of alarm, he smiled. "Let it be as you will. I have always wanted to go back to Avalon. . . ."

Two days' journey brought them to Sorviodunum. Viviane felt ill, realizing how close they were to that circle of stone where her life with Vortimer had begun, but, then, she had been sick with anxiety for the past three days. She knew that the jolting of the horse litter must be hurting him, but all her skill could barely hold the infection at bay. Vortimer was a strong man; surely he would be cured if they could reach Avalon. And so they went on, and shortly after leaving the town turned onto the ancient trackway that led westward across the hills.

On the second night, they camped on a round hilltop above the road. The place was much overgrown, but as she moved about seeking firewood, Viviane realized that the top had once been leveled and surrounded by ditches and earthen walls to make a fortress such as men built in the ancient days. She said nothing—she knew spells to quiet such spirits, and she did not want to alarm the men.

They were anxious enough, for, while she was gone, Vortimer had been restless, muttering about battles. They thought he must be reliving the battle of Rutupiae, where he had gotten the wound, but when she listened, she heard other names—the Brigantes, Father Paulus, and sometimes he babbled of Gesoriacum and Maximian.

The firelight showed her how gaunt he had grown with even a few days of fever, and when she uncovered the wound she was appalled to see the telltale dark streaks of mortification raying up toward his groin. But she cleaned and bandaged it as usual and did not speak of her fear.

That night, she sat late, sponging Vortimer's heated body with cool water from the spring. If it had been drawn from the holy well, it would have cured him. Without intending it, she fell asleep, still holding the cloth.

She woke to Vortimer's cry. He was sitting bolt upright, babbling of spears and enemies at the gate, but this time he spoke in an archaic version of the speech the marsh men used. Frightened, she called him, first in that language, and then in their own. And at that, recognition came back into his eyes and he collapsed onto his blankets, breathing hard. Viviane pushed more wood onto the coals, and the flame leaped up once more.

"I saw them . . ." he whispered. "Painted men with golden necklaces and bronze spears. They looked like you. . . ."

"Yes . . ." she said softly. "This is a place of the ancient ones."

He looked at her in sudden fear. "They say that from such a place the fairy folk can take you."

"I wish they would. We should come all the sooner to Avalon."

Vortimer closed his eyes. "I think I shall never come there. Take me back to Cantium, Viviane. If you bury me on that shore where I won the battle, I will guard it, and the Saxons will never again settle there, whatever other British port they may hold. Will you promise me that, my dear?"

"You will not die, you cannot!" she said frantically, clutching his hand. But it was hot, and so thin she could feel his bones.

"You are the Goddess ... but you would not be so cruel as to keep me alive in such pain...."

Viviane stared at him, remembering that first ritual. The Lady had given him victory, and now, as She had promised, She was accepting his offering. And Viviane, as a priestess of the Goddess, had been the means by which that promise had been made. She had meant to help Vortimer, and herself to escape the magic to which she had been born. And all she had accomplished was to bring him to this lonely death where the ghosts of ancient warriors haunted the hills.

"I have betrayed you ..." she whispered, "but I never meant to—" She held his wrist and felt the pulse flutter frantically.

Vortimer's eyes opened, darkened by pain. "Was it all for nothing, then? Was all the killing in vain? Hold on to me, Viviane, or I will go mad again. Let me at least die sane!"

Abruptly she understood that he was calling on her as a priestess, and that if she failed him now she would have betrayed him indeed. She could *see* the life in him wavering like a dying flame. And although she wanted to cast herself upon his breast, wailing, she nodded, and forced herself to remember lessons she had hoped never to be grateful she had learned.

Viviane took his hands, and held his gaze until his breathing matched her own. "Be easy ..." she whispered. "All will be well. As you breathe out, let go of the pain...." His energy steadied, but it was low, so low. For a little while they sat in silence; then his eyes widened.

"The pain is gone ... my Queen...." His eyes fixed on her, but Viviane did not think it was herself that he was seeing. "May the gods watch over you ... until we meet ... again."

Automatically her lips began to move in a chant that had once been sung in far Atlantis for the deathbed of a king. *This time, at least, I am here to ease your passing!* she told herself, and then wondered from what lifetime that thought had come. She felt his fingers tighten on her own. Then he let go of her hands, and of life itself, sighing like a man who, having fought to the end, sees, beyond hope, his victory.

Chapter Twenty-three

"One is for the Goddess, who is everything...." Igraine's smile was like the sunshine. Harvest was past, and the year was turning toward Samhain, but here, by the shore of the lake, the light was dazzling, flashing from the wavelets and gleaming from her bright hair.

"That is so, my sweet," said Taliesin, looking down at her. "And can you tell me what is two?" Beyond the blue water the land had ripened into all the colors of autumn beneath a pale sky.

"Two ... is *somethings*, things that She turns into, like the Lord an' the Lady, or Dark and Light."

"That is *very* good, Igraine!" He put his arm around her. This child, at least, he was allowed to love.

His gaze moved toward that other daughter, who walked along the shore, her cropped head bent, pausing from time to time to gaze away toward the Watch Hill where they had buried Vortimer. Almost two moons had passed since the marsh folk had found her with his body at the old hill-fort and brought them back to Avalon, and still she grieved. She had begged them to let her take him back to Rutupiae, but it was too dangerous, with the remnants of the Saxon host still ranging that shore. Was that why her face had grown so thin? And yet this gauntness had not affected her body. As she turned, her silhouette dark against the bright water, he could see the lovely shape of her breasts—

"An' three is when the Two have a baby!" Igraine exclaimed triumphantly.

Taliesin let out his breath in a long sigh. Viviane, whose chest had always been almost as flat as a boy's, had a woman's shape now. Why had she not told them that she was carrying a child?

Was I right?" Igraine tugged at his sleeve impatiently.

"Indeed you are...." At five, she was as bright as any little one he had ever known, but of late she seemed to need reassurance as she had not before.

"You will tell Mama, please? An' she will be happy with me?" The words carried clearly in the still air, and Viviane turned. Her eyes met Taliesin's, and he saw the sorrow in them turn to anger, as if she were remembering her own childhood. Then they gentled, and she came quickly and took the little girl into her arms.

"*I* am happy, Igraine. When I was your age I could not say my lessons half so well!"

That was not quite true, thought the bard, but by the time she was six Viviane had been sent away with Neithen. In the years between, she had forgotten, and had it all to learn over when she returned to Avalon.

"Now you may run along the shore and look for pretty stones." Taliesin bent to kiss the child. "But do not go out of sight, or into the water."

"Igraine is confused, and no wonder," said Viviane, looking after her. At this season there was not much danger; the level of the lake had fallen with prolonged dry weather, so that one could practically walk across. "Ana no longer has time for her, has she? I remember how it was when she began to turn away from me...."

Taliesin shook his head at the bitterness in her tone. "But she was so loving when Igraine was a baby—"

"Some women are, I have been told. They enjoy being pregnant and adore little children, but do not seem to know what to do with them when they begin to have minds of their own."

"You are wise," he answered, accepting the truth of her observation. "I am sure you will not make the same mistake with yours...."

Viviane sat up, all color leaving her face so suddenly he thought she would fall. "My child?" Her hand went in an instinctive gesture of protection to her belly.

"You are expecting, I would guess, around Beltane—my dear, surely you knew!" But she had not. As Taliesin saw the color come and go in her face, that was clear. He reached out and gripped her hand. "Come now, this is reason for rejoicing! I suppose it is Vortimer's?"

Viviane nodded, but she was weeping—for the first time, he realized, since she had brought her lover's body home.

◁ ◁ ◁

At Samhain, when the dead come back to feast with the living and the Goddess completes Her half-year of rule and transfers sovereignty to the God, the people of Britannia went in procession from village to village, singing and cavorting in costumes of straw. The folk of the marshes traveled in boats with torches whose light ran across the water like liquid flame. On the Christian isle, the monks sang to repel the evil powers that walked on this night, when the doorways opened between the worlds. From time to time some hapless monk, scuttling between the church and his cell, would see the lights on the water float into the mists and disappear. Those who glimpsed this did not speak of what they had seen. But for the people of the marshes it was a time of rejoicing: on this night, as on Beltane Eve, they completed their circle on the Isle of Avalon.

◁ ◁ ◁

The Lady of the Lake sat on a throne of lashed branches covered with a white horsehide, facing the bonfire they had built on the big meadow below the holy well. Soon it would be midnight, and the people were dancing; the earth throbbed to the stamp of bare feet and the beating of their drums. She bore the sigils of the white mare and crescent moon of the Goddess on breast and brow and nothing more, for on this night she was the priestess of the Great Mother for them all.

It was not yet time for the feasting, but the heather beer had been flowing freely. The beer was not very alcoholic, though a pleasant buzz resulted if you drank enough of it, but Ana drank spring water from a cup of horn bound in silver. Like her ornaments, it was very old. Perhaps it was the inebriation of the drumming that made her want to laugh. Watching her daughter begin to glow with the beauty of early pregnancy, she had felt ancient, but tonight she was young once more.

She gazed at the top of the Tor, where torches flitted like fairy lights against the dark sky. In a sense that was what they were, for it was said that those spirits who had neither passed beyond the circles of the world nor been reborn might dwell for a time in Faerie. On this night the priests and priestesses of Avalon made of their bodies an offering, allowing the spirits of the ancestors to displace their own so that they might feast with the living, and those who at any other time would shun ghosts or the fairy folk equally, on this night welcomed them.

Viviane was watching the Tor as well, with an intensity that her mother found disturbing. Did she think her lover was going to come back to her? Ana could have told her otherwise—for a year and a day the dead stayed in the Summerland, for the healing of their souls. Even too much grieving could hinder them, and they must not be summoned back until that time had passed. But a soul with unfinished business in the world might linger. Was it grief, or guilt for something left undone, that haunted Viviane?

Someone threw more wood on the fire, and Ana's gaze followed the exploding sparks upward until they were lost among the cold fires of the sky. It was nearing midnight, and her anticipation grew. Then from the watcher by the well came a ululating cry that pierced through the noise of the dancing. The torches were moving, winding down the Processional Way around the Tor. The drummers lifted their hands, and silence spread like a spell.

Very softly, the drumming began once more, an insistent heartbeat that throbbed in the flesh and the earth below. The people drew back, crouching down by the food they had brought for the feasting, as the ghostly procession neared. The faces of the priests were whitened and their bodies painted with signs that had been ancient when the priests of Atlantis came over the sea to this isle, for this was a very old magic. Ana did not recognize Taliesin among them, though it was hard to be sure. No one knew in advance where the Horned One's lot would fall, but her pulse quickened in anticipation.

Stepping in unison, the ancestors circled the fire. The people began to call out names, and as they did so, the anonymous white faces seemed to alter, taking on personality. Now an older woman cried out in recognition, and one of the dancers, limping and mumbling like an old man, left the line and sat down beside her. A girl, perhaps their daughter, knelt before him, patting her belly as she begged him to reincarnate in her womb.

One by one the ancestors joined the feasting. Viviane, who had watched them come in with a desperate hope in her eyes, turned away, weeping. Ana shook her head. Perhaps next year, if Viviane still desired it, she would see Vortimer and show him their child.

Her lips twisted. She herself had borne her first babe much younger, but it still did not seem right that her daughter should be pregnant. At the Giants' Dance, she had felt ancient; her courses had stopped for several moons and she had been ready to proclaim herself a crone. But then they had returned. Ana thought now it was worry that had stopped them. She was still in her prime.

A marsh woman knelt before her with a platter, offering strips of beef still smoking from the fire. Her stomach growled, for she had come to the ritual fasting, but she waved them away. Around her, the feast continued. Some of the ancestors, satisfied, left the bodies who had hosted them, and the priests were taken away to wash off their paint and get some food for themselves. Ana felt a tingling in her flesh and knew that the astral tides were turning. Soon the ways would open between past and future, linking the worlds.

From the pouch at her waist she took three tiny mushrooms, brought to her by one of the wisewomen of Heron's tribe. They were still plump and fresh; her mouth puckered at the bitter taste, but she chewed carefully. She was riding the first wave of disorientation when Nectan came to her, bowing.

"It is time; the well is waiting. Let us see what fate it holds. . . ."

Ana swayed a little as she rose, smiling at the buzz of mingled apprehension and curiosity that swept through the crowd, and the old

Druid steadied her. Together they moved up the hill. The Mirror Pool lay still under starlight, the reversed image of the Hunter of Worlds striding through its depths as he mounted the sky. Reflected firelight swirled dizzyingly across the surface. The High Priestess waved the torchbearers back, and silently the people took up position around the pool.

Viviane stepped forward to look into the water, as she had each Samhain since her first vision in the Pool, but Ana grabbed her arm.

"Stupid girl, you cannot See while you are carrying a child!"

That was not entirely true—it was difficult, for when a woman was pregnant she was more firmly connected to her body than at other times, and the energies she channeled could be dangerous for the baby. But as Ana pushed past her daughter, she knew that was not why she had stopped her from claiming this task.

She blinked, forcing her eyes to see normally for just a few moments longer. It was time to show them all why she was still High Priestess of Avalon.

A piece of sheepskin had been placed at the edge. Nectan assisted her to kneel, and very carefully, for now the mushrooms were reaching full potency, Ana gripped the cold stone. The discipline of long practice locked her muscles. Her long hair fell down to either side, blocking peripheral vision. She stared down into darkness and her eyes lost focus. One deep breath steadied her; another, and a shudder racked her frame; with the third breath, her awareness floated free.

The ripples in the water became hills and valleys. The crossed rays of ley lines veined the land with light. Tonight those tracks were thronged with spirits hastening toward the flickering Samhain fires.

"White Mare, I beg you, speak to us." Nectan's voice came floating from the world she had left behind. "Tell us what you see."

"The land is at peace and the ways lie open; the dead are coming home. . . ."

"And what of the coming year? Will rain and sun bless our fields?"

Grey filled Ana's vision and she coughed, as if she were drowning.

"Fill your storehouses and repair your houses, for a wet winter is coming, and all the lowlands of Britannia will lie beneath the floods. . . ." Somewhere back in that other world people were murmuring unhappily, but Vision rushed onward. "In the spring, I see more storms, and rivers overflowing their banks across the fields. It is a hard year that comes to you, and a thin harvest. . . ."

There was a pause. Ana floated in a place beyond time, watching rainbow patterns form and fade.

"But will we have peace?" Nectan's voice pulled her back toward the world. "Will Britannia be safe from danger from men?"

She was shaken by sudden laughter. "Men live in this land—how can it be safe from them?"

Another voice, her daughter's, interrupted. "Will the Saxons come again?"

Sight spiraled dizzyingly, showed her the grey sea and the lands beyond it, where brown floodwaters spread across the low-lying fields. Ana's lips moved, but, gripped by the vision, she did not hear her own words. She saw drowned men and cattle, and a harvest worse than the one she had foreseen for Britannia. More seasons passed, equally wet, though not so cold. After a time men began to dismantle their halls and build warships from the timbers. She saw armies hosting, the three keels in which Hengest had fled multiplying a hundredfold.

"No—" Ana heard herself denying the vision, but she could not escape it. "I don't want to—"

"What do you see?" Viviane's voice was implacable.

"Five winters pass, and the Saxons gather, winging like the wild geese over the sea. And they are many—there have never been so many—and they fall screaming upon our shores. . . ."

She whimpered, wanting to reject, to deny, the knowledge that forced itself upon her. She had to stop this disaster! They had suffered enough; she would do anything to keep this from coming to be—

"Ana, it is enough!" Nectan spoke sharply. "Let the vision pass; let darkness sweep it away!"

She sobbed as his voice grew softer, calling her name, soothing her fears, guiding her home. At last she opened her eyes, and collapsed, shivering, into his arms.

"You should have known better than to ask her that last question," said someone.

"Should I?" she heard Viviane reply. "This is no more than what she did to me...."

🔹 🔹 🔹

Viviane lingered by the Mirror Pool as the others assisted her mother back down to the fire. She was tempted to look into it herself, but the Pool rarely revealed its secrets to more than one seer at a time, and in any case, she dared not risk her child. Vortimer's child. Into what kind of world would it be born?

He had begged her to bury him on the Saxon Shore, but they had not allowed her to take him there. And even in extremity Vortimer had not believed that his spirit could ward more than one small part of Britannia. On the Watch Hill, she thought, his power would be amplified, and he could watch over all. But if she was wrong, then she had betrayed him even in his burying.

Five years ... If Ana had seen truly, Vortimer's great victory had bought them no more than that in which to set Britannia right again. But Viviane had no heart for more fighting; all she wanted was to crawl into a soft nest and wait to bear her child.

When she returned to the fire circle, she saw that her mother had begun to recover from her trance and was sitting on her throne once more. *She should be in bed,* Viviane thought sourly. Ana looked exhausted, but the marsh folk bustled around her like bees, and moment by moment she was reviving. *Why does she need reassurance?* Viviane wondered. *For more than twenty years she has been queen of this hive.... But at least I can go to bed if I want to,* she thought then. *No one will even notice I am gone!*

She turned to take the path through the orchard and stopped short. Someone, or Something, was watching, standing among the trees just on the flickering boundary between the firelight and the dark. *It is a shadow,* she told herself, but it was not altered by changes in the light. *It is a tree*— But she knew every tree in the orchard, and there should be nothing there. Heart pounding, she extended priestess-trained senses outward, and felt: *Fire . . . darkness . . . a predator's lust and the terror of its prey . . .*

Viviane whimpered, and as if it had heard her, the Other stirred. Branching horns emerged from among the branches, wreathed round with crimson autumn leaves. Below, firelight glowed on a patchwork of hides and gleamed from ornaments of copper and bone, and then on muscular legs as He stepped from among the shadowed trees. The antlered head turned; from shadowed sockets came a red glow. Viviane stilled, eyes widening, and an ancient wisdom warned her not to run.

Someone saw her reaction and pointed. Once more, all that great gathering grew silent. With deadly grace, the Horned One moved forward, carrying a spear that she had last seen leaning against the wall beside the Grail. He paused before Viviane, and His swinging ornaments tinkled a moment and were still.

"Are you afraid of Me?" His voice was harsh, and cold. He did not sound like anyone she knew.

"Yes . . ." she whispered. The point of the spear drifted idly from her throat toward her womb.

"There is no need to be . . . yet. . . ." The spear swung away. Abruptly He seemed to lose interest and paced on.

The strength went out of Viviane's limbs, and she sank shaking to the ground. The Horned One passed among the people, ignoring some and brushing others with His spear. She saw strong men tremble; one woman fainted away. But others stood straighter when He had spoken to them, with the light of battle in their eyes. At length He came to stand before the Lady's throne.

> *While the sun shone high and strong,*
> *Earth our Mother labored long;*
> *Soul and body She has blessed,*
> *Comes now the time for Her to rest.*

"Lady of Summer," He continued, "the season of Light is ending. Resign to Me your sovereignty." The fire had burned low; his shadow, monstrously magnified by the angle, reached toward her chair.

The priestess faced him without flinching, white and proud. "For six moons all that lives has rejoiced in my radiance; by my power the earth bore fruit and the cattle grew fat upon the hills."

> *"Bounteous was Summer's reign:*
> *Harvested the golden grain,*
> *Ripened fruits are gathered in,*
> *Winter's food is stored within."*

She too spoke the words of ritual, but she spoke as a priestess, while the Being beneath the Horned One's mask was something more. His reply was not unkind, but it was implacable.

> *"The autumn wind plucks leaf from tree,*
> *From barren fields the chaff blows free.*
> *From summer's warmth to winter's cold*
> *Now you are changing, growing old.*
> *While leaf and branch prepare to sleep,*
> *The red stags through the woods do leap,*
> *When wind makes blood sing in the vein,*
> *The time has come for Me to reign.*

"Your harvest is gathered, your children grown. It is time for the darkness to triumph, and Winter to rule the world."

"I will not let You have it. . . ."

"I will take it. . . ."

Ana stood up, and if she was not the Goddess, still she clothed herself in the glamour of the priestess, and seemed as tall as he.

"Dark Hunter, with You I will make a bargain. . . ." There was a murmur of surprise. "For now we have peace, but I have Seen that the enemies of Britannia will come once more against her. I offer You myself, now, in this sacred hour when our powers are equal, that we may make a child who will save her from her foes. . . ."

For a moment He looked at her. Then He tipped back his head with a growl of laughter.

"Woman, I am as inevitable as the falling leaves or the failing breath. You cannot bargain with Me. I will take what you give Me, but as for the outcome, that is already written in the stars, and cannot be altered." The spear swung forward to hover above her breast.

As He moved, the firelight fell full upon her body, and Viviane saw with pity how her full breasts had fallen, and the silver scoring of childbirth upon the soft skin of her belly.

"Mother"—she forced the words past the ache in her throat—"why are you doing this? This is not part of the ritual—"

For a moment Ana looked at her, and Viviane heard, as if in memory, *"I never give reasons for what I do...."* Then her lips twisted in self-mockery and she turned back to face the Horned God.

"Spring to Summer," she said, taking a step toward him. "Summer to Fall—Life and Light I give to all...."

The spear wheeled and the point sheathed itself in the ground. "Autumn to Winter," he answered, and people breathed more easily, recognizing the familiar words, "Winter to Spring—Night and rest the gifts I bring."

"Your ascent is My decline"—they came together—"All that You shall lose is mine. Ever yearning, forever returning, in the Great Dance we are One...." His arm went around her and they embraced. When they parted, His garments shifted and one could see that beneath them He was very much a man.

Then the Horned One lifted the Lady in His arms and bore her away, and the night air trembled to His deep laughter. In another moment there was nothing but the spear, triumphantly upright before the empty throne.

Nectan looked at the shocked faces before him and cleared his throat, trying to retrieve the rhythm of the ritual.

"Summer's golden time is done
With the waning of the sun;
After Winter's snow and rain,
Summer's joy will come again!
All that was prisoned is set free,

The season's cycle circles on!
Now is the power of change released
As we have willed, so be it done."

But what was it that Ana had willed? Viviane wondered as she gazed toward the shadows into which they had disappeared. And what would now be done?

⊛ ⊛ ⊛

As the year drew on to Midwinter, the sense of dread that had gripped the community on Avalon since Samhain began to lift, for the weather held mild for the season, and clear. People whispered that the Lady's offering had been accepted and the disasters she had prophesied forestalled, for by the solstice Ana was sure that she was with child.

There was a great deal of speculation among the priests and priestesses. Children had been born often to those who went apart at the celebrations at the Beltane or Midsummer fires, but Samhain, despite the invitations to the ancestors, was not a festival of fertility. Some laughed and said there was no ritual reason to forbid it, only that at that season you would have to be in trance or truly inflamed by passion to enjoy lying with a man on the cold ground.

Only Viviane still worried. She remembered too vividly how Ana had labored with Igraine, and that had been five years ago. Could she survive another birthing now? Viviane went so far as to suggest that her mother use the herbs the priestesses knew of to cast the babe forth, but when Ana accused her of wanting all the attention for her own child, they quarreled more violently than they had in years, and Viviane said no more.

It was shortly before the feast of Briga, when the world ought to have been showing the first signs of spring, that the first storms blew in. For three days high winds lashed the treetops, driving the clouds before them like an attacking army, and when the winds at length began to withdraw, they left the land beaten and helpless before the rain.

For most of Briga's month and into the month of Mars the rains continued, in downpours or misty drizzle, with scarcely a glimpse of the sun. Day by day the level of the lake crept upward, until it had passed its normal waterline and begun to reach for the high-water marks left by ancient floods.

The thatching of the roofs was saturated, and water slopped over the lintels to pool upon the floors. It seemed impossible to get any clothing dry. The air stayed so damp that even inside the temple moss grew upon the stones. Most days the clouds were so low they could not see across the lake. At those rare times when they lifted, the view from the top of the Tor showed them a world of pewter-colored water stretching all the way to the Sabrina estuary and the sea. Only the sacred islands and the ridge of the Poldens still lifted their heads above the flood, and, to the north, the distant Mendip Hills.

On the isle of Inis Witrin, the monks must be wondering if their God had decided to send a second Flood to wash humankind away. Even on Avalon there were whispers. But the time had passed when the Lady could have safely rid herself of the child, and in truth, though all others grew sallow and thin, the Lady of Avalon bloomed, as if this pregnancy had granted her youth once more.

It was Viviane who suffered, that damp and deadly spring. As always, by the equinox their stores were growing scanty, and this year it was worse, because water had ruined some of the food. She ate her share, mindful of the child, but though her belly grew, her legs and arms were like sticks, and she was always cold.

After Beltane, they said, it would be better. Viviane, gazing over the hard mound of her belly, could only agree, for it was in that month that she would be delivered of her child. But before the warming weather brought the sunshine, it brought sickness, a low fever with nausea and aching muscles that in the old or weak—and there were many of those—turned all too easily into the lung fever and carried them off.

Nectan died, and the Druids chose Taliesin to replace him. Old Elen went as well, and that was not unexpected, but all were shaken when Julia followed her. Little Igraine fell sick, and would have none but her sister to nurse her, and she was scarcely out of danger when Viviane began to feel the first symptoms herself.

She was sitting by a fire which seemed to have no power to warm her, wondering which of her herbal remedies she could use without endangering her child, when the door opened and her mother came in, drops of rain still glittering on her cloak and her hair. There were silver strands among its dark waves now, but on Ana they seemed an ornament, not a sign of age. She shook the water from her cloak and hung it on a hook, and turned to her daughter.

"How is it with you, my child?"

"My head aches," Viviane said sourly, "and if there were any food worth eating, I would not be able to keep it down."

Her mother, she thought, looked well nourished. Her sagging breasts had filled out again with pregnancy, and though her belly had rounded out, she had not yet reached the ungainly stage which Viviane, who felt like a cauldron on legs, was now enduring.

"We must see what we can do to help you—" Ana began, but Viviane shook her head.

"You had no time when Igraine was ailing. Why should you bother with me?"

Ana's face flamed, but she replied evenly, "She asked for you, and I was nursing Julia. The Goddess knows there has been work enough for all of us, this dreadful spring."

"Well, we cannot complain we had no warning. How gratifying it must be to know yourself a true oracle—" Viviane stopped short, appalled to hear her own venom, but exhaustion had sapped all her control.

"It is terrifying," her mother snapped, "as you should know! But you are ill, and do not know what you say."

"Or perhaps I am simply too tired to care," Viviane replied. "Go away, mother, or you and I may both regret my words."

For a moment Ana stared at her; then she sat down. "Viviane, what has gone wrong between us? We are both bearing new lives—we should be rejoicing together, not trying to tear each other apart."

Viviane sat up, rubbing her back as her temper began to fray. She told herself that pregnant women were easily upset, but only her mother had ever had the power to drive her so completely past reason.

"Together? I am your daughter, not your sister. You should be looking forward to becoming a grandmother, not giving birth to another baby of your own. You accused me of jealousy, but wasn't it the other way around? Once you knew of my condition, you got with child yourself as soon as you could!"

"That was not why—" Ana began.

"I don't believe you!"

"I am Lady of Avalon, and no one doubts my word! You were a disobedient girl who should never have been made priestess." Ana's eyes darkened and she seemed to expand as she too gave way to rage. "What makes you think you will be a decent mother? Look at you! Even at my age I am in better condition. How do you expect to bear a healthy child?"

"You cannot say that! You must not!" screamed Viviane, hearing her own worst fear. "Will you ill-wish me now, so near my time? Or perhaps you have already. Was it not sufficient that you should have all the care and energy of the others? Have you drawn the strength from my child to carry your own?"

"You are mad! How could I—"

"You are Lady of Avalon—how can I tell what spells you know? But from the moment you conceived, I began to ail and grow sickly. You gave yourself to the Hunter. What powers does He give one who carries His seed in her womb?"

"You accuse me of betraying my oaths?" Ana's face went white.

"Oh, I am sure it was done for the most noble of purposes. You would sacrifice anyone or anything to your notion of the will of the gods! But this is my oath, mother. You shall not sacrifice *me*, and you shall not harm my child!"

Rage had suspended all awareness of her aches and pains. Ana was replying, but she could not hear. Shaking with fury, Viviane grabbed her own cloak from its peg and slammed out the door.

Once before she had run, but now Avalon was truly an island.

Viviane pushed off in the first boat she could find, and used the pole to thrust it out into the water. Made ungainly by pregnancy, she found it surprisingly hard to keep her balance in the punt, and awkward to pole, but she persisted. She had tended the people of Heron's village often enough in the past—surely they would take her in now.

It was not precisely raining, but mist lay low upon the marshes, and the wind was damp and cold. It chilled the sweat on her brow, for indeed she was out of condition for such exertions, and soon her backache was far worse than it had been before. Gradually, the anger that had impelled her flight faded, first to impatience to reach the other shore, and then to fear. It had been months since she had worked any magic. Would the mists obey her call?

Carefully she stood, for here the waters were too deep for the pole and she had been paddling, and lifted her arms. It was hard to let go of the self that had been fighting so hard to carry her child, hard to let her anger at her mother go, but for an instant Viviane achieved it, and she brought down her arms with all her might and cried out the Word of Power.

She felt the balance of the world shifting around her, and fell. The punt bobbed wildly beneath her and shipped some water, but did not overturn. Viviane could feel the difference—the air somehow heavier, and a dank, muddy smell on the wind. Before she could get upright a cramp rolled through her belly, short but severe. Clutching the rim of the punt, she doubled up, waiting for it to pass. But as soon as she sat up, she felt another. There was no nausea, and that surprised her, but when a third cramp rolled through her belly, surprise gave way to consternation. This could not be labor! It was a month too soon!

Babies were not born in a moment, and she had been told that a first child especially took some time. She could see a huddle of trees dim in the distance; pausing for each contraction, she paddled toward the shore. At least, she thought as she reached it, she would not give birth in the middle of the lake. But her pains were still coming strongly, and she was beginning to have an unhappy suspicion that the backache she had thought the onset of illness had in fact been early labor.

She remembered also how swiftly the marsh women she had attended sometimes had their babies, and she was much like them. She wished devoutly that she were safe in one of their villages now. It occurred to her that she had cursed herself far more effectively than she had accused her mother of doing, that in fact her foolishness might cost her own life, or that of her child.

I will never, she thought, gasping as another contraction doubled her over, *allow anger to cloud my judgment again!* Warm liquid trickled down her leg; she realized it had been doing so for some time.

Viviane managed to get above the mud on the shoreline, though there was no place where the ground was dry. By the time she reached the trees, she realized she could walk no farther. But there was a spot beneath the thick foliage of a large elder bush that offered some shelter. She spread her cloak beneath her and curled into its embrace.

And there, somewhere between noon and sunset, she gave birth to Vortimer's child. It was a daughter, seeming almost too fragile to live, but tiny and perfect, with hair as dark as her own, who mewed faintly as she felt the touch of the wind. Viviane tied off the cord with the lace from her gown and cut it with the little sickle knife of a priestess that never left her. She had enough strength to put the child to her breast, held snugly against her body within her gown, and to pull the cloak around them. Then she could do no more.

Viviane fell into an exhausted sleep, protected by the elder tree. It was there, as twilight began to veil the marshlands in shadow, that a hunter of Heron's people found her and carried her to his home.

Chapter Twenty-four

Viviane sat on the Isle of St. Andrew beside the new-made grave beneath the hazel trees. The ground was moist but not sodden. After the festival of Midsummer, the storms came less frequently. That gave her some comfort. She did not like to think that little Eilantha would have to lie in the cold rain.

From here she could see across the Vale to Inis Witrin. She was sure she had located the spot correctly, the analogue in the world of men to the place where they had laid Vortimer on the Watch Hill of Avalon. The Goddess had said that the Great Rite would make Vortimer a king—but the kingship she had given him had been in the Otherworld. Perhaps Eilantha's father could keep her safe there, since in this one her mother had failed. Three months only, Viviane's little daughter had lived, and at the end was scarcely larger than Igraine had been the day she was born.

Viviane's full breasts still ached fiercely, leaking milk as the tears slid from her eyes. She crossed her arms, hugging herself fruitlessly. She had not bothered to seek out the herbs that would dry up that flow. Time would do it for her all too soon; until then, she welcomed the pain. She wondered if in time her tears would cease to flow as well.

She heard a step on the path, and looked up, expecting to see the hermit monk who kept the chapel on this hill. He was no Father Fortunatus, but neither was he one of those who thought all women snares of the Devil, and according to his lights he had been kind to her. The sun was behind him, and for a moment she could see only a tall shape against the light. Something about it reminded her of the Horned One, and she stiffened. Then he moved, and she recognized Taliesin.

She let out her breath in a long sigh.

"I am sorry I never saw her," he said in a low voice, and, looking into his worn face, Viviane knew that he spoke truth, and forebore to ask him why he should care.

"They said she was a changeling," she said instead. "When Eilantha began to ail, the women of Heron's village said it was because one of the fairy women had substituted her own sickly babe for mine while I lay sleeping after she was born."

"Do you think that is true?" he asked gently.

"The fairy folk breed rarely. I do not think they have enough children, healthy or ailing, to account for all those who die in the lands of men. But it is possible. The Lady of Faerie knew about my child—she told that hunter who rescued me where to look. I was too weary to speak even the smallest spell of protection, and we were alone."

Her own voice sounded flat in her ears, and he looked at her oddly. The marsh folk had been afraid to speak to her of the baby, but what did it matter? Really, she could hardly think of anything that mattered now that Eilantha was gone.

"Do not torture yourself with such thinking, Viviane. In such a year as this, many babes have died who were born safe and warm at home."

"And what of my new brother, the Defender of Britannia?" she said bitterly. "Are they drinking his health now on Avalon? Or is it another daughter to supplant Igraine?"

Taliesin winced, but his expression did not change. "The baby is not yet born."

Viviane frowned, counting back to Samhain. If her own babe had come early, then Ana's was certainly overdue. "Surely you should be with her, holding her hand. There is nothing that you can do for me. . . ."

He looked down. "I would have come to you, my daughter, but

the word that Heron brought us was that you wanted to be left alone."

She shrugged, for that was true, though there were times when she had needed him, and thought that if the Druids were as wise as they believed, he should have known.

"It is your mother who has sent for you, Viviane—"

"What, again?" She began to laugh. "I am a grown woman now. You may tell her that never again will I dance to her tune."

He shook his head. "I phrased it badly. It is no order, but a request that I bring you. Viviane"—his composure broke suddenly—"she has been in labor now for two whole days!"

It serves her right! came her first thought, followed, in the next instant, by a rush of fear. Her mother couldn't die. Ana was the Lady of Avalon, the most powerful woman in Britannia; like the Tor itself, loved or hated, she had been something to push against, the foundation upon which Viviane had built her own identity.

Thus spoke that part of herself that Viviane had thought buried in Eilantha's small grave. But the part that had learned so painfully to think like a priestess told her it was only too possible. And it was clear that Taliesin was afraid.

"I could not even keep my own baby alive," she said tightly. "What do you expect me to do?"

"Only to come to her. She needs you to be there. *I* need you, Viviane." Something tormented in his voice reached her, and she looked at him again.

"You were the Horned One, weren't you?" she said softly. "She is bearing your child." Suddenly she remembered how He had touched her belly with His spear.

His face was hidden behind his hands. "I don't remember. . . . I would never have agreed to it if I had known."

"No man can claim to have fathered a child to the Lady . . ." she quoted softly. "It was not your doing, Taliesin. I saw the God, and did not know the flesh He wore was yours. Get up now, and take me home."

◁ ◁ ◁

"Oh, Viviane, I am so glad you have come!" Rowan hurried out of the Lady's dwelling and hugged her rather desperately. "Julia had not finished teaching me, and I don't know what to do!"

Viviane shook her head and looked up at her friend. "My dear, I have had even less training than you—"

"But you were with her the last time, and you're her *daughter....*" Rowan was looking at her with an almost avid intensity that reminded her of the way people sometimes looked at the Lady of Avalon. It made Viviane uneasy. "I heard about your baby. I'm so sorry, Viviane," Rowan added, rather belatedly.

Viviane felt all expression leaving her face. She nodded stiffly and brushed past the other girl and through the door.

The scent of blood and sweat hung heavy in the shadows of the room. But not yet death—Viviane had learned too well the odor of mortality. Her breath caught as her eyes adjusted to the gloom and she saw her mother lying on the straw. Claudia, the only other one of the priestesses who had borne more than one child, was sitting beside her.

"She's not walking?"

"She walked the first day, and much of the second," Rowan replied in the same whisper, "but not now. The contractions have slowed, and the opening to her womb is smaller than it was before...."

"Viviane—" Weak as her mother's voice was now, it still held that exasperating note of command.

"I am here." Viviane managed to keep her voice steady, despite her shock at her mother's ravaged face and misshapen form. "What do you want of me?"

Amazingly, the reply was a thread of laughter. Then Ana sighed. "Perhaps we could begin with forgiveness...."

How could her mother know she had sworn never to forgive her? There was a low bench by the bedside; suddenly aware of her own exhaustion, Viviane sat down.

"I am a proud woman, my daughter. I think you have inherited that from me.... All those things I most dislike in myself I have fought to eradicate in you. With little success." Her lips twisted wryly. "If I had kept my temper, you might have kept yours. I did not mean to drive you away."

Her gaze went inward as a contraction rippled across her belly, but Viviane could tell it was a weak one. When Ana relaxed again she bent forward.

"Mother, I will ask you once only. Did you work magic to take strength from me or my child?"

Ana's eyes met hers, and Viviane was shocked to see them filling with tears. "Before the Goddess I will swear that I did not."

Viviane nodded. Ana's labor must have begun about the time her little Eilantha died, but if there was a connection, she did not believe it had been made by her mother's will. And this was not the time or place for her to blame the Goddess. They might yet have some bargaining to do.

"Then I will forgive you. If I am like you, I may need forgiveness myself one day." She wanted to weep, or to scream, but she could not afford to waste the energy. She thought her mother was too exhausted to feel much emotion now.

Ana's lips twitched, but another contraction was coming. She rode it out, but when it was done she looked perceptibly more tired.

"Are you thinking on what you can do for me? You have not the knowledge; indeed, I doubt that even Julia could help me now."

"Three days ago I watched my little daughter die, and there was nothing I could do..." Viviane said thinly. "I will not let you go without fighting, Lady of Avalon!"

There was a pause. "I am open to any suggestion," Ana said with a faint smile. "I was never easy on you, and it is fitting you should rule me now. But more than my life is at stake here. If nothing else serves, then you must cut me and take the child."

"I have heard of that among the Romans, but it kills the mother!" exclaimed Viviane.

Ana shrugged. "They say that a High Priestess knows her time, but perhaps that is a skill we have lost. Reason tells me that the child and I will die anyway if the babe is not born. It is still alive—I can still feel it move—but it won't live if this lasts too long."

Viviane shook her head helplessly. "This is what I feared when I begged you to be rid of it—"

"My daughter, don't you yet understand? I knew what I risked, just as you did at the Giants' Dance when you lay down upon the altar stone. If I had not understood this danger, it would have been no true offering."

Viviane bowed her head, remembering how Vortimer had spoken before he rode to battle. For a moment, she glimpsed a meaning to all this pain. Then the sight of the woman before her brought her back to the present. But thinking of Vortimer had given her an idea. She took Ana's face between her two hands and held her gaze.

"Very well. But if you die, you will die fighting, do you hear?"

"Yes . . . Lady—" Ana grimaced as her belly clenched once more.

Viviane got to her feet and went to the door. "I want this open, and the windows as well, so that she can get some air. As for you"— she gestured to Taliesin—"bring your harp, and tell the others to get their drums. I have seen music give men strength in battle. We will see what it can accomplish here."

Throughout the afternoon they fought, riding the rhythms of the drums. A little before sunset, the laboring woman's back arched and she strained, and for a moment Viviane saw the birth opening ridge around the curve of the baby's head. Claudia supported her as again Ana pushed, her features contorting, and again.

"The head is too big!" Rowan looked up with scared eyes.

"I can't do any more." Ana sank back from her last effort with a defeated sigh.

"You can!" said Viviane grimly. "In Briga's name, this baby *will* be born!" She laid her hand on the hard belly and felt the muscles begin to move. "Now!"

Ana sucked in breath, and as she began to strain Viviane drew upon her belly the ancient sigil, and then pressed down with all the force she had. Power shocked through her hands, and the laboring woman heaved beneath her. She felt something give way, and Ana screamed.

"The head is out!" cried Rowan.

"Hold on to it!" Ana's belly contorted again, less strongly, and

Viviane pressed again. From the corner of her eye she saw the rest of the child emerging, but her attention was on Ana, who had fallen back with a groan.

"It's over! You've done it!" She glanced over her shoulder. "It's a girl!" From the baby came an outraged yell.

"Not ... the Defender," Ana croaked. "But she will have a part ... to play ... all the same." She drew breath with an expression of sudden surprise. A strangled sound from Rowan made Viviane turn. Still holding the baby, the other girl was staring down at the bright blood that gushed from Ana's womb.

Viviane swore, grabbed a cloth, and jammed it between Ana's thighs. In a moment it was soaked through. The baby continued to wail in furious protest as they strove to stop the bleeding, but from the woman on the bed there was no sound.

After a time, the blood slowed to a trickle. Viviane straightened and looked at her mother's white face. Ana's eyes were still open, but they saw nothing. Viviane caught her breath on a sob.

"Mother ..." she whispered, and she knew not if she spoke to the Goddess or to the woman who lay so still before her. "Why? We had won!" But there was no answer, and after a few moments she leaned over and closed those staring eyes.

The baby was still screaming. Moving stiffly, Viviane tied off the cord and cut it. "Wash and swaddle the little one," she said to Rowan. "Cover her." She motioned toward the body, and abruptly sat down.

"Sweet Goddess," said Rowan presently. "How will we feed her?"

Viviane realized that the front of her gown was wet and her breasts were throbbing in response to the baby's cries. With a sigh she undid the lacing at her neck and held out her arms.

The baby butted frantically at her breast, mouth gaping, and Viviane yelped as it closed around her nipple and her milk let down. Even at three months, her own daughter had never sucked so hard. The child coughed, lost the breast, and drew breath to yell, and Viviane hastily guided the nipple back in again.

"Hush! It is not your fault, little one," she whispered, although she had wondered what kind of soul would choose to incarnate at Samhain. The newborn had Igraine's coloring, but she was much bigger, far too big a child for a woman of Ana's size to bear, even if she had been young.

Why should this child live when her own had died? Her hands tightened involuntarily, and the baby whimpered, but did not let go. And that, she supposed, was the answer. Viviane forced her fingers to loosen. This one was greedy for life and always would be.

Other people came in. Without real awareness she answered questions and gave commands. Presently they wrapped Ana's body and carried it away. But still Viviane sat, holding the now sleeping baby in her arms. She did not stir until Taliesin came in. He had aged since that morning, she thought dimly. He looked like an old man. But she let him lead her from the shadows of the chamber into the brightness of the day.

⊲ ⊲ ⊲

"But Viviane *must* agree," said Claudia. "We might have chosen Julia as High Priestess, but she is dead too. Really, we've never discussed the succession. Ana was not even fifty years old!"

"Can we trust Viviane? She ran away . . ." said one of the younger Druids.

"She came back," answered Taliesin heavily. He wondered why he was arguing, why he should try to force his daughter, if she was his child, into the role that had killed her mother. His ears still rang with that last, dreadful cry.

"Viviane is of the royal line of Avalon and a trained priestess," said Talenos. "Of course we will choose her. She is very like Ana, and she is already twenty-six years old. She will serve Avalon well."

Dear Goddess, it is true, thought Taliesin, remembering how beautiful Ana had been when she bore Igraine, and how much Viviane had looked like her with the little one, whom he had named Morgause, in her arms. At least she had been able to fight for her mother's life, while he could only sit and wait. And Viviane was allowed to show her grief. He could claim the dead woman as neither beloved or lover, but only as his High Priestess. *Ana*, his heart cried, *why did you leave me so soon?*

"Taliesin," said Rowan, and he looked up and tried to smile.

Shock and grief had marked all their faces; Ana's daughters were not the only ones who wept because their mother was gone. "You must tell Viviane how much we need her. She will surely listen to you."

Why? he wondered. *So that the burden can kill her too?*

He found Viviane in the orchard, nursing the baby. He supposed it did not take the Sight for her to guess what he had come to say.

"I will care for this little one," she said tiredly, "but you must choose another High Priestess for Avalon."

"Do you think yourself unworthy? That argument got me nowhere when the choice of the Druids fell on me...."

She looked at him and almost laughed. "Taliesin, you are the noblest man I know, and I am a green girl. I am not ready for such responsibility; I am not fit for it; I do not want it. Is that reason enough for you?" The baby, falling back into the swift sleep of infancy, let go the breast, and Viviane covered herself with her veil.

"No ... and you know it. Your mother was training you for this, though she never expected to pass on the power so soon. You are very like your mother, Viviane...."

"But I am *not* Ana—*father*. Think!" she added suddenly. "Even if there were no other reason, the rite by which the Arch-Druid consecrates the High Priestess is one we cannot do...."

Taliesin stared at her, for, indeed, he had forgotten. Ana had never told him if he had begotten Viviane, but in every way that counted, he had been her father since she was fourteen years old. At this moment, however, he did not feel that way. She was so much like her mother— why could she not *be* her mother, now, when he needed her so?

A groan he had not expected escaped his lips and he stood up, trembling. Abruptly he understood why Viviane had fled before.

"Father—what is it?"

He thrust out his hand as if to ward off a blow, and his fingers brushed across her soft hair. Then he was in motion, his long stride carrying him swiftly through the trees.

"Father, must I lose you too?" Her cry followed him, and the baby, waking, began to wail.

Yes, he thought wildly, *and I must lose myself, before I shame us all. Ana would not allow me to give up my body to the Merlin, but I must call on him now. There is no other way. . . .*

449

⊲⊗

Lady of Avalon

⊲ ⊲ ⊲

Taliesin was never to regain much memory of the hours between that moment and nightfall. At some point he must have slipped into his chamber and retrieved his harp, for, when the long dusk of midsummer gave way to darkness, he found himself with the sealskin case in his arms, standing at the foot of the Tor.

He stared up at that sharp, stone-toothed summit, black against the glow of the rising moon, and committed his spirit to the care of the gods. He had climbed it so many times, his feet knew the way. By the time he reached the top, if he reached it, the moon would be in the sky. And when he came down again, if he returned, he would not be the same. At his initiation, the path had seemed to lead not up the hill but through it, to that place beyond human comprehension that lay at the heart of all realities. Then the smoke of sacred herbs had aided him. But since that time he had given his soul to music. If the power of his harp would not help him to the place he sought, he would not get there at all.

Taliesin adjusted the straps that held the harp against his body, reached out with his right hand, and drew the first sweet music from the lower strings, choosing the mode which was used for the most ancient magics, the harmonies whose use, prolonged, had the power to open a way between the worlds. With his left he stroked upward, releasing the notes in a shimmer of sweet sound. Again and again he drew forth the music, moving slowly forward, until suddenly he glimpsed an answering shimmer in the grass.

He felt the path solid beneath his feet, but when he looked down, the ghosts of grasses waved around his calves, and then his knees. The harp sang forth his delight in a series of triumphant chords as Taliesin walked into the Tor.

The holy isle existed in a reality that was perhaps one level removed from that of the world of humankind. One forgot, living here, that beyond Avalon there were other levels, stranger spheres.

Around the hill Taliesin trod the sacred way, and inward and around
again. That first time he followed this way, it had brought him to the
crystal cave hidden in its heart, but now he could sense that the path
was rising. Hope lifted his heart, and his fingers flew faster as he
strode on.

He was all the more surprised to come to a barrier. His music faltered as the light around him grew. The barrier shimmered; a figure
was standing there. Taliesin took a step backward and so did the
Guardian; he moved forward and the Other came to meet him; he
looked into its eyes and saw that it both *was* and *was not* himself.

Taliesin had done this before, at his first initiation, with the symbols of mirror and candle flame. This was the Reality. He stood still,
reaching for calm.

"Why have you come here?"

"I seek to know in order that I may serve. . . ."

*"Why? It will make you no better than other men. As life follows life, every man
and every woman shall come at last to perfection. Do not delude yourself that going
forward will free you from your problems. If you take up the burden of knowledge,
your road will be harder. Would you not rather wait for enlightenment in the course
of time, like other men?"*

Was the Voice his own? Surely these were things he knew. But he
saw now that he had never understood them before.

"It is the Law that if one truly seeks he cannot be refused
entrance to the Mysteries. . . . I offer myself to the Merlin of Britannia, that through me He may save this land."

*"Know that you alone can open the gateway between what is without and what
is within. But before you can attain to Him, you must face Me. . . ."*

Taliesin blinked as pale flame flickered into being above his head.
In the mirror the light burned as well. He gazed, appalled at what he
saw within, for the face before him shone with a terrible beauty, and
he knew now what he would be losing if he persevered in the purpose
that had brought him here.

"Let me pass. . . ."

*"Three times you have asked, and I may not refuse you. . . . Are you prepared to
suffer for the privilege of bringing enlightenment to the world?"*

"I am. . . ."

"Then may the light of the Spirit show you the way. . . ."

Taliesin stepped forward. Radiance sparked and shimmered around him as he became one with the figure in the mirror, and then the barrier was gone.

But he was not surprised, as he completed the next turn in the path, to find his way blocked once more. This time it was a pile of rock and earth that quivered as if at any moment it would come crashing down.

"Halt—" At the hissed command, a little loose soil came sliding down. *"You cannot pass. My earth will cover your fire."*

"Fire burns at earth's heart; it will not extinguish my light."

"Pass, then, with your fire undiminished." What had been solid turned to shadow and misted away. Taliesin took a deep breath and went forward.

Around the hill he passed, and around again. The chill breeze that moved always through these passageways intensified until it was a gale against which he could hardly stand.

"Halt! Wind blows out your fire!"

"Without it no flame can live; your wind but nourishes my flame!" Indeed, as he spoke a great light blazed up above him; then subsided again as the wind faded away.

He went forward, shivering as the air became damp and cold. Now he could hear water dripping with that same relentless power that had half drowned the world. In the winter just past, he had learned to fear the rain. The moisture in the air increased, and his flame began to gutter.

"Halt. . . ." The Voice was liquid and low. *"Water will quench your fire, as the Great Sea of Death will swallow up the life you have known."*

Taliesin struggled to breathe as the air turned to mist around him. In the next moment, his light was gone.

"Be it so," he croaked, coughing. "Water puts out fire, and death will reduce this body to its elements. But hidden in the water is air, and these elements may recombine to nourish a new flame. . . ." He knew that, but it was hard to believe it. He fought to breathe in the darkness, and the water filled him, and he sank into a dark and dreamless sea.

⚛ ⚛ ⚛

This was not how he had expected it to be.

The spark of consciousness that had been Taliesin wondered what had become of his harp. He could not even feel his body anymore. He had failed. In the morning, perhaps, they would find his abandoned body on the Tor and wonder how a man could drown on dry land. Well, let them wonder. He contemplated the thought without emotion. He floated, and gradually, in that place which is beyond all manifestation, he let volition, and memory, and identity itself dissolve, and found peace.

He could have stayed there until eternity came to an end, except for the voices.

"Child of earth and starry heaven, arise——"

"Why would you disturb one who has finished with the world and its torments? Let him rest, safe in My cauldron. He belongs to Me. . . ."

It seemed to him he had heard this conversation before, but then it was the male voice that had brought the darkness.

"He has vowed himself to the cause of Life; he is pledged to carry the sacred fire into the world. . . ."

This too he had heard before. But whom were they discussing?

"Taliesin, the Merlin of Britannia summons you. . . ." The voice rang like a gong.

"Taliesin is dead," the female voice responded. *"I have swallowed him."*

"His body lives, and he is needed in the world."

He listened with more interest, for it came to him now that he had been called Taliesin once, long ago.

"He is gone," he said. "They needed more than he could give. Take the body he left behind and use it as you will." There was a long silence, then, surprisingly, a man's deep laughter.

"You must return as well, for I will need your memories. Let Me in, my son, and do not be afraid. . . ."

The emptiness around him began to fill with a Presence, huge and golden. Taliesin had drowned in the Darkness; now he burned in the Light. The Darkness had enfolded him, but this radiance was penetrating slowly but surely to his center. Though he was afraid, he recognized that acceptance of this possession was what he had been offering, and in a final act of self-sacrifice he opened the door to let the Other in.

For a moment he saw the face of the Merlin, and then the two became One.

The passageway around him glowed with light. The Merlin gazed upward, and saw, blurred and shimmering as if he looked through water, the first radiance of the dawn.

Since sunset, when Taliesin had not come in for the evening meal, they had been searching. None of the boats were missing, so he must still be on the island, unless of course he were floating in the lake somewhere. Viviane, alternately weeping and cursing, understood now how he must have worried when she ran away. If her skill on the harp had been more than rudimentary, she would have tried to sing him home. But Taliesin's harp was gone as well. It was that which gave her hope, for, even if he sought death for himself, he would not have allowed the instrument to be destroyed.

When Viviane came back out of the house after giving Morgause her predawn feeding, the torches of the searchers were still moving through the orchard, their flames flickering pale in the lightening air. Soon, she thought, the sun would be rising. She turned toward the Tor to check the eastern sky and stopped short, staring.

The hill had become transparent as glass, and a light was shining through it that was not the sun. As she gazed, it intensified, rising until it blazed from the top of the Tor. Gradually the hill became opaque beneath it, and as the dawn sky grew brighter, the radiance atop the Tor modulated so that she could see, first a figure, and then that the figure was Taliesin's. But he *shone.* . . .

Shouting, she began to run toward the Tor. There was no time for the stately spirals of the Processional Way. Viviane scrambled upward, clutching at the turf when her bare feet slipped on the dew-drenched grass. By the time she reached the top her breath came in tearing gasps. At the top she halted, clinging to one of the standing stones.

The man she had seen stood in the center of the circle, arms lifted in salutation to the rising sun. She stared at his back, biting back her cry of greeting. This was not the man she had called "father." The clothes and the height were Taliesin's, but his posture and, more subtle still, his aura were not the same. The glow in the eastern sky intensified, unfurling banners of rose and gold. Then she looked away, dazzled, as the newborn sun burned up over the edge of the world.

When Viviane could focus again, the man had turned to face her. She blinked, seeing him first in silhouette, outlined in flame. Then her vision adjusted and she saw clearly for the first time what he had become.

"Where is Taliesin?"

"Here . . ." The voice was deeper too. "As he adjusts to my presence and I become accustomed to wearing flesh again, he will dominate more often. But in this hour of Omen it is I who must rule."

"And for what is this hour propitious?" she asked then.

"For the consecration of a Lady of Avalon . . ."

"No." Viviane shook her head and let go of the stone. "I have already refused it."

"But I demand it in the name of the gods. . . ."

"If the gods are so powerful, why does my mother lie dead, and the man I loved, and my child?"

"Dead?" He lifted one eyebrow. "They are no longer in the body, but you must know that you will see them again . . . as you have known them before. Do you not remember—*Isarma?*"

A shudder shook her thin frame as she heard the name that Ana had called her when Igraine was born. Hearing, she glimpsed, brief and vivid as fragments of dream, all those lives in which they had been linked, in each one striving to carry the Light a little farther. . . .

"In this life, Taliesin has been a father to you, but it was not always so, Viviane. But that does not matter. It is not the union of the flesh but of the spirit that is of importance now. And so I ask you again—Daughter of Avalon, will you give meaning to all the suffering you have seen, and accept your destiny?"

Viviane stared at him, thinking furiously. He was offering her a power beyond that of kings. Her mother had lived all her life safe on this isle, and never really used it. But Viviane had seen the enemy. In the world where Rome had ruled, Avalon could be no more than a legend, preserving the ancient wisdom, but reaching out only rarely to guide the affairs of men. Now all things were changing. The Legions were gone, and the Saxons had destroyed all the old certainties. From this chaos a new nation would emerge, and why should it not be guided by Avalon?

"If I agree," she said slowly, "then you must promise that together we shall prepare the way for the Defender—the Sacred King who shall place the Saxons under his heel and rule forever from Avalon!" It seemed to her that this had always been her role, with Vortimer, and before that, when she had been High Priestess of Avalon in other lives, and the spirit of the Defender had lived in other men. "To this purpose I pledge this life, and I swear that I shall do whatever is necessary to bring these things to pass."

The Merlin nodded, and in his eyes she saw an age-old sorrow and an ageless joy. "The King will come," he echoed, "and he will rule forever in Avalon. . . ."

Viviane let out her breath in a long sigh, and came to him.

For a moment he stood smiling down at her; then he knelt before her and she felt his lips brush each foot in turn.

"Blessed be the feet that have brought you here—may you be rooted in this sacred soil!" He set his palms over her arches and pressed down firmly, and Viviane felt her soul reaching down through the soles of her feet, extending deep into the Tor. When she breathed in once more, its power came rushing back upward, and she swayed like a tree in the wind.

"Blessed be your womb; the Holy Grail and the cauldron of life"—his voice shook—"from which we are reborn. May you bring forth blessings." As he touched her belly, she felt his kiss burning through the cloth of her gown. She thought of the Grail, and saw it glowing crimson as the blood that had gushed from her mother's womb, and then she *was* the Grail, and from her, life flowed ever outward in pain and ecstasy.

She was still shaking when he kissed her breasts, hard and firm with milk for the child.

"Blessed be your breasts, which shall nourish all your children. . . ."

As the power fountained upward, her breasts throbbed with sweet pain. They were full now for a child that was not her own, and she understood that, although in time to come she might bear others, she would always, in a sense, be feeding those who were her children not in the flesh but in the spirit.

The Merlin took her hands, and pressed a kiss upon each palm.

"Blessed be your hands, with which the Goddess shall work Her will. . . ."

Viviane thought of Vortimer's grip slackening in hers as he died. She had been the Goddess for him then, but she wanted to give life, not death. She hungered to touch Igraine's bright hair and Morgause's silken skin. And yet, as she flexed her fingers and felt their strength, she knew that whichever they were called to deal—life or death—that they could do.

"Blessed be your lips, that shall speak the Word of Avalon to the world. . . ." Very gently, he kissed her. It was not the kiss of a lover, but it filled her with fire. She swayed, though she was too firmly rooted to fall.

"My beloved, thus I make you High Priestess and Lady of Avalon, that your choice may confer sovereignty upon kings." He took her head between his hands and kissed the crescent moon upon her brow.

Light exploded within her skull, and Vision was opened; together they whirled through a thousand lives, a thousand worlds. She was Viviane, and she was Ana. She was Caillean, calling the mists to hide Avalon; she was Dierna, burying Carausius on the sacred hill; she was every High Priestess who had ever stood upon this Tor. Their memories awakened within her, and she knew that from this time forward she would never be entirely alone.

And then awareness settled back within the confines of her skull. Viviane was aware of her body, and found that she could move her feet once more. And yet she saw the man before her with doubled sight, the standing stones were glowing, and every blade of grass beyond them seemed edged with light. She knew then that she, as well as Taliesin, had been forever changed.

By now the sun was well above the eastern hills. From here Viviane could look down upon the lake and all the sacred islands and see, nearer still, the people of Avalon, gazing upward with wonder in their eyes. Taliesin reached out and she gave him her hand.

Then the Merlin of Britannia and the Lady of Avalon came down from the Tor to begin the new day.

The Faerie Queen Speaks:

A woman-child with my face rules now in Avalon. A moment ago, it was her mother; a moment hence, perhaps the daughter of Igraine, who so resembles my daughter Sianna, will come. There have been many High Priestesses since the Lady Caillean passed and my daughter took up the ornaments of the Lady of Avalon. Some of them inherited by right of blood, and some because an ancient spirit had been reborn.

Priestess or Queen, King or Mage, again and again the pattern alters and re-forms. They think it is the blood that matters, and dream of dynasties, but I watch the evolution of the spirit which transcends mortality. That is the difference—from life to life and age to age they grow and change, while I am forever the same.

It fares likewise with the holy isle. As the priests of this new cult that denies all gods but one tighten their grip on Britannia, the Avalon of the priestesses moves even further from the knowledge of humankind. And yet they cannot ever be wholly divided, as we of Faerie have found. The spirit of the earth transcends all dimensions, and so does the Spirit that stands behind all their gods.

A new age is coming, when Avalon shall seem as distant to them as Faerie does now. This girl who rules now upon the Tor will use her powers to try to change that destiny, and the one who comes after her will do the same. They will fail—even the Defender, when he comes, will conquer only for a little while.

How could it be otherwise, when their lives are but moments in the life of the world?

It is their dreams that will survive, for a dream is immortal—as am I. And though the world should change entirely, as its events have their reflections here, so there are places where a little of the light of the Otherworld shines through to the world of men. And that light shall not be lost to humankind so long as men still seek solace in this holy earth called Avalon.